Yours Pictorially

Illustrated letters of
Randolph Caldecott

Yours Pictorially

Illustrated letters of

[signature: Randolph Caldecott]

Edited by Michael Hutchins

FREDERICK WARNE

Published by
Frederick Warne & Co Ltd: London
Frederick Warne & Co Inc: New York
1976

Library of Congress Catalog Card No
76-2923

ISBN 0 7232 1981 8

Printed in Great Britain by
William Clowes & Sons, Limited
London, Beccles and Colchester
923.676

For Mary and Emily Kate
With my love

Contents

Acknowledgements

For permission to reproduce the letters of Randolph Caldecott I am grateful to the Librarians of the Houghton Library, Harvard University; the City Library, Sheffield; Shropshire County Library; the Library of the University of California; to the Directors of the Fitzwilliam Museum, Cambridge, and the Victoria and Albert Museum; to the Archivists of the East Sussex Records Office; and to Williams and Glyn's Bank Limited.

I was also helped by Miss Judith Chantry, Mr Paul Collet, Mr Richard Gatty and other members of the Gatty family, Mr Ruari McLean, and the Local History Librarians of Chester, Manchester, Sheffield and Newcastle, and the Librarian of the Caldecott Library, Whitchurch, Shropshire, to all of whom go my thanks.

Foreword

The first of Randolph Caldecott's picture books that I saw was a tattered copy of *John Gilpin*. I had gone to the rare book shelves in the library of Camberwell School of Art and Crafts to prepare a lecture on 19th century colour printing techniques, and among the books I took down was 'Mr Cowper's diverting history'.

I was at once fascinated by the evidence of Edmund Evans's skill as a wood engraver and printer and delighted by Caldecott's illustrations: how stiff and formal and serious seemed the other illustrations I saw that day. I began to buy his picture books and then, thanks to the efforts of a colleague, the school was presented with some of the actual wood engravings for *The House that Jack Built*. I planned to write a text to accompany these engravings, did some initial reading and found that although his illustrations have delighted children and adults for a hundred years, very little had been written about Caldecott.

My researches deepened: what originally was to be the background reading for a short text proved to be the beginning of several years' involvement with Caldecott and Evans. When the successors to Edmund Evans went out of business in 1971, I acquired the wood blocks that they still held, and I began to work on a biography of Caldecott. As I have said, there was little published material, but in Henry Blackburn's *Randolph Caldecott*, issued in 1886, the year Caldecott died, were quotations and reproductions taken from a few of Caldecott's letters.

Unexpectedly the wood engravings were extant: might the letters have survived?

Slowly I located them in libraries and museums in England and America. Although my original intention was to draw on them for the biography, their uniqueness as a collection of letters soon became apparent: here was all the charm and wit of Caldecott's picture books, but on an intimate level, shared until now only with his friends.

How fortunate for us that his correspondents treasured the letters, for a hundred years or so after they were written we can enjoy them anew. I hope the letters printed here will give readers pleasure, for I have gained much enjoyment from their discovery.

Michael Hutchins
Orpington, 1976

INTRODUCTION

I

Randolph Caldecott was born the son of a shopkeeper[1] at Chester in 1846, and forty years later, when he died at St Augustine, Florida, he had gained an international reputation as an illustrator of children's books. Only Walter Crane and Kate Greenaway came close to the critical concord and public popularity that was his during the 1880s.

Just fourteen of Caldecott's forty years were spent as an artist, and during this time he worked in many media: his oil paintings were exhibited at the Royal Academy and leading London galleries; his water colours and reliefs were bought by national museums; he had some reputation as an interior decorator; and he designed a campaign medal for the Royal Mint.

Caldecott was in his middle twenties before he thought seriously of shrugging off one career and taking up the more chancy profession of artist. At fifteen he started as a clerk in the Whitchurch office of the Whitchurch and Ellesmere Bank, and here he stayed until 1867. It was a quiet town, midway between Chester and Shrewsbury, and was the market centre for these undulating acres of dairy land. Much of the bank's trading was done in farmhouses and in the halls of the minor squirearchy. Caldecott made many of these rounds, and in both the bank's time and his own spare time during these adolescent years the young banker's clerk gathered in a store of visual memories of the towns and villages of north Shropshire and south Cheshire which in later years the illustrator was to use in so many of his books.

While he worked at Whitchurch he lived in the farmhouse home of a young married couple, William and Charlotte Brown, at Wirswall, a hamlet two miles north of the town. The earliest letters in this book were written from Wirswall and Whitchurch when he was eighteen and nineteen. Each carries a sketch or two—quick pen jottings which show little how he was to develop, though they already indicate that he drew as readily as he wrote a letter. One sketch[2] is the earliest appearance of a bill-poster adding his new message to an already over-burdened wall: it was the basis of a scene Caldecott was to use again and again at the head of a letter.

He left Whitchurch for the head office of the Manchester and Salford Bank when he was twenty-one; and in Manchester, for the first time in his life, there was an artistic world with which he could make contact. If Whitchurch gave him a store of memories on which he was to draw in later life, Manchester gave him the first opportunities which took him from the banker's stool to the illustrator's desk.

It was not long after his arrival that some of his drawings appeared in

Will o' the Wisp, a humorous weekly. Their publication gave him pleasure, but brought its own fears:

'I suppose you will receive a *Will o' the Wisp* this week. As I know at present, there will only be one sketch by me—the rest of the space being this month devoted to a new artist, who I dare say will eclipse me.'[3]

In May 1870 he spent some days in London and met Thomas Armstrong (later Art Director at the South Kensington Museum) who, though his elder by fourteen years, was to become his closest friend. Much later in the year some drawings which he left with Armstrong were shown to Henry Blackburn, the editor of *London Society*. These were accepted, and the first appeared in the February 1871 issue. Other drawings from this batch were to be seen in April, June and July, and others appeared during the rest of the year. For them Caldecott received £30.[4] It was as much as a quarter's salary paid him by the bank, and was sufficient encouragement for him to quit Manchester for London.

II

The letters he wrote during 1872, his first year in the capital, show plainly the delight he took in his new work:

'You know how devoted I was to business when I was a quill-driver; well, now I am still more devoted, and hope by a strict attention to business and by still supplying the best article at the lowest price to merit a continuance of the favours which the nobility, clergy, &c.'[5]

His friendship with Thomas Armstrong gave him an immediate entry into the du Maurier-Whistler circle, all of whom were older and already successful artists. He was conscious of the disparity between their success and his own position, and could boast that he

'very often . . . squatted for an hour in the evening with the greatest master of drawing in line that we have'.[6]

In these early insecure years Caldecott was willing to undertake any commission that might come his way, and made a half-joking offer to one of his Whitchurch friends:

'I have just got into a new workshop next door at the back, and there I light my stove and carry on my business. Do you want a sign-board? or an equestrian statue? or an elegant wallpaper?'[7]

Such diversity of work was, in truth, unnecessary: within two years of leaving Manchester Caldecott established himself as a freelance magazine illustrator.

Most of his early work was connected in one way or another with Henry

2

Blackburn. *London Society* was edited by Blackburn until June 1872; he and Caldecott spent a month in the Harz mountains which resulted in a series of articles in the *Graphic* and *Harper's Monthly Magazine*, and in a book; they were fellow correspondents for the New York *Daily Graphic*; and when Blackburn was appointed art editor on the *Pictorial World* he immediately engaged Caldecott. Later they were to visit Vienna for the New York *Daily Graphic*, and Brittany, which resulted in more magazine articles and a book, *Breton Folk*.

The opportunity to make a comparable reputation as a book illustrator came in January 1874 when James Cooper, the wood engraver, proposed that Caldecott should illustrate extracts from Washington Irving's *Sketchbook*.

Cooper persuaded Caldecott to undertake the illustrations more easily than he was to persuade a publisher to take the book, once complete. It was first rejected, but then Macmillans took it. While Cooper was making the wood engravings, Caldecott began illustrating more extracts, which were to be published in a second volume. The first, *Old Christmas*, was published in November 1875; as the text was already well known, the critics, naturally enough, concentrated on the illustrations. The *Graphic* and the *Pictorial World* were generous with the space allotted to the book and with their praise. Arguably they were being kind to a fellow-contributor; in fact they were heralding Caldecott's future career, when he would be better known as an illustrator of books than as a regular contributor to weekly journals.

More and more books to illustrate came his way. For Macmillans he illustrated Louisa Morgan's *Baron Bruno*. It was the first children's book he attempted, and the stories and his illustrations are quite unlike what was to become his normal work for children. The stories resemble some of Grimm's tales, and the drawings are heavily detailed and over-finished, like the early drawings for *Old Christmas*. Alice Comyns Carr, wife of the London art critic of the *Manchester Guardian*, wrote a series of articles which Caldecott offered to illustrate if they were to be published as a book, and this, *North Italian Folk*, appeared in 1878. Another book with Henry Blackburn, begun in 1874 and put aside, was completed.

In addition to this, and his painting and modelling, was his work in the *Graphic*. His first coloured illustrations in this most popular of fashionable weeklies appeared in the Christmas number for 1876; they were based on his *Old Christmas* drawings and made two pages. From then until the summer number of 1886 when it printed the last of his illustrated stories, virtually all Caldecott's magazine illustration appeared in the *Graphic*. From it came most of his regular income: by 1882 he was paid for

'a *Graphic* page . . . (tell it not in Gath)—30 guineas or more—and I am meditating raising that price'.[8]

His oil paintings were never as popular as the water colours, especially those of his picture-book illustrations, but he exhibited fairly regularly from 1876. A direct request to paint a portrait would be gently but firmly turned aside, for as he knew well, it was difficult to keep caricature out of his work:

'I fear that I ought not to approach Mrs Green brush in hand—my brush is not a very reverent one.'[9]

The reliefs he made were more successful. Many of them, particularly those of animals, show a sure grasp of anatomy: one is aware not only of the tension of a surface but of the masses beneath which give it its form. The trouble he took was considerable. When he was working on a terracotta model of a cat crouched ready to spring, he had three cats about him in the studio, one a skeleton, the second dead, and the third alive. He took as much care about the colouring of his work:

'I intended it to be much greener—like some old bronzes. It is rather black I think—like certain old bronzes, but not of so pleasant and poisonous a hue as I could wish.'[10]

He was understandably bitter that 'artists say I am only a clever amateur'.[11]

III

By 1877 Edmund Evans needed a new illustrator if he was to continue with one particularly successful part of his engraving and printing business. For twelve years or so he had produced children's books which Walter Crane had illustrated, but now Crane did not want to produce any more sixpenny titles. Evans was the most skilled engraver and printer of coloured illustrations in England and Caldecott a relative newcomer, but Evans made only one stipulation when he asked the young man to illustrate two picture books: they were to cost a shilling.

The stories, and how they were to be treated, were entirely Caldecott's choice. He made a blank dummy book and rapidly drew 'a number of sketches in the rough, page for page as they will appear'.[12]

The dummy for *The House that Jack Built* shows how close the printed book was to these first sketches. Detailed descriptions can be as easily written from the few lines on every page of the dummy as from the printed book itself.

Before publication day Caldecott sailed for France, and when the books were reviewed he was staying at Cannes, where:

'2 or 3 notices have been read by the visitors to this hotel and I am asked if I am any relation to the gifted artist. 30,000 of each book, *Gilpin* and *House*, delivered to Xmas—50,000 of each expected to sell straight away. Hope so. I get a small royalty—a small, small royalty.'[13]

Without exception the reviews were full of praise. The enthusiasm of *The Times* reviewer was carried along for three hundred words and it was natural

4

that he should end with a comparison with Evans's former protégé:

'In a few strokes, dashed off apparently at random, he can portray a scene or incident to the full as correctly and completely, and far more lucidly than Mr Crane in his later and far more elaborate style.'[14]

Caldecott—as an illustrator of picture books for children—had begun spectacularly.

So confident was Evans that the plans for the next pair were already advanced. Caldecott wrote:

'Some of those designs [for *The Babes in* the *Wood* and *The Mad Dog*] were made when I was very very stomachily seedy at Florence and most were arranged and planned there. I scribbled out the plan of 1 book in the train between Florence and Bologna.'[15]

Until the end of his life Caldecott was now committed during the spring and early summer of each year to selecting the titles, planning and producing the original drawings for a pair of picture books.

The subjects he chose were a curious mixture of traditional nursery rhymes, pieces by 18th century writers, and nonsense made up by himself. There was one title, written mainly by a friend, which uncharacteristically Caldecott used without acknowledgement. In its review of *The Three Jovial Huntsmen* the *Manchester Guardian*[16] chided him for not admitting that Edwin Waugh had written the main part of the rhyme. Caldecott explained the reasons why no author is credited, and, he implied, the reviewer should have noticed the additions, for:

'I supposed all Lancashire people knew *Old Cronies* by heart.'[17]

Successful though the books were, Caldecott became dissatisfied by the returns they gave him. His royalty was raised, but he thought

'that the only way for me to get more is by raising the price of the books—putting them in stiffer cover apart from first and last pictures. Or should I threaten or stick out or something? Do you think ½ of the present sale would be found for a ²2/– book'?[18]

Despite these thoughts the picture-book series continued. They were first published singly, then in collections of four, and finally in two collections of eight. The second eight-part collection was completed in 1885, but for a while Caldecott was unwilling to do this:

'As to future Picture Books. I do not want to do any more of this kind: but I shall be glad to hear if you and Routledges have a strong opinion that a couple more should be done. Of course Routledges run little risk and will perhaps wish to make up another 4 and another 8 volume: but it is of no use doing other 2 merely to make up volumes to oblige them—if a fair sale may be relied on for us, well and good—I'll consider it.'[19]

He made two more picture books, however. They were published after he sailed for America, where he died on 12 February 1886.

IV

Any of the sixteen picture books, which are most people's introduction to Caldecott, tells something of the man. The prodigality with which he drew shows at once how fast he worked and that even the shortest text gave him a long sequence of ideas.

His great rivals, who also had the benefit of Edmund Evans's skills, were Kate Greenaway and Walter Crane. All three illustrated *Sing a Song of Sixpence*. Kate Greenaway, in *April Baby's Book of Tunes* has just one illustration; Crane, in *Baby's Opera*, puts the verses and four small illustrations on a single page; Caldecott made eight coloured and twenty-two black-and-white illustrations.

The difference between the three books is far more than just this. By changing a word in the title—his book is *Sing a Song for Sixpence*—Caldecott adds a dimension to the original rhyme which is completely lacking in Crane's and Miss Greenaway's pages. He tells a story which is far more complex and involved than appears at first reading.

Here, and in every picture book, is certain evidence of the clever amateur —the clever man who, in the older sense of the word, loves to draw. They show just how accomplished an illustrator he was, for at no point does he merely put the words of a text into visual form. With each illustration Caldecott adds something quite unique to the story.

Why was the maiden forlorn in *The House that Jack Built*? Because, says Caldecott, she had seen the dog tossed, killed and buried. Why, in *The Frog who Would A-wooing Go*, did the frog ask the rat to go with him to Miss Mouse's house? Because he was too shy to go wooing alone.

Caldecott has his chosen text as initial inspiration, but his skill as a story-teller takes over. It is this, the ability to weave one story around another, coupled with the mastery which produces pictures not fixed in time, that makes his picture books as enjoyable today as when they were first published.

V

For information about a partnership which resulted in three very popular children's books we have both Caldecott's letters and those of Mrs Ewing, who wrote the stories. From them we can see how the work of illustrator and author began and flourished; how during the production of a book they complimented and criticised each other; and just how their most popular tale came within an ace of failing altogether.

At the start of their collaboration Caldecott could be thought of as the senior partner: his picture books had made him as well known in the nursery as the drawing-room, and although Mrs Ewing had already written far more books than he had illustrated, she had not achieved the success that was his.

Caldecott had been asked by Miss Gatty, Mrs Ewing's sister, to provide a coloured illustration for *Aunt Judy's Magazine*, and Mrs Ewing would write a story based on this picture. Writing to explain her weaknesses as an author, Mrs Ewing suggested that:

'What I should like best of all would be if you would do a rough coloured sketch of anything that pleases you, and if you would pack it up with one or two pen and ink scratches of *any* quaint groups or figures that float before your mental retina!' [20]

But by the end of the letter she describes in detail the illustration he was to draw:

'If the coloured sketch would be easily concocted out of a laddie with an aureole of warm yellow hair on a red-haired pony, full tilt among the geese over a village green (the geese to include pretty frightened members of my sex!) . . .' [21]

Inspired by the drawing (or the note she gave him) Mrs Ewing wrote *Jackanapes* for the October 1879 edition of *Aunt Judy's Magazine*. By the following July she had decided to publish it as a book, and asked Caldecott to make ten illustrations and half a dozen initial letters. He put off this work for as long as he could, and did not become immersed in its production until 1883. Nominally the Society for the Promotion of Christian Knowledge was the publisher, but handled only its distribution: it was the author and illustrator who controlled the production up to the time the bound books were delivered to the publisher. Evans was to print it, and Caldecott acted in part as Mrs Ewing's intermediary, discussing estimates, royalties and production plans.

An edition of 10,000 was published in October 1883.

'At first Smiths said they would not take *Jackanapes* in *paper* covers. Then they said they would not put "anything" more of the kind—coloured boards or otherwise—on their stalls until Xmas. They were "glutted".
. . . The 2,000 first printed and bound in *paper* all sold off in a fortnight or so—and the publishers—Society P.C.K.—ordered 500 more copies from E. Evans. Meanwhile, tinted boards were being prepared for rest of 10,000 edition, printed; but unbound.
Cost of new cover (same designs) borne by author, engraver and printer, and *me*.' [22]

It had not been the easiest book that Caldecott had worked on, but encouraged by its immediate success in spite of Smiths' temporary embargo, he and Mrs Ewing began to prepare another of their *Aunt Judy's Magazine* stories for book publication. In its own way *Daddy Darwin's Dovecot* was to be as troublesome as *Jackanapes*, and in the letters concerning it we are given an insight into the difficulties which accompanied changes in the reproduction of illustrations between 1880 and 1890. In 1880 the wood engraving was, as it had been for six decades, the chief medium for book illustration. By 1890 it had lost this place to the photographically prepared process plate, and before the turn of the century even Edmund Evans was forced to admit:

'I used to employ two rooms full of assistants at one time, now they [his sons] can scarcely keep the engraver employed.' [23]

But in 1884 process techniques were not perfected. To save wood engravings or photo-process plates from wear, electrotypes were usually made and the illustration was printed from these rather than the expensive and easily damaged originals.

A wood engraving is made on box wood about 23 mm high and the printing surface stands higher than the non-printing areas. Normally large white areas were about 2·5 mm lower than the lines which were to print, a depth which produced good electrotypes. Photographic process plates are made by etching zinc plates with acid, and in these early days it was impossible to etch the zinc deeply without destroying the line which was to print. This shallow depth of etch could produce poor electrotypes and, consequently, badly printed illustrations.

Most of the faulty illustrations in *Daddy Darwin's Dovecot* can be traced to poor etching and faulty electrotypes. Unfortunately these imperfections were compounded when, by an oversight, Evans printed the book in black ink and not in the brown that had been stipulated.

For the third book which Mrs Ewing, Caldecott and Evans were to produce together, *Lob-Lie-by-the-Fire*, they returned to wood-engraved illustrations.

Mrs Ewing died before the book was completed, and other, half-formed plans ended with her death:

'... if my best and tersest and most finished writing combined in one volume with your finest and freest work, such as in the best of your toybooks, we might command a success that would make haggling over a few pounds for engraving worse than folly'. [24]

VI

Randolph Caldecott's letters cover more than half his lifetime. The earliest that is printed here was written when he was only eighteen, the last just three months before he died.

The early letters show him growing up in a country town, a town he was to remember twenty years later and which can be seen clearly in the last pic-

8

ture book he was to make. Through them we can trace his friendships: with young men who worked, farmed and hunted in north Shropshire; with older men, closely attentive servants of a bank whose routine Caldecott escaped; with wealthy socialites into whose circle the successful illustrator was welcomed.

His first year in London was full of new excitements. The lightly boasted pleasure he takes in the company of the famous; the journeys he makes through Europe; the hints he drops of where his illustrations may be seen: all are described with an obvious, innocent enjoyment.

Before his marriage Caldecott lived for six years in an apartment at 46 Great Russell Street, opposite the British Museum. At the beginning of September 1879 he moved into a house at Kemsing, a tiny village near Sevenoaks, Kent. Wybournes was an old-fashioned country house and until his wedding day in March 1880 it was bachelor's quarters:

'I have no curtains and no carpet in this room; but I have 2 Scinde rugs on the floor; I have borrowed the drawing-room fender (its only piece of furniture) and a few things from the dining-parlour, and I am warm and cosy. My bedroom just holds a bed and an adjoining room holds the other things.'[25]

Chief among its advantages, Wybournes was close to Chelsfield, the home of his fiançée, Marian Brind, who lived

'about 7 miles from here (nothing to a good horse)'.[26]

He and his wife stayed at Wybournes until September 1882. The house was burnt down at the turn of the century, but it is still possible to recognise corners of the gardens from his sketches.

In June 1882 he took a twenty-one-year lease on 24 Holland Street, a tall narrow-fronted Georgian house which stands in a small, quiet street close to Kensington High Street. Much time was spent that summer searching for another country house; though when they had decided upon Broomfield, a large house hidden in the lanes of Frensham, Surrey, there were annoying delays:

'Broomfields house is so dirty that we cannot put our furniture and things in order yet. And the Bogles only left on Friday last—2 servants there still . . .'[27]

It was not a successful move. Caldecott regretted leaving Wybournes, and they lived at Frensham for only three years.

Many letters were written while he travelled in Europe. At first his journeys were made on specific journalistic assignments: to Austria, the Harz Mountains, to Brittany, but it soon became possible for him to escape English winters, and in alternate years he would spend four or five months—November to April—abroad. It would be wrong to consider these trips as holidays. As an illustrator armed with a commission he could set up his studio anywhere:

picture books could be made as well in Menton and Florence as in London.

He gives us glimpses of a way of life which has vanished. How strange it seems to us that if Caldecott travelled from, say, Cannes to Rome in December and January he could stop at any town en route and *expect* to meet friends. How different, too, was travelling: a carriage-drive from Frensham to his parents-in-law at Chelsfield, no more than sixty miles, would take as long as a rail journey from Genoa to Paris, and, like that journey, would involve an overnight stop.

Each letter tells us something about the man, but naturally the most revealing are those written over a long period to one correspondent. His life is best shown in those written to William Clough, Frederick Locker and Frederick Green, but for information about his work we owe much to Mrs Ewing. That enthusiastic, practical woman wrote to Caldecott not only about the books they co-produced but also about his picture books. She did not simply praise them—as did so many—she criticised them minutely, compared his work with other illustrators, suggested additional titles he might illustrate. Her sharp approval drew from him much that is half-hidden in his work.

Sketches tumbled from his pen as he wrote to friend or business colleague. It was as though the man couldn't stop drawing: in the two hundred and fifty or so letters which have been collected here, there are over a hundred illustrations.

The letters are a unique record—in his own words and in his semi-private pictures—of a man who was 'not only an artist gifted with an inimitable specialty, but . . . also one of the most gentle-hearted and generous men';[28] the clever amateur whose picture books have remained for a hundred years favourites with succeeding generations of children and adults.

1. Both the *Dictionary of National Biography* and Henry Blackburn in *Randolph Caldecott, a Personal Memoir of his Early Art Career* state that Caldecott's father was an accountant, but on Randolph Caldecott's birth certificate his father, John, is described as a hatter.

2. Letter to John Harrison, 16 February 1865; *see* p. 191.

3. Letter to John Lennox, 27 September 1868; *see* p. 209.

4. Letter to Henry Blackburn, 16 January 1872; *see* p. 20.

5. Letter to John Harrison, 27 August 1873; *see* p. 196.

6. Letter to William Etches, 5 February 1873; *see* p. 57.

7. Letter to William Etches, 1 January 1874; *see* p. 65.

8. Letter to Mrs Ewing, 15 December 1882; *see* p. 90.

9. Letter to Frederick Green, 3 February 1883; *see* p. 170.

10. Letter to William Clough, 29 August 1878; *see* p. 30–1.

11. *Pall Mall Gazette*, 16 February 1886.

12. *ibid.*

13. Letter to William Clough, 13 December 1878; *see* p. 33.

14. *The Times*, 14 November 1878.

15. Letter to William Clough, 8 November 1879; *see* p. 38.

16. *Manchester Guardian*, 20 November 1880.

17. Letter to *Manchester Guardian*, 24 November 1880; *see* p. 252–3.
18. Letter to Frederick Locker, 24 November 1880; *see* p. 232.
19. Letter to Edmund Evans, 5 November 1884; *see* p. 73–4.
20. Letter from Mrs Ewing to Caldecott, 4 August 1879; *see* p. 75.
21. *ibid.*
22. Letter to Frederick Green, 6 November 1883; *see* p. 176.
23. In a letter dated 6 October 1897 to a Mr Jones.
24. Letter from Mrs Ewing to Caldecott, October 1884; *see* p. 119.
25. Letter to William Clough, 8 November 1879; *see* p. 38.
26. Letter to Horatia Gatty, 17 January 1880; *see* p. 145.
27. Letter to Frederick Green, 11 October 1882; *see* p. 170.
28. *Manchester Guardian*, 29 November 1880.

PUBLISHER'S NOTE

The letters are arranged in alphabetical order according to the recipient.

EDWIN AUSTIN ABBEY

1852–1911

Edwin Abbey was one of many Americans who settled in England during the latter part of the 19th century. He trained as an illustrator in Philadelphia, but made his reputation in New York on *Harper's Weekly*, to which, for a short time, Caldecott was a contributor. In 1878 Abbey came to England, where he settled permanently after 1880. Abbey was successful not only as a book illustrator but as a water colourist and mural painter.

[1]
Broomfield, Frensham, Farnham, Surrey
30 June 1885

My dear Abbey,
  A happy new July to you! Have not got a Railway Guide at this moment, but tomorrow—Wedy—shall be happy in that possession, I hope. Will then tell you of trains for Sunday or thereabouts. We

are in middle of our hay-making, but shall leave a little of the roughest grass on a hill-side for you to mow. I see you at it!

Genial N.E. winds are blowing. Bees buzzing. Ponds smelling. Roses blooming. Men drinking.

All is divine!

So no more now from yours rurally,
R. Caldecott

WILLIAM HENRY AMYOT

A Newcastle solicitor who also wrote many articles for the *Gentleman's Magazine* and the *Athenaeum*.

[2]
Broomfield, Frensham, Farnham, Surrey
25 February 1883

Dear Sir,

I am very much obliged to you for sending me copies of 2 Nursery Rhymes and for accompanying them with a complimentary letter.

That of *The little market woman*[1] is very well known and often appears in Children's Books—illustrated and otherwise: and I seem to know a version of the other. But however much or little they may be known I should not care if it suited me to use them—this at present it would not do—I am grateful to you for bringing them to my notice notwithstanding.

I am, dear sir,

Yours very truly,

Randolph Caldecott

1. The rhyme is:

> 'There was a little woman
> As I have heard tell,
> She went to market
> Her eggs for to sell;
> She went to market
> All on a market day
> And she fell asleep
> On the King's highway.'

It had appeared in Walter Crane's *Baby's Bouquet* four years before.

THOMAS ARMSTRONG, C.B.

1832–1911

Armstrong was Caldecott's closest friend in London: they met almost daily, many holidays were spent together, and Marian Caldecott was godmother to the Armstrongs' only son.

During his youthful art studies in Paris, Armstrong made life-long friendships with George du Maurier, Thomas Lamont and Sir Edward Poynter, and he later introduced Caldecott to this circle. He was a busy interior decorator, working particularly in the north of England, and on several of these houses he and Caldecott were collaborators. For seven years, from 1881, Armstrong was Director for Art at the South Kensington (now the Victoria and Albert) Museum, and for his work there was created C.B. in 1898.

[3]
Brazenose Club, Brazenose Street, Manchester
29 June 1871

My dear Armstrong,

My dear Armstrong,
    It was fortunate for me that you gave that sketch of a 'Seaside drama' to Mr Bradley, for two or three days afterwards I had a letter from Swain,[1] who asked me to put a scene on the wood for approval, as Shirley Brooks[2] had said that the subject would do—with more gentlemanlike men and a prettier girl.

I sent one block to Swain, who returned it as too sketchy and asked me to try again. I did so; and he then sent me blocks for the other scenes. After these had been in his hands a few days I received a note from him to say that they were accepted, and if I liked to send any more drawings to him he would shew them for approval.

So I look forward to seeing myself in 'Punch' shortly.[3]

Now this is pleasing to me, and I have no doubt that, considering the trouble you have taken, it will also be pleasing to you, to whom my thanks are due.

I am making one or two things to send to Mr Blackburn[4] shortly.

16

Thomson will tell you more about this city and its inhabitants than I can—
I believe he is in London.

Hoping you are well, I remain,
Yours faithfully,
Randolph Caldecott

P.S. I have thoughts of framing Swain's last letter!

1. Joseph Swain (1820–1909); he controlled the engraving of illustrations in *Punch* from 1843 to 1900.

2. Shirley Brooks (1816–1874); editor of *Punch* 1870–4.

3. Caldecott's first drawing in *Punch* was in the issue for 22 June 1872.

4. Henry Blackburn (1830–1897); editor of *London Society*. He became a close friend and collaborator of Caldecott. *See also* pp. 20–1.

E. J. BAILLIE

Honorary Secretary of Chester Art Conversazione and later Honorary Secretary of the first management committee of the Grosvenor Museum, Chester.

[4]
24 Holland Street, Kensington
19 March 1883

Dear Sir,

I leave here for Broomfield, Farnham, Surrey tomorrow or Wednesday and I shall be glad if you will kindly send *address* for Package of Pictures &c, direct to H. J. Murcott, Framemaker, 6 Endell Street, Long Acre, WC; also to Mrs Austin, Fine Art Gallery, Cardiff (who will forward a picture); also to H. G. Seaman, Esq., Manchester and Salford Bank, Mosley Street, Manchester (who will perhaps be able to send 3 contributions).

This will save time. If writing to me it will be best to address here up to Wednesday morning.

I suppose that you will not want me to pay the carriage both ways. All my exhibitions are to be returned to Holland St.

The temporary mounting and framing of the drawings will be an expense to me which I shall be happy to bear for the sake of the cause in which you are interested.

The works will be insured against fire, I suppose.

Yours very truly,

R. Caldecott

[5]
Broomfield, Frensham, Farnham, Surrey
26 March 1883

Dear Sir,

I am much obliged to you for the care and attention which you are giving to my contributions to your exhibition.[1] Those from London and Manchester have been sent off to Mr Lamont—started on Thursday last, I believe. And I hope he will receive an oil picture of Frogs from Cardiff.

I shall be obliged if they are all returned to 24, Holland Street, Kensington. You have my hearty wishes that a successful result will reward you for your exertions in this good cause.

At 19, Pepper St in your city reside my step-mother and her 3 daughters, who are not rich enough to regard ˢ4/– as other than an important sum. If it could be done as a favour to me and to them, they would be glad to receive an order of admission to the exhibition. Should, however, this be against all rules, pray pardon me for having suggested it, and believe me,
Yours very truly,
R. Caldecott

1. The drawings were sent to the loan exhibition which accompanied the annual exhibition of work by students of Chester School of Art. Among the twenty-six frames which Caldecott submitted were eleven unpublished drawings for Aesop's *Fables*.

HENRY BLACKBURN

1830–1897

It was due chiefly to Henry Blackburn's encouragement that Caldecott left Manchester for London: in 1871 *London Society*, of which Blackburn was editor, was the first journal of any consequence to publish Caldecott's drawings. Originally a civil servant who turned editor, author and lecturer on illustration, Blackburn was very aware of the change that the new techniques of process engraving were to make to illustrators and wood engravers. Caldecott made many drawings for *Academy Notes*, which Blackburn edited, and he illustrated many articles and two books which Blackburn wrote.

[6]
Brazenose Club, Manchester
16 January 1872

Dear Mr Blackburn,

I beg to acknowledge the receipt of a cheque for thirty pounds for my drawings in "London Society"[1] last year, and to thank you for the same.
Yours faithfully,
Randolph Caldecott

P.S. As you suggest we can talk about rate of payment &c when I next see you. The cheque is welcome and I am grateful to you for your encouragement. R.C.
P.P.S. On second thoughts, I send a detached receipt. R.C.

[7]
46 Great Russell Street, London WC
21 August 1878

Dear Blackburn,

I enclose you sketches of 4 drawings which I have made—suitable, I think, for article on artists' haunts.[2] I hope you will think so—I propose to add a small upright one as an initial 'cut'—an old peasant and child—costume as in margin. These drawings are 'dessins à la plume' and do not pretend to the elegance of the illustrations to the Wye (see Mag. of Art, posted tonight). They would, however, gain a little in quality by being reduced a little in size—which will be necessary, for they are all (except the man going forth to his labour) wider than a page of the Mag. (I speak of those I have here ready to go to Cassells). There is more quality in the *drawings* than in

20

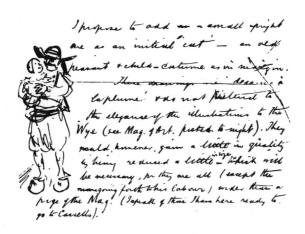

these sketches; but not much more *work*—except in the view of Pont Aven over page.

Perhaps Cassells would have preferred something like the *Wye*. I hope you won't. I can make another or 2 if you order me. A small one or 2—eh? Let me hear, and if Cassells will send, or shall I send and when?—if they'll do. Yours faithfully,

R. Caldecott

I hope you are all well. Kind regards. Will write to Mrs Blackburn. But I wish to send this at once. R.C.

1. This payment was for a total of seventeen illustrations and decorations which appeared in *London Society* between February and December 1871.
2. Reproduced in *Magazine of Art* September–December 1878.

DAVID BOGUE

For a year, 1881–82, Bogue was the publisher of *Aunt Judy's Magazine* which was edited at this time by Horatia Gatty (*see* letters 114–144). The small circulation of the magazine may have contributed to his bankruptcy in that year.

[8]
Wybournes, Kemsing, Nr Sevenoaks
23 August 1881

Dear Sir,

At Miss Gatty's request I send you direct a design for new cover of *Aunt Judy's Magazine*.[1] She wishes it put in the hands of engraver at once, I believe—and thinks that this will save time.

There accompanies it a piece of paper—the best of the patterns of coloured paper which I received—upon which I have scribbled.

It is your proposed plan, I believe—to print a tint of warmer brown upon the engraving so as to throw out the figures.

May I have proofs on white paper and also on tinted paper in order that I can touch where necessary and also apply the tint for copying?

Yours very truly,
Randolph Caldecott

1. It was for the November 1881 issue, the first for which Bogue was the publisher.

WILLIAM CLOUGH

1838–1905

Caldecott and Clough were fellow clerks at the head office of the Manchester and Salford Bank from 1867 to 1872. Clough remained in the Bank's employ for the rest of his life, and was the only one of Caldecott's special friends at the Bank to outlive him. The letters and drawings which Caldecott sent Clough were sold at Sotheby's in 1925.

[9]
with T. Armstrong, Esq., Wynnstay Grove, Fallowfield
6 October 1876
Friday morning

Dear Clough,

My friend Armstrong—who is staying with his father (mentioned above) —wishes me to ask you to come up here this evening if you would like to see me. He will be pleased if you can do so, and so shall I!!! I am only just recovering from a little illness which might have developed into a great illness and I do not like to go out much—the weather of this morning not being promising—otherwise I should go down to the Bank.[1] I came on Wednesday and go away from here tomorrow. I shall look into the Bank tomorrow or Monday or Tuesday.

Yours affectionately,

R. Caldecott

P.S. 7 o'clock tea, 3rd house on right in Grove. I have asked Lang.

[10]
46 Great Russell Street, London WC
17 December 1876

Dear Clough,

I was contemplating a reply to your kind note of 9th October, when I received your still kinder one of 3rd of December. It is exceedingly pleasing

23

to me to hear that you like *B. hall*[2] and do not think it worse than *Old X*. I know that the great swells—some of them, anyway—think "Paradise regained" as good as "Paradise lost". I think my artist friends here prefer the *B. hall* to *Old X*. I have heard of a fine review, but perhaps may come some depressing ones. Anyhow, it is cheering to have a few people speak well of one's efforts, and though one would like all to do so, one must not expect it. As far as I've got, people say they like *B. hall*.

And I have received cheering letters and heard encouraging remarks about the *Graphic* Xmas sketches.[3] So I suppose I must struggle away, although I am not worth quite so many corpses as I fancied last summer. But the summer is past, the harvest is ended, and some of the wheat is very light, and I am amongst the mildewed. I am very glad to have your opinions about my works: but don't be afraid of criticising.

You enquire about my health—I am jogging along very well, I think. No irregular habits. But such a lot of work waiting to be done in so many ways that on Thursday next I think of flying away to the Riviera and staying at Mentone or somewhere near—where I can find something to draw and somewhere to draw it—for 2 or 3 months. Plenty of sunshine and lemons.

Thank you for your letters and their kind observations. I hope you and your people are all well. With kind regards, believe me,
Yours faithfully,
R. Caldecott
P.S. "Merry Xmas, Yah!!"

[11]
Splendide Hôtel, Mentone, France
16 February 1877
posted 17th

Dear Clough,
This blessed place is usually called by its Italian name, but, as it is now France, I suppose we must adopt the French—Menton—in our postal communications. Two bays—an east and a west—the east full of consumptive people I believe—people who house before sunset—not been there yet—only

smelt it from afar. West bay for the robust. I am in the west bay, and as to housing before sundown, why this blessed evening I have been drinking in a confectioner's shop with Armstrong who arrived on the Riviera di Ponente 13 days ago. I'm worth several corpses yet. Thank you for your kind enquiries in your letter of 20th January. Don't run away with a wrong idea because I have come to Mentone. People come here for lung diseases. My lungs are considered all right. Would bear inspection if hung on a butcher's door-post and called lights. Which reminds me that I reached Monaco—a few miles west of this—on 26th of Decr and left on 8th of Feby. A lovely spot. A principality. A casino with gaming tables. Such larks. You can lose a lot of money. The frequenters—(here shed a tear).

Balmy weather. Blue sea. Clear sky usually. No rain since beginning of January. A trifle then. Mountains close up to sea. Curious little towns and villages stuck on the hill tops—1000s of feet above sea. Went to one yesterday. A,[4] I, a donkey, and a woman. I rid ass up hills. Usually walked down. The woman, as is usual, came to see after the donkey which was a female of the name of Garibaldi. Had lunch under the olive trees—purple anemones agrowing all around. Can't describe it.[5] Orange and lemon orchards—full of fruit.

Living in hotels rather dear here. Plenty of English. Several Manchester folks in this. One lady very civil—offered to lend me a book—did so. Has a nice niece. Hope you are quite well. Might pick up a dowager or an invalid cheap here.

Italian border 2 or 3 miles east. Shall go on east in a week or two perhaps. Kind regard to all friends. Thank you for your letter.
Yours faithfully,
R. Caldecott

[12]
(Hôtel de Gênes), Genoa
13 April 1877
3.30 p.m.

Dear Clough,
I have just read your note—welcome—of 27th ult. Have read it in the garden of a *caffé*. Am in the garden *now*. Over my head are orange trees with bright fruit—30 feet high—Japanese medlars, drooping miniosas (or something else); round about are pink azaleas and other flowers, several marble statues, lamps &c., and a few waiters. I've just made a sketch of the garding—perhaps [it] will appear some day—am not doing ought for *Graphic* at present, though. Had a cup of coffee—forbidden beverage. 'Twas to keep awake after [a] bottle of grignolino secco—not up to much, left half.

This garden is between 2 old palaces in the Via Nuova, which is a narrow, cool street with nothing but palaces right and left. Now not used by the owners, I think. Plenty of marble round—a little dirt, and a hell of a noise. Yelling, sqwalling, sculping, knocking, rowing, &c. I never was in such a noisy hotel as the Hôtel de Gênes in my life—a chequered one.

I hope you are better. Glad you say so. I heard of Oxford Road branch, M[anchester] & S[alford]. Cuckoo have you in Isle of Man? Nightingales here in a cage, and some blasted cockatoos or paroquets, as if not noise enoo already. I go on to Rapallo, 30 miles east in day or 2. Hôtel d'Europe, Rapallo, Italy. 8 or 10 days there—return home.

I thank you for nanny goats. Got none myself. Very pleased to hear what you say of *Graphic* things.[6] 1st letter was not what I intended to appear, I had made *another* and sent it, but we or they muddled it. So I have one unseen. They are all my property, and are larger much.

Tell Lang address. Kind regards,
Yours faithfully,
R. Caldecott
As if I didn't know what *teem* means, or *sheed*[7] either. R.C!

[13]
Hôtel Belle Vue, Santa Margherita, Italy
Friday, 20 April 1877

Dear Clough,
I don't know how it is: but, somehow, directly I have mealed I wish to open my bosom to somebody. Your letter came this mng. Thank you!

I've just asked the gossoon how the devil he appelles this hotel—says as above. Well, the bay in which Porto Fino, St M., and Rapallo are situate is in front thro' window—old town of Chiavari in distance. Sestri-levante also, far away eastern headland of bay of Spezia. Sea blue, sky blue and white.

Walked over rather warm from Rapallo this mng., $1\frac{1}{4}$ hours slowly—reposed and dozed in church for $\frac{3}{4}$ hour. Like ritualistic churches, always open, cool retreat, but no smoking.

Came into this place—walked up stairs, banged doors with my camp stool —ristorante being locked. Landlord appeared at last. Then rough waiter. Have fed. 6 cutlets—God knows what of—bread, small bottle of wine, cheese = 160 centesimi.

I am pleased to hear you went to B[lack] and W[hite] Ex[hibition] P[rivate] View. Glad that noble patron of art has purchased those drawings. Man of discernment!

What mean you by "Pelican of W'ness"? I have *sent nothing* to R.A. Ex.[8] Meant to send *Storks* painted 1875 but too much bother to get it from owner's house in country. Other day I drew some Pelicans and a lady drew trees and background—perhaps paint it this summer.

Want to be back for *press day* R.A., 2nd May. Promised to help a man. Best day to see. Alone in a room sometimes. You mention exam. on Cromwell. I am much obliged to you. But if I had thought you would have liked the story, I would have mentioned it sometime since. Pardon my neglect. Adoo!

Yours faithfully,

R. Caldecott

[14]
46 Great Russell Street, London WC
9 November 1877

Dear Clough,

I hope you are quite well and everybody belonging to you.

Your remark about having got my scrap of paper was a bucketful of comfort to me for I posted it at Rugby in company with a billet writ unto a lady whose good opinion I possess and am anxious to retain, and I had not received the reply for which my heart yearned. So I was afraid that the porter into whose lucrous hands I put these letters had played me false. Your note, therefore, was a pleasure—as usual—and a relief—as an extra—howbeit—I still yearn with regard to the other billet.

Quite well? There is no news. I have read your anecdote. It is now nearly 3 years since I gave up telling that story. *I* always said it was Darwin who replied "There's a divinity doth shape &c."

I thank you very much for the newspaper containing the account of the M. & S. Bank. I had no idea that I did once belong to so wonderful an institution.

I met a man in the country who had read the article and he also sent it to me.

A prophet sometimes gets honour in his own countree, eh?

Kind regards to all friends and yourself from

Yours faithfully,

R. Caldecott

P.S. I write to Lang, and address to 47 Mosley Street, right?

[15]
with Dr George, Whitchurch, Salop
3 May 1878

Dear Clough,

How are you? Happy new May to you and all! Thank you for your note of 18 Apl with story—divorce desired—very good. I have told it and it has given unalloyed pleasure. Only one man said he had heard it before.

On Monday was the R. Academy Artists' Day. I have a picture[9] there—oh, so dreadfully, dreadfully hung! Too high for the interesting details to be discovered, and so opposed in tone and key to the picture below it that all the many charms of its effect and general aspect have faded like the tracery of frost.* So badly placed it is and so sad and looks that I won't make a sketch for Academy Notes (Blackburn's) although desired. The Grosvenor Gallery private view was Tuesday. I have a small bas-relief there.[10]

Amen. I agree with your suggestions about war, Russia, and what not. Adieu! Regards to friends.
Yours faithfully,
R. Caldecott

   * I have sold it to Mundella, the tribune of the people.

[16]
46 Great Russell Street, London WC
22 June 1878

Dear Clough,

I am sure you will join me in wishing myself many happy returns of the day. Let us drink! It is my birthday—my monthly birthday. Therefore, as a little treat, I write unto you.

I have had your letter of 7 May, St Helens, on my table since the 8th ult. I regret that business and pleasure and idleness have combined to prevent me from writing earlier. And what weather too! Are you quite well? There is nothing much in that letter requiring direct reply. So I thank you for it and assure you that I have noted your remarks—especially some in a poetic strain and luscious. Were you quite well when you wrote them?

And you have written again! Nice of you! And you ask me if I am reproducing *Boar hunts*. Now that is encouraging. I have had many encouraging letters lately and yet have not become excited. In fact I have calmly said Dam it! and laid them aside. I am demoralized, O Clough! but I *am* having the said *Boar hunt* reproduced 6 times—in an exact manner, I hope. Not in *expensive* metal but in metal. They will cost me somewhat, however, and if I can sell them at a price sufficient to pay me for the labour of the whole I shall rejoice. My art will be glad and my ills will hop. Soon, oh soon do I expect to hear of the reproductions and their cost, and then will I let you know how much I shall want for each. Thank you.

I have to-day received a note asking me if I paint portraits of horses and if so, prices according to size.

On Monday last Mr William Langton, late the managing director of the M. & S. Bank came to visit me and sat a while a-talking. He looks very well, and talks very practically on art—landscape water colour particularly. He asked me to go and see him at Ingatestone which I shall do, if I have time, during the summer.

To the friends that are about you I send greetings.

No more at present. Amen!

Yours faithfully,

R. Caldecott

29

46 Great Russell Street, London WC
29 August 1878

My dear Clough,

Are yer quite well now?

I should have written unto you—even from the land of Brittany, the land of cider and sardines—before now; but to confess the truth, the sitting on Inn benches, under pretence of studying and sketching the forms of the passersby, for a month is somewhat unhinging to a mind dwelling in a body not over-robust.

However, I have been back a fortnight now, and the peaceful air of Bloomsbury and the seclusion of London have calmed my spirit and soothed my nerves. So I settle down to a little correspondence.

I wish to tell you—in answer to enquiries which you made time back—that I have sent a metal reproduction of my *Boar Hunt* to Manchester—to the forthcoming exhibition. You will there see it, probably.

If you care to have one at the price named, do not take the one exhibited, for it was sent during my absence from town, and I fear that the colour is not very good. And besides, somebody else *might* fancy the one in the exhibition. I intended it to be much greener—like some old bronzes. It is rather black, I think—like certain old bronzes, but not of so pleasant and poisonous a hue as I

could wish. I judge by 2 or 3 which I have here—and which I shall have made greener in a *permanent* way. So if you do want one, please write to me and say so. If not, please write to me and tell me to go to that bourne (the lower and warmer one) from which no sculptor returns.

N.B. A very beautiful book on Brittany[11] will be out next spring.

Kind regards—and to friends.

Yours faithfully,

R. Caldecott

[18]
46 Great Russell Street, London WC
1 October 1878

Dear Clough,

Whilst basking in the sunshine of the smiles of some amiable and agreeable damsels a week or 2 ago, I pulled your last letters out of my pocket—being desirous of a riddance of pocket-filling stuff—and I re-read them—I

did—and got off by heart what you had written so that I might comment thereupon when next I wrote unto you, which I now do, greeting.

But, Oh my Clough, I have forgotten most of what I learnt—perhaps those smiles dried up the matter before it could sink into the memory. Indeed there are still soft and susceptible spots in my bosom which none who regard this outward severity, this austere calm, this forbidding aspect, these walls in which the yellow lichen is beginning to grow, would give me credit for. A sunny smile will make me forget serious subjects—sometimes. But, ah, I

31

remember that you spake feelingly and tenderly of diseased children! I wonder whether it was the hospital for which I sent a drawing from Mentone —it fetched, I rejoiced to hear, ten guineas at a bazaar. It is indeed a dreadful question to ponder on—the inheritance of disease and its relation to a creator called Good. Many charming drawings—coloured—did I see on Sunday of children and child-life done on paper by Kate Greenaway, in whose company I passed the last week-end at Witley, near Godalming. We were staying in the same house,[12] I mean. She has not a sunny smile: but the book which will contain the drawings—added to bits of lines by herself—ought to be a success. Out at Xmas, I am afraid not. Not to be ready. Spring perhaps. One guinea.

George Eliot, who lives at Witley, suggested that K.G. should go and see some twins at a neighbouring village. We drove on Sat. afternoon—a party—and 3 of us produced sketch-books and made a grand pencil charge upon the village. A history of the twins was kindly given by the mother, how they lived together, ate together, slept together, walked together, did everything together. Interesting. My opinion was that they were 2 fat, ugly children who looked as though they laid down to their food and slobbered it up. We all thought them to be of the porcine genus.

Wasn't Sunday a glorious day! I communed alone during the morning in a pine wood. I would describe it, but if you go into a pine wood and open your eyes, ears and nose and take off your hat as the sun glances down through the tree tops, making the insects to hum and the perfume to spread, why, you will save me trying to do what I cannot.

I leave these rooms at the end of this week, and then shall be without a home. I shall go wobbling about the country until about the 20th, when I shall return to town and prepare to migrate on the 26th to a clime where rheumatism is mute and where the orange tree flowers all day long. This address will find me. You talked of seeing me soon. I hope I shall not be out of town if you are coming up.

By the way, I have a metal *Boar Hunt* of a fine colour—greenish like an ancient bronze. If you do want one, you can have this—10 guineas—'tis framed. But do not take it unless you wish. Of course you won't, if you don't like. What a—No more!

I am in the middle of a large number of Breton subjects. Touching up the sketches, re-drawing, &c, &c. I have also 3 small pictures to finish, and some drawings for Locker's *London Lyrics* to make before I go, besides odds and ends. I enclose a few odd sketches—may amuse you.

Respects to friends.

Yours faithfully,

R. Caldecott

[19]

Hôtel Gray et d'Albion, Cannes, France
13 December 1878

My dear Clough,

2 of your notes lie before me: 17 Oct. and 4 Nov.—are you quite well?— I am sorry about not replying to 1st earlier. Never mind. Busy. Glad you like *Boar hunt*, and were pleased with L'pool Ex. generally. Thank you for cutting from *Daily News* re some other book—*Our Village*, which Cooper wanted me to do—and comparisons of artists with me.

Hope Kendal is better, my kind regards to him, please. Good tale, very good tale, about owl and bargee. We always admired it at school.

I am flattered and pleased by your writing so swiftly to tell me that the effect of the *House that Jack built* was upon you so marvellous. Better? 2 or 3 notices have been read by the visitors to this hotel and I am asked if I am any relation to the gifted artist. 30,000 of each book, *Gilpin* and *House* delivered to Xmas—50,000 of each expected to sell straight away. Hope so. I get a small royalty—a small, small royalty.[13]

Some blackguard has been intimating in Punch's Almanack—which I don't think a very great one this time—that the weather here is always fine. I believe it usually is. I believe that the moon slides gracefully through a summery sky on most Xmas days and that the cock robin would go on piping from the palm tree's verdant branch if he didn't happen to have been stalked and slain for food long, long ago. At present don't let's talk of the weather. The said blackguard's drawings have lost much from reproduction and printing, I hear it said in the billiard-room here.

I expect every minute to hear the electric dinner bell tingle thro' the large and spacious also commodious and suitable for families and gentlemen hotel in a minute or 2. Then must I sit next the president—a deaf Tory, opposite to an American family, and on my right a Viennese Chew, next to him are further Children of Israel, and opposite them again is a man whose ancestors resided down in Judee. He wants a borough. Wife upstairs unwell. 42 or 3 dine. Tonight I have to play whist instead of one of the Hebrews—it's Friday night, do you see. Moses forbade whist on the Sabbath. (Levit. Chap. &c.)

I beg to enclose a few odd sketches—failures—if of use to you, keep them; if not, give or throw away. *If of use—then* get from John Heywood or elsewhere a copy ($1/–, or *less*, I fancy) of Waugh's "Old Cronies, or Wassail at a Country Inn" and post it to Mrs Blackburn, 103 Victoria St., London S.W., first folding down the page on which comes a song of 3 huntsmen huntin and hollerin and findin nothin: but having had a rattlin day,[14] and I shall be eternally indebted to you. Send it as soon as may be decently convenient: do. Before Xmas. Lovely things in W. Crane's *Baby's bucket*.[15]

Adieu! A Merry Xmas to you and yours at home, and with kind regards to each, Je suis
Yours faithfully,
Randolph Caldecott

[20]
Albergo d'Inghilterra, Rome
28 March 1879
night-time

Dear Clough,
Consumption be damned! It's consumption of cigarettes and chianti—capri and Falernian. I have as fine an appetite as a man could wish and as strong a drinketite as in the glorious 'Crown' days (nearly). But a few months of feeding at tables d'hôtes has given me a chronic dyspepsia. No more of it (table d'hôte). I left Mentone for Florence hoping to get well by change of air. By the way, we had some fine girls at Mentone. If I had been a young chap—ah, ah! There were some cross-bred Dutch and English—5 of 'em, and hadn't we a time at the carnival, eh?

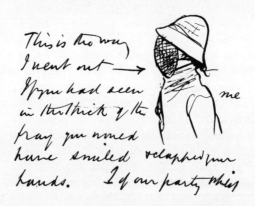

This is the way I went out. If you had seen me in the thick of the fray you would have smiled and clapped your hands. 1 of our party whilst scaling a balcony—at my innocent suggestion—received so many confetti (plaster peas for throwing) and dust that when he descended his brother and I held him (he was over 6 ft) up by the legs in the middle of the street and shook the stuff out of him—out of his neck-hole and interstices generally. What fools we all were!

But I met friends, and at Pisa—just as our trains were starting I changed my mind for here. All the same to me. Ancient old town. Ruins—very. Principally old bricks. Galleries of art. Plenty of society. The feast of reason and the flow of coat-tail. Dukes and artists. Princes and politicians. 1 of my friends is always at the Minghetti's. Can't get her away. So I'm going to leave her and bolt to Florence (In Roma will be a voice heard, &c).

Doctor says this place too relaxing for me now—unless I go and take a villa on the Alban hills. Must come here some Dec., Jan., Feb. Been here 17 days. Leave on Sunday 30th.

Are you quite well? And all friends? "The artist's friends?" eh? especially "W.C."

I shall be in London in May, if not before. No more at present. Kind regards.

Yours faithfully,

Randolph Caldecott

[21]
14 Albion Street, Hyde Park, W
24 May 1879

14, Albion St,
Hyde Park.
W.
24 MAY. 1879.

Dear Clough,

Thank you for your greeting—your welcome! How *are* you? Tollol?[16] I received with joy, and with interest perused, *your poetical note* to foreign parts —you certainly asked for a photograph, and you ask again. But because you want a photograph of me it does not follow that I send you one. It would follow, however, if I had 1 to give you; but I haven't. I had some took at Cannes about New Year's day—Lord bless you, they went off rapidly—they were for the most part promised ages ago, and those not promised were divided equally amongst some newly found acquaintances who professed much love and esteem for me. I'm going to see some of 'em tomorrow— Sunday—Americans. I thought of having some fine *cabinets* taken at Florence (I was last done in '73 before this Jany); but evil fell upon me in the shape of neuralgia in the stomach and my rounding countenance dropped, flattened and hollowed until I was ashamed of myself. So I was done not. Never mind, next batch—about 1887.

I'm not sure of the value of Lang's idea (tho' obliged for it). The cards are only dummies; and the fact that the mind only contemplates the cardly kings and queens as dummies, and that people *play* with the kings and queens —*throw them away* sometimes, put *their aces on them* indeed, may perhaps conduce to a properer estimate of human majesty than if kings and queens were sent into exile by some families and sympathized with and brought back and firesidely nourished by others. Besides there is a significance in having a knave always handy—next in succession. (But as the knave never—except in Euchre and 1 or 2 other games—upsets the King or Queen, perhaps the Royalists might use this fact of an omnipresent but never supreme knave as an argument in the favour of their sway.) Eh! The selection of substitutes would be difficult. The monosyllabic names now in use, ace, king, &c, are good in that aspect.

I fear that those who play cards most would prefer royalty.

No more now. I hope all well.

Yours faithfully,

Randolph Caldecott

P.S. Further, 'nobody' thinks much of kings and queens, and they ought only to think of the game—so their attention is not led away.

2nd P.S. K. Greenaway's book[17] will be a guinea book, I believe. Our *Brittany* will appear in autumn—perhaps a guinea.

[22]
Hôtel de Paris, Trouville, France
27 August 1879

My dear Clough,

While it rains in this Trouville I will amuse myself by writing a line to

36

you. It has rained in gusty showers here and there have been squalls about for several days—not a cheery prospect for our voyage from Le Havre to Southampton tonight. A man is with me—an artist of a sort—he is a nice man—he riseth betimes in the morning, he goeth out into the market-place, where he buyeth fruit—grapes, ripe and right sweet; or large slices of melon, luscious, and lo! very good for breakfast in my chamber. These we eat by the open windows to the pleasant sound of shouting garçons, of shivering bushes, of clattering dishes, and of the voices of birds—to wit, the whistles of the prisoned parrot and the shriek of the caged cockatoo. With all this, I cry aloud about once a day 'Happiness, where art thou?'

You may, O Clough, have read the notes to "Flirtations in France" in S. No. of *Graphic*. You may. Let me tell you that the last 40 lines were substituted for my short winding-up sentence in order to fill up the space, and that I am not responsible for 'spoony-hugging' and sundry jokes to be found in the last lines. I made the editor cry 'Peccavi!'[18]

Are you quite well? And all friends? My respects to 'em.

5 Langham Chambers, Portland Place, W, will find me.

The friend waits upon the *plage*. There are not many tip-top, right nobby, A.1., smashing swells here: but there are some nice-looking and interesting folks.

Adieu!

Yours faithfully,

R. Caldecott

[23]

Kemsing, Nr Sevenoaks

8 November 1879

Dear Clough,

on this Saturday night

Dear Clough,

On this Saturday night—this 8th of November—me—being alone in an house of Wybournes in the village of Kemsing—write unto thee greeting.

How are you? Your note of 1 Oct. is before me. I was sorry when last summer they said unto me "Mr Clough has been and called, Sir, during your absence, Sir!" Better luck next time. I shall be at 5, Langham Chambers mostly during the winter: for this place is not yet in proper order. I have had to move out of the dining-parlour into the 'Study', or what you choose to call this little panelled room, this afternoon, because when the wind is in its present quarter the chimney smokes a wee. I have no curtains and no carpet in this room; but I have 2 Scinde rugs on the floor; I have borrowed the drawing-room fender (its only piece of furniture) and a few things from the dining-parlour, and I am warm and cosy. My bedroom just holds a bed and an adjoining room holds the other things.

The parson has called and found me 'out'—I returned the visit and found him 'from home'. There is nobody else to know in the village. He has many daughters: but, Lord bless you, they'll have no chance![19] Too late! Again those words that sound so mournful must be said.

My work which is coming on will be best done in town, so I shall go thither on Monday, and be here very little until next Summer, perhaps, when I expect to get advantage out of the place in the way of conveniences for the study of beasts and landscape. Not having, therefore, much use for my mare —a goer—I am going to let a friend buy her, and buy another horse myself in the Spring.

The roughest, weediest, couchiest bit of fallow in the county is part of my take and I was grimly joyful today to see 4 horses, 2 men and a strong plough tearing up the clods and driving through the tangled fibres of the couch-grass. On the rest of the land is tethered the black and white cow of a neighbour at a charge of ˢ2/– per week. Oh, I *am* farming, I can tell you.

I have and had no proofs of certain books called the *Babes* and the *Mad Dog* or I would cheerfully have sent 'em along to you. Some of those designs were made when I was very very stomachily seedy at Florence and most were arranged and planned there. I scribbled out the plan of 1 book in the train between Florence and Bologna.

I told Kate Greenaway something of what you said re her book. Here is a note from her for you to look at. Perhaps you will send it back. She is—as you ask—nearly 30, maybe more, and not beautiful.

By-the-bye will you send me sometime a copy of Waugh's "Old Cronies, or Wassail at a Country Inn"—6d or 5d or 8d or 2d it is. I'll carefully owe you the money. When are you coming up? I shall be in England until March, I think. I hope all your family circle is well. Kind regards.
Yours faithfully,
Randolph Caldecott

Wybournes, Kemsing, Nr Sevenoaks
11 March 1880
10.30 p.m.

My dear Clough,
    "There were 3 ravens sat on a tree;" but the above 3 are not ravens. Somebody's going to stop—or put a stopper—on 1 of the 3. It is the 1 in the middle. He only seems quite alive to the seriousness and severity and gravity of the occasion. The 3 are waiting until what they consider to be the proper moment for entering the adjacent church and taking up their stand at the Hymeneal altar—and it's the middle 1 who's to be wed. This waiting on a rail has not taken place yet. It is a sketch of a probable scene on the 18th morning of this month—if fine weather. For your ancient companion of the ledger and the scales of brass purposes to drive in a dog-cart—most rustically— with his best-man[20] and his curate (for to assist = one Alfred Caldecott, of Christchurch, Stafford) to some decent and comfortable railing near the church at which he has invited his wife-elect to meet him on the aforesaid morn. They will be in good time, and rather than irreverently loll on the altar-rails for $\frac{1}{2}$ an hour, they will, until the fitting moment, enjoy the balmy March breeze, listen to the love-lay of the lark, let their hearts beat responsive to the warbled praisings of the tuneful throstle, kick their heels about and over the verdant pasture, and perchance inhale the fragrant weed.
    2 of them will do these things for sure. The 3rd will no doubt rest solemnly on his perch, he will not let his heels wander in the air and he will hold the railing with firm and elegantly-gloved grip. His wonted acrobatic performances in such positions will not be seen. The muscles of his back will be rigid. His tongue will cleave to the roof of his mouth; and he will yearn for a glass of the 'Crown' stout. His thoughts will wander from the contemplation of his coming contentment and happy companionship to the days—the past days—of his gay bachelorhood, and ever and anon he will ask himself if he really put the ring in his pocket. This man will be the bridegroom of the day.
    His companions—whose minds will be at ease—will trifle lightly with the serious moments that are passing rapidly away. The banker—F. B. Seaman—

will feel right glad of a 'day out' in the country, and the parson will rejoice in the coming opportunity of trying his 'prentice hand at a marriage service.

Chelsfield is the church, and the house of the bride's father is very near it. The graveyard and his garden have a common wall, so it will be a walking wedding, of course.

Now let me thank you for your kindly gift of remembrance—it is a very capital book and I prize it. Your sending me this is a pleasant surprise: for, my dear Clough, thy memory will ever hold a place in my cherished cogitation of former days for its own sake, and thy person will continue to be before me sometimes, I trust, when you visit London (we expect to be there from middle of May to mid. of July) and when you come to see us in the hop-country, will it not?

I wish I deserved all the expressions of your respect and affection which you so heartily convey to me in your note. I did not know that I could be so well thought of and I have shewn it to Miss Brind[21] by way of a testimonial.

I am very glad to have your good wishes and those of your family circle. To me it is a real satisfaction to know that people think and wish well of me. I desire to be at peace with all good and worthy folks for I value their blessings.

No doubt many of my old companions in "calling out the debits", in "taking of bills", and in "balancing of tills" will be interested to know that in addition to having been successful in making a position in my new profession I have also been successful in winning the woman whom, of all others in the world, I wish to make my wife. The inhabitants of the earth are not altogether disagreeable to me. If I had wished to be cynical and bitter, a mere mocker without helping towards amendment, the folk with whom I have passed my life have been so very benevolent and cheering that such a wish could never have taken enough hold of me to be seen affecting my temper and my life.

You say, bold flatterer, that *she* must be very good to deserve me. Her friends say that I am a lucky man and am to be unaffectedly congratulated—so I think. Therefore all ought to be well and future happiness secured.

Before the 18th I hope to send in the 8 page drawings for 1 of the next Picture Books[22]—I have, however, not done much visible work of late. (Pardon me, my public!)

We expect to reach Venice some time in April—that month is a refreshing and a lovely one in north Italy—according to my experience and the narratives of others.

Give my kind regards to your mother, sister and brothers, and say I thank them for their good wishes; and remember me to all friends who ask after and take an interest in me, whether bankers, accountants, fiddlers, yarn agents, lawyers, artists, teetotallers, or gentlemen.

Now, my Clough, I will say Good night—Peace be around thee! And, by-the-bye, keep your health—I was sorry to hear of your sickness. You are better, I hope. Adieu!

Yours faithfully,

Randolph Caldecott

P.S. Tell James Williamson that I am glad he thinks of me. I wish him all health. His picture will reach him soon after I next catch sight of it. Meantime, does he want a mare, 15.2, chestnut, a gay goer; and a tandem, old fashioned Holland and Holland dog-cart? I must have a sober 4-wheeler and a big, flopping horse.

My regards to Mr Walter Smith. I hope *he* is well. R.C.

2nd P.S. I enclose a sample of the kind of letter[23] with which I have been much afflicted during the last few months. R.C.

[25]
Wybournes, Kemsing, Nr Sevenoaks
5 September 1880

My dear Clough,

Nearly 2 months after date pray receive this reply to your kind note of 14th July congratulating me on having safely returned from honey-mooning. We did return safely to our native land and sojourned 2 months in town (until the 13 July)—then after a visit of 2 or 3 weeks to friends we came here —to this sequestered spot amongst the hops, a county where most things seem to flourish. I never saw the by-rabbit-admired sow thistle grow to such dimensions as it does in our garden, nor the insinuating bind-weed grapple more tightly or intrude so impudently. On the other hand our marigolds and our poppies—pink scarlet, double, treble, single—and our lilies and our various other fine and gay flowers have equally astonished and more pleased us by their hardihood and prosperity.

The fallow-land, which was enough to make a man who has self respect left him wipe his eye with the lease in which it states that the 'Agricultural Holdings Act' must not apply, now bears more than $\frac{1}{2}$ a crop of fine oats. Did I learn farming for nought? The very best plum tree breaks down under its reddening load. The dachshund bitch is &c, &c. But I will not trouble you with further accounts of our fertility.

Thank you, we are well.

Only 2 Xmas books[24]—no third. I do hope you will look leniently on these works produced at so trying a time of my life. How can they be funny? Wait till next year for the funny ones.

I must go back to mention that the harvest-bug[25] has been very prolific this year. Likes chalky land. This is very chalky. We have had a dreadful time about here.

I am trying to work—sketching at present—getting hold of new methods.

We are quite well, I repeat, and so is the horse—barring a few of his feet (bit of 'thrush')—and the Russian pony (one Menschikoff by name—Menshakeoff, I mean it to be spelt) and the dogs.

You'll come this way as soon as you can you say. That is right and just. Adieu now—Sunday night—bed-time. Busy tomorrow, breakfast each day 8 sharp—no nonsense.

Our very kind regards, my Clough!
Yours faithfully,
Randolph Caldecott

[26]
Hôtel de l'Europe, Menton, France
13 May 1881
7.30 a.m.

My dear Clough,

I do not recollect if I thanked you for your flattering and complimentary and poetical and imaginative letter of the 26th of November last. It now lies before me and calls for a note of acknowledgement—if I had not already, before finding it in my writing case, been wishing, yearning, striving to write to you.

It is very pleasant to have a few people—friends—in the world who can see so much mind and talent and beauty in one's little achievements, and who do not mind mentioning it: for I do like a touch of well-worded praise. I think that I *may* deserve it—yet, my Clough! whenever I am praised I feel more or less of a humbug—oftentimes more, sometimes less.

Well, I am glad that you liked the last little books. I am now busy with 2 more. While we have been here I have done part of one and have been practising sketching round this beautiful place. It is a marvellous region. All the senses are pleased and interested. The eye sees such types of mankind, such luxuriant vegetation—oh the wild flowers, and the roses of the gardens—such seas and skies, such rolling olive woods, such weird pines! The ear rejoices in the song of the nightingale, the cry of the peacock! the croak of the frog! and the crack of the artistic carter's whip! The nose revels in the rosemary, the wild thyme, the garlic, the orange and the lemon flower! The palate delights in the japanese medlar; the *canneton aux olives,* and the mountain honey (by the way, the missis is now putting the honey-pot on the breakfast table and I must leave you for a minute—tea, bread and butter and honey—an early meal, and we do enjoy it—pardon me).

To resume—we ran away from Kemsing on 6 April to escape the east winds which had then been blowing too too long. My friend—Thomas Armstrong—went over to Paris with us to meet his bride[26]—the whole family party dined with us—and we left them to their wedding ceremonies—and reached here on 9th. The Armstrongs joined us here a week afterwards. He has several canvasses being made into pictures of subjects found here. You will probably see 1 or 2 at Manchester autumn Ex. We 4 have often taken out in the afternoon sketching and tea-making apparatus and have set them going in the woods—under the pines or the olives.[27]

At the Fine Art Society in New Bond St. are being exhibited nearly 300 of my original drawings. A number have been sold, I hear.

We shall be back in England end of month and be in town about 4 weeks from 7 or 8 June—probably. Let us know if you go up—do! We wish to see you. Hoping all of you are well—with kind regards
Yours faithfully,
R. Caldecott
P.S. My dachshund is not a mother yet—I'll let you know when there are puppies. R.C.

[27]
with F. Locker, Weylands, Cromer till early next week
11 August 1881

Dear Clough,
    Quite well?
    Yours will be a happy home for any puppy. I don't know when I can send one up to town for transmission to you.
    It would take my man all day to go up and start him fairly and return to Kemsing. It takes us nearly 2 hours from house to town.
    —However, as soon as I can manage it, I will—
    Do you know of anybody in town who is travelling towards Manchester? Or will be rather?
    We *want* to send off the extra 3 pups (there are 5 altogether. Funny dogs!)
    Glad you had a cheerful holiday. Raining here and has been blowing.

I have every interest in sales at Grundy's—I believe and hope. The Fine Art Society sent them down—and to be sold (if possible) on the same terms as when with them—I thought. At prices agreed on by me with F.A. Society and a small commission to F.A. Society on sales. Let me know if you think otherwise. Adieu!

Yours faithfully and now as ever, Amen,

R. Caldecott

P.S. Cromer is full of Hoares—bankers, I mean—and their kidney, Gurneys, Birkbecks, Fowell, Buxtons, &c, &c. This is one of their houses. Head of Bank in London and wife who live next house dined here Tuesday. Adieu! R.C.

[28]
Wybournes, Kemsing, Nr Sevenoaks
25 August 1881

Dear Clough,

The pup will leave Euston tomorrow*—Friday—at 12.10, reaching M'chester 5.30 p.m. Meet it. The guard will probably have received a hint about receiving something on its arrival. She—the puppy—left here this morning—sorrowful farewell!

I write now to Chorlton upon Medlock also.

Yours sadly,

R. Caldecott

  * In a hamper addressed to Mosley St. as you direct.

[29]
Wybournes, Kemsing, Nr Sevenoaks
25 August 1881

Dear Clough,

The puppy—the small one—"the masterpiece"—will leave Euston to-morrow, Friday, at 12.10 train and should arrive in Manchester at 5.30 p.m. in the evening. Meet that train. The guard will expect something—he will have a hint to that effect from the man who puts the beast in the train. She and a sister left here this morning with sorrowful hearts behind.

The father of my bitch (the puppy's mother) belongs to Otto Weber,[28] the animal painter, and I believe is a very good and well-bred dog—the mother belonged to the Queen, who gave it to the late F. W. Keyl,[29] the animal painter.

Let me know of safe arrival.

Yours faithfully,

R. Caldecott

P.S. The father of the puppy belonged (until it was stolen a week or 2 ago) to

A. Nattali, of Christy, Mansom and Woods[30]—and is a handsome dog—
Black and Tan. He has often been to Kensington Palace, and, I believe,
Buckingham Palace also. R.C.

I write now to Mosley St. as well (for hamper directed to Mosley St.).
R.C.

[30]
Wybournes, Kemsing, Nr Sevenoaks
4 September 1881

My dear Clough,

On Friday evening reached our station and yesterday evening our house
the hamper of grouse. We were agreeably and pleasantly surprised and shall
enjoy them much. We like "them things", and return you our liveliest thanks
—(If I had known such a bountifully replenished hamper was coming as a
"returned empty" I would not have mentioned the carriage of the full basket.
My P. Card left here a post too soon—it takes 2 posts to get from Manchester
here).

We hope Brownie will do well and be a comfort and a joy to all of you.
Her mother is an incorrigible fawner and jumper about and begger.

Pardon more this Sabbath morning—I am very busy preparing to go to
Exmoor tomorrow. We go first for a week or so to "Royal Oak", Winsford,
Dulverton, Somerset.

I am very busy with work also. Our best regards. At lunch I shall think
of you thro' the palate. Adieu!
Yours,
R. Caldecott

[31]
6 Via de' Servi, Florence
11 December 1881

My dear Clough,

Quite well? We were very grieved to hear of the death of Brownie, I can
tell you. You shall have another puppy whenever we can send one. Poor little
things! They have all had a bad time of it, I believe. Topsy, the black and
tan, who resides at present at Wybournes has been nearly naked—quite so on
head—better now, I hear. Toby, who lives there too, and whom we are
going to keep, got thro' more easily. (Topsy belongs to the Armstrongs—
Director, Art Department, S. Kensington). Another, that went to the place
where her father hailed from when he wasn't stolen, has had a dreadful
badness, we heard. This is all very painful—I must make it up to you some
day.

Here we are! Settled until April, I hope. Rooms in Brazilian vice-consulate, where they do for us nicely—not cheap. Salon, study, dining-room, bedroom, dressing-room, &c—comfortable in most ways—Winter begun—rather cold sometimes, and today there is rain. Wood fires and marsala. Turkeys and roasted chestnuts—wish I could eat, or even drink!

There are plenty of people whom we know and are knowing here—and artists exist of various degrees of skill. There are men who can sculp lace, flounces, frippery, and eyelashes in marble—also socks falling round the juvenile leg. Yes, sir!

Goodbye! A jovial balance to you and all my ancient cronies—each and every—shake their hands for me, shed a tear, and go back to your seat. The advantages I gained by a sojourn at the M. & S. Bank will always tell on my life.

Addio!
Yours faithfully,
Randolph Caldecott

[32]
Wybournes, Kemsing, Nr Sevenoaks
22 August 1882

My dear Clough,

I lunched yesterday and both of us today off cold grouse and enjoyed myself and ourselves. Your present was very welcome and touched me in a tender part. I have had your name on a slip of paper before me for some time past—have been daily for writing to you. Our kind regards and thank you for so pleasantly reminding me that I have not written to congratulate you on having received benefit from your voyage to and sojourn at Madeira. Nice place, eh? I hope you keep better and are really well now. What a vale of suffering this is! Eh, what?

I wish I were not so busy or I would go down and give Lang a "shove o' side of the head".

We are much occupied with changing of residence—contemplated this month—to be effected next.

Nearly have we settled about a cottage near Farnham in Surrey—3½ miles from station. Go down and have a 3rd look at it and a talk this week—have to stay all night and be cajoled into taking over disgusting and undesired fixtures!

Then we are just fitting up a small house in Kensington (24, Holland St.) in whose garden I shall erect a small studio before winter. 21 years' lease!

No more now. My blessing to all belonging to you and to ancient cronies.

Adieu!
Yours faithfully,
R. Caldecott

P.S. This is an important letter—so I pack it with some rough protective stuff. R.C.

[33]
Broomfield, Frensham, Farnham, Surrey
8 July 1883

My dear Clough,

Much obliged for your last note—14 June—full of interesting remarks and donderings. Happy man to be in such a humour! Wish my vulture (established with beak well into my vitals—which beak he twists now and then) would allow me to display some of the hilarity of my youth or your age.

I *was* nearly hilarious the other evening at a dinner of men assembled to join together in putting down publishers and picture dealers—most of us were surprised at finding ourselves at the meeting of this club and left without understanding its exact objects and rules altho' each member (and there are no other members than were present and who have signed *menu*) got up and tried to explain everything. The dinner was at the Blueposts in Cork St. The *menu* is somewhat curious—I enclose it, begging for its return not more mashed about than necessary. You will observe that 1 publisher—Osgood— did force his way in. You will see some known names—Gosse,[31] Lang,[32] Dobson,[33] Carr,[34] King (author of *Democracy*) &c.

The etching is by Abbey.[35] The meeting ended in mild Poker at Long's— or rather Bong's in Lond St.[36]

Thanks for 1 or 2 of your sentences.

Remember me to Lang, Dutch, and all well-wishers—I yearn to embrace them once more.

We have come down from London where we have sojourned since Easter and the damned monotony of the sweet smiling verdurity of the country has only been broken during six days by a notification that the Queen has been pleased to allow the Institute of P. in Water Colours to—words fail me! Art improves by being called "Royal", however. So I will say little. Prices are rising at once—ah, a thought!

Agnews and I have dealings now. I am 2 drawings (water) in their debt.

Farewell!

Yours,
R. Caldecott

P.S. Punch R. B. Wallace's head for me—not angrily: but firmly, and ask him what he is doing in reply to any mild appearance of enquiry which he may put on. R.C.

P.S. Monday mng. Just off on an expedition—driving—for the day. Perhaps you would like an autograph of Walter Crane—if so, here it is—if not, here it is also. Why you should like it, I do not quite know. Why you should not, puzzles me. He is a clever man: but he does not enough follow his natural bent. He is in the thrall of the influence of the early and most intellectual Italian painters and draughtsmen.

I enclose 1 of my sketches for 3 *Jovial Huntsmen*.

How's Lang? I am *about* writing to him. Kind remembrances to those around you from

Yours

R.C.

Don't forget to give greetings from me to all the Bank officials and gentlemen. R.C.

[34]
Broomfield, Frensham, Farnham, Surrey
16 November 1884

Dear Clough,

Last Sunday about this time I found myself writing to you. Our letters crossed.

I am glad to have your good word for the *Picture Books*[37] of this year— also for *D.D.D.* The illustrations in that book—some of 'em—do not come out very well. The children a-singing especially. It is very flattering of you to desire to possess it; but I do not at present think of divorcing it from the rest of the set. I have been asked about one or 2 more. The original of the frontispiece—which is a drawing somewhat apart from the others in style, &c—was bought from me at the time I made it for *Aunt Judy's Magazine*, 2 or 3 Novembers ago. The 'mag' used it and some friend of the Editor's bought the original drawing—or you should have had it *cheap* with pleasure.

Glad to here about your puppy—Treu.

The mother of the pup I sent you—by name Lalla Rookh[38]—disappeared 2 or 3 months ago. I had been exercising her after breakfast, and her son, and a beagle—Countess. While tying up Countess—Lalla went off with Toby —hunting in woods, I believe (we had to keep her up about that time on account of game adjacent). Toby returned 1 p.m. She never. Either smothered in rabbit-hole—or picked up by earliest arrivals of hop-pickers—a bad lot came to the neighbourhood of Farnham this year. Toby has since developed in intellect and friendliness. He converses at times with us.

Riding with a young Hook (son of the painter) other day—his nag made mine run away—he could not control his—she'd bucked and he'd lost a stirrup. After a smashing gallop on hard road I managed to turn on to common and amongst heather and soon over we went. All wind knocked out of me—25 miles an hour was the rate—thorough-bred mare. Was in a draper's window this autumn. When Hook came up sent him on to warn Missis as mare had gone towards home. I walked back and all ended happily.

I'm pretty well, thanks. Be thou well!

Yours,

R. Caldecott

24 Holland Street, Kensington
4 January 1885

My dear Clough,

Thank you very much for your kind greetings for new year. We reciprocate. Be happy!

Wonder whether you ever saw these fine concentrations of Whistler's—to be found on other side of this leaf. They are part of catalogue of a small exhibition of his held last season.

Yours,
R. Caldecott

[36]
Broomfield, Frensham, Farnham, Surrey
1 March 1885

My dear Clough,

Would that I could wish you and Dutch a happy New March! What is a man to say more than that the death of his friend causes him many a half-hour's cogitation of a melancholy colour? I was about to write a stirring-up note to the thin invalid when I received a letter from his son Frank announcing the death. And I was talking about Dutch to Armstrong about the time of this last scene—in consequence of a remark on the case by H. G. Seaman in a recent letter.

I shall miss Dutch—tho' I saw and heard from him little of late yet there was always a possibility of his stepping on the scene before my vision in his uncompromising and dark-toned manner. Poor man, he did not deserve such a complication of disorders (I am wondering which of them I have got inside me). His honesty deserved a better time than he had on earth—although he was better off and I should suppose had a happier life than most men of his means. Where would you have found such a wife for him? He was lucky over that step in life. I am writing to her by this post. It is very good news to hear that the Bank have behaved generously. How much? He was over 20 years, or about that period, in the Bank, I think.

Much obliged for the City newspaper[39]—Waugh had already sent one, according to his weekly custom—and glad to hear your remarks about my little works. Ah, if, if! But too late!

The paper gave me the 1st intimation of the sale of the pictures. There may be an official communication in town—whither we go tomorrow for 6 days.

"Serener air!" eh? I've had rather an uncomfortable time as regards my 'innards' since about 20 Dec. Shall go abroad next winter, probably. Leave here at Michaelmas. Sell a fine hunter. Give away an excellent cob. Shoot a beagle and drop a tear!

Yours,
R. Caldecott

Broomfield, Frensham, Farnham, Surrey
18 August 1885

My dear Clough,

I am very much obliged to you for sending me the photograph of our friend Walter Smith. I appreciate your thought of me, and the occasional stare which I shall direct upon the portrait will conjure up not unpleasing sensations. I shall be reminded of times gone by, of troubles, of yearnings, of ambitions. Smith has been a bright example to other clerks in having such a steady respect for his work. I believe he did his duty as well as a man can do.

As for me, I am sure I must have caused him moments of dissatisfaction and uneasiness. There was seldom visible in me any steady sober respect for the work of the bank.

I am sorry to hear that you are not well. What is the matter with you? To take holidays in such pleasant lands and to return home not benefitted is a melancholy state of things. And not to be able to take exercise looks bad. I should like to think that you were groaning without sufficient cause. Tricycles and bicycles are not sympathetic machines to me.

I enclose 2 of our failures. Keep 1 if you care about it and give the other to Lang if he cares about it. Hope he is well.
Yours,
R. Caldecott
P.S. A fire began on 10th on the common 2 or 3 miles from here. Not out yet. Must have already burnt some thousands of acres of heath, gorse, and fir plantations. R.C.

Dear Clough,

Very sorry not in when you called.

Have to go out now 12.20 on business—shall be at Union Bank, Holborn Circus until 2 or 2.15. Then Newman's, 24 Soho Square—then Fine Art Society, 148 New Bond St. at 3 and after. Then visit to Dickinson's Gallery, same street. Then probably—*possibly*—Arts Club, Hanover Square—Here to dinner at 7.15. If I do not see you between now and then—come here and take luck with us (we have new servants) at 7. Do! My wife says so.

Can you return with us to Farnham tomorrow—train 2.45 p.m. Waterloo —Do if you can—we are more fixed up there.

I hope you will come this evening and tomorrow.
Yours aff.
R.C.

1. The Manchester and Salford Bank.

2. *Bracebridge Hall* was the second book by Washington Irving which Caldecott illustrated. It was published for Christmas 1876, and followed his success the previous year with *Old Christmas*.

3. In the Christmas number of the *Graphic* were eight illustrations from *Bracebridge Hall* and a double page of coloured illustrations by Caldecott based on the scenes he had drawn for *Old Christmas*.

4. Thomas Armstrong.

5. He illustrates the lunch at the head of this letter. Caldecott is bearded, Armstrong has a moustache.

6. These were the *Letters from Monaco* which appeared in the *Graphic* of 10 and 24 March 1877.

7. Lancashire and Cheshire dialect words. *Teem* means to pour liquids fast or to rain heavily; *sheed* is an undefined measure of land.

8. Caldecott did not exhibit at the Royal Academy until the following year.

9. It was *The Three Huntsmen*, which was bought, as Caldecott says in the postscript, by A. J. Mundella, the Member of Parliament for Sheffield.

10. *A Boar Hunt.*

11. *Breton Folk* by Henry Blackburn, illustrated by Caldecott and published by Sampson Low, 1880.

12. That of Edmund Evans, the engraver of both Kate Greenaway's and Caldecott's children's books.

13. Caldecott received three farthings a copy.

14. This was to be the basis of *The Three Jovial Huntsmen*.

15. *Baby's Bouquet*, published by Routledge.

16. Tolerable.

17. *Marigold Garden*; however, Caldecott over-estimated the price.

18. I have erred!

19. He was already engaged to Marian Brind.

20. F. B. Seaman.

21. His wife-to-be.

22. *The Three Jovial Huntsmen* and *Sing a Song for Sixpence*.

23. Written in childish capitals, it says 'Please Mr Caldecott, draw me Little Bo-peep next time. Dorothy Dunnell.'

24. *The Three Jovial Huntsmen* and *Sing a Song for Sixpence*.

25. *Tetranychus autumnalis*. Gilbert White in a letter to Thomas Pennant, dated 30 March 1771, describes them as 'very minute, scarce discernable to the naked eye; of a bright, scarlet colour'. They are 'very troublesome and teasing at the latter end of the summer, getting into people's skins, especially those of women and children, and raising tumours which itch intolerably'.

26. Mary Brine.

27. The sketch above the address shows the party 'sketching and tea-making'.

28. Otto Weber (1832–1888); painter of landscapes and animals, among whose paintings was *Doughty and Carlisle*, pets of Queen Victoria.

29. F. W. Keyl (1823–1873); animal painter; student and close friend of Sir Edwin Landseer.

30. The Fine Art auctioneers.

31. Sir Edmund Gosse (1849–1928); poet and man of letters.

32. Andrew Lang (1844–1912); poet and folklorist.

33. Austin Dobson (1840–1921); poet and author. He wrote a short introduction to *The Complete Pictures of Randolph Caldecott*.

34. Joseph Comyns Carr (1849–1916); art critic of the *Manchester Guardian* and one of the men behind the establishment of the Grosvenor Gallery. Caldecott illustrated

North Italian Folk by Alice Comyns Carr, his wife.

35. Edwin Abbey. *See* p. 13.
36. Long's Family Hotel in New Bond Street.
37. *Come Lasses and Lads* and *Ride a Cock Horse* and *A Farmer Went Trotting*.
38. His dachshund is named after the heroine of a poem by Tom Moore.
39. The *Manchester City News*.

JAMES DAVIS COOPER

1823–1904

With Dalziel, Evans and Whymper, James Cooper was one of the most successful wood engravers of the 1860s, when wood engraving was particularly successful as an illustrative medium in English books. Like Dalziel and Evans, Cooper planned many books, choosing a text, commissioning an illustrator and superintending the engraving and printing. This was how he and Caldecott worked together, first on *Old Christmas* and then *Bracebridge Hall*. He also engraved Caldecott's illustrations for *Breton Folk*, some magazine illustrations and other minor pieces.

[39]
46 Great Russell Street, WC
15 August 1877

Dear Sir,

I am much obliged for proofs, which don't require touching from me as far as I can see.

I like No. 27 as rendered by you, but if you will allow me to again refer to the subject, I think you are not always fortunate about the position of your name. In this, the effect of the boy's foot being partly sunk in the dust is lost by having the name so close. The *sc.*[1] at least ought to come out. There would have been no harm in putting the name at the bottom edge of the cut.

You may think me too particular about this. As for myself I would rather leave out my initials than have them to interfere with the drawing—and I often do so—and in these slight drawings every little tells.

Yours very truly,

R. Caldecott

---

1. *sculpsit*: engraved by.

MRS DAWSON

[40]
24 Holland Street, Kensington, W
28 October 1885

Dear Madam,

I looked at the "Rotten Row" drawings yesterday. I made them during the first year (1872) of my coming to London; but I quite forget into whose hands they passed from mine. I believe they were exhibited at a "Black and White" Exhibition in 1872, which was held at the Dudley Gallery in the Egyptian Hall.

The people represented were characters that I saw: but I did not know their names.

It would be a very difficult thing for one to put the true money-value upon these sketches.

I am, dear Madam,
Yours truly,
Randolph Caldecott

ROBERT DRANE, F.L.S.

1833–1914

Robert Drane was a pharmacist whose chief interests were English and Welsh porcelain (he has been described as the 'greatest exponent of comparative collecting'), and, as his fellowship of the Linnaean Society suggests, the close observation and classification of animals and birds. He is credited with the recognition of two sub-species of birds, and he was the first to record the existence of *Evotomys skomevensis*—Drane's vole.

[41]

96 Park Street, Grosvenor Square, W
22 June 1880

Dear Sir,
    Your note of 22 May is very complimentary to me—in it you tell me you are going to *preserve* for future generations a copy of my volume of *Picture Books*.[1] I am very glad. I hope others will do the same, and that future generations will feel blessed, be content, and not knock the nose off my statue.
Yours pictorially,
Randolph Caldecott

---

1. *R. Caldecott's Picture Books*, which contained the first four picture books: *The House that Jack Built, John Gilpin, Essay on a Mad Dog, The Babes in the Wood.*

WILLIAM BAKER ETCHES

1847–1935

Caldecott and William Etches were young men together at Whitchurch. Etches was at this time a solicitor's articled clerk, who lived with his grandfather at Broughall House, a mile or so from the town.

[42]
46 Great Russell Street, London WC
5 February 1873

Dear Will,

Your letter does equal honour to your head and heart. (This is not original, and it doesn't quite apply; but no matter.) I thank you much for it.

Don't mention Coal to me. I am being ruined by the beastly stuff. I used to pay 9d a scuttle for it. I don't know how much now, for the best coal is $12/- a ton dearer than then. It is now $48/- or more here per ton. When the fire wants mending I put on pieces with my forefinger and thumb. Artists are usually improvident persons. I shall spend my time at my club until the weather becomes warmer. Something is wrong about coal. I shall agitate. You'll see my name in the papers—took chair at a meeting of Patent Bohemian Selfsupporting Democratic Blazers to frame a petition to Parliament. "Meeting closed with the usual vote of thanks to the chairman."

Ice, eh? Dirty snow here.

I should like to have been with the gallant ten in the run you describe. It is not likely that I should have lived with them had I been out, for a variety of circumstances combine to make me a steady and calculating sportsman. In fact, I calculate too much. Nevertheless, moreover, but, I thank you for offering me your steady animal. My life is a precious one, the eyes of the world are upon me, and I have lost somewhat of that much admired, greatly envied, free, gay, dashing, devil-may-care, adventurous, heroic, and reckless spirit which lent to my youth an excitement and a charm (here I turn away and drop a tear—a manly tear—for as the years go by I change. I am not as I was).

> "But I am sad, and let a tale grow cold,
> Which must not be pathetically told."

Some of these days I shall be setting up a studio in your neighbourhood so as to model horses, cows, dogs, &c, into which line I am going. Your well-bred shorthorns are not in the eyes of those superior beings in whom artistic genius asserts her rampant sway considered picturesque enough. Some rough shaggy Scotch beasts are more in our line. But don't let this influence you in the matter of purchasing stock for profit. I shall regret having mentioned it if you do. Please don't.

As you wish, I have executed at immense personal risk and sacrifice of time a sketch in the hunting field. The price is three guineas. You need not send it. It will do when I see you next. Anybody else who may require similar productions must send the cash with the order. Stamps not taken. P.O.O's to be made payable at Gt. Russell St., W.C., cheques to be crossed Union Bank of London, Holborn Circus Branch. (N.B. No reduction on taking a quantity.)

I very often am squatted for an hour in the evening with the greatest master of drawing in line[1] that we have. Such a small pipe he smokes.

Jim stayed here the first two nights of his sojourn in town, and I have not seen his face since. He must stick at his work—that's my advice. Perseverentia et patientia, &c.

I hope you are all well and with kind regards to Mrs Etches and Miss Etches—I very nearly wrote "Amy"—
I am, dear William,
Yours faithfully,
Randolph Caldecott
P.S. I should much like to have the photograph which Amy—I mean Miss Etches—so kindly says she will send. If she would wish one of mine, say that when the weather gets better I hope to be able to have some taken and would issue them as soon as possible afterwards.

46 Great Russell Street, London WC
29 March 1873

My dear Will,

I never saw the University Boat Race before, and I very nearly never saw it again, as you shall hear.

So many reports of the race are written—a whole steamboat load of reporters following the race—that I may be allowed to let off a few remarks on the subject. Personal impressions literally.

The morning was very foggy in town, the sun looking like a pink wafer. I got on board a steamboat, went about a hundred yards, when the vessel moored itself to a pier to wait for the departure of the fog. So then I took train, and the train took me up the riverside. Lovely day outside town. Miles of people and carriages. Lots of good-looking girls. Scores of 'nigger' minstrels, troubadours, coco-nut and stick-throwing proprietors. Popping of champagne corks from the carriages. Hundreds of adventurous people in small boats and on river barges. Charming garden parties on pleasant lawns. Fat ladies on horseback. Swells in four-in-hand drags. Cads in cabs. Beer served through the windows of the inns. Hardy pleasureseekers seated on broken-glass-bottle-topped walls. Nimble youths swarming trees, securing places of advantage at the ends of boughs, and then falling down on to the heads of the pleased multitude. A few hand to hand contests. Much shoving. Bawling of police. Treading on toes. Upsetting of stands commanding fine views of the race. Hats off! Cheers. Here they come! There they go! Cambridge winning. Tide flows over osier beds. Happy payers of $5/-$ each up to their knees in water. Wash of the steamers undermines respectable elderly gentlemen taking care of their plump partners. They struggle. They slip. Down they go. Damp just below the back of the waistcoat. Strong men carry timid people on their backs through the water. Foot in a hole. All roll over together. Jeers of the populace. A rush. Several benches and forms with rows of British ratepayers slide about in the mud. Clutching of neighbours. Lurch. Splash. Over they go. Swearing. All safe to land. Plenty for the money. Not only good view of the race; but wet legs and damp clothes—some wet and muddy all over.

So much for other people. I—after the race—walked along the river bank and was soon in the closest crush and squeezingest mob in which I was ever a party—and I have been in a few. Between the water and a high wall were a carriage road and footpath. There was a close row of unhorsed vehicles of every description; and a swaying, surging crowd of all classes of folks moving each way. And in addition, horsed carriages and people on horseback trying to get along. Then did ladies scream and infants cry. Then did protruding elbow find soft concealement in yielding waistcoat, and tender faces unwillingly repose on manly bosoms. Corns were ground. Bonnets said farewell to chignons. Chests had no room to sigh, lips that seldom swore spake grunted oaths, and unknown forms were welded together and blended in sardine-like harmony. Then slid the purse and fled the watch. (A gentleman near me lost seventy pounds.)

I found myself one while jammed up against a pony carriage driven by a fair-haired damsel. I clutched the rail, the crowd pressed, my toes were near the wheels, and my noble form doubled up on the wing. The vehicle turned part round, the pony objected, and eventually the persevering crowd made me lift the carriage off two of its wheels. The girls screamed and raised their hands in supplication (I believe they thought that I desired to overturn them). I managed to get away, and spying a nook under the stern of a drag and the splashboard of a cab, I crept therein, and was joined by others. Into this temporary haven we dragged a fair young girl from amongst the swaying crowd and kicking horses. She shed a few tears on one man's shoulder, and her bosom heaved so much that I dropped one or two tears in sympathy, which refreshed me and comforted her. After some time, when there was a little more room, she went west to look for her lost friends, and I went east and saw her no more.

The police told me that the crush and crowd were greater than heretofore.

I enjoyed the sight of the many thousands of people; it was good fun to watch the manner of passing away the time before the race. This was about the best.

I noticed one young creature busily engaged in sketching the people. I mentally sketched her. Here she is—and this is the man she was sketching.

So you will observe that there is very much to be seen besides the boat race. As for that, you only see the fine fellows glide easily and beautifully past for a moment—unless you have a good place by paying for it at an extortionate rate, or by doing the civil to people whom you know that have a house on the river side.

Most people were adorned in some way with dark or light blue ribbons to shew their partizanship. Many glorious ladies were attired in blue from head to foot. I observed that the light blue predominated—not so much for the sake of good wishes to Cambridge, but because the fair creatures considered that the lighter tint suited them better. Mark the deception! Moral—it is not prudent to give persons credit for the best motives without careful and due consideration.

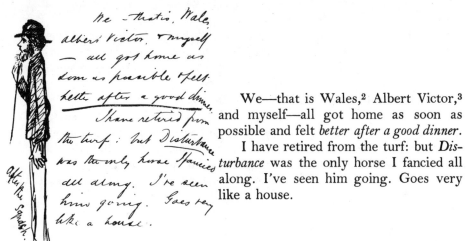

We—that is Wales,[2] Albert Victor,[3] and myself—all got home as soon as possible and felt *better after a good dinner*.

I have retired from the turf: but *Disturbance* was the only horse I fancied all along. I've seen him going. Goes very like a house.

Thank Mrs Etches and Amy for kind enquiries about my cold. My voice is now more harmonious and winning than ever. A dying swan would be ridiculous in comparison. I am all right again, thank you, and hope that Mrs Etches' cold is gone.

Say unto Amy that a magnificent portrait of me is in preparation and will be forwarded shortly, together with some remarks on the application of the language of flowers.

I hope you are all well, and with kind regards to each, remain, my dear William,

Yours faithfully,

Randolph Caldecott

P.S. 31st inst. On a review of the preceding I feel somewhat timid about sending such an effusion, although it is all true; but trust that you will make every allowance for the probably variegated state of my mind and body on Saturday evening. R.C.

Vale!

[44]
22 October 1873

My dear Will,

The fortunes of your family are still interesting to me—although most of you have not reaped as much benefit as you might from the many opportunities of receiving wisdom as ye sat at my feet. (That's a little vague.)

Therefore—ergo—argal—let me know some day something about you. When the wind sighs amongst the dark fir tops, and breeze roughens the surface of the muddy moat, when the cozy curtains are drawn across the windows, and a fresh log of old cherry-wood is thrown upon the fire, then take up thy pen and write words to cheer my pent-up and melancholy spirit.

I can tell you no news from here, for you know not Smith of the *Daily Delirium*, and Jonesbrownson of the War Office ranks not with your acquaintance. Gambooge the artist is a stranger to you and Mudgroveller the sculptor is not of your company.

They are all well, though! Very well indeed.

I—humble I—have been daubing this day in clay with a sculptor of Chelsea—a Frenchman of note.[4] And now I contemplate dining. For what we are going to receive, &c. I heard Mark Twain lecture the other day. It was very hearable. He says lots of dry and humorous things.

I think I have about got over the waiting time before dinner—so I will conclude hoping that you are all very well.

Kind regards to Mrs Etches, John, Harry, everybody!

Turn over and

I remain,
Sweet William,
Yours faithfully,
Randolph Caldecott

[45]
46 Great Russell Street, London WC
3 November 1873

Dear Will,

I was delighted to get your long letter — sparkling and humorous, original and well seasoned, as usual.

I should think that most of the late calves you talk about would be reared—or rather attempted—even all the bulls —and no partiality for

"Harvesting the Root Crops"

colour—even if they have no tails and are not good-haired 'uns.

I congratulate you much on passing your exam. I do indeed. What larks we'll have when you final!

I expect Arthur up here next week, and perhaps a brother of mine[5] for his B.A. honours exam. I'm busy myself, I am. Up to elbows in "slutch".[6] Coin scarce. Got any? You must have had a lot on your mind: but it's a great mind, you know. As you say, probably no fellow ever had so much on his mind as you have of late—except one—that's me, that is.

I hope you picked up a good hunter, and had a good day on Saturday. I shall have to take some of my hunting this season with the Queen's Staghounds in Bucks. There is a little place[7] where I can go and live all winter if I like, and work as much as I like, get drunk when I like, and on what I like.

I wrote to Jack, and have heard from Jack. I rejoice in his successful start. May he hold out!

There does seem to be many packs of lawyers about. Perhaps foxes are plentiful.

I thank you so much for your photographic portrait. It is capital! It is much too lovely (as young ladies say)! I like it. I'll owe you one of mine, meantime take this. By Broughall, I had such a crop at Paris! Came out this sort of thing. Oh, so nice!

If you get tickets for the Crystal Palace Show, and don't want them, do send them to me, and I will try to go down. As for sketch of turkey—*it is no joke*—if you win, will see about it.

Thank you for offering me a turkey treat. I accept it: but don't send it yet. If your offer will stand, I'd rather wait a little.

You are not married then? Ah, Will, as each of my young friends gets married I feel older and sadder, and yet see more for me to toil and struggle for. Though I get somewhat stouter without, yet I feel a little hollower within, and as nature abhors a vacuum, let's open a bottle and take a deep, deep, &c.

Please only send original and new conundrums.

Kind regards to Mrs Etches, and Harry, and rest.

Yours faithfully,

Randolph Caldecott

[46]

46 Great Russell Street, London WC

1 January 1874

Dear Will,

Thank you much—it was a very fine turkey—a remarkably fine ditto

—especially for a country turkey.

I thought of clasping your manly digits this gay season: but stern fate wills it not. I am filled with anxiety, my mind is very troubled; yea, my spirit groaneth, for I have much things on hand and I have girded up my loins to do them.

I have just got into a new workshop next door at the back, and there I light my stove and carry on my business. Do you want a sign-board? or an equestrian statue? or an elegant wallpaper? Anything in that line I shall be happy to attend to, and hope that by a steady &c, &c, to merit a continuance of that &c, &c, which the nobility, clergy, &c, &c, have for so many &c so liberally &c, &c.

Disbelieving, heathen! I was at two meets of the Quorn[8] a fortnight ago, and shall probably be at another further on. The master offered me a room in his house if I liked to accept it.

I rejoice to hear of the Salopian run and regret that you were not there. Your name then might have been handed down to history—I mean posterity —(I've been dining out—the clock has struck 1 A.M. Friday).

Kindly keep your pecker up until I see you again.

I hope you are all jolly well, and with kind regards to Mrs Etches and Amy, and all you may have in the house—also a happy new year (original remark) to you all—I still remain,
My Sweet William, my cabbage rose, my early pea,
Yours faithfullee,
Randolph Caldecott

[47]
Winchelsea
4 April 1874

Dear Will,
    Being rained up in a charming inn, looking out on the fine old churchyard

depicted above, I think of you and feel remorse at not having written to you of late. My letters always do you much good. Improving your health by curing the spleen.

I and a cove walked here from Hastings yesterday—Friday—about 10 miles over hill and dale, through shady lanes and over fertile flats, down steep cliffs and along the stony shore of the sounding sea.

This is a delightful modern town—a stranger would call it a village—built about the middle of the 13th century after the former town was swallowed by the sea. It is on a hill and commands a fine prospect with a good view of the sea looking towards sunny France. This is the only inn and is opposite the fine old ivy-covered half-ruined beautiful church, from the pulpit of which I have this morning addressed a scanty audience.

But while I write the rain ceases, the sun comes out, we order food, drink draughts, send away our luggage, and prepare for a walk to Rye, a nice place which we can see from here, and another of the old Cinque Ports.

I shall feel a man again after this atmosphere, and ready for my work, which is waiting for me in a more "wanted" state than I like. I am very busy.

Let me hope that you are swimming away lustily and with grace down the stream of life. I hear that you will run a galloway[9] at Bangor.

Some friends of mine have just bought a place near Bangor, which I must visit when I next attend the steeplechases.

Some people in this house have just begun to play a regular stomach-twisting organ and to squeeze out of it a fine, soul-subduing tune.

I was going to ask how you all are, and how Jack is getting on—I will give him some excellent advice when I see him—and how many lambs you have, and the average per yow,[10] and how much violets you have growing, and the quantity of primroses that have come; but I have no more time. We must away over the country to Rye. It stands out above the level shore and the flat meadows on rising ground with a useful-looking church as a centre.

But away! Good bye! Kind regards to Mrs Etches, Amy, Dick, Charley, Harry, Artie, Jack and all.

Yours affectionately,

R. Caldecott

H. Blackburn, Esq., The Cottage, Farnham Royal, Nr Slough, Bucks.
22 June 1874

Dear Will,

We are in the middle of our hay harvest, and a very bad crop much of it is. The cherry harvest is also now on with a very fair yield. We are glad of this, because our bird scarer has made a dreadful noise lately, holloing, and rattling, and clacking, and asking all passersby beneath a certain social scale what o'clock it is. This going on from half past six a.m. until seven p.m. took away much of the charm of the sequestered spot ("the world forgetting, by the world forgot") in which my melancholy spirit now seeks quiet and calm.

Some friends have lent us a cottage. We pay the wages—half the parish clerk's time, and a buttoned-boy in the house as butler, footman and cook—and he can cook, too. By Jove, you should smell some of his soups! A matron steppeth in from her own household to do the chamber department.

We do our work in the loose-box, capitally fitted up and cool. An American hammock swingeth in one corner inviting repose. Table and chairs and our utensils desire us to work. I can do my present work better here than in London and feel better.

A good pony; and an intelligent ass, who combineth with beauty of outward form a tractable disposition, sore ears and an amiable temper; a 4-wheeled carriage, and a 2-ditto ditto form our means of locomotion over a very delightful country.

I wish that I could knock about more, for there are charming places near here: but I am committed to work. Here we can retire early if we wish.

We know a few very fine people round: but we are unassuming people and fall back on our own well-stocked cellar or on (for my part sometimes) the 6d ale of a neighbouring pub.

My companion, Mr Lamont,[11] is an artist of note, and a worthy man who has seen much of the world and its inhabitants, of whom he once married one, but she went aloft and left him a lonely widderer.

So no more at present from yours faithfully, hoping that all are well and Jack and Mrs John safely settled in the house, to whom my kind regards as also to Mrs Etches and Amy who I hope have recovered from the measles, if they had them.

R. Caldecott

[49]
Hôtel du Conseil d'Etat, Rue de Lille 59, Paris
9 May 1875

Dear Will,

Having at last found a retired spot, where there is nothing to disturb the calmness of an evenly-balanced mind, I find time for a little letter-writing. I am the more disposed that way because this is a quiet Sunday afternoon, and on this Sunday there is little going on here except the annual picture and sculpture exhibition, the usual museums and galleries and palaces of art, horse-races in the Bois de Boulogne in the afternoon, and the theatres and opera at night. Therefore, to w*hile away the tedious hour, I perform a duty and do myself a pleasure in writing to thank Mrs Etches and you, and Amy too, for your kindness during my late visit to Shropshire.

*If this H is of no use here, keep it until I see you again.

I went down to Shropshire and the adjacent counties to study nature thus:

I returned to London again last Tuesday night, and on Wednesday evening I came with a painter to Paris to study art thus:

and very delightful it is; but there are so many miles of pictures &c that it is really hard work, and deserves a good reward. (Let us here offer up a short hope that the said reward will come.)

The weather here is fine, the trees are in leaf, the gardens are full of lilac trees in full "blow", the chestnuts and laburnum have unfolded their blossoms, asparagus is an inch and a half thick, my bedroom window is open at night, and we sit out in the air until bed-time.

The French are a polished people, and so are their floors and stairs. If you manage it well you can easily and quickly descend the stairs of any of the public palaces in this manner (the dotted line represents the course taken).

69

Opposite to this hotel—the other side of the street—is a large building for the Council of State. It is being repaired after the damage it received during the late seige, &c. Two floors of this house were burnt, but now all is well.

Whenever you can come over for a day or two let me know—I shall probably leave here on Tuesday (11th) myself—I'm sure you'll like the place and people.

So no more at present. With kind regards to all, every one, I am, dear Will,
Yours faithfully,
R. Caldecott

[50]
46 Great Russell Street, London WC
19 August 1875
1 A.M.

Dear Will,
I was very pleased to receive so prompt a reply from you—a reply so prompt that it is a matter of much wonder to the few who are left in town that

My dear Noble,

From
what Beckley says you seem
twist somebody to write to you.
I should have written long long
ago: but it was suggested
that I had better not, — I
could not quite see why though.
However, I apologise for my
neglect, and hasten to assure
you that it is with great pleasure
that I sit down to the duty
this fine Sunday evening,
when all good folks are at
worship, & where I should like

Opening page of letter to Matthew Noble, 13 June 1869 (p. 255),
written before Caldecott embarked on his art career. A drawing at the
head of his letters, incorporating the address, became almost a standard
practice with him.

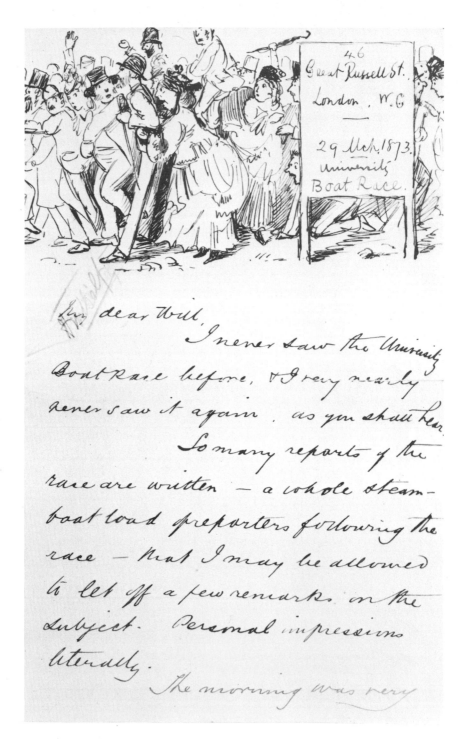

My dear Will,

I never saw the University Boat Race before, & I very nearly never saw it again, as you shall hear.

So many reports of the race are written — a whole steam-boat load of reporters following the race — that I may be allowed to let off a few remarks on the subject. Personal impressions literally.

The morning was very

Opening page of letter to Will Etches, 29 March 1873 (p. 58), describing the Oxford and Cambridge Boat Race of 1873: 'the closest crush and squeezingest mob in which I was ever a party'.

clothes — some wet & muddy
all over.

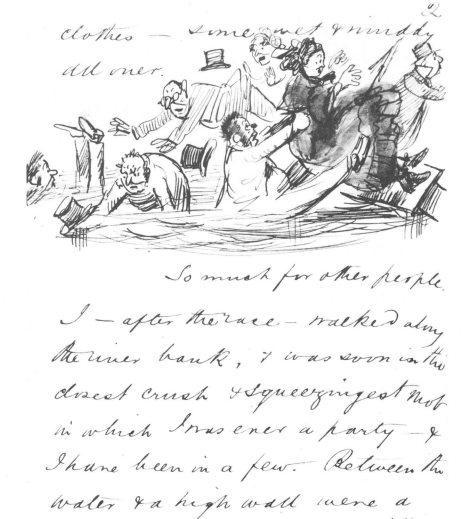

So much for other people.

I — after the race — walked along
the river bank, & was soon in the
closest crush & squeezingest mob
in which I was ever a party — &
I have been in a few. Between the
water & a high wall were a
carriage road & a footpath. There
was a close row of unhorsed vehicles
of every description; & a swaying
surging crowd of all classes of
folks moving each way. And

Extract from letter to Will Etches, 29 March 1873 (p. 59). Drawing
depicts onlookers at the Boat Race falling into the river when their
bench overturns.

than heretofore.

I enjoyed the sight of the many thousands of people; it was good for me to watch the manner of passing away the time before the race. This was about the best.

I noticed one young creature busily engaged in

Extract from letter to Will Etches, 29 March 1873 (p. 60). 'Swells' in a carriage drinking champagne before the start of the Boat Race.

sketching the people. I
mentally sketched her. Here
she is ——
& this is the man
she was sketching

So you will
observe that there is very
much to be seen besides the
boat race. As for that, you
only see the fine fellows
glide easily & beautifully
hast for a moment ——
unless you have a good
place by paying for it.

Extract from letter to Will Etches, 29 March 1873 (p. 60). Drawing shows a young woman in the Boat Race crowd sketching a Negro minstrel.

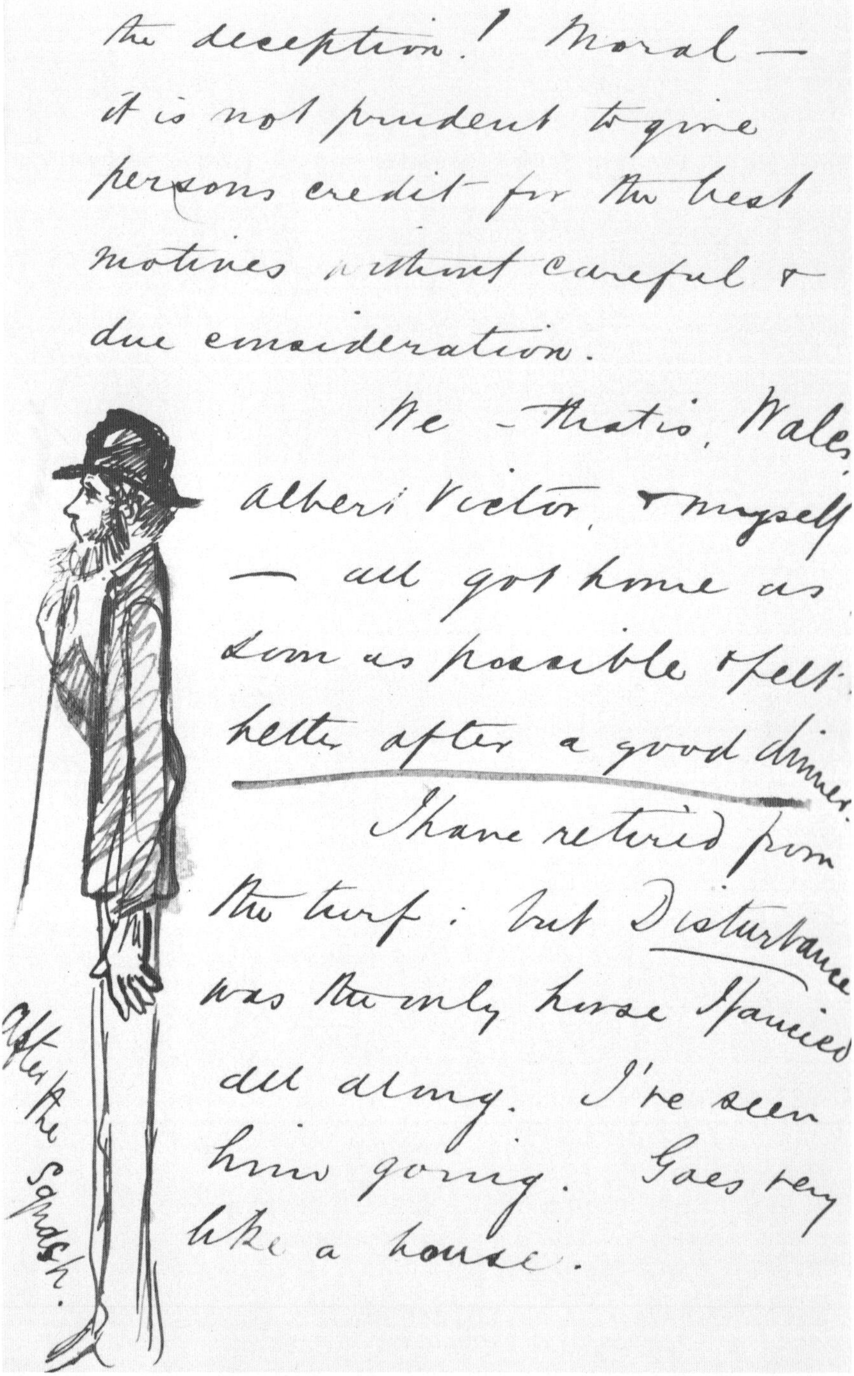

the deception! Moral —
it is not prudent to give
persons credit for the best
motives without careful &
due consideration.

We — that is, Wales,
Albert Victor, & myself
— all got home as
soon as possible & felt
better after a good dinner.

I have retired from
the turf : but Disturbance
was the only horse I fancied
all along. I've seen
him going. Goes very
like a house.

After the squash.

Extract from letter to Will Etches, 29 March 1873 (p. 61). A self-portrait of Caldecott 'after the squash' of the Boat Race.

Tail-piece of letter to Will Etches, 22 October 1873 (p. 62). Caldecott frequently finished his letters with a drawing after his signature.

Opening page of letter to Frederick Green, 6 January 1880 (p. 167), in which Caldecott invites the Greens to visit him in his new house. This coloured letter-head drawing charmingly anticipates the visit.

it did not find me out of town either treading the vine-clad hills of Italy, driving along the dusty poplar-arrayed roads of sunny France, or becoming happily—and sweetly—forgetfully bedrunken unter der Linden. But no, my sweet William, I am here. The Bloomsbury sun blazes on my feverish brow as I try to toil on in the arduous sphere I have chosen. The juice of the grape, the water of the seltzer, the essence of malt, the mist of Ben Nevis, even the liquor of Apollinaris are unavailing. I am not happy. Why is this, why, oh, why? 'Tis because you come not. The chambers, the handsome suite of apartments which I chose for you echo not to your laced-boot's tread. The voice of revelry is not heard there. The spirit of intended carousal dozes curled up in the corner, held to the wall by the accumulated cobwebs of a melancholy summer.

You speak of miseries. I weep. But the wise Frenchman has said that we bear with wonderful resignation the misfortunes of others. We do indeed. How are you? My soul is amongst the wheelbarrow, the machine twister, the fowls, the black pigs and the turkey-cock of your farmyard!

Commend me to each, every and all. My love to your landlord. Kind regards to Mrs Etches, to Amy, to Mrs Jack, Jack and the young Jacks, including Ajax. Farewell! We may meet again. Let's hope not.
Yours faithfully,
R. Caldecott
P.S. Say unto Mrs Etches that I shall write to her soon about the photograph.

[51]
Hôtel de la Ville, Florence
3 April 1879

Dear William,
You brought a tear of pleasure to the eye of the exile—that homeless and wandering man—by your little note received a while back on the sunny Riviera. Think of me sometimes leaning with pensive cheek upon bony hand gazing over the blue sea or running an enquiring eye over the ruins of Caesar's wine vaults—or sometimes fondling the soft long ears of a melancholy ass which bears a fair, straw-hatted and parasoled burden on some hilly excursion.

I'm getting an old fogy now, Will! People put their daughters and nieces under my charge for walks in romantic valleys or for prowls on promenades to view fireworks.

By-the-bye, we had a fine lot of girls at Mentone. If I had had out a $\frac{1}{2}$ dozen of smart young fellows I could have married them all comfortably. There was 1 batch of 5 girls, half Dutch and $\frac{1}{2}$ English. Mother a widow— money—3 of 'em very good looking—Uncle to give 'em away—a Baronet. (Mentone quite smelt of baronets before I left—I've got to hunt up the grave of one's first wife here.) I had not decided which to make up to when I was called for and hurried away to Rome by 2 ladies. There I abode about 18 days, and then gave them the slip, coming here where the air is purer and more exhilarating than at Rome during this time of the year. Still, we had a time at Rome. Some people whom I know arrived at this hotel yesterday— wherever one goes one is sure to be dropped on by somebody.

While I write the sound of the Arno dropping over the weir makes a rushing outside. My window gives on to a road, on the other side of which is the river. The principal spot in Florence for living. Hope it is not dear! I know a man who lives in a villa here and suppose I must look him up.

I trust you are 'getting on' and are all comfortable at Bell o'hill—I forget name of house. With kind regards to Mrs Etches and Amy (many happy returns of Sunday to her) and hoping all well.

Yours faithfully,

R. Caldecott

1. George du Maurier.
2. The Prince of Wales.
3. Prince Albert Victor.
4. Jules Dalou (1838–1902). A sculptor best known for *Triumph of the Republic*. He worked in England 1871–80.
5. Alfred Caldecott.
6. Mud; a northern dialect word.
7. Henry Blackburn's cottage at Farnham Royal.
8. The Quorn Hunt in Leicestershire; he was illustrating an article for the *Graphic*.
9. A small horse, under fifteen hands.
10. Caldecott has spelt the word—ewe—as most countrymen pronounce it.
11. Thomas Lamont (died 1898); water colourist. He was a great friend of Thomas Armstrong and George du Maurier.

EDMUND EVANS

1826–1905

Perhaps the most famous of all 19th century wood engravers, Edmund Evans's reputation was made by the colour engraving and printing which he undertook from 1853 until his retirement in 1892. Evans was the engraver and printer of the coloured illustrations which Caldecott (among others) made for the *Graphic*, and for Mrs Ewing's stories, but their most important partnership resulted in the sixteen picture books which were published from 1878 to 1885.

[52]
24 Holland Street, Kensington, W
5 November 1884

My dear Evans,

Much obliged for all the copies of **D.D.D.**[1]

Printing does seem to me to be a puzzle—because the appearance of the illustrations in the book is different from the proofs. If I had known that the process blocks would not have printed clearer I should have begged for your old-fashioned wood-engraving.

I don't know—but I should have thought the paper unsuitable for clear printing. If the illustrations did not depend so much upon line, but relied upon breadth of tone and shadow, perhaps this style of printing would have been successful. And I cannot understand—as I told you—how those eyes in the key-blocks of 2 or 3 of the pages in Picture Books came so dimly—and the lines on one girl's dress on p. 3 of *Come lasses* came out not at all. This is, I suppose—or rather, faintly conjecture, the result of trying to keep the lines and dots light in the engraving—altho' the girl in last coloured page but one of *Come lasses* was meant to have dark eyes.

I thought the rendering of the faces this year better than ever before in the engraving—also the reproduction of the spirit of the touch all thro'—in fact, I think the engraving was a little over done in delicacy and some lines might have come out stronger than they have done. One or 2 artists who saw early proofs were well pleased.

I think that there are many good things in the tinting of the pages and that something even higher (!) than we have done together might be tried. Something to frame. Decorative things to sell for framing. I have talked of a set of hunting scenes—you know. Perhaps we may try one, or a picture of a separate subject, and see how the public or Fine Art Society will receive it.

As to future *Picture Books* I do not want to do any more of this kind: but I shall be glad to hear if you and Routledges have a strong opinion that a

73

couple more should be done. Of course Routledges run little risk and will perhaps wish to make up another 4 and another 8 volume: but it is of no use doing another 2 merely to make up volumes to oblige them—if a fair sale may be relied on for us, well and good—I'll consider it.

I wish to turn my attention to something else. I have an idea of another single book at $2/6$ or so which might be successful. Books of several shillings seem to have difficulty in finding many customers in England. America is the place to publish more expensive books in.

I heard of a guinea book published there last year which sold 6,000 in America and 120 or 150 copies here. The subject being thoroughly English and beautifully treated—by the way, I'm not sure if it was not a 2 guinea book.

Suppose we begin with a decorative picture of oval shape—about 10 or 12 inches high. It would have to be carefully printed—and could not we use the warm grey more for a groundwork of tone and shade?

We go back to Broomfield this aftn.

Yours very truly,

R. Caldecott

Mrs R.C. says *D.D.D.* is a "lovely little book"!

[53]
Broomfield, Frensham, Farnham, Surrey
27 September 1885

My dear Evans,

Thanks for slips[2] of letterpress.

I have made one suggestion—change of 'grand' for 'great' in panjandrum. I think it most likely that it should be 'grand': but I happen to have gone by the 1st reading sent me and I have called him the *Great* on the cover &c. so we had better be consistent all through.

Goldsmith was always called 'doctor' when spoken to by his comrades and when written of by his contemporaries, I believe.

I have an edition of his essays and poems 1782 in which he is called in title 'Dr. Goldsmith' and in notes at foot of pages is always referred to as 'doctor'.

We put in *Mad Dog* 'Written by Dr. Goldsmith'.

Yours very truly,

R. Caldecott

1. *Daddy Darwin's Dovecot* by Mrs Ewing, illustrated by Caldecott and printed by Evans.

2. Galley slips: type not made up into pages, but pulled as proofs on long (50 cm or more) slips of paper.

JULIANA HORATIA EWING

1841–1885

Mrs Ewing was one of a family of writers for the young: her mother, Margaret Gatty, wrote many books, founded and was editor of *Aunt Judy's Magazine* which subsequently Juliana Ewing and her sister Horatia Gatty edited.

Caldecott and Mrs Ewing collaborated on three books: *Jackanapes*, *Daddy Darwin's Dovecot* and *Lob Lie-by-the-Fire*. It was a close partnership in which, as these letters show, each contributed more than just the text or illustration. Like Caldecott, Mrs Ewing suffered from ill-health, and she died in May 1885, while *Lob Lie-by-the-Fire* was in the press.

This section begins with four letters from Mrs Ewing to Caldecott for which his replies are not extant. Other letters from Mrs Ewing are placed chronologically, as are two letters written by Marian Caldecott, acting as her husband's secretary, and a reply, and one letter to Major Ewing.

[54]
4 August 1879

My dear Mr Caldecott,

My sister is writing to say how good it will be for "A.J.M."[1] if you *are* able to let me have a coloured sketch to write to before very long—but I am sure we neither of us want you to feel the least "hustled", so don't get (metaphorically speaking!) out of breath.

But I am now becoming so nervous under the honour of interpreting you! that I want to give you a hint of my weakest points—than which nothing is stronger—and one is that I am an absolute, hopeless, unredeemable stick at *mere* middle class modern life. A rising young family in sandboots and frilled trousers with an overfed mercantile mamma will simply congeal my few brains. I only say this because I fear that you may try to *draw down to me* and give me a subject ready-made for a writer of nice little stories!

It must inevitably seem to you that the more obvious and everyday the situation the more help you have given me, but the truth is, nothing is *so* hard as to extract the pathos that lies beneath "Philistinism". Forgive my saying that though my art may do it, I doubt if yours can! You only with your "fateful lines" burn in upon one's brain for perpetual contemplation what it takes such large efforts of human and super-human sympathy to forget!!!

Tell me if you would prefer me to give you the least suggestion.

What I should like best of all would be if you would do a rough coloured sketch of anything that pleases you, and if you would pack it up with one or two pen and ink scratches of *any* quaint groups or figures that float before your mental retina!.

Putting them together will be *my* game! and I hope you may think it worth the candle. But trust my imagination please, and if you will send me several *scraps* I shall be very grateful.

Yours very sincerely,

Juliana Horatia Ewing

P.S. and N.B! Don't give me a fat baby with a coral[2]—though all England would rise up and call you blessed if you did—and put in dogs or ravens or cockatoos or any such babies at your will.

Lady's postscript: It has this moment struck me that you have profound sympathy with horses, and with the haunting memories round old houses. Don't be afraid of trusting me with the ghost of a posting house, horses, highwaymen, and an old postillion.

But N.B. if you do let your genius run along an old coach road give me one sketch of an almost baby lad learning to ride "like a jackanapes never off"[3] on a donkey (but not, oh *not*!!! at the seaside).

Take it any way you like. If the coloured sketch would be easily concocted out of a laddie with an aureole of warm yellow hair on a red-haired pony, full tilt among the geese over a village green (the geese to include pretty frightened members of my sex!),[4] give me the decayed post house and postillion in pen and ink. Or, if easier, give me a military sequence!! (easier to me, perhaps!!).

Any child scenes you like:

Child with stick (to ride); hobby horse; rocking horse; donkey; or pony!!!

2. Country yokel (lad of 16) watching cavalry regiment in Autumn Manoeuvres. The soldiers might be approaching an old stone bridge marked 'Blown up'.

3. *Any* scene of horse and trooper caressing each other. (I knew of one man who cried like a woman when his horse was sent to another troop.) They are very kind to them as a rule.

4. Trooper falling from his horse in battle, or riding hard, *anyhow with another man's body laid across his saddle.*

And if in this or any horse sequence you like to have a man riding with a woman. (Do you know Browning's poem of the Ride?)[5] If in the coaching days, on a pillion!

Tell me if suggestions hamper you.

[55]

Ecclesfield Vicarage, Sheffield

21 August 1879

My dear Mr Caldecott,

If I tell you that your letter pleased me almost more than the sketch I

76

fear your modesty may lead you to underestimate my entire delight and satisfaction with the latter—so I won't say so!

I will only say how very pleasant it is to find that you have not taken very justifiable "huff" at suggestions which might have seemed presumptuous, and how very grateful I am to you, 1st for doing it at all (the full favour of which I assure you I don't underestimate!), and secondly for trying to do it to please me! It is very pretty of you to leave me so many graceful openings for refusing to be inspired by your drawing but I cling to it as tightly as 'our' hero to his red pony, and my head *will* be stupid if I can't hammer something out of it to illustrate you!!

Please forgive a very stupid expression of delight and thanks—I am rather prostrate after the pursuit of science up and down Sheffield streets—it being the British Association!! I can hardly say that we found Mr Mivart's speech worth headaches—and I spent most of my time in trying to sketch that most picturesque Professor—Allman (reminding one of Grimm's Professor Knowall!!) on the back of my programme. Naturally I longed for the cunning of your fingers—but we really also wished for you yourself. There was much to draw! Allman himself would be at once a puzzle and a triumph to your pencil, his attitudes, gestures, facial expression, and the nervous play of his hands change ceaselessly.

Not that I should like you to do a "Summer Number of the B. Association" (you have given a prize to "cheek" and so must expect more!). *On the contrary*, as I sat "listening" to Mr Mivart and thinking of other things (!!!) I quite arranged my theories in my own head—and came to the conclusion that when a painter puts down the *mere* results of observation (such as a table d'hôte—or a platform-full of Professors!) it is like the innumerable people of *my* trade who think they have written a novel when they have strung together a couple of dozen portraits from their acquaintance, instead of soaking their brains in the said results of observation, and using the stored-up "traits" to subserve the purposes of the Ideal!!!!!!

I now feel horribly like the *Transcendental Lady in the Wig* in Martin Chuzzlewit!!! and without getting further out of my depth and into disgrace with you—will only say that if by any amount of brain-thrashing I can fit the design with words the least worthy of it—and please you one half as you have pleased me, I shall be very proud—as well as
Very gratefully yours,
Juliana Horatia Ewing
P.S. I am writing to secure attention to your discretion. I consider it "mean" in my sister to be sending you O. Wendell Holmes,[6] which she says she is going to—Allman would be an ideal model for the hero, but I don't want you (such is female inconsistency!) to become *too* classic in your sympathies! I should like you to draw the "literary and artistic" line just where it would include *Mrs Ewing illustrated by, or illustrating, Mr Caldecott!!!*

Ecclesfield, Sheffield
23 July 1880

My dear Mr Caldecott,

I am sending you a number of "Jackanapes" in case you have lost your
other.

I have made marks against places from some of which I think you could
select easy scenes; I mean easy in the sense of being on the lines where your
genius has so often worked. I will put some notes about each at the end of my
letter. What I now want to ask you is whether you *could* do a few illustrations
of the vignette kind for Jackanapes, so that it might come out at Xmas.
Christmas *ought* to mean October! So it would of course be very delightful if
you could have completed them in Sept. and as soon as might be—But do
not *worry* your brain about dates. I would rather give it up than let you feel
the fetters of Time, which when they drag at one's work, make the labour
double. But if you would begin them and *see* if they came pretty readily to your
fingers. I shall only too well understand it if after all you can't finish them as
you would like in time for this season!

In short, I won't press *you* for all my wishes!—but I do feel rather disposed to struggle for a good place amongst the host of authors who are
besetting you, and as I am not physically or mentally well constituted for
surviving amongst the fittest, if there is *much shoving* (!) I want to place my
plea on record.

So: 1. Will you try? 2. Will you kindly tell *me* what it is your duty as a
family man, making hay while the sun shines, to charge apiece; or rather
what your terms will have risen to by September 1880!

Respectfully suggested scenes to choose from (Please forgive pencil: I
am trying to combine letter-writing with oxygen in the garden and within
the sound of the language of lawn tennis players—a quartette—young and
good looking who are alluding to the last no. of Punch!!!)

Initial T out of the old tree on the green with perhaps *to secure portrait*
the old *postman* sitting there with his bag—à la an old Chelsea Pensioner.
1 A lad carrying his own long-bow (by regulation his own height) and
trudging by his packhorse's side, the horse laden with arrows for Flodden
Field (9 Sep. 1513). Small figures back view (!) going westwards—poetic
bit of moorland and sky.
2 If you *like*—the portrait of the little Miss Jessamine in church.
3 to 5 You may or may not find some bits on p. 706 such as the ducking in
the pond of the political agitator (very small figures including the old Postman, ex-soldier of Chelsea Pensioner type). Old inn and coach in distance;
geese (not the human ones) scattered in the fray.

The Black Captain, with his hand on his horse's mane, bigger (so as to
secure portrait) and vignetted if you like. Or *small* on his horse stooping to
hold his hand out to a child, Master Johnson seated in a puddle, and nurses

pointing out the bogy; or standing looking amused behind Master Johnson (p. 707).

6   Pretty vignetted portrait of the little Miss J., ¾ length about the size of p. 29 of *"Old Xmas"*. Scene girl's bedroom—she with her back to mirror, face buried in her hands "crying for the Black Captain"; her hair down to just short of her knees, the back of her hair catching light from window and reflected in the glass. Old Miss Jessamine (portrait) talking to her "like a Dutch uncle" about the letter on the dressing table. Aristocratic outline against window and (as Queen Anne dies) "with one finger up"!!!!! (these portraits would make No. 2 needless probably).

7   Not worthwhile. I had thought of a very small quay scene with slaves, "black ivory", and a Quaker's back! (Did you ever read the correspondence between Charles Napier and Mr Gurney on "Trade and War"?)

8   A very pretty elopement please! Finger post pointing to Scotland—capt. *not* in uniform, of course.

9 or 10   Hardly. Too close to the elopement, which we *must* have!

11   You are sure to make that pretty.

12   Might be a very small, shallow vignette of the field of Waterloo. I will look up the hours &c, and will send you word.

13   As you please. Any part of this chapter.

16   I mean a tombstone like this [*sketch of flat-topped tomb*] very common with us.

17, 18   I leave to you.

19 or 20   might suit you.

21   Please let me try and get you a photo. of a handsome old general!! I think I will try for Genl. MacMurdo, an old indian hero of the most slashing description and great good looks.

22   I thought some comic scene of a gentleman in feather bed and night-cap with a paper—"Rumours of Invasion" conspicuous. Might be vignetted into a corner.

23   Might be fine and go down side of page; quite alone as vignette or distant indication of Jackanapes looking after—or up at him.

24   Should you require any military information for any scene here?

25–26   I hope you could see your way to 26. Back view of horses—Lollo the 2nd and a screw, Tony lying over his, holding on by the neck and trying to get at his own reins from Jackanapes' hand. J.'s turned to him in full glow of the sunset against which they ride; distant line of dust and "retreat" and curls of smoke.

The next chapter requires perhaps a good deal of 'war material' to paint with—and strictly soldier type faces.

27   The cobbler giving his views might be a good study with an advertisement somewhere of the old "souled and healed cheap".

28   This scene I think you might like. And please, on the wall have a hatchment with dulce et decorum est pro patriâ mori (excuse my bad latinity if I

have misquoted).

29 Would make a pretty scene, I think.

and 30 would make me too happy if you scattered pretty groups and back views of the young people, "the Major", and one together in one of your perfect bits of rural English summertime.

If there were to be a small vignette at the end, I should like a wayside calvary with a shadowy knight in armour, lance at rest—approaching it from along a long flat road.

Now please (it is nearly post-time) forgive how very badly I have written these probably confusing suggestions. I am not very well, and my head and *thumb*(!) both fail me.

If you can do it, do it as you like. I send the letter I wrote as it is biznizz. Also I will send you a photo. of an officer who will do for the Black Capt., and will try to secure a general also. If you could lay your hands on the Illustrated No. that was "extra" for the death of the Prince Imperial—an R.A. officer close by the church door helping in one end of the coffin is a very typical military face.

Yours,

J.H.E.

It was very kind of you and your wife to have us to see your sketches. I hope you are taking in ozone in the country!

Yours ever,

J.H.E.

[57]
176 Finborough Road, S. Kensington
17 November 1880

My dear Mr Caldecott,

How can I bless you enough for "the Huntsman"[7] and the sweet little inscription—or how can I *kuss*[8] you enough for rolling up your lovely books—and letting that fiend in everyday clothing, the male or female postmaster expend his or her spleen in stamping and crushing works of art which they mayn't steal? Let me tell you *we* never send one of the Toy Books without due protection of millboard—and we have already sent the Jovial 3 in all directions—not only across country as is proper at this season but across the sea! The Pig is of course a universal favourite—and he is delightfully comic —and very naked—but I think my favourites of all are pages 19, 20 and 21. The boy and *the bird* at page 20 are so living a picture of "bursting with happiness" in the sweet seasons of youth (and hunting) and all outdoor and country joys that it makes one feel young again and strong again to look at them!

18th. I had to stop yesterday for a bad headache.

I hope you will not set it down to ingratitude, for I am *charmed* with my

80

huntsmen. I must also say how very much I admire the Song for Sixpence. When you showed us the sketches I remember being so greatly struck with that happy thought of genius by which you had put the arras with the hunting scenes behind the young king and queen. The effect is grander and more royal than any vista of vast rooms could have been. But as I have once or twice been "cheeky" enough to express my grudge of your pencil being used to immortalise sea-side trippers or other ungraceful episodes—I must say how intensely I am charmed by the peculiar *grace* of the song. The king in his counting house is exquisite, his pictures and knick-knacks are admirable but the teachings of tradition, the dignifying effects of state—and the general pressure of *noblesse oblige* in that most royal and most fascinating little couple and their surroundings are most refined and most perfect. Not perhaps the least in one sense, though the tiniest, is the deliciously dignified little pair and their page issuing from the distant yew hedge archway. (I have a great theory that the shallow steps of old big houses and the height of the yew hedges taught people to walk with grace and dignity.)

And after all this—I believe you won't believe it anything but the military element which makes me so delighted with "The Song"! And I'm free to confess that it adds its usual sparkle to the scenes of everyday life!

And oh, *how* well you'll do soldiers some day when you're too big a swell to do anything for me!! Pages 24 and 25 are *too* good! The girl is a model of pose and grace, but dear old sentry-go is delightful, though I trace a tendency to treat with some levity the Defenders of our Hearths and Homes(!) especially about the legs. But the "portrait of an officer" in the frontispiece is all that could be wished and I think you must allow that he adds much to the picture. Page 30 is perfect. The distant group—the *rage* of the blackbird (I *do* congratulate you on having expressed by almost identical strokes fury there, and rapture in the bird on p. 19 of The Huntsmen)—the beauty of the maid and the *prompt support of the military* are truly excellent. Finally it may seem an impertinence to congratulate you on the virtues of honesty and thoroughness—but it is very pleasant to see you surpass yourself where your success is already sure and you might *scamp*.

Shall you ever be able to do Jackanapes for me? But I fear my work doesn't "fetch" your sympathies as yours does mine! I quite agree with you that you could not do it otherwise than with the care you give to these. But I think we could afford you your just terms; and I should like them in this style rather than more highly finished (as in Bracebridge Hall) to go with the coloured frontispiece. I hate to bother you—but I know that when I hold my peace other people snatch you, and you know I have a charming letter of yours signed "your future illustrator". How wrong it is to break faith with a lady. I know I need not impress on your chivalrous mind! Large be your royalties on these nice books!! I know you (or *ye*) will be glad to hear that more than $\frac{2}{3}$ of the 1st edition of my new Xmas book was taken by the trade in about 3 days.

My love to your wife. I am sending her a little volume of mine—written many years ago, in its new edition.
Yours gratefully,
J.H.E.

[58]
Wybournes, Kemsing, Nr Sevenoaks
25 November 1880

My dear Mrs Ewing,

I was glad to hear from you once more—altho' grieved because you shew signs of weakness by breaking off in the middle of a letter on account of headache.

I was not aware that the *Picture Books* suffered so much at the hands of the Post people—and I am sorry to hear that yours was knocked about. Shall I send you another? I hope you did not happen to get one which had its last picture gummed to the opposite page—such a one I am afraid I sent to somebody—the last picture had suffered from the superabundant paste. Do tell me—if you got it. Millboard and card are not sold in this village—but I really thought the books would go through quite comfortably as I made them up.

It is very pleasant to me—to us—to have your good opinion of these last books.[9] You are 1 of those at whom I feel that I specially aim when I am making the drawings.

N.B. the drawing on p. 29 has got so much tilted that the girl and the sentry are both off their balance—which is the printer's or engraver's fault and not mine.

Yes, I have gradually been approaching the military. I fancy it must be because of the vast number of my wife's relatives who are men of war. I come of a peaceful family. My brother[10] has lately been elected a fellow of St John's

Coll., Cambridge and he lectures on English Literature and takes prizes for Political Economy. I apologize to you for him; but expect to receive sympathy from you when I tell you that I begin to feel a tingling of pride as I call to mind once seeing in my very early childhood a yeoman relative shewing us upon his lawn how he had won the very sword which he flourished around his bucolic head.

Let us approach with reverence the subject of "Jackanapes". I wish that I had time to illustrate it—altho' you have made me quite timid about my power to do it as you would like.

You went into the matter so thoroughly and exhaustively in your letter on the subject that I felt quite awed at the contemplation of what I should have to "attend to" if I undertook it.

But I assure you that it would not be right for me to do it at present. It would occupy the time which ought to be devoted to the production of about 50 drawings for a book to appear in a year from now, said book having been promised long ago and now fixed for the coming year—and, to confess the truth, I doubt whether I shall be able to get it done.

We are glad to hear about the sale of your new book, which we shall get. We hope you are better in health now.
Believe me,
Yours very truly,
Randolph Caldecott

[59]
Greno House, Grenoside, Sheffield
23 November 1881

My dear Mr Caldecott,
I am so glad to gather from my sister that you are yet in England. I thought you had gone abroad, and did not know where to catch you to pour out my delight and gratitude for the Gaffers![11]

It is hardly possible fitly to tell you how I appreciate the sympathy you have shown and the trouble you have taken in depicting the scene and all its local colour.

In the latter you have been quite marvellously successful. It would amuse you to hear how many people "hereabouts" know the exact spot in "the Shroggs" wood where you *must* have sat to sketch the dear familiar scene— or at least that I must have made a rough sketch and sent it to! [you]. An enthusiastic Yorkshireman, a young coal owner (*not a coal heaver*! and highly cultivated, who builds cottages on his property and *guides* his workmen in matters of furnishing and decoration!) delivered a sort of lecture to me on the subject the other day! He walked over here and complained that he had been hunting about in the neighbourhood of "the Shroggs" for the precise point of view and not *quite* hit it. "But one knows the gaffers, of course.

83

They're Yorkshire, and Yorkshire *of this district"*. This exclusion of the other Ridings amused me much.

But it *is* true! You have given the spirit of the men and the spirit of the country, and I know what that means as to careful reading of my M.S. and kindly sympathy with the home life thereof! Many, many thanks!

Now I want to, and I have had to do it in such a tearing hurry, I want to get out, but I could not resist daubing down a remembrance of a scene in the village here [that] I have been sketching this morning.

I have so often longed for you this glorious November, amid the autumn fires of the red and golden woods and the sandstone walls, and old women and bonny children gathering sticks after the equinoctial storms!!!

I hope you gain some comfort from knowing that "whatsoever things are pure and whatsoever things are lovely" in home scenes of landscape and of humanity—always tempt one to say "How like Caldecott".
Ever gratefully yours, with best regards to your better half,
Juliana Horatia Ewing

[60]
12 Lung' Arno della Zecca Vecchia, Florence
4 December 1881

My dear Mrs Ewing,

I am very glad to hear from yourself that you like the "old Gaffers"—that they suit the story and the locality in the remarkable way which you so flatteringly describe in your complimentary letter. What I have done is a simple thing; and lo! you say it is something wonderful. I hope it will always be my luck to please my patrons—and especially you, for I really believe you look into, and about, and around, and up and down one's little bits of sketches in the most critical way; and if it were not that I know you to possess a larger bump of imagination than falls to the skulls of most critics I should be much afeared. But you are good—if there is not much in a drawing your imagination will supply the necessary interest and romance, poetry and story.

I should be very pleased to make a few little vignettes to *Jackanapes* for the purpose you name.

When I *have* time!

"Stay, fleeting Time!"

I cannot make any more promises, "indeed 'deed truth" (as I used to say when a child and I meant it). I have a large quantity of work promised to be done between now and next August, and I have had to give up the present carrying out of some drawings which have been expected any time during the last few months and which I began 2 months ago. They are postponed and much trouble has been taken about them—not only by me.

I do not dislike military subjects—it is only that military people are not generally remarkable for strength of head. I am tending towards cavalry and artillery subjects—I assure you—slowly; but surely: but I've no details, &c, around me yet to work from.

This last month I have done almost nothing—owing to travelling, &c. We left Rome 5 November, and a month means something in the way of work.

I am much obliged to you for your little sketch—it is full of character, and suggestion of detail too. A useful mem.

Beautiful weather here now. We hope you enjoy clearer skies and are in better health, and with our—Mr and Mrs R.C.'s—best Florentine regards, believe me,
Yours faithfully,
R. Caldecott

[61]
Wybournes, Kemsing, Nr Sevenoaks
24 May 1882

WYBOURNES,
KEMSING.
Nʳ SEVENOAKS.

My dear Mrs Ewing,
    You throw yourself
on my mercy—

now I throw myself on yours.

24 May 1882.

My note the other day was short and unexplanatory because I had just given orders for the execution of a nice lady dachshund. I am just as stern today (altho' I speak of mercy); but I will dissemble and seem to wish to be kind.

Now for it—since you first proposed the illustrations to *Jackanapes* I have wished to make them and up to this I have had no time to do them. I have not let other new adventures take up my hours—I have been merely doing my year's promised work, which will not be completed until end of August, I expect, and I thought that perhaps your drawings might be made in Sept. or Oct.—altho' I want those months for painting and modelling amusements and studies. I really cannot touch anything besides what I am busy with until end of August or beginning of Sept.

Before then I have to make at least 120 drawings—none of them large, but most requiring invention and many requiring careful execution. These are for 4 books—or rather what remain to be done of them—I have made a number of the drawings. The most important of these books will be the 1st part of a series (probably) which I promised to undertake about 5 years ago— and I must go on with this year's part now. Each part will be complete in itself—so I need not go on with it afterwards if not successful at first display.

I am actually not doing a temperance society's card which is wanted: and I do not know when I can again take up a small book of animal subjects which I began last year for importunate flatterers.

Before I could approach *Jackanapes* I should have to find out some details of costume—military.

Lastly—and as explanation of my incoherent remarks—I am not well just now—I thought I was when I wrote the other day—and it is pleasanter to read the *Field* than stick up to a table—and more enjoyable to throw oneself about like a boneless puppet at times. Therefore I could not put on a spurt at present. To-day we go to 14 Sheffield Gardens, Campden Hill, W,[12] until 5 June—and I wish we didn't—at this moment.
Yours faithfully,
R. Caldecott

[62]
Wybournes, Kemsing, Nr Sevenoaks
6 June 1882

Dear Mrs Ewing,
    It is good to be here sometimes—we have just returned from a little ride and feel all the better for it.
    On Monday I saw "the other party"[13] and the result of our confabulation is that we cannot let the S.P.C.K. have the publishing of our little work. I will tell you the reasons—perhaps—when I next see you.

Apart from the business view of the matter, there is a cause for satisfaction in my breast at this our decision. If my friend Walter Crane had his drawings rejected, and afterwards saw *Fables* by me rushing out (by the millions which you promised) from the S.P.C.K.'s mansion, it would not be pleasant to him (and he's sad about a lost baby at present); and if he found out that I knew that his drawings were under consideration when I sent mine in, and if I found out that he knew that I knew this, it would be unpleasant for me, for I could not meet his eye with that steady honest grasp that has, &c, and should, &c, &c. If his are published I will be calm, and if there should be a fight it will be fair.

Thank you and Miss Gatty for the interest you take in the matter. Our kind regards.
Yours faithfully,
Randolph Caldecott
P.S. Military subjects—I went to see the Generals at Trooping of Colours on Saturday last. R.C.

[63]
Broomfield, Frensham, Farnham, Surrey
29 November 1882

My dear Mrs Ewing,
You are very kind to take so much trouble in my behalf and I shall be much obliged to you if you will retain my letter to Mr Bryan and send it to me when you have time to cram it into an envelope. Then, in returning the other valuable letters to that gentleman, will you take the trouble to mention that you have sent mine to me, and if he should afterwards demand it from you please take up a postcard and refer him to me. What a bother!

Thank you—when the wind is in a cold quarter all the chimneys smoke, including the funnel of a stove which we have just tried; the front door requires a Hercules to shut it; the drive-gate drags heavily on the gravel; the cold blast pierces the wall of the dining room; the rats scuttle noisily under the drawing room; the new nag ran away with us on Monday (my wife, the groom and I all pulled and kept her straight and no harm was done—Mrs R.C. pulled most womanfully); we are eating away at some very ancient hens which I took over; matters are not yet settled with the late occupier, who has requested me to apologize; and I have had to pay his tithe—Otherwise we are quite comfortable.

We *are* knowing a few people about. On Sunday we drove over—3 miles —to Hook's (R.A.)[14] and lunched. He has a very pretty property. Farnham is three miles to our north. We are near open heathery commons, pine woods, the river Wey, and we see the Devil's Jumps from the windows. I refer to some hillocks and not to the personal activity of the "oud lad".

(I'm trying hard to fill up my paper before I get to *Jackanapes*—can't do it, though, with honour!)

In the matter of *Jackanapes*—I thought you would have reminded me of it when the time came of which I spoke. Perhaps it is well you did not. We lost much time and had a great bother over moving from Kemsing to here. I have a fine long letter of suggestions somewhere. Will you, however, be kind enough to say now how many drawings you would like and their sizes, and when they should be ready? And do you think you could get me any details of the costumes you want? It would help me much. I am really very busy indeed and am obliged to hunt 2 days a week—or 3 a fortnight—for health's sake.

I *do* rejoice over the 3,000 and the 3,200. Mrs R.C. encloses thanks for your message and her love to you.

Yours faithfully,

R. Caldecott

[64]
24 Holland Street, Kensington
5 December 1882

Dear Mrs Ewing,

Thank you for your enclosure.

About "reminding" me—I am sorry to say that everybody has to remind me that the time has come when I have promised to do something. So you must forgive me. I have your former letter of suggestions which I will make as much use of as I can. It is the military costume of which I have hardly any details. I called at that shop[15] in Lower Regent St. yesterday—had sold all prints of a time gone by.

You must not *think*—let alone *say*—that your work does not please me or 'attract' me. If you knew with what avidity I seized upon *Laetus sorte meâ* and how I express myself about your writing when I ever have a chance you would not so misunderstand me. The truth is—I have such an opinion of your force that I feel timid about illustrating you.

And I know I shall not come up to your expectations about *Jackanapes*. I believe I have 1 or 2 copies somewhere at Broomfield: but I am not sure whether they have got themselves into a handy place yet.

And have I not gone to live near Aldershot? And do not the enclosed attest my rampant delight in military scenes?

I will enquire about the little matters on which you require information.

Who will engrave and print the book?

Yours very truly,

R. Caldecott

[65]
9 December 1882

My dear Mr Caldecott,

One thing I *won't* let you say—that there is the remotest fear of your not being able to "satisfy me".

It's a moral, mathematical and mechanical impossibility that you could fail to do so.

I am too "far-gone" a lover of your pencil; and if the designs proved entirely different from my expectations, I should only see deeper designs in your work, and expound you as Ruskin does Turner!!!!

I doubt if you know, and it seems almost impertinent in me to express, the charm your work has for me.

We must say very nice things of each other behind each other's backs, if you express $\frac{1}{100}$th part of what I am constantly expressing in the way of admiration!

I think you stand alone!—For an 'all-roundness' of genius in "illustrating" humanity, and human surroundings, with a delicate dexterity that is delicious to anyone who has *any* knowledge of *your* art, and with an absence of tricks and mannerism which seems to me only to be found in the highest order of any art whatever!

And this is not because I fail to appreciate that we are very rich just now in character sketchers of very high order. I am devoted to du Maurier (think him vastly superior to Leech!) He draws the finest breed of men, women and children with a fineness of perception worthy of Vandyke. And the *grace* of his pencil, at times, in certain things in Punch (such as those girls and youngsters riding tricycles and bicycles) stirs me with a sense of pleasure that only very fine work gives one as a rule. For pose and beauty of youthful strength in "thoroughbred" humanity he has had no predecessor to touch him in his own line of art, I think.

And yet—I think you have no peer! And, as I said some days ago to Mr McClure, I believe your work will be gathered up again and treasured by those who *know* and *love* their fellow creatures—the world around them— and the gifts of hand and eye—when Mr Crane and Miss Greenaway are out of fashion for the mass and fatiguing to the elect!!!!!!

Don't weary yourself in telling me about your not being up in the details of military life. I gather that you say this in a kind and thoughtful explanation of not having helped me with "Soldiers' Children".

Not that I accept any reason for that, but the unworthiness of the lines and your own over-workedness. (I think it more kind than I can say that you have done the other!)

If it had been possible to your time and inclination to do one design (coloured) for it—as a frontispiece to a volume of child-verses—I think you might have found a scene non-soldiery.

Your embryo hero on his red pony is so delicious. I think I should have

89

suggested to the lines "There's a man in uniform to bring the letters, but he's nothing like our old orderly, Brown. I told him—through the hedge— "Your facings are dirty, and you'd have to wear your belt if my father was at home." And oh, how he did frown!" A rather crabbed-looking old postman (without a belt!) poking in his bag for the letters. (The captain's wife (as pretty as you please!) coming anxiously to the door with her little girl and doll, and the younger boy in dark blue knickerbocker turn out *if you like*). These rather *more* in the background, the principal figures being the postman and—The embryo military man, about the age of your pony boy, having pushed a fair flushed face, and very upright attitude, through the honeysuckle hedge. Any village green details you please. Time, *present day*.

N.B. You will of course let Mr Bell—or us—know how deeply, *besides gratitude* the magazine is in debt for the water colour design.

[What will you] say are ①, your charges *per design*; ②, can you be ready by March; ③, can you do *Daddy Darwin* or not till another year?
Yours,
J.H.E.
P.S. *How* I laughed over Signor Dante Allighretti[16]—in costume—doing the stern parent. The mixture of the s[tern] p[arent] *and* the classic poet is irrisistible!

[66]
Broomfield, Frensham, Farnham, Surrey
15 December 1882

My dear Mrs Ewing,
I have all your recent letters before me and I have much to say on the subjects treated therein: but I can only say some of it now.

You wish *Jackanapes* to make a book of 48 pages without titles, &c. Have you calculated on the probable space which the cuts will occupy? And do you wish any of the illustrations to cover the whole page? Drawings the size of the *Household Troops*[17] would require all the page to look well.

On the question of price—I ought to charge for a drawing the size of *H. Cavalry* 6 guineas; and for ½ that size 4 guineas; and for an initial or finial 2 guineas. (The originals to be my property). This is not quite at the rate I get paid for the *Graphic* work or for other employment. Space has something to do with it and number of designs in the space—well a drawing of each size mentioned above would occupy space &c such as I should usually charge 20 gs for. For a *Graphic* page I get—(tell it not in Gath) 30 guineas or more—and I am meditating raising that price. This will perhaps help you in coming to a conclusion as to whether it is worthwhile to employ me. (Miss Thompson got £400 for a picture 25 inches by 18 the other day and it is offered at 500 now!)

I can let you have the drawings by middle of March—but you can be

90

going on with the reproduction of the drawings as I send them in.

The amount of work which I should consider would *fully* illustrate *Jackanapes* would be as much as a Picture Book.

I should prefer a royalty on the book because then I should only be paid according to results. This, however, would be difficult to arrange, I doubt not.

You get a halfpenny on a shilling book, you tell me. I suppose there is not much colour-printing—if any—in the books. I should want at least a penny on J[18] unless a circulation of over 20,000 were guaranteed: and I think that I should in that case still want my penny!!—so covetous and griping are we in these days of house-fitting-up.

I am making a rigmarole—thinking over the matter before you, as it were.

On making further calculations I see that the above-mentioned prices are rather too low: but if you will kindly tell me how many drawings you would like at 7 gs, 5 and 3 guineas, and how you are influenced by these sums, I will do my very best to come to terms.

You tell me to 'put a price that will pay me'—and I am not sure that I am doing that—I cannot tell how long the drawings will take me and how many trials I have to make over each subject. Pray be frank with me and give me your opinion of these prices. I should not charge *more* than the last named sums to you.

I could not undertake *D. Darwin* yet.

I am about to write to decline Jane Austen's works (private!)—and this I do with sorrow.

In what war was Jackanapes slain?

Thanks for last copy of story.

I should be very pleased to meet the Rouge Dragon[19] at Herald's College during the Xmas week and have a look at costumes. If he cannot be there at my time I should be very much obliged for a sketch of the hussar you desire. I must also get some details of the horse's trappings.

The *Household cavalry* sketch belongs to a private book[20] of my own which will probably be issued (without letterpress) in 2 or 3 months time. I believe you might have the loan of it, if you really wish to do something with it.

The shininess of some coloured prints[21] is due to the paper on which they are printed—generally. My Pict. Bks are done on soft paper. This reminds me that perhaps I misunderstand you: but do you think the brown ink drawings in the Pict. Bks are done by a "process"?[22] They are engraved on wood. At present I consider wood safer than "process" (altho' I have wept copiously this morning over some proofs from wood-cuts).

If we come to terms—and we are sure to come to some sort of terms—I should not desire to do more than touch up the proofs of cuts before the printing. I would prefer not to arrange with Evans or Cooper. The latter is rather dear, but he takes great care with my work. The *H. cavalry* is a *rough proof* of a cut by Evans.

I do not mean that I would rather that E. or C.[23] did not have the work.

I don't think I care much about the coloured illustration to *Jackanapes* which you used before. Do you truly want to serve it up again?

Pardon disjointed remarks, want of lucidity, and the evidence of an avaricious disposition which pervade this letter—written on my knee.

Yours very truly,

R. Caldecott

[67]
Broomfield, Frensham, Farnham, Surrey
19 December 1882

My dear Mrs Ewing,

Your letter of the 17th came to my hand too late for me to send this reply by to-day's post.

I hoped you would not have written to the S.P.C.K. people until you had expressed to me your opinion of my "business terms". The principle upon which we go—"we" meaning all virtuous illustrators and designers—is to get as much as possible out of the people who deal with us as a pure matter of business. I should have no scruple in touching the very bottom of a publisher's coffer. I am sorry to say that I know them a little too well. I hope I am not wrong in supposing that the Society should be treated in the same way.

But when my dealings have been with authors and engravers (at such times as they take risk and a special interest[24] in the matter dealt with) I have been somewhat indifferent as to the money (speaking within bounds) wishing to do as good work as I can, and to please the author, or satisfy the engraving-projector.

All this means that, although the prices I quoted to you are not as much as I could occupy my time with earning (supposing I wished to accumulate lucre) yet I should like to illustrate *Jackanapes* to your satisfaction, to the applause of the critics (whoever they are) and to my own glory; and that, therefore, I am quite ready to fall in with any arrangement which seems to you the best. It will pay me somehow—if I am successful. So, if you can tell me how many designs you would like, I will name a lump sum for all. Or if you will tell me how much can be afforded, I will do as much as I can— as much as Time and Avarice will allow me. Never mind further details than this. If your sum—should you mention a sum—seem small I will propose that I receive something more after a certain number of editions are run through. I trust to you to get as much for me from the Society as they can afford, but I do not wish to *surpass* the terms of my last letter. I think, and [suppose] that the book[25] must not be more [than] a shilling.

My talk of r[eturn] was as if the book had been given to me and I did it thoroughly—[I get] more than a penny[26] on my Pictu[re Books] of course, because there is no author.

92

My tendency towards royalties is [the] result of a foolish feeling of wish[ing] to be paid by results. A royalty brings in very little if the [sale is] not large.[27]

Do not think I do not consider the author's deserts. I look upon the author as removed from the baser herd of printers, paper-makers, binders, packers, illustrators, and publishers who must be paid as tradesmen. An author is much above that sort of thing—except in profits (as a rule) and in these the deserving author *should* be pre-eminent always.

I was much interested in your remarks about du Maurier. He is great: but cannot be compared with Leech in "passion". To descend to detail— Leech's women were dolls; but his men were suggestions of finer individuals than du M's. The latter would have been as happy in following out one of several other bents—Leech must have drawn. I will not refer to Walter Crane now.

We have to thank you for a visit from Mrs Harold Browne, her daughter and son (of Tilford, not Frensham). I only was at home to receive them.

[Part of this letter is missing]

P.S. Evans and I get from Routledges 5¼d per book and they stitch them. R.C.

[68]
24 Holland Street, Kensington
1 January 1883
A Happy New Year!

My dear Mrs Ewing,
I saw E. Evans the other day—but I had not your letter with me in which you mention the size and number of pages you wish *the book* to have. I shall send him these particulars and he will make a dummy book and then calculate the cost of engraving, printing, binding, paper, &c. We shall then see how many drawings can be engraved for a fair sum—as for me, I shall make as many drawings as Evans can engrave, &c for 4½d—supposing that sum will allow me something of a royalty—as I believe it will. The paper you want will be expensive, perhaps.

Meanwhile, if you have anything to add to your former letter about size, &c, kindly tell me before Evans makes up the dummy. And if you are in a hurry—as I shall not be able to get your letter until my return to Broomfield on Thursday or Friday—it would save time if you would be so good as to put down the particulars of pages &c over again on a P.C. and address it to 24 Holland S.

(I think I told you that I should be at Court Lodge, Chelsfield,[28] for Xmas and afterwards (where I write this)—your letters have been to Broomfield, however. Yet no serious delay has occurred.)

It seems to me that it will be best for you to leave the getting out of the book to Evans and me—after you have told us all you wish done. We will try to follow your instructions and submit paper, &c, &c for approval.

I should think we could do what you require for 4½d—but I'm not quite sure—you are so particular!

I am glad to see your Seccombe birthday book:[29] but I fear the cuts are too small for one to make out details by. You see as I do not understand the insertions and attachments of the various rigging and straps about accoutrements a mere suggestion is not enough.

I called at a Regent St. shop a week or 2 or 3 ago—had sold out all prints likely to be useful to me. I will look in elsewhere.

I will keep the Secretary's[30] letter until I write again. He offers fair—and trusts in you.

Yours very truly,

R. Caldecott

[69]
Broomfield, Frensham, Farnham, Surrey
29 January 1883

My dear Mrs Ewing,

At last I am able to send you a dummy book for your inspection. E. Evans says there are 4 leaves too many in it—by mistake.

If he prints 10,000 copies and I make as many drawings as are shewn in the dummy in pencil—but not quite so large and of higher quality—he can let you have them for 4½d each. This would give me £50.

The number of drawings you see are 13[31]—1 frontispiece and 12 ½-*pages*. I do not know whether he counts on the former cut of *Jackanapes* as the frontispiece: if he does, I would like to arrange for using that elsewhere and make a new drawing for the frontispiece—I should have to pay for the extra engraving.

This is calculated at 1 printing only. I proposed to do 4 pages, 10 ½-pages and 6 vignettes, which would leave me £30 19. 8 after all expenses of paper, engraving, and printing were paid. The cover to be mere printing—no design engraved.

You will see specimens of printing in 2 colours.

I should approach the subject more carefully when making the designs than the pencil mems. might seem to warrant. They do not pretend to illustrate your story—so do not try to puzzle them out. They are larger than they ought to be, please to remember, when regarding the arrangement.

If other things seem right I am quite willing to make the amount of illustrations which I first proposed, i.e. 4 pages, 10 ½-p. and 6 vignettes—it was Evans who suggested the 1 page and 12 ½-pages.

94

We spent an agreeable evening and morning at Farnham Castle the week before last. Mrs Caldecott sends her love. I send a wish that you will say exactly what you think and want about the subject of this note. Don't mind me!

Yours faithfully,

R. Caldecott

[70]

Broomfield, Frensham, Farnham, Surrey

4 March 1883

My dear Mrs Ewing,

Re *Jackanapes*. Mr E. Evans writes and says "I did not calculate on *saving* anything by buying an electro[32] of Bell—I only estimated the cost of new cuts—besides, Mr Bell writes, in reply, that he will not sell an electrotype of it—but will sell the whole, colour block included, at $\frac{1}{2}$ its original cost, and he wants to get rid of 1000 printed plates. So I say—let it alone altogether—it will take off from the new look of the book to use an old illustration".

I think I agree with E.E. in this.

"The $4\frac{1}{2}$d will include binding, but not a design for cover—I reckoned on using one of the inside cuts for cover—the extra printing for type *black* and cuts *brown* would be £30 on the 10,000—about $\frac{3}{4}$d per copy." He says he could let you have reprints after the first 10,000 at $3\frac{1}{2}$d a copy. He says further that "some arrangement ought to be made with the S.P.C.K. to take a given number a time or I may be left with some thousands on my hands".

If more copies are required than 10,000 I think I should have some little interest in them—as the £50, which is what I should receive if no further expense be added to the present estimate, is not an exorbitant sum—but I do not know whether the $3\frac{1}{2}$d a copy would include me—I will enquire about this.

I should like the copyright to be *yours* if it can be so arranged.

All this sounds as though we considered the designs were going to be in great demand.

I shall be in town on Tuesday and for a week or 2 afterwards and should therefore like to see you and find that you are in better health. I could try to wait upon you at Warwick Road.

Meantime, believe me to be,

Yours faithfully,

R. Caldecott

P.S. I have just received your note of yesterday 3rd. I was not aware that I have yet failed to carry out what I think of doing—the time mentioned is not yet up? And I could not begin until it was definitely settled as to how many drawings would come in. The question of money has not influenced *me*—it only tells on the engraving.

But I must not boast—I only received E.E.'s last letter yesterday. I wanted your birthday book a little while—I am much obliged for its loan: but I'll return it at once. You must not trust artists with valuable documents. R.C.

[71]
Broomfield, Frensham, Farnham, Surrey
4 March 1883

My dear Mrs Ewing,

The post-boy was waiting this morning when I wrote a hurried post-script to a letter already indited to you. Then I had no time to express great sorrow at the disturbance in your mind caused by my apparent neglect of *Jackanapes*. Pray do not feel very uncomfortable, for I intend to make the drawings during this month of March—on referring to your letters I see that they were asked for "in March", and I never meant to begin before this month had blown itself in. There will not be much engraving to do and not much printing so that I think there will be ample time to get it gently out before the publishing time.

My Picture Books—on which I depend for some of the necessary luxuries of life—are barely begun—1 drawing only not quite finished is all to be seen; and these books are wanted for publication as early as *Jackanapes* and have twelve coloured plates between them. Yet you are wise to "remind" me—Evans reminds me of the Picture Books, somebody else reminds me of other things, and I am in daily expectation of being reminded of various neglected works—not wickedly or intentionally neglected. I am putting aside a cherished plan or 2 for the sake of *Jackanapes*. I do not think I have undertaken anything "fresh" since I promised to actually make designs for your book. "Lewis Carroll"[33] did me the honour to apply to me the other day; but he did not flatter me as you do—at least, not much—he asked for specimens and samples.

I should not have been so anxious, *perhaps*, to get the correct costumes if you were not so particular about them. If you remember, when you suggested my going to see your brother[34] at H. College[35] I said that if I knew he would be there I would pay a visit to the college in Xmas week: but I had no reply. (However, as I cannot get prints, I must go there, I suppose.) I only mention this because you reproach me with not having been to the college.

On re-looking at your Birthday Book I think I must ask you to let me keep it for a week or 2 longer. It may be useful; but if you cannot rest without it, I will make mems. from it and return it at once. It has been reposing quietly and peacefully in a corner of my "private secretary"; and it looks in quite as good health as when its poor battered body first came to me.

If you do not think E. Evans's prices low enough do not hesitate to get an estimate from somebody else.

It is very pleasant to me to hear that my slight scribbles of "cavalry" &c are inspiring you.

I will trouble you with no more remarks at present—except one—which is—I do not like to hear of your being tired.
Yours very truly,
R. Caldecott

[72]
24 Holland Street, Kensington
7 March 1883

My dear Mrs Ewing,
Your letter of 5th came this morning.
I should like to go and lunch with you and Miss Sulivan to-day—the weather is so cheerful and summery that it almost tempts one to take a holiday—but please excuse me for not accepting the invitation kindly sent. If I went out to luncheon I should never be able to keep any promises about work. Should it be convenient, I will look in upon you some afternoon between 4 and 6, towards the end of the week.

I will write to your brother and ask him when he will be at the College.

In 2 or 3 letters back I quoted Evans's estimate for printing in 1 ink. Then you referred to 2 inks as if you had not noticed the proposed 1 ink. So I asked Evans again about 2 inks—that is why he says that the 'extra printing' would cost £30 or so more. He only calculated on 1 ink when he made out that there would be £50 for me.

The 3½d after 10,000 would not allow me any royalty: but I do not want much beyond being associated with you in any success the book may have—it is really not worth considering from a money point of view (after 10,000, I mean)—I only desire the excitement of thinking that a pound or 2 might someday drop in! Suppose I had a halfpenny per copy (or is that too much)—that would be £2 for each 1,000 over 10,000. I hope the sale will reach far beyond that. It is not quite a new book and I should think that might be against it.

Do you know—I am afraid that the plain cut of Bell's coloured plate would not be in character with the other cuts. He must know that we do not want the colour blocks—or they would have been asked for.
With kind regards to Miss Sulivan,
Yours very truly,
R. Caldecott

24 Holland Street, Kensington
10 March 1883

My dear Mrs Ewing,

On my return here I found a letter from Mr E. Evans which he had not sent direct, as he should have done.

He wants to know whether the 1st 10,000 will be all taken from him and paid for, and "how many would each edition of re-prints be? For, of course, a small number is more expensive than a large one in proportion, and would these editions be paid for if they sell or not?"

I have told him that I am writing to you, and I have asked him to say how much 2,500, 5,000 and 10,000 copies would be after the 1st 10,000, supposing they were ordered in such quantities.

I have also said that I believe he is to be paid for what he is asked to print —that, in fact, the S.P.C.K. will *order* the editions, and that he is not supposed to be a speculator in the matter.

If I have said wrong, kindly mention it. I will send on his reply as soon as received.

We are very pleased with your verses because of so many natural touches that exactly describe and hit off the children in the *Spectators*.[36] You might know them—Do you think you could—would it be possible—am I impertinent in wishing that you might see no harm to your work if you changed the name of *Alice* to *Maggie*, and *Spot* to *Spike*. *Dolly* is like the original, very; but I won't ask about that.

Some of the remarks about the donkeys are the putting into words what my ideas were when I sketched the *Household cavalry*. The "flat of the sword" business too.

I hope you are better and are going to be quite robust.
Yours very truly,
R. Caldecott

24 Holland Street, Kensington
13 March 1883

My dear Mrs Ewing,

Over the leaf you will see the figures of Evans's calculations for various editions of *Jackanapes*. The expense of engraving will—of course—only be borne by the 1st 10,000.

I can be included in the 1st edition either by Evans receiving 4½d a copy or by an outside payment. Perhaps it would be best to arrange it by paying 4½d for the first 10,000. Subsequent editions could be paid for according to Evans's statement of what his charges would be. He wishes it to be well-understood that these charges are calculated on the plan of his being paid for what he is ordered to print—sell or not.

Yours very truly,

R. Caldecott

P.S. Very much obliged about change of names "Alice and Spot".

Engraving			
1 page for frontispiece	4		
& 12 half-pages	24		
	____		
	£28		
or 2 pages &	8		
10 half-pages	20		
	____		
	£28		

or other charges to equal a like total

1st edition of 10,000, 48pp.			
Paper and binding at $1\frac{3}{4}$d	72	18	4
Setting type	6		
Printing	30		
	_____		
	£108	18	4
Reprinting 10,000			
Paper and binding	72	18	4
Printing	30		
	_____		
	£102	18	4
Reprinting 5,000			
Paper &c	36	9	2
Printing	19	10	
	_____		
	£55	19	2
Ditto 2,500			
Paper &c	18	4	7
Printing	12	15	
	_____		
	£30	19	7

24 Holland Street, W
21 March 1883

My dear Mrs Ewing,

"It would nearly double the expense of printing *Jackanapes* to have 3 pages only in 3 printings instead of one; for the sheets would have to pass through the press for these 3 pages—if printed separately they would be an extra expense in binding as well." Thus E. Evans.

He cannot say what initials, &c, would cost till he sees what I draw. They might cost $10/- to $20/- each. (We'll—you and I—put 2 or 3 in anyhow.) He says not worth £5 to purchase old frontispiece and "will give book a secondhand look". "Excuse me expressing my opinions unasked for." (E.E.)

Samples of the cover paper can and will be obtained.

Please decide as soon as possible as to how many and what sizes illustrations you will have—I want to get at them.

I was at War Office yesterday. Colonel Deedes very kind and attentive, thank you!

To Broomfield, Farnham, 5.5 this aftn. Return Thurs. or Friday next week.

I hope you are getting stronger.

Yours,
R. Caldecott

Broomfield, Frensham, Farnham, Surrey
24 March 1883

My dear Mrs Ewing,

The electro would be worth £5 to Mr Evans if he saved paying for the drawing of a design as well as the engraving of it: but in this case it makes no difference as far as the draughtsman's charges are concerned. At the same time we may note that if Mr E. bought the electro he would lose the profit on the engraving of a new design at £4 the block. It would therefore be a loss to him. This, however, he has not considered of any consequence and it has not affected his calculations.

Still, if you want him to buy the electro at £5 you must remember that you are taking £1 from the rest of the engraving money and the profit on one block out of Mr Evans's pocket. In short, the electro is worth less than nothing to him and he does not want it. He will use it, of course, with pleasure—perhaps—if you really wish it.

As I understand your last letter, I need not put this matter before him again for any decision or opinion; and unless you write and say "buy *it* at £5" I will make my plans without it.

I cannot see how Mr Bell can be ill-used by your not buying *it*.

I think it will be best not to trouble about any royalty for Mr Evans; but to work on his prices last sent in.

As to what you get from the S.P.C.K. I must let you arrange all that. You know how I calculated to be remunerated on 1st 10,000—on subsequent editions I do not mind what you give me. $\frac{1}{4}$d, $\frac{1}{2}$d or 1d—just exactly what you like. Do not let the question trouble you further.

Now I will proceed to plan according to suggestions in this your last letter.

I am glad to hear of Major Ewing's return.[37] Post-boy waits.

Yours very truly,

R. Caldecott

[77]
Broomfield, Frensham, Farnham, Surrey
21 August 1883

My dear Mrs Ewing,

Jackanapes. Of course I had proofs of the engravings and marked them for alteration. Others I pasted—no, I did not—I marked and numbered where the cuts were to come in on a copy of *Jackanapes* which I sent to E. Evans and I marked the frontispiece properly. Before it was engraved I told Evans to keep it as large as possible. It *has* lost by reduction.

Since then I have—until from you—heard nothing at all of the book in any way.

I hope that my part will be a success—yours is assured, because so many have passed their opinion upon it, and because the interest that new readers will take in the story will make them excuse the bits of cuts if they are not satisfactory—besides, they'll be so excited that they will hurry past the illustrations.

I am very pleased to be included in the re-publication of the story; but I do not want you to think that I have 'a great notion' of the importance of my designs to the volume.

I am glad to have your kind remarks on some of the cuts and to hear what Sir P. Douglas said (a visitor here now went to school with a daughter of his).

We should like to visit Taunton—I hope it suits your health—thank you; but see no way to make time.

Our kind regards.

Yours very truly,

R. Caldecott

P.S. I return proof with thanks. In saying I had not heard in any way of *Jackanapes*, I did not mean the *business* part, I assure you. R.C.

[78]
Broomfield, Frensham, Farnham, Surrey
12 October 1883

My dear Mrs Ewing,

Your note of 10th reached me in aftn. yesterday and I reply as soon as I can in order to return Evans's and McClure's[38] letters—the former I should have returned before—which are herewith.

I have no doubt that your plan of dividing cost of coloured boards is a good and right one *if the Society*[39] *will agree to it*. As for me, I am content to fall in in any way you like—as I told you—because I have made no calculation as to what money I might or should receive for my share—and am prepared to receive whatever can be afforded in the way talked of some months ago—I forget at this moment what we said about it.

As to Evans—it looks as though he could very easily afford a reduction of 8 or 10 per cent on his total bill (which would include cost of the coloured boards). I have no doubt that his work has been done rather more carefully and that the materials are really a little better or more costly than the Society's, and that his going about it is more expensive to him than the Society's to them. Yet the margin seems too large according to Mr McC.'s estimate. I think, too, that as you have been more particular about all the details and the materials and the manner of working-up than is usual with authors or people who put work in Evans's hands, he may have felt that the extra attention required of him should be reckoned in the bill. This is only an idea, you know. To have things done exactly as one wants, and as well, necessitates expenditure of money besides time.

Yet again, I say, I am surprised at McClure's estimate as compared with E.E.'s—and I am glad you have told E.E. about it.

I am of opinion that E.E.'s charge for engraving is not too much. I should not like to think that it had cost less—if it had, I should feel that a mistake had been made and the drawings not had a decent chance. I have

arranged for the book to be asked for at Chester, Manchester, Cambridge, T. Wells, London, &c. I found copies of it at Cornish's in Holborn. Let me know, please, if I can do anything more.
Yours sincerely,
R. Caldecott

[79]
Broomfield, Frensham, Farnham, Surrey
15 October 1883
8 A.M.

My dear Mrs Ewing,
On Friday I sent from here the cut of Jackanapes and the duckling tinted in blue and buff. Miss Gatty is here and yesterday we talked over the subject of this cover and agreed that the above-named cut is not so interesting in aspect and so likely to attract gazers and purchasers as could be wished. We think a soldier should be outside—Miss Gatty also saying that the baby is not sufficiently characteristic of R.C.

A new design—even simple—which I would make—would cause a further delay of 2 or 3 days: but I now propose and humbly suggest that the present cover design be tinted in blue and red—I send a rough specimen—in a lighter ground of pale buff. The little chap at top would come darker than in this specimen.

So I am off to Farnham to telegraph to Evans asking him to wait until tomorrow morning—Tuesday—when he will receive from me a tinted cut of this design—and from you a telegram to say which he is to go on with—this last or the baby and duckling.[40] I think this when tinted will do what can be done for the book.

If it had been originally settled to have a separate design for cover I should have put therein a soldier very prominently.
Yours very truly,
R. Caldecott
P.S. I don't think you should have given in to McClure; but I am content.
R.C.

[80]
Broomfield, Frensham, Farnham, Surrey
18 October 1883

My dear Mrs Ewing,
I have not made any comment on your kind and thoughtful remarks about the profits which may accrue from the sale of *Jackanapes*—as I read them in your letter of 12th. All will be well, no doubt. I have ever been of opinion that one should not make profits over an unsuccessful work. The new cover

ought to produce a fair sale; but it cannot compete with the full and complete manner—and pretty—in which your book of "soldier's children" has been produced for ˢ1/-.

When I said the other day that you ought not to have given in to S.P.C.K. I meant as regards their sharing in the expense of covers. I have no doubt that for trade purposes and for money-making to all concerned a gayer aspect was essential to the book. However, I fall in cheerfully with your arrangement.

You ask me the question "Is it true that E.E. is not an engraver?" I thought you knew something of how the "wood engravers" manage their affairs. I will try to explain a little. E.E. has learnt thoroughly his profession and worked at it closely, and as artistically as is usual in this century, for many years (so I believe). But as it is impossible to make any money by sticking to the bench and graver and trying to engrave each block which he engages to do with his own hand, he has called in the assistance of sundry youths whom he has educated in his own style, and when they have become accomplished engravers he has endeared them to him by means of regular weekly payments of money. And in course of time he has felt so satisfied with their ability that he has been content to superintend their work and to give advice and make suggestions thereon at such moments as he could spare from his growing occupations of waiting in publishers' lobbies, of corresponding with authors, of seeking out suitable materials to his trade, of discovering draughtsmen who might be trusted to return to him a block of wood with a fair design pencilled thereon instead of selling it for a few immediate pence, and of interviewing such artists as called upon him either to solicit employment, to request instant and inordinate reward for work done, or to point out that his engraving of their drawings was "sickening" (I quote the word usually used).

Then he has bought certain machines and engaged accomplished workmen to take off the impressions from the blocks, and, further, to produce such letterpress as may be wanted to accompany the cuts. He has also secured the services of book binders and of those who stitch covers on to regulated masses of printed matter—in short, he has prepared himself to get out and produce in its completeness an illustrated book—plain or in colours.

Now it will be very evident that the employment and direction of so many men and of so much machinery, and the necessary pleadings with publishers, explaining to authors and combats with artists, must unfit a man for quiet steady work such as is required from a true engraver, who should have unclouded eye and unshaking hand.

Therefore E.E., Cooper and others wear tall silk hats, have extensive establishments, and seldom, if ever, touch a block themselves.

Artists who know the unhinging effects of the modern wood-engraver's habits of business prefer that his instructed assistants and called-in help shall execute the engraving of their drawings. I could tell you how an engraver

104

recently waited hat in hand on a publisher and how that publisher gnashed his teeth at him, foaming at the mouth, and being beaded with perspiration, all about something not directly affecting either of them.

I could tell you of an artist calling upon a "real" engraver; but it is too dreadful and the post goes.

More some other time, I have wearied you now.

Another 500 copies of *Jackanapes* have been sent for and delivered.

Yours very truly,

R. Caldecott

[81]
Broomfield, Frensham, Farnham, Surrey
Tuesday to Friday (*and after if frost comes*) at 24, Holland St., Kensington.
9 December 1883

My dear Mrs Ewing,

I have been during the last cold day or 2 pondering heavily on the subject of *Jackanapes* profits, and the conclusion which I have arrived at is that if E. Evans will without demur pay $\frac{1}{3}$ of cost of coloured covers or will take 10% off the bill you can honestly allow him to do so and not be wakeful at nights with the thought that he is unhappy or discontented with his share of the profits.

As you suggest, he probably takes care of himself all through. I trust him, as I think I must have told you, from a remark which you make; but I have no means of checking or auditing him, which makes it less noble in me to leave matters in his hands and gratefully accept what money he allows to dribble thro' his fingers into my outstretched and hungry palms.

I do not go so far as to recommend you to trust him so implicitly. As regards my publications, I can check the amount delivered to Routledges by referring to them, I suppose; but I cannot tell how much profit Mr Evans gets on the books.

I have an impression that little bits of carelessness and inattention in our friend are the result of his having much to do. I think, however, he keeps a clear head—I know that he is able to remain calmly at his country-seat[41] 8 miles from here 3 days out of the 7 of which each recurring week is composed, as perhaps you are aware.

I am the more firmly of the opinion expressed in the 1st paragraph of this letter when I reflect that if E. Evans pays the $\frac{1}{3}$ or 10% you will consider me rightfully entitled to £50 on the 1st edition of 10,000. I suppose we did say something of my having that sum if it could be afforded. Anyhow, when you come to settle please to pay me that sum if you find it fair; and less if after late changes and events you think I ought to have less. I shall indeed be grateful if you can afford me a penny royalty on other editions. Of course, I am considering that you will take for yourself at least what you originally thought you would get—if you do not get that on 1st edition, neither must I.

I am rejoiced to hear that *Jackanapes* is selling. I thought it would. You have given pleasure to many people by the story, I hear.

Kindly tell me what *initials*,[42] when and how, and I'll do my best—as if you were a defunct or undiscoverable or unasserting author.

Yours faithfully,

R. Caldecott

[82]
Broomfield, Frensham, Farnham, Surrey
16 December 1883

My dear Mrs Ewing,

Your difficulties are indeed great. I should resist all attempts of S.P.C.K. "to take something off" agreed price until my last gasp, and my very latest faltering words should be "mere publishers!"

As for E.E., I do not comprehend the way of doing business; but, I am beginning to think that I shall make the experiment of asking how much he or somebody else will "produce" a book for me—myself—and then I should see what a publisher would give me. There is, however, a quantity of bother and trouble over that sort of thing which perhaps I am well out of.

I have experienced some annoyance over "Breton folk" with S. Low and Co.—I am a partner in the book.[43] I have told them I have found them out—they could not actually deny it, and in one detail they admitted and corrected an error. This is a different kind of arrangement from what I hint at trying.

As to my charge—I shall be perfectly satisfied from a business point of view with the £50 (if it be possible) and 1d royalty afterwards. If the sale were likely to be anything approaching my *Picture Books* I should be more than satisfied. I could not afford to do the *Picture Books* if the circulation were to fall much—and I am quite prepared for this event because of the ever-increasing competition of the many lovely and imaginative publications which are spread about in window and on stall.

For about the same quantity of work as in *Jackanapes* if a sale of 20,000 were guaranteed I could accept a penny royalty all thro'! This would pay as well as some other work which I do, more than some, and less than some. So now you know. Please to remember, however, that I should not like in any case—of anybody's—to be a pocketer whilst the other parties interested put nothing in their fobs; and I should not like, therefore, in case of failure, to insist on the guaranteed sum—so why need a guarantee be spoken of? And I should not like to accept a sum down and afterwards to see the book selling like mad.

[The rest of this letter is missing]

The Court Lodge, Chelsfield, Kent
31 December 1883

My dear Mrs Ewing,
   When we are at home we live in *Surrey*—altho' Aldershot is in *Hants*.
   I hardly know where to begin, for I have several letters of yours before me. I must apologize for not replying earlier to some questions—correspondence time has been taken up just lately with the affairs of a destitute family who don't deserve help.
   I do not know why I said that E.E. would take discount off his bill—yet I think he would, if paid within a certain time after sent in.
   "Have I any reason to believe it customary for the engraver and colour printer to do so?" This comes after "of course the printer and binder take off discounts for Mr E". E.E. is the engraver and colour printer himself—i.e. pays men on his premises regular wages to work the machines.
   Yes, I should think he would do as I have said—take off if payment not too long delayed.
   'Tis true, I could not afford to give as much work as in *Picture Books* and pay Evans and an author as well. But if I put less work in I can afford to take less remuneration.
   As *Jackanapes* has reached 20,000 (or will do, I suppose) I shall be content with 1d royalty all through—I said something like this before, I believe. Will that help you?
   I'll drop a hint about the ink—I think it *too bad* to have used the black under the circumstances.
   Please tell me some time about "Spectator".
   I must have a specimen of E. and Binger's *photo*-lithographic[44] reproduction of a drawing of mine before letting them do a lot. Best, would it not be?
   I rejoice about the turn the linen binding has taken.
   Yes, I did read and enjoy "Laetus sorte mea". But I think I should not be able to do it justice. Very modern dresses—and I should have to hunt up scenes and details at Aldershot, &c, which would take up time and perhaps not please the many who know all about them.
   Happy new year! I rush to post this.
Yours very truly,
R. Caldecott
P.S. I'll tell you about *Darwin's Dovecot*. Have a cup—silver with bas-reliefs—*offered* to me to design—hundreds of pounds. R.C.

Broomfield, Frensham, Farnham, Surrey
22 January 1884

My dear Mrs Ewing,
   I hope that during the interval which has elapsed since I last heard from

you you have not been continuing your warfare with publishers and book-producers.

I saw Mr E. Evans on Saturday last at his country seat—nine miles from this. In speaking of *Jackanapes*, he only referred to the Society (S.P.C.K.) as 'dreadful screws' and said that they had a reputation as such. In accordance with your remembered behests I asked why was not *Jackanapes* printed in brown ink. He replied somewhat vaguely—and said the ink used *was* a sort of brown, but not the right kind. I gathered that he did not change the colour out of malice and indeed hardly knew how it happened.

I fear that he does not attend closely enough to the details—or to the carrying-out of the details—of the work which he undertakes. And he seems not to be as careful after his own interests as he should be; if I may judge by the fact that he had entirely overlooked a sum of £50 in his transactions with me.—This omission was against himself.

"D.D's Dovecot" would, of course, make a nice illustrated book; and, if you would entrust it to me, I think I could make the drawings in April—not before. I would make as many drawings as you can afford to reproduce. If you think of having it fully illustrated and by yours obediently, could you be so good as to lend me any little sketches of the villages, farmhouses, churches, &c, &c of the locality in which the scene of the story is laid—or of any details of local costume.

I shall be very busy until April, and during that month also, of course; but I could arrange to fit the "Dovecot" in, I think, hope, and believe—if you wish it.

What a fine, open winter—it suits me admirably. I am looking forward to the N.Easterly winds of spring—they won't suit me. I hope the weather is agreeable to you.

Yours very truly,

R. Caldecott

[85]

Broomfield, Frensham, Farnham, Surrey

7 March 1884

Dear Mrs Ewing,

I am sorry to read that you have not been in good form for work lately. I hoped your troubles in that way were over—that you had got permanently stronger. I think the changeable weather has not been good for the heads of many people.

I have not the "Illustrated" to which you refer me.

As to process-paper[45]—if you will tell the people to send me a bit to try on I will make an experiment with pleasure, but I do not care for any that I have tried hitherto in the case of drawings that should have a little more refinement and expression than rough sketches. I am not satisfied with wood as a rule—

especially in faces. Yet the process drawing—as far as my experience goes—does not allow one to make little, but important, alterations. And I am not genius enough to be able to do without alterations.

My method of going at once at the design on the very piece of paper which is to be the needed drawing frequently results in the necessity of slight modifications of proportion or expression in the figures. I feel bolder if I know that a knife or some Chinese white will clear away too wild a line or too clumsy a touch.

Most processes produce a wiry line in the printing.

I have not yet commented on your kind suggestions about R. de Coverley—I think you spoke of Steele as most to be admired in those papers—I like some of Addison's and one of Budgell's:[46] but those papers have often been proposed to me—and J. D. Cooper—tired out—got another man to do them for *him* a year or 2 ago.

After going head over heels in the muddiest lane imaginable a fortnight ago I saw a fox killed at bottom of George Eliot's[47] late garden and then went to see E. Evans close by—in bed, but cheery—I have not heard whether he is at work again.

Yours very truly,

R. Caldecott

P.S. Would the original drawings be saved[48] or destroyed by your process; and if not, would they be as nice to keep as when made on *transfer paper*? R.C.

[86]
24 Holland Street, Kensington, W
7 April 1884

My dear Mrs Ewing,

I think the specimen of coloured printing with text is a success—I return it with thanks.

You will think one long in answering your note of 3rd. Things have happened.

I *have* a copy of *D.D.D.* at Broomfield; but I will have it sent up—if I do not go down on Satdy for the finish of the hunting season. I constantly come across in odd places the copies of "Jackanapes" which I used to lose so readily.

This is indeed the month, and by the end of it I will have the drawings made if you will decide quantity and size.

I think it will be a good plan to use the old cut as plain frontispiece and use title page for cover with a tint or two.

As to all the cuts being on full pages—I think that would be well if you will be able to print enough illustrations in that way—that is, if you will be able to afford the printing of so many separate leaves. But perhaps I do not understand—the printing of those pages *may* be done at same time as the type, if so I cannot see how they can dodge it so as to print the 'cut' pages well enough, as you say 48 pp at a time is a less careful method. I am getting muddled—so I will not continue on this part of the subject.

The cuts would look very valuable with wide margins—they would have to be small in size I suppose to save expense in engraving—but they would give a different character to the book.

Mind, please, that I do not care who prints the book as long as it is decently done.

Thanks about French Edition—I am pleased they so compliment you. I have nothing to suggest about it.

Yours very truly,

R. Caldecott

[87]
28 May 1884

Dear Mr Caldecott,

Bizness!

I am leading a life again with "Jackanapes"—"Drat the boy!"—and S.P.C.K. who are doing me out of $\frac{1}{4}$d a copy to which I am entitled!! But I have got something and hasten to share the crust.

You were good enough to say that 1d royalty would satisfy you if we passed 20,000, and if you remain of that mind I thank you—and render count accordingly.

Mr Evans and his binder differ as to numbers to the trifling extent of 1,700 copies which adds to my labours—but the lowest estimate anyone makes is 24,000 (S.P.C.K. admit *that*!). And 24,000 pennies I believe to = £100 (but a lady visitor will converse on social topics whilst I am writing letters, a thing that does make me so inclined to use bad language! so *check* my statements).

You have had £66. 13. 4. £100 − £66. 13. 4. = £23. 6. 8. Do it not? I enclose cheque for £23. 6. 8. If I have done you less than justice say so. I have sent in a claim for payment for 1,878 beyond this. When I am paid, you shall be. How are you getting on with *D.D.D?* I hope to be able to do it with E.E. He offers better terms if I will risk 20,000.

Yours very truly,

J.H.E.

[88]
The Longest Day—so they say! 1884

My dear Mr Caldecott,

I am shocked to recall that I omitted to say that a catastrophe had be-fallen the pinafore of one of the little workhouse damsels in Sacred Song. We are in a plague of greenfly—as my roses know too well!—and when I was putting the sketches together a greenfly got between and perished on that pinafore, and I knew it not until I found his corpse. I thought it best to leave it to you to remedy this with a touch of chinese white. But did you see it? Or will E.E. engrave that blemish? I will despatch a postcard to him.

At first I swore by every power a wilful woman can invoke, that nothing should induce me to allow these drawings to be reduced at all, but I fancy we should blunder if we changed shape and price. But it is a *grievous pity*. Set in the middle of a blank page the size of your later picture books, D.D. facing the board would be a gem indeed. Of course it must go in sideways, and so must the workhouse children.

I am unhappy about binding. The cover of Jackanapes is its one blemish in my eyes. The colouring is about as crude as the application of prussian blue and brick red in 2 printings could be, and yet it is not roughly effective at a distance—on a bookstall, for instance. And I hate the 'boards', which curl and bend and break. I much prefer the toy book covers. But if the Trade *will* have boards I suppose it must!

Yes. The initials are A. O. F. T. J. T. D. A. L. D. C.—do what you like. Title page to be:

Daddy Darwin's Dovecot

A country tale

by Juliana Horatia Ewing

author of "Jackanapes" &c

illustrated by Randolph Caldecott

(don't *you* put publisher's name!)

I enclose cheque for £1. 12. 0 for the 384 Jackanapes—which S.P.C.K. think I ought to *give* them—but have paid me for under protest! Please check my calculations!

Indeed I did see about the £100. I was very seedy and worried to death just then. I hope you count money after your best friends. You ought!

Yes. The proposal to do D.D.D. for "1d fee" if 20,000 were guaranteed did come from you. You afterwards qualified it by saying that if the 20,000 did not sell, you would not claim your pennies. But a bargain is a bargain, and I took no notice of your qualification!!!

I am going to risk the 20,000 altogether so as to diminish printing expenses. I am not much afraid. And *now*!!

If the public don't know that—"D.D. faces the board" for a gem when they see it (sideways!!!!)—I give up the taste of my age!! I am longing to see more. I took a fly and went straight over to Heatherton to show those to old Sir Percy Douglas. He really *screamed* with delight.

111

A *military* friend has had your bas-relief framed for me, and it *does* look well. Deep red plush, gold and black. Post waiting.

Yours very truly,

J.H.E.

[89]
24 Holland Street, Kensington, W
23 June 1884

My dear Mrs Ewing,

The 3 drawings are in E. Evans's hands—I did not notice the egg on the pinafore. No matter—anyway.

(Much obliged for the £1. 12s/– royalty on the 384 which the Society tried to 'do' you out of. "Jackanapes" total £91. 12/–).

Do you know I have been so charmed for a long time now with the aspect one end of a stationer's window in High Street, Kensington—wherein are displayed eastwards 2 copies of "Jackanapes" side by side: and I have thought them (from a passer's-by point of view) very attractive. Not that *I* claim much: but for a shilling book of such a size I think they are fairly attractive to the eye—attractive as bait, you understand.

I shall be glad to receive any suggestions which you may be kind enough to make—I fear, however, that as the cover design has to be the title page too some amount of "quality" must be put in it—it must not merely be "catching" from afar—from the top of an omnibus or out of the passing window of a railway carriage. And it is hardly big enough to make much display.

Punch cover is only noticeable (except when you are close to it) by its familiar aspect—and that is a good cover.

Then you are aware that things in too large a scale on title interfere with frontispiece.

We go down to Broomfield on Monday to look after the hay—11 acres.

Yours very truly,

R. Caldecott

[90]
Broomfield, Frensham, Farnham, Surrey
6 July 1884

My dear Mrs Ewing,

Here are 2 drawings corrected. I have taken out and put in again the face of young lady and boys and have added terrier. I have also taken out and re-put in chin and mouth and eye of young lady in garden. (I have also made the chin lighter in Phoebe Shaw returning from church: but I do not return it for inspection.) And *all* this in warm weather and with hay still about. Better if you had had the drawings in the month of April! You are not even decided

112

yet—process or engraving? I wished to know which before making the drawings—I should not have used white for process. (Remarks about process further on.)

Your letter is interesting because of the remark about my heroines having passed their first youth and I feel quite pleased that you have made it. Mrs R.C. is—and has been—of this opinion—and so am I to a great extent (explanation further on). But the instance which you give—p. 17, "Milk-maid"—I do not feel to be applicable. I have smoked a cigarette over it and I consider the girl to be only about 20—and the mother in the frontispiece to be old enough to have a son of 17.

And I cannot allow that the parson's daughter was not—before alteration in face and figure—quite correct for 19. I am not saying that she was nice; but, according to my experience, possible and even common. The healthy country people that I have known—milkmaids and parsons' daughters—have been quite women at 19. And I maintain that altho' I seldom represent, or try to represent, girls of 15 and 16, yet my young women are seldom more than 25—generally about 20—and at 20 the first bloom of youth is certainly over. You will smile at my assured way of putting it. I find that many artists —illustrators—fight shy of representing the age of 15 or 16. It is, however, a difficult thing to draw small faces in ink so that all observers shall agree as to the age represented. And 'figures' vary so much that one cannot lay down laws about them.

I may remark here that milkmaids in the dairy districts that I know do not marry as early as those in your experience.

What you say of chins is true—I make a note of it—but the suggestion to 'give a touch more size to the eyes' makes one think that one must be careful in accepting—or rather in acting upon—criticisms of this kind. Mr Blackburn used to say that I was the only man who would alter—I like to do so when I am sure it would be better, although the certainty may be forced upon me by a critic who regards things with different eyes from mine. I have altered the eye of the lady in question: but I have made it rather smaller. It was monstrously large before and not in its right place. It is a very cheap way of making a pretty face to draw large eyes, and then the effect is not intellectual, unless the brow is massive—which will tend to give an imp-like look to the head. Of imps there are 2 kinds—small-brained and large-brained.

I have always been struck by the truthful value given to faces by artists who know how to keep down the eyes. Du Maurier is good in this way— Leech was not so in female faces—in *woodcuts*—and they often looked rather silly.

If I had enlarged the eye in question the distance from eyebrow to under-lid would have been greater than distance from under-lid to bottom of nostril.

Pardon me for going into these details: as you are a good and valued critic I can pardon myself.

P.S. Monday morning 8.30

I wrote somewhat hastily and jerkily yesterday and now I see that I have forgotten several things. The post-boy has not yet come—so I will scribble further.

Do not think I have been doing your work hurriedly or carelessly. The drawing of *D.D. and P. daughter* is one of 5 made, and I was obliged to let one go at last.

My *Picture Books*[49] are not yet completed, and other matters press upon me: but I do no work hastily.

The proof of verses about Tiny and Toby I return. I am much obliged to you for offering its illustration to me, but I really cannot go into the question beyond saying that I cannot undertake anything more—however small—at present.

I have time to add that of all dogs—all kinds of dogs—I think I have least sympathy with pugs. I have very little sympathy with the kind of human people they seem to me to represent in the doggy world.

You will do me a service if you will always be kind enough to say what you think about drawings—in detail and generally. Some people let one drift to ruin by not giving true opinions.
R.C.

[91]
Broomfield, Frensham, Farnham, Surrey
10 July 1884

My dear Mrs Ewing,
I am very sorry to hear of your indisposition—I would not have bothered you with a letter if I had known. *I will settle with E.E. about reproduction.*

Here are 3 drawings for your inspection—I hasten to send these off to-day —drive specially to post—because I think the initial A may cheer you up a bit.

Rain—rainy—and my hay not all up.

We return to Holland St. No. 24 on Sunday—Better return these things there, if you please.

Hoping you are better again and will stay so.
Believe me,
Yours very truly,
R. Caldecott

[92]
My brother's rooms in St John's College, Cambridge
Thunder and lightning all round and rain falling
15 August 1884

My dear Mrs Ewing,
Your letter of 8th only reached my hand yesterday. I thought of waiting to reply until I could send the rest of the drawings to *D.D.D.* which consist

of 5 or 6 initials. I have 1 or 2 ready, but the heat of the weather has prevented me from doing the others. Therefore I write to prevent you from becoming anxious. E. Evans is not waiting for the initials; and they will be made during the next few days, I very firmly believe.

Last week was a whole holiday—we were visiting the F. Lockers at Cromer, and the only things that I really did were to read a novel or 2 and to board a mission-smack bound for the herring fleet in the North Sea to counter-act the effect of the Dutch gin-boats. I commended the enterprise and blessed the minister and his crew. Mr Samuel Hoare, who lives at Cromer, is the chief promoter of the mission, and he arranged for the smack to lie off Cromer for a day. This reminds me that I have had my eye on the initial atop of page 8.

I have been writing and writing to Evans about the proofs and experi-ments and shall hear again from him in a day or 2. I may see him by going over to Witley on Saturday next or Sunday—if not too warm across the commons.

A week or 2 ago he asked if the old engraving of 2 Gaffers was to be used, saying that you had not decided and that you seemed inclined not to use it. To which I replied that I understood that you doted on that illustration and would perish straight away if it were left out; and that, as it would be little or no expense to use it, the book should of course by all means have the benefit of it.

I think it would look more distinguished to have it uncoloured.

Your letter before the last has in it something requiring my attention and my remarks; but it is in my bag at the Vicarage—I must, therefore, leave my reply until I am at Broomfield again, which will be on Thursday evening, I hope.

Your friendly enjoyment of my *Bull* is of much value to me. I like encouragement. Locker liked the process proof of the D.D.D. drawings— not so much the *process* part as the *design* portion.

On Saturday last I was at a private meeting in some rooms at King's College of the Cambridge branch of the Psychological[50] Society. Thunder rolled around and lightning flashed thro' the windows during the séance, and the lady smoked cigarettes. The evening was devoted to the cross-examination (chiefly by Profs. Sidgwick[51] and F. Myers[52]) of 2 Theoso-phists—a Russian stout lady who has written strange books and an eminent Hindu (or some sort of dweller near the Himalayas). Amusing, interesting, but not convincing. Some very notable Cambridge men were present, and I thought I detected incredulity in most of the countenances.

Yes, it has been hot, and is still warm.

I dare say I mentioned to you that—on second thoughts, it is not worth troubling you about.

Yours very truly,
Randolph Caldecott

115

Broomfield, Frensham, Farnham, Surrey
22 August 1884

My dear Mrs Ewing,

I have not yet answered your questions about what I propose to do with the original drawings of *D.D.D.* I think I shall put them into a book with the letterpress pasted on the opposite pages—perhaps add a few flourishes—get the book neatly bound, and offer the whole thing to the highest bidder. And *Jackanapes* the same—those are lying somewhere just as I received them from the engraver. But probably I shall not have time to put together either of the books. I am complimented by your asking about the originals of those you like best.

I have—perhaps you have also—told E. Evans that you want the frontispiece to *D.D.D.* printed in colour. He is going to use a *process* reproduction of title for cover and engrave the design on *wood* for title page.

The other day I saw a little pencil sketch by F. Leighton in a gift book— young girl with chin very separate from throat or whatever that part of body is called under the jaw. Now as to eyes—large eyes. Perhaps I did not put down the proportion—or explain what I mean—very exactly or correctly. There are of course exceptions to every rule—and there are people with large eyes who do not look insipid and childish—some who look extra-intelligent, when they have large foreheads as well, without being impish. But these exceptions are a dangerous type to the draughtsmen—they are very difficult to represent without an appearance of exaggeration and amateurishness, and a smaller eye deeper sunk in the head will, as a rule, be more suggestive of practical common sense (perhaps not of genius—to the multitude). I do not wish to be too personal: but I may say that what you point out about your own face is a little surprising to me—I thought the proportions were different from most people's—yet not quite as you say. I believe that *this* is why you are so sentimental—if you will pardon the remark! You know you specially referred to your preference for sentiment beyond everything else in one of your last letters.

And about youth and beauty—what I said about 15-year-old girls and most of the other remarks referred chiefly to the class from which milkmaids come, I think—and my experience of Shropshire and Cheshire milkmaids is that in the majority of cases they lose the elasticity which you admire and which I adore very soon after 15. They become set in form and thick-armed, and one knows into what attitudes they will fall. At about 15 or 16 one oftener sees those unconscious "flowing" movements which belong only to young animals than in older girls. I am not speaking of *women*—although *my* "milkmaid" I meant to be a *woman*. And I am not here speaking of other classes than peasants and servants. Woman is a vast subject and I must not enter upon it now. I may, however, just mention that our housekeeper at Holland

St. has a daughter of 15 whose somewhat slow but easy movements are very charming and impossible to represent "plastically". She is curiously bred, and has attained her full height, but will not be a rounded woman for 2 or 3 years or more—she is not angular at present. I knew a family—country lawyer's—9 children—girl at top and girl at bottom of list. Girl at top was more girlish in form and movement when she was 21 than the girl at bottom was at 16.

This is my second turn at this letter—I have much correspondence and I fear that I do not take sufficient care in writing my letters—so you must not consider my remarks of such value as you seem to say they are to you. I am very pleased indeed to read any critical suggestions and comments which you ever care to make—they are always useful and interesting to me.

I believe—in my haste—I spoke of the *Psychological* instead of the *Psychical Research* Society in one of my recent letters.

The sketches which you kindly lent me I now return in their tin case—dangerous-looking as it must be to the P.O. people.

We overtook E. Evans and his family in the road yesterday when driving —had no time to talk on business with him—but we write to each other pretty often. Tomorrow early a friend and I set off to drive to Tunbridge Wells—sleeping at Horsham. I hope you have lost the headaches and are better now.

Yours very truly,
R. Caldecott

[94]
Broomfield, Frensham, Farnham, Surrey
21 October 1884

My dear Mrs Ewing,
Much as I like the story, I do not yearn to illustrate *Laetus* as much as *Lob*. I could not do both without breaking promises to other people.

Lob is longer than *D.D.D.* or *Jackanapes*. Will it not be published at a higher price and a more important book made of it?

When you can be kind enough to tell me about how many "cuts" you want, I will lay my plans and try to adhere to them.

Process is cheaper than wood.[53] I will make the drawings with a special view to process and if reproduced by Dawson's dodge[54] they will come out better than the process blocks of *D.D.D.*

I saw some results of Crane's drawings at his house the other day—and they were satisfactory.

But I must admit that I shall have to shunt—for the occasion—my indelible brown ink bottle, and take to the more tedious and brutal lamp-black, which cannot be tinted over—because it is black and because it would run. Yet—why should not black and white drawings be executed with a black ink on white paper or card?

The 'sojer' would make a fine coloured frontispiece or cover to *Lob*.

Believe me—happy to do my best with such an opportunity as *Lob*—
Yours,

R. Caldecott

P.S. We thank you for letter received this morning. R.C.

[95]

[October 1884]

Dear Mr Caldecott,

I am greatly obliged by your letter. It more than confirms the convictions which took some shape in my letter to ye of yesterday: that we must arrive at some better understanding about the seeing through the press of the books we do together, and in which we have both of us a continuous pecuniary interest.

Some slowly gathering distress on this head rather culminated when I told you the other day: ①, about the cover D.D.D.; ②, about Mr Evans' promised improvement of the process by touching with the graver, and you replied that as to the first you could not remember, and having done a drawing invariably dismissed the subject, regarding disappointment in the result as inevitable, and as to ②, that Mr E. had sent you proofs supposed to be touched, and that you could see no improvement whatever.

As to ①. This seems to me much what it would be if I wrote out my share of our books fairly and neatly, and left the blunders of the printer-compositor to an overruling providence in a spirit of pessimism. And as to ②, I was aghast! because I had carefully written to Mr E.E. to refuse the responsibility of deciding on the method of production of your most beautiful drawings, and to give him the most explicit charge to refer to and satisfy *you*, and I would endorse your verdict. *And* I wrote to you to say that I had done so, and had made the sole condition that of *your* satisfaction. It was trying to find that you had been quite dissatisfied and had neither told me so nor forced Evans to content you.

Your friend says the book has suffered from economy. He may be right, but it has suffered quite needlessly if this so.

When you showed symptoms of taking to D.D.D. as you never did to Jackanapes (in which you only kindly *pleased* me) and said you wished you had "carte blanche", I gave you carte blanche by return of post. I wrote jubilantly to S.P.C.K. and E.E., and said I had done so. I was prepared to spend extra money for the pleasure of having you at your best. I put no limit to cost of engraving, I only told E.E. to let me have an early estimate of general expenses that I might know where I was. I put no limit to numbers of drawings, being more than willing to engrave all you would do. And when you had done what you thought fit, it was you who wrote and said "This is the last".

Evans, not I, proposed "process". He wrote and said "I am going to try process" and he afterwards wrote an elaborate account tending to show that engraving and process each had disadvantages, and that perfection was best arrived at by the truthfulness of process touched up with the graving tool. I felt nervous, and emphatically told him that I was no expert and that he must apply to you and satisfy you. To make it more secure I wrote and told you that I had so referred him.

I never tried to cheapen the outcome under the head of illustration. I am never likely to—till I change the perhaps insane conviction that if my best and tersest and most finished writing combined in one volume with your finest and freest work, such as in the best of your toybooks, we might command a success that would make haggling over a few pounds for engraving worse than folly.

Eventually Mr Evans wrote and told me "Mr Caldecott fully agrees with me in deciding that process touched afterwards is the best", and he promised to do this with his own hand.

To every after remonstrance I have been told that I had only seen rough copies, and when he reported you as satisfied, I felt my mouth closed.

You say if you "had dreamed of such a result as the children in Sacred Song, &c, you would have remonstrated".

Did Evans not send you proofs? Had you forgotten that I committed the matter entirely to the question of satisfying you?

I hardly know E.E.'s object in the matter unless that he dislikes my wish to save on printing and paper: not by getting worse of either, but by not paying fancy prices. I pay much more for the paper (according to S.P.C.K.) than I ought, and yet I have bought enough for 25,000 to cheapen it by E.E.'s advice, and have printed 20,000 though S.P.C.K. only take 10,000.

I suspect the paper is not good for process, though nice enough and "laid" and dear! and the same as the first edition of J.

But I have another notion. I think it is less the process than the *printing* that is at fault, and I told E.E. so by return of post on getting my copy. The only good one I have is the *last*, and the letterpress of that is much clearer also. Moreover Phoebe's mouth was *there* in the proofs, or I am much mistaken. It is bad printing.

But the only question now is how to avoid future failure.

Will you kindly tell me, if you remember, whether E.E. *did* submit his first attempts at process to you, and ask your orders in the matter.

I want to learn if he conveyed *my* orders (viz. that the use or not of process was to be for you to decide, and I told you that I referred him to you).

I don't pity the public much.

It gets a good shillingsworth, but it is galling to have one of Phoebe's sweet eyes almost omitted in the title, with an effect of cataract, and her mouth absent elsewhere.

I made for E.E. a sketch of the top of one of the workhouse heads with an "aureole of smudged brown ink".

He has not replied yet. We must hear what he says.

[The rest of this letter is missing]

[96]
24 Holland Street, Kensington, W
29 October 1884

My dear Mrs Ewing,

If I had not received your letter this morning at Broomfield Mrs R.C. would have written to you on the subject of *Lob* this afternoon. But now I will leave *Lob* for a moment and say a word or two in reply to your last. I will begin by summing up *D.D.D.*—if the *process* reproductions and wood cuts had been as good in the book as the proofs submitted to me I should have had nothing to say about the book beyond a remark about a little experience gained for the benefit of future books. The point is that I could not tell that some of the illustrations would come out so unsatisfactory in the book. The proofs were taken on totally different paper. I understood that you had selected a paper, and I believed that E.E. would not have accepted it if it would not take the impressions of blocks well. He is the best man to judge of that.

I was surprised when *process* was first mentioned—it was mentioned in this way. I received proofs from E.E. shewing that he had already gone to expense of reproduction by *process*—and although I doubted a little—having understood that you had contracted for *engraving*—yet when I submitted the *process* proofs to and got words of approval from men of sound judgement in these matters—to Mr Blackburn (who fancies himself the best judge in the world of this kind of thing[55]) amongst others, and when I recovered from my surprise and judged the proofs on their merits, and was assured by E.E. that they would come out all right in the end—after I had questioned him on the subject—I let the *process* pass.

I have an entry in my diary of 12 July "E.E. agrees with me about *engraving v. process*; but must use latter for these *D.D.D.* drawings or book cannot be got out to pay. Will have *process* blocks touched and print from electros". Only if I had felt certain of the failure of *process* could I have comfortably interfered after he had gone to expense in *process*, and have upset the arrangement about cost which I believed you had after much trouble come to with him.

After seeing 1 or 2 more of the little initials in *process* I felt that it would be safer to have some *wood engraving* to mix with *process*; and therefore and because I thought the delicacy of that particular drawing would suffer, I asked him to *engrave* the title—the result was that he also *engraved* the rest of the initials. The proofs of wood engraving I carefully—very carefully,

120

but not 'exactingly'—'touched'. The eyes of Phoebe were all right, of course. As to 'touching' the *process* blocks—it was E.E. who proposed to do it, and it was I who told him boldly that I could not see any difference after 'touching'; *but this was of no importance*—I did not think they required 'touching': but I gave my opinion after he so pointedly pointed out that he had been at 'em. The beauties of *process* are present without 'touching'—or are absent.

And now, if you will hear me—but read not if you are not strong and cheerful—it is not worth the trouble—I will just make a small comment on your letter as I re-read it.

My remark about expecting disappointment in results of reproduction—when you spoke of *D.D.D.* cover—was more general than particular, and my above statement about 'touching' engraving proofs will shew you that I do look after these things as much as I can. The draughtsman can never get a *perfect* reproduction of his work and he must pull up somewhere in his expectation. There is no analogy between his 'touching' and an author's correcting of proofs—the latter can get what letters of the alphabet that he wants exactly printed. There are only twenty-six and the type is made by machinery. Punctuation not absolutely necessary! but can be insisted on and any amount of accents &c introduced at pleasure and with certainty.

Your remark that "I had been quite dissatisfied and had neither told you so nor forced Evans to content me" is answered in the early part of this letter. I was not dissatisfied beyond the degree above mentioned, but I was somewhat doubtful.

You truly gave me 'carte blanche' in reply to a remark of mine: but *my* 'carte blanche' I saw to be impossible. And your saying that it would be a "blunder to raise the price" and Evans saying that "the book cannot be got out to pay" rather modified what I thought *you* meant by 'carte blanche'.

I did say "this is the last" because we had settled that there were to be 10 or 11 initials and 5 or 6 other illustrations, and "this is the last" did not mean what I might have done, but that what drawings could be reproduced to pay had been executed according to our arrangement as to number.

The quotation from E.E. of a letter of mine to him about my agreeing with him on the advantages of *process* is bare—the context, I think, was of importance. At the same time, I may repeat that if the book had been like the proofs, what I hoped for would have happened. I see that *process* is suited to the hopeful temperament.

You ask 'Did Evans send me proofs?' He did, and passable ones, as I have said.

I have taken more interest than you credit me for in these books and would have made more drawings for the money I receive: but I have understood that in addition to my enormous charges the publications could not stand unlimited engraving. I believe that to Evans I offered to pay part of extra expense in being specially careful about "Jackanapes"—I think it was "Jackanapes"—it might have been *D.D.D.* I feel vague here.

And I do not think it fair for you to continue to suppose that I do not feel drawn to your books. You credit me with no pulls in other directions. I assure you that I am very pleased that you—the author of your books—wish to have me as an illustrator. I am no flatterer and seldom do I gush—my brother, whose exuberance I had to check, used to say there was apparently much of the *nil admirari* about me. I was a dissembler.

I must confess to not feeling as free in the presence of a living author as in that of one defunct—the longer the better. This is because I have a great respect for the author's feelings. I do not see how an entirely independent illustrator can please an author who goes in for more than money-making.

If you like I will go into the question of what it is fair for me to receive, and I will explain further anything which I have not made clear and which is worthy of enquiry. Perhaps I am one of those who serve the paviours of Pluto.[56]

I really hope you are well again.

Believe me, yours very truly,

R. Caldecott

[97]
Broomfield, Farnham, Surrey
3 November 1884

My dear Mrs Ewing,

Last week Mr Caldecott was at Kensington and I here; even had I been with him probably he would have preferred to manage his correspondence with you himself. I have always wished, and used to hope that I might sometimes act as secretary to him, but he is more particular than anyone I know, and has always said that it is less trouble to him to do it himself. He now thanks you for your letters. We are both very sorry to hear about your throat and hope you are better.

He promises that the information you give him shall not go further to *anyone*. Thinks your letter to E. Evans is to the point.

Have you come to any conclusion as to the price of "Lob"? It seems a difficult question, because in England 3/6 books do not generally have a large sale, and yet "Lob" will be a great deal for a 1/–. R.C. will make as many drawings for it as can be reproduced. Also, if you decide upon the more expensive arrangement he is quite inclined to act accordingly and to do the best that he can to look after his work. He will probably have some experience in the reproduction of similar drawings before the printing of "Lob" and the bargain with them is that they shall be reproduced to satisfy him. So that will be a help. He fancies that Dawson's and the Direct Photo Etching Co. seem the best processes.

We will do what we can in the matter of the paper, before the drawings are put in hand. We may probably be able to get advice from some "fellows" who know a good deal about it, and I shall be delighted to send you specimens, and help *when I am allowed*. R.C. says it certainly is the *quality* of the reproductions that must be changed for a 1/– book. I feel so wrathful with Mr Evans. He cannot give himself any trouble to speak of.

As the copyright of the frontispiece of D.D.D. was sold to "Aunt Judy" R.C. cannot have further payment for it, he says. I return Arrowsmith's mem.

I believe we have to-day found a married couple to suit us. We hope so. They are living in the neighbourhood, and we have been wildly advertising for a month!

With love.

Yours very sincerely,

Marian Caldecott

[98]

6 November 1884

My dear Mrs Caldecott,

Many thanks for your letter and R.C.'s messages.

1   I know he sold us the D.D.D. picture. What I meant was, that in asking if he could afford to do as much for Lob as he did for D.D.D. for a 1d royalty, I forgot that the coloured frontispiece had not been part of the work done for "penny fee". Thank him much for his good offer to do for Lob what we can afford to produce.

2   I think we shall be wise to try and effect it at a shilling.

3   I should like—I know he would like—us to do it ourselves, not to let S.P.C.K. do it as then we should be in trammels and difficulties might arise about copyright. Also about getting the best form of process, &c., &c.

4   I am venturing to use his name in arranging this with S.P.C.K., namely saying that he prefers to keep control of matters, &c., whilst we propose to "meet" Mr McClure's views by doing it for 1/– if possible.

5   I think on Wyman's estimate I may manage this if I risk a large edition, which with R.C.'s good help I am more than willing to do.

6   I think it may be *safer* to use black ink instead of brown. But if R.C. will collect opinions as to which prints best whatsoever process he decides to use, then that I will have. And if he decides that it is safer only to have full pages, no initials, I am willing, but I doubt this being needful.

7   I enclose E.E.'s letter. He doesn't like to be in the wrong, but we shall see a change in the next edition.

With love and a 1000 thanks,

Yours,

J.H.E.

[99]
Broomfield, Farnham, Surrey
8 November 1884

My dear Mrs Ewing,

"Lob" covers 88¼ pages. That comprises the title on the page before the beginning of the story, but not "contents", real title page or anything else.

R.C. begs me say that he thinks Cruickshank's 2 designs are in his worst style, and that they would be so utterly different in spirit and treatment from what he will do himself, that it would not be well to use them.

That is "freely spoken", I think.

Yours very sincerely,
Marian Caldecott

[100]
Monday 24 November 1884
Confidential

Dear Mr Caldecott,

I enclose cheque for £83. 6. 8—1d royalty on 20,000 D.D.D.

I now want to ask you if you are likely *to be in town* soon, and can see him there, on the spot *with the blocks and presses*, or if this *impossible*, will you kindly endeavour to see E.E. at Witley as soon as you can on the subject of future impressions of D.D.D.

I have spent a good deal of time and eloquence on the subject with the result which the enclosed letter will show you. Mr Evans *prefers* the "softening" effects of smudge on the faces, and the aerial perspective gained by the occasional failure to print of things in the background!! The dicta of people who are not professional artists on art subjects does not, naturally, carry any weight. I could only reply (which I did) that I did not share his views and must see proofs with damped paper, &c, &c, before next edition. He said a darker ink would be better. I enclose his specimen.

I also enclose some process proofs which Mr McClure took (without consulting me) and sent to me intimating that that would cost 9d the square inch.[57] I suppose neither he nor your friend who regretted the cheap production will believe that I have paid £1 each for engraving all the *initials* (and *look* at page 12) and that my share of the 20,000 is not quite a 1d royalty.

I have had great difficulty in getting fresh proofs—Mr Evans is so thoroughly satisfied as things are. I have insisted, on the grounds of submitting them to you, to satisfy you, having been my original and only order on the subject. I hope you will kindly have the question out with him.

Your opinion must have weight with him. Moreover it is the credit of your share (not mine) of the book which is at stake, and you have every right to complain.

Mr Bell thanked me for the copy I sent him, and said "The designs are very nice but they seem to be reproduced by some inferior photo-process and don't come out like the Toy books". This is pleasant—when 13 of the 17 are wood engravings!

I have enclosed 2 of the *original proofs* as sent me by E.E. That is how he can do them, if he will. *He* considers them inferior to the later ones. Will you kindly express your views on that question with no uncertain sound?

I am particularly anxious that you should investigate and discover why the *top* has been taken off Daddy D.'s head. It makes him look *commoner* and less distinguished.

Love to the wife.

Yours very sincerely,

J.H.E.

N.B. If you find E.E. out at Racquet Court his "Mr Miller" is a very satisfactory substitute. Please return my old proofs—don't leave them at Racquet Court. I told E.E. to send you 6 copies; I hope you received them.

[101]

Broomfield, Frensham, Farnham, Surrey

28 November 1884

Dear Mrs Ewing,

I devoted Wedy to the study of the **D.D.D.** illustration question and to going over to Witley—where I red-bearded Mr Evans in his den.

I began the talk by saying simply that I should be much obliged if he would prepare fresh blocks of the "D.D. before Board" and "Children" either by another well-known process or by engraving and at my expense. And I should have been glad if he had fallen in with this suggestion. However, after making him confess that the proofs which I have marked Q.B. are not quite the thing—which I did by pointing to the exact spots which are smudged, filled up, &c—and that the head of D.D. in Board scene is different from the 1st proofs (marked R. in left-hand top corner), he stated that it was his serious opinion that if he printed the next edition from the *zinc* blocks (from which proofs R were struck) instead of *electro* casts from the said zinc blocks (which he has used in those copies already printed) the result would be as satisfactory to us as the proofs marked R. He made a few remarks about the softening of lines in backgrounds, &c; but I would not stand them. His letter (enclosed) dated 27th inst will shew that he admits what I insisted upon—that the electros used must be bad—very bad.

I also enclose—marked D.F.M.—part of the proofs sent me when he was arranging the cuts and type and which was the last I saw before the book appeared. You will admit, I think, that I was not wicked in passing this. But now I hear that it was printed—this cut of children—from the *zinc*—therefore it is not a proof of what was to appear in the printed book. Which will account for some of my surprise when I saw the book. When the proofs marked R were sent E.E. said that he should print the book from electros and said it in a way to make me believe that the result would be better than R proofs : and I had no reason to suppose that D.F.M. was not from the boasted electro.

Enclosed also are proofs from the original *zinc* pulled yesterday—after my interview—I think I prefer the XO—it is in lighter ink, which seems to me to suit *D.D.*'s headpiece better than the darker on which E.E. appears to be sweet. The idea of his speaking of clearness—he says "shews up the work more clearly"!! when he admits that he likes muddle.

If, however, you do not like any of these proofs X.O., X.O.A., X.O.B. good enough, or would rather not risk the *zinc* (which E.E. feels sure about) I will tell him to get fresh reproductions (engraved or otherwise) made *at once* at my cost. Do not hesitate to say what you really wish.

Observe that the mouth of *Phoebe* in Bergamot scene appears in all these proofs.

E.E. could not explain the faults in my *Picture Books* about which I think I moaned unto you.

Anything left unexplained here—please write about.

Yours very truly,

R. Caldecott

[102]
29 November 1884

My dear Mr Caldecott,

If ever you were "wicked" you have made noble amends!—I fear at the cost of a day's hunting.

For my own part I feel as if having bruised my knuckles against stone walls 20,000 times—the monstrous impediments had yielded—and "things" are once more "what they seem"—smudge is smudge and not "tone"—and the peculiar (and to me entirely new) art quality of "touchiness" will be hereafter confined entirely to the productions of E.E.'s leisure hours, in that lovely upper chamber which I wish you had the likes of!

What *can* he mean by it!

Now as to your very generous offer. It would have pleased me much to hear that E.E. had at once responded "No, no, if matters can't be put straight otherwise, the cost must be my affair!"—but I am not the less sensible of *your* kindness.

I do not, however, see any need to do more than print from the zinc, and I am quite satisfied with the proofs you prefer.

I have *repeatedly* told E.E. that I will *not* have a darker brown. It is insufferable that the results should not correspond to specimens.

I had proofs of Jackanapes in brown and it was printed in black. When I remonstrated (and asked you to remonstrate) there was no result. Eventually he said he had with infinite care selected and preferred a darker brown, and a darker *brown* he maintains that it is to this day! It is very tiring! I have not described half the difficulties I have had to get pulls! But—basta!

Thank you very much. I think you had best give the final orders, so I return the proofs with my remarks for you to send to E.E. It is nice to see Phoebe's sweet face again! and D.D. like himself!

I wish I had not lost hope of amendment, and sent Ruskin a copy out of this edition!

Poor E.E. He'll think thunderbolts are abroad—I wrote last night to say I could not risk 20,000 in each edition, and to ask him if he would print 10,000 on the same terms, adding that a London printer had tendered to print 72 pages, a 20,000 edition, for less than $\frac{1}{2}$ his charges! I soothed down the dose with a cheque on D.D.D. account for £287. 2. 8!!!

I told him also that I have given in and am letting Mr McC. print Laetus himself, and pay me my royalty. I have not the *strength* to fight with, and it is a disastrous waste of time.

He alone knows if he prefers to lose a job sooner than be content with moderate profits. I'd let him fleece me a little, and I fancy it would pay him to do my work reasonably, and as he pretends he is going to do it, and be my bulwark against my publisher, and save me from detail worry. To take fat profits, fail in the production, leave me the fighting, and retire with "touchiness" to his artistic domain among the pines is madness all round!!!

Again my *many thanks*.

Love to the wife.

J.H.E.

Mr McC. says he will want 10,000 more D.D.D. soon after Xmas. It is selling 400 a day at present. Did I tell you *entre nous* E.E. has offered me *my own terms*—of either a lump sum or a royalty, if I'll do him a tale for Kate Greenaway to illustrate. So he must have a margin!

[103]
Broomfield, Frensham, Farnham, Surrey
7 December 1884

My dear Mrs Ewing,

1stly, excuse me if I seem impertinent in saying that I cannot be responsible for the total loss of any MSS., drawings, proofs, cheques, drafts, or bills of exchange which you may be kind enough to send me by post. It was a mussy[58] that any portion of your package containing "Old Father Xmas" reached us. The envelope was nearly 'all-parted' from the contents—and if the insides had got scattered you would have had no letter of your own back again to tell the tale—saying "I only am escaped"—Because "Saturday" and

"J.H.E." are the only clue to the sender or writer of the letter. Mind, I am not interfering—if you choose to risk the things without name or address, don't blame me if jigging about in hard leather bags, in pockets, or in bottoms of carts on rainy days wears off the envelope, and the documents neither reach me nor are returned to you.

I mention this to save you possible trouble and annoyance—you might have to *rewrite* something—and so waste time and energy.

D.D.D. I sent to E. Evans the proof from zinc with your notes in pencil at back—and I repeated the substance of your remarks. I said he must print in that ink to oblige us. Told him he must watch the zinc, and if it shews signs of breaking down it must be renewed or a sufficient substitute be provided. I also observed that it was the risk to *my* reputation that I was thinking of and that made me very uneasy, anxious and unable to sleep o'nights and prevented me from becoming sleek and fat (I did not use these exact words). I hinted at the possibility of a demand for 10,000 more after Xmas.

Your accounts of the coming to terms with E.E. about printing &c are interesting—so interesting that the contemplation of the subject in all its bearings causes my left hand to slowly rub my chin, one eye and eyebrow to bend towards the earth—as musing on the fact—and the other eye and eyebrow to arch towards the heavens—as peering into the future.

I have not yet made up my mind about *Lob*. I should like to do it well and in a manner that will be best served by engraving, I think. It is to be a shilling book, I believe. If I make what I should consider "sufficient" illustrations for the book, will you be prepared to have them engraved? If so, I think the book would have a better chance of being a permanent publication and one that no family should be without. Having now gained much knowledge you would save on the printing—but you must have good printing. E.E. has engraved my picture books more faithfully than before—altho' he has occasionally erred on the side of "refinement". Kate Greenaway's books are well-engraved and carefully printed. Have you seen them? At foot of page 101, Mavor's Spelling[59] is a very *choice* bit. Don't ask me to explain why I do not like Cruikshank's[60] illustrations to *Lob*. I should have to use violent language about a very clever man. I note what you say about a "Trade Honour" story.

I have read "Old Father Xmas" and thought it over—and I do not think it will suit me—the characters don't interest me enough. I am a little "kept back" in the matter by not wishing to make too many promises for the future or too many plans. Besides *Lob* I have 2 other books before me, and must concoct 2 last Picture Books soon as possible for E.E. Am now tinting some summer *Graphic* things and drawing out for Xmas 1885. I think you saw an oil sketch of *'Twas the fiddler play'd it wrong*—Agnew has bought it. He bought my *Hussar* in the spring (at Grosvenor Gallery).

Thanks for proofs of colour printing. The verse books seem very clear and neat—if *bon-bon* boxy. I have seen none of them by daylight yet—so the colour may be worse than I think. I should think the *C.Pictorial*[61] was an advance for process and colour with type: but the style of drawing must be quite decorative to suit it. The 'sanguine' illustrations are best—but all black is more like nature than all red lines.

Yours very truly,

R. Caldecott

[104]

Thursday evening

My dear Mr Caldecott,

I will amend my ways! My sister recommends a "cartridge paper bag shaped" sold at the stores! Thank you much.

Your letter was charming. I hope you have a pencil note of your own thoughtful and prophetic attitudes therein described.

Re Lob, I will *certainly* engrave if you wish it, and by *wish* I mean if you decide that this is best.

But I clutch *my* chin, and release it in confusion. For R.C. says K.G.'s books are charmingly *engraved* and printed, and instances *Mavor* and quotes a page. And I *entirely* agree that the reproduction is "tender and true" (like the love of the north!) and E.E. writes to me "R.C. approves Miss K.G. in Mavor and praises the production. They are printed from electros exactly similar to those of D.D.D. and with no more care or pains".

"Is things what they seem? Or is visions about?"

Do you believe him? I could swear—if it were proper!—that the results are mighty different! and I fancy it may be because he has more direct pecuniary interest in K.G.'s work. But then I release my chin once more, for *on the whole* the colouring of your books is charming, and that of K.G.'s is past description bad! Blue noses, pink chins, blue superimposed on yellow with edges of each, and such a *daub* that the lines of the folds of the green garment are invisible.

Then my ideas swim once more!

Look at that page you quote in Mavor, and then look at Jack March in the workhouse garden in D.D.D. The former electro and the latter wood engraving, if E.E. correctly informs us! He says Mavor was printed by the same men as well as the same process.

Doth he speak truth? Whichever we do, one thing will have to be made clear. If we employ E.E. (and I always lean to bearing those tyrants we have rather than fly to others that we know not of!) he must do it under contract to satisfy—on pain of moving elsewhere.

What colour do you ambition? More than cover and frontispiece?

If process like Mavor would be good enough for the crown drawings and frontispiece and cover satisfy your dreams of colour, we *might* squeeze it out for $1/-, but we will rise to $2/- if necessary.

I fancy the question of price rather resolves itself into "small profits and quick returns" versus larger profits and slower returns.

In *one* way the higher price would pay me better, because I am a sort of residuary legatee of the concern. Where I *don't* get the best of it is that I don't *begin* to get anything till after the first expenses are paid, which in the case of colour blocks is heavy.

But I want to make "what no family should be without" and will do it one way or the other.

Tell me what colour you wish for. Also if you wish for engraving rather than 'Mavor' process.

Yours in haste, and much muddled,

Juliana Horatia Ewing!

Villa Ponente

Taunton!!!

[105]
Taunton
2 January 1885

Dear Mr Caldecott,

Major Ewing is writing for me, as I am in bed. I have been ill for a fortnight and must not use my brains at present. So I can't go into even "Lob". Roughly my idea is that we shall be wise to keep to a shilling unless you *had* had any special wishes about bursting into colour. We must have some colour on the outside, where the Highlander might blaze. I think, in spite of its length, that all you are likely to do may, without further colour, be accomplished for a shilling at a low printing estimate and economy over paper, not in quality, but in buying quantity, and *my* getting the discount off instead of the printer doing so.

If you feel inclined that we should work it through Evans: I mean, if you are *satisfied* that you could make him produce it properly (and, I must add that my present illness makes it a *sine qua non* that you should kindly see that *your* share of the work is done due justice to, and that the responsibility for this should not be a three-cornered affair and rest partly on me).

I will, as soon as I am fit for business, write frankly to Mr Evans to tell him that "Lob" is proposed and that you have undertaken it, and, giving him all details, offer him the chance of estimating for the work on a scale to cover our royalties; to satisfy you in the reproduction of your drawings and to satisfy *me* as to general effect and the expenses.

I see nothing to hinder your proceeding with the drawings at any leisure moment, as the book will be the same size as Jackanapes. If you are seeing Evans and feel inclined to talk matters over with him, I am quite willing that you should tell him that my only hesitation in going into the affair with him is first, the printing expenses, and secondly, that I wish *you* to have a process of reproduction that you are satisfied with. There *is* a "third", which is that

130

this new process of colour-printing employed by S.P.C.K. would undoubtedly be good enough for the cover, and something like 50 per cent cheaper. But if Evans could satisfy *you* and could estimate expenses with *me*, so as to get out our two royalties, I like him and I should prefer to do it with him.

No more today, but good wishes for 1885, and, with love to the missus, Yours ever sincerely,

J. H. Ewing

P.S. I have managed a letter to Evans to this effect, so you can discuss it.

[106]
24 Holland Street, Kensington, W
4 January 1885

My dear Mrs Ewing,

We were much concerned to hear from Mr Evans that you were ill and forbidden to work—and we wrote to Miss Gatty to enquire about you; but she has not yet replied. I am now glad to find that you can say as much as you have done in your note of the 2nd.

At present I will not trouble you with any further remarks upon the subject of the illustrations to "Lob"—meantime I will try to see E.E.—it will be difficult to see him, and I shall probably have to write. He leaves town so early in the afternoon.

I may just remark, however, that, in answer to some comments which I made on "Mavor" when puzzled by your news of the illustrations being *process*, I have heard thus from E.E. "Who told you they were by process? I did 3 by our process—viz. pages 33, 100 and 101 (pages 103 and 107 are also our process) but I worked on them with the graver as I did on **D.D.D.** Miss Greenaway not liking them, *I did all the rest on wood.*

"I have always regretted *Mavor* paper was so thick; but the surface is certainly better than the ribbed paper[62] Mrs Ewing always had a fancy for."

This last sentence is in answer to searching questions of mine as to surfaces for printing. I don't believe in your paper for cuts; but I am not an expert in papers.

Do not trouble about anything for a time—I shall have something definite to say when you are better.

We thank you for your good wishes and send greetings for New Year to you and Major Ewing.

Yours very truly,

Randolph Caldecott

Broomfield, Frensham, Farnham, Surrey
25 January 1885

My dear Mrs Ewing,

I am very glad to find that you are so much better—I believe you will beat me in the end. *I* do not sleep quite as well as I should like, and of late I have been 'queer'—a strong dislike to exertion having seized me for its own.

'Tis amusing about the size of presses at Racquet Court.

E.E.'s letter which you send me is most interesting. He quotes me as writing "how tenderly and dearly". No. No, I wrote "clearly". And if this is the letter which caused you to write to me that E.E. told you that *Mavor's* illustrations are by same process and everything as process used in *D.D.D.*— why, I must laugh aloud. E.E. calls out to me "Who told you *Mavor* was by process?" I reply "Mrs Ewing". *Is* this the letter in which he informed you of it? Because I read that he only says that the electrotypes were from the same people and were printed from on the same presses as *D.D.D.* The electrotypes would be taken from wood-blocks (except in the instances he excepted—and the printing of those distinctly shews process results) as is usual nowadays—the cuts in nearly all publications and books when large sale is expected being printed from electros. Altho' by the same people, the electros used in *Mavor* would be deeper than *D.D.D.* because the wood allows a better and firmer cast to be made than the process metal original. The unnecessary dots and dirtiness in *D.D.D.* were owing to *shallow* electros., you are aware.

Perhaps I am foggy in my remarks—or I may be fogged in my understanding of this intricate question—if so, pray forgive me.

Don't forget that the paper used in *D.D.D.* might not have been the best for the purpose. I think it was not.

I should be much obliged to you for a look at the book of Scotch characters if you can send it to me.

And if you have any notions about the kind of house—have any particular house in your mind—or have any sketch or photograph—that would help me in delineating "Lingborough" I should be further obliged.

As you speak of "John Brown" becoming white-headed I must place his birth about 1800 I suppose —also, as you speak of rumoured invasion afterwards. What sort of dress or gown stuff is "tabbinet"? And may I ask if in the north they call a cow house a stable. In Cheshire a cow house is called a "shippon"—evidently a name belonging to the habitations of sheep originally.

I am wanting to begin "Lob"; but it will not be in "leisure time" that I shall attack it.

You are always flatteringly alluding to the style of my *Picture Book* vignettes—now do you think—I mean, now don't you think that style too slight for "Lob"? Not enough quality for a real book—a book to be read. Looks cheap? Would be not expensive to engrave, I believe.

Not able to write more.

Hoping you have slept well since you last wrote.

Yours,

R. Caldecott

[108]
24 Holland Street, Kensington, W
25 March 1885

My dear Mrs Ewing,

It's a very short time since I heard a rumour that you were ill, and I am very sorry to find—through Miss Gatty's kindness in replying to our en-quiries—that rumour has not been a story-teller (in an old meaning of this term).

We are, however, very glad that you have made a decided turn towards recovered health, and our hope will be that the next news will come from your convalescent self.

I will not bother you with more now—except to say that the time for doing the *Lob* drawings approaches, and to thank you for cheque: but why have you troubled about it at present?

With our best wishes for your speedy recovery, and kind regards to Miss Gatty.

Believe me, yours very truly,

Randolph Caldecott

[109]
Broomfield, Frensham, Farnham, Surrey
20 April 1885

Dear Major Ewing,

I hope that by this Mrs Ewing is quite well again and able to give atten-tion to the publication of her books. If she *is* well enough, will you kindly tell me whether I may send her some drawings to look at and to what address? I do not want to bother her in the least if you think that I had better defer troubling her. I wish her to get perfectly restored in health, if possible.

Yours very truly,

R. Caldecott

N.B. Frensham is not in *Hants*.
Broomfield, Frensham, Farnham, Surrey
24 April 1885

My dear Mrs Ewing,

We are very sorry to hear that you have had such a serious illness and that you are not well yet—only "progressing". Please go on progressing.

I do not know whether it is a wise thing to do—to send you these drawings to look at—they may annoy you: but possibly you sometimes wonder if I am proceeding with the illustration of "Lob".

I know that E. Evans wants to be at the engraving—he has been bothering me for a long time—and I have not made one drawing for my *Picture Books* yet. Do not trouble to write yourself—and defer the matter if you think there is something that you can deal with better when you are well again.[63]

Thanks for Miss Gatty's post card and for returning these drawings to 24, Holland *Street*, Kensington, whither we go this afternoon.
Yours very truly,
R. Caldecott
P.S. 11 drawings there are here for your inspection and criticism (but, as I have hinted, they can wait in my hands and not be sent on to E.E. if you cannot now consider them as seriously as you would wish).

Soldier and cockatoo scenes not done yet.

I have not yet got Highlander's costume of the time—I wonder if a Major in the Black Watch whom I know could help me. The dress cannot be much different from the present—and there are Highlanders at Kensington Barracks—or were. R.C.

1. *Aunt Judy's Magazine.*
2. Toy of polished coral for children cutting teeth (O.E.D.).
3. Shakespeare: *King Henry V*, Act v, sc. ii.
4. This is basically the illustration Caldecott produced.
5. *The Last Ride Together.*
6. *See* letter 115 to Miss Gatty.
7. *The Three Jovial Huntsmen.*
8. Curse.

9. *The Three Jovial Huntsmen* and *Sing a Song for Sixpence*.

10. Alfred Caldecott.

11. The frontispiece of *Daddy Darwin's Dovecot*.

12. To stay with Thomas and Mary Armstrong.

13. His brother Alfred, who had made the translation of Aesop's *Fables*. It was published by Macmillan.

14. James Clarke Hook (1819–1907); painter. He lived at Churt, a tiny village to the south of Frensham.

15. William Carter's book and print shop.

16. A splendidly profiled character in *Mr Oakball's Winter in Venice*, an illustrated story in the *Graphic* Christmas number for 1882.

17. From a series of three illustrations from *A Sketch-book of R. Caldecott's*: Mrs Ewing wrote sets of verses for *The Cavalry* and *The Spectators*.

18. *Jackanapes*.

19. Mrs Ewing's brother, Alfred Scott-Gatty (1847–1918), was at this time Rouge Dragon Pursuivant at the College of Arms. He later became Garter Principal King-of-Arms.

20. *A Sketch-book of R. Caldecott's*.

21. The shiniest coloured illustrations of the period were cheap chromo-lithographs, and the cause is not the paper surface but rather the thickness of the layers of ink and that one ink layer is often printed over part of another.

22. Metal printing plates in which the image is first produced photographically and then the non-printing parts are etched away.

23. Evans or Cooper.

24. It was common at this time for a publisher to act solely as a distribution agent. Authors, as Mrs Ewing, would deal directly with the printer of their books, paying them for the printing and binding, and would then sell the books to a publisher, who would distribute them under his imprint. Many of the more famous illustrated books were the responsibility of the wood engraver. He chose the text, commissioned the artist and undertook production. James Cooper (not Macmillans) asked Caldecott to illustrate *Bracebridge Hall* and *Old Christmas*; Edmund Evans (not Routledge) suggested that he did the picture books.

25. *Jackanapes*.

26. After receiving three farthings for the first four picture books, Caldecott's royalty was now a penny-farthing.

27. A small part of this letter has been cut away.

28. The home of his parents-in-law, Mr and Mrs F. W. Brind.

29. *Lieut.-Col. Seccombe's Army and Navy Birthday Book*, illustrated by Thomas Seccombe.

30. Of the General Literature Committee of the Society for the Promotion of Christian Knowledge.

31. Eventually *Jackanapes* contained ten illustrations, a decorative title page and six decorative initial letters.

32. This is an electrotype of the key-line drawing of the coloured illustration to *Jackanapes* which appeared in *Aunt Judy's Magazine* in October 1879.

33. In his diary for 4 February 1883 'Lewis Carroll' wrote, 'Heard from Mr Caldecott who would like to draw for me, but is too deeply engaged to undertake anything at present. I must try and engage him for some future time, and could then feel encouraged to work definitely at a new book.' B.M. Add. MS. 54346.

34. Alfred Scott-Gatty.

35. Herald's College, an alternative name for the College of Arms.

36. An illustration from *A Sketch-book of R. Caldecott's*.

37. From Ceylon. His army service, first in Malta, then Ceylon, and his wife's ill-

health, kept Major and Mrs Ewing apart for four years.

38. Mrs Ewing's chief contact at the Society for the Promotion of Christian Knowledge.

39. The Society for the Promotion of Christian Knowledge.

40. The baby and duckling drawing finally appeared on the back board of the book.

41. At Witley, Surrey.

42. For *Daddy Darwin's Dovecot*.

43. With Henry Blackburn, the author.

44. Emrik and Binger were well-known London chromo-lithographers, though obviously at this time they were experimenting with photo-lithography.

45. Paper with a very smooth surface, used in photo-process reproduction.

46. Eustace Budgell (1686–1737); a cousin of Addison and an occasional contributor to the *Spectator*.

47. George Eliot (Mary Ann Evans) lived at The Heights, Witley, 1876–80.

48. The use of photography to print a negative of the original drawing on to box wood for engraving gave an extra source of income to the illustrator of the 1870s. No longer was the drawing destroyed, as it was when he drew directly on the wood. Now if his books were successful he could make more money by selling his drawings, and it was this extra income that Caldecott was anxious to preserve.

49. *Ride a Cock Horse to Banbury Cross*, *A Farmer Went Trotting* and *Come Lasses and Lads*.

50. This should be 'Psychical'. Caldecott corrects this in his next letter to Mrs Ewing.

51. Henry Sidgwick (1838–1901); first president of the Society for Psychical Research, 1882–5.

52. Frederic Myers (1843–1901); one of the founders of the Society for Psychical Research in 1882.

53. Process engraving at this time varied between four pence and a shilling per square inch. The cost of the wood engravings for *Jackanapes* was approximately 2s 3d per square inch.

54. Over many years Alfred and William Dawson devised a number of techniques for making letterpress plates. The one Caldecott refers to here was 'wax engraving'. A stylus is used to make the drawing through the wax ground on a brass plate. Once the illustration is complete, the large white areas are built up with more wax, and finally an electrotype is made from this mould. It was a complicated technique but was used until the First World War.

55. In addition to his work as a civil servant, editor and author, Henry Blackburn was an 'instructor in drawing for the press by new processes'.

56. In Canto VII of Dante's *Divine Comedy: Inferno* the hoarders and spendthrifts are forced to spend their time rolling huge rocks.

57. This compares with approximately 2s 3d a square inch for wood engraving.

58. Mercy.

59. Edmund Evans proposed that William Mavor's *Spelling Book* should be illustrated by Kate Greenaway and Caldecott. According to Spielmann and Layard (biographers of Kate Greenaway), Miss Greenaway would not consent to the partnership. However she more than toyed with the idea, for she produced a rough design for the title page, naming herself and Caldecott as illustrators. Evans's comments on the process engravings disagrees with p. 129 of Spielmann and Layard.

60. George Cruikshank illustrated the first edition of *Lob Lie-by-the-Fire*.

61. *Coloured Pictorial*.

62. Laid paper. Illustrations with detailed shading, especially coloured illustrations, needed a smooth-surfaced wove paper if they were to print well.

63. This was not to be; she died 13 May 1885.

ANNIE ADAMS FIELDS

1834–1915

Mrs Fields was the wife of the American publisher James T. Fields, and was New England's best known literary hostess of the 1860s and '70s. As an authoress she published several biographies and books of verse. She made various trips to Europe, and her letters to Caldecott were written after the death of her husband, when she was travelling with Sarah Orne Jewett, who was to become her constant companion.

[111]
6 Via de' Servi, Florence
24 March 1882

Dear Madam,

Yesterday I received your note of the 6th inst.

Your former letter did not reach me very quickly—owing to the illness of a friend in England—but I replied to it, and posted my reply here on the 13th February. I said how sorry I am that I cannot undertake what you so flatteringly wish me to do—I mentioned my admiration of the ballads—some of which I knew before you wrote—and I told you that I am too busy to make more promises and that I have to decline to work in collaboration with several personal acquaintances and friends who are well known as writers and composers of songs. I believe I wrote all this.

I again cannot help thanking you for the compliment which you pay me and for the interest which you take in my designs.

I hope to be in London in June—my permanent address is the Arts Club, Hanover Square, W.

Feeling sorry that you have been troubled to write twice, I am, dear Madam,
Yours very truly,
Randolph Caldecott

[112]
Wybournes, Kemsing, Nr Sevenoaks
2 August 1882

Dear Mrs Fields,

I hope to have the pleasure of calling upon you tomorrow—Thursday— at a quarter before 5 o'clock—and I shall be glad if you have found it convenient to be 'at home'.
Yours very truly,
R. Caldecott

THE FINE ART SOCIETY

Most of the drawings which Caldecott sold during his lifetime were sold by the Fine Art Society.

[113]
Broomfield, Frensham, Farnham, Surrey
29 November 1883

Dear Sir,

In this instance I accept the 1½ guineas each for (Q. of ♡♡♡) vignettes. If not too late.

I only received your letter last evening after dark and post-time—I had been out hunting. We are 4 miles from telegraph office. I [will] try to send a telegram in for you this morning.

Yours very truly,
R. Caldecott

HORATIA GATTY

1846–1945

Editor of *Aunt Judy's Magazine* and Mrs Ewing's sister. Although Caldecott is remembered more for his illustrations to Mrs Ewing's books, he made, at Miss Gatty's request (and often insistence), many illustrations and designs for *Aunt Judy's Magazine* which are comparatively little known. After Mrs Ewing's death, during the production of *Lob Lie-by-the-Fire*, Miss Gatty worked with Caldecott to publish the book.

[114]
5 Langham Chambers, London W
31 July 1879

Dear Miss Gatty,

I am much obliged to you for the M.S. of the song—it is very kind of you to copy it for me, and I will make somebody sing it to me.

Also for the magazine as a specimen of the kind of work you require in the way of illustration. It will be very difficult to get anybody who will do such respectable work as C. Green's.[1] If I can help you, I shall be glad. I will keep the matter present in my mind.

It is just possible that you may see the summer number of the *Graphic*. Therein is a series of illustrations by me, and the letterpress accompanying—bearing the frivolous title of *Flirtations in France* —is also attributed to me—bearing my initials—but I am not responsible for the last 40 odd lines containing one or two *dreadful* remarks and jokes—these were *added* instead of my winding-up short sentences—to fill up the page. It is not an important matter to the world at large: but I should be sorry that any friends of mine credited me with what I object to.

Believe me,
Yours very truly,
Randolph Caldecott

[115]
Hôtel de Paris, Trouville
25 August 1879

Dear Miss Gatty,

I am very pleased to hear from you and Mrs Ewing in so joyous a strain

as regards the drawing which I sent you. You would not have surprised me if you had returned it "with thanks". I earnestly hope that it will serve your purpose.

You have kindly offered to send me the *Professor at the B Table*.[2] I will, however, not let you take this trouble. The book I have read and admired, smiled and sighed over. On the point of its adaptability to illustration by *my* pencil I must differ from you. 1stly the book is almost too good. 2ndly none but an American, or a man or woman who has lived much in Boston, could do it.

To succeed in the serious portrayal of fine types and characters of a strange nation is an achievement—I believe—beyond the power of any man. Even a peasant is, as a character and an individual, best delineated by an artist of his own land. Delight may be given to and praise received from a painter's countrymen by and for his pictures of 'life' in another country; but not much of those things would be stirring about during the contemplation of the pictures by a countryman of the other country.

America I look upon in many things as another country. Yet it is so connected with England—we should *hear their* criticisms—that this point must be considered in dealing with its peculiarities.

After this lucid explanation of my feelings on that subject, I pass on to considering your friendly suggestions regarding my pen and ink pictures of life.

You look on them from the literary point of view, and I dare say you are right more than wrong. From the artistic standpoint, however, they should also be regarded. A view from that lofty mound—and a fine one—is that which sheweth that it is as much the manner in which a work is executed as the choice of subject which is of importance: and that a mean subject may be raised to distinction by an artist's treatment.

Now, as I believe very much in realistic work—not in opposition to—but as equally worthy with—ideal work—when the object is to teach, enlighten, or—(same thing)—innocently interest and amuse—I wish it to be fairly judged as to its *reality*. Its reality is its strongest or *only* reason for existing. I admit that some of the subjects which I choose fail and are unnecessary when they are not as realistic as I can exhibit them. And I am content to consider that they—my attempts at realistic drawings—are *all* unnecessary if people say they are not "like". I do not think that I often fully succeed—I rarely do anything like what I want—but I believe that the exact representation of ordinary people and life is not a bad thing to shew to the people who live that life, and as I see in the works of others so very, very little exact and true representation of it, why I—with great self-denial, for I yearn for pure forms, graceful lines and noble subjects—rush in—pencil in hand—and let drive at the people. Some say I hit them—anyway they pay well for it—which last fact brings out my self-denial in startling relief!

I can understand that many of my subjects do not interest the upper class:

but I also consider the larger (and more-purchasing) middle-class. This class (I have observed) is as human—as tender of heart—and as deserving of respect for its sympathies—as any other class. If it is not so refined as the upper we must gradually and gently lead it through those things with which it sympathizes to a more exalted state. First catch its attention by realism, reach its sympathy by judicious choice of subject, then by gentle doses of idealism it may be drawn into a hopefully contemplative condition.

I notice that Mrs Ewing regards some of my *sketches*[3] as intended *pictures*. A study of a man or group of men is not always and need not be a *picture* or a *novel*.

I will write to Mrs Ewing—for whose note I am grateful—when I am clearer in the intellect than tonight. I wonder whether you will make any meaning out of my pen-wanderings over this paper.

My side of Sevenoaks is the north—I believe—about 4 miles from middle of town. 1st station on branch line from Otford to Maidstone—Kemsing. A sequestered village sheltered by chalk downs, or high land of some sort.

At the top of this letter is a fine text for a homily on the legitimate aims and true scope of pictorial art, to which might be added an appendix on grace being beauty in motion.

This is the end.
Believe me to be
Yours very truly,
Randolph Caldecott
P.S. I return to London Thursday morning.

[116]
5 Langham Chambers, Portland Place, W
29 August 1879

Dear Miss Gatty,
Thank you for your note expressing more thanks than I deserve, and for the drawing. I have coloured the latter and to-day left it personally—I mean that I took it—with Mr Evans, the Engraver and Colour printer, &c. He will look after it. If you are writing to Mr Bell, you will perhaps tell him that the matter is in hand, or not, as you think well.

You ask me to say in how much money the Magazine is indebted to me. I will send a "bill" in to Mr Bell—it will be on the consideration that *you yourself* and not Mr Bell have the original drawing that I left with Mr Evans. If, however, you do not arrange this—on second thoughts, I think I can make no difference.

I hope the result will be satisfactory to you and Mrs Ewing and everyone concerned.
Believe me,
Yours very truly,
Randolph Caldecott

[117]
Wybournes, Kemsing, Nr Sevenoaks
5 October 1879

My dear Miss Gatty,

Pray pardon me for not answering your note of 30 September earlier. It did not reach me direct and I expected to see the magazine before writing. But I have not seen it—I fancy it is reposing at Langham Chambers. I am much obliged for it and I will tell you my opinion of the result of the engraver's and printer's efforts and my thoughts about the story after I have seen the number.

I am trying now—I have just returned here from some visits—to get some work done in this retired and rustic spot while the weather keeps fair. The beasts of the field are attracting my attention now and I hope to make something out of them. I *hope*, for some things which I shall do will be experimental. I shall try to infuse a little poetry into the subjects, perhaps. If I don't idealize a wee I shall be safe to caricature. Let no man or woman ask me to make an exact representation of his or her head in clay. There would be words in the end.

Because I am, and must stay, here for a time I shall not be in town again yet awhile—for which I am sorry, as I should have taken pleasure in calling to see you and Mrs Ewing before she starts for Malta.⁴ Present my wishes for a cheerful journey to her, and say that as far as sketches are concerned I am behindhand with everybody. Time beats me easily. I have, however, some suggestions of what Mrs Ewing likes as subjects which I will preserve against easier times than just now.
Believe me,
Yours very truly,
Randolph Caldecott
P.S. The picture of the boy and pony is—I think—at my chambers.⁵ You shall have it all right. R.C.

[118]
Wybournes, Kemsing, Nr Sevenoaks
10 October 1879

My dear Miss Gatty,
    I have not been able to look
at the magazine which
you kindly sent to me
until now—this afternoon
—I have been—and
often am—away from home,

142

so that your letters have not reached my hand until too long after their despatch from your hand. And now I have only just time before the postman comes to write to say that I think Mrs Ewing's story very well concocted—but I ought not to use that word; because it is very clear that my drawing had but little to do with the invention of the story. I like the story and I think others must do so too. I do not know Mrs Ewing's writing enough, I perceive from this—and when opportunity serves I will become better acquainted with it. The story is much better than the illustration—this latter has been very fairly reproduced, I think. A little thin, but not the usual faults of coloured prints.

The original drawing I shall send you when I am in town.

Please present my kind regards to Mrs Ewing and the repetition of my wishes for a good and pleasant voyage (I hope she is better) and forgive my present haste. If I do not write now—Sunday will intervene between the writing and receiving.
Yours faithfully,
Randolph Caldecott

[119]
Wybournes, Kemsing, Nr Sevenoaks
7 November 1879

My dear Miss Gatty,
I have written to Mrs Gatty to say that I expect to have the pleasure of being at 131 F. Road on Tuesday afternoon—because I go to town on Monday from here. I shall be but little here during the winter, I am sorry to say, for my work—that which I must be at during the next two or three months—can best be done in London.

I was much concerned to hear of the breaking down of Mrs Ewing on her journey towards Malta, but I hope to find her better in health when I see her, and in good spirits. They must both—good health and spirits—be very necessary to her—as to all people who do brain-work—perhaps the people who don't do brain-work like to have them too, but I have a sort of feeling that it does not much matter if *they* are upset now and then.

I am very glad you like my Picture Books:[6] especially that you prefer the *Babes* most—because those who have told me their likes hitherto seem to enjoy the *Dog* better than the other.

With kind regards to yourself and Mrs Ewing, and hoping to see you on Tuesday.
Yours very truly,
Randolph Caldecott

[120]
5 Langham Chambers, W
19 November 1879

Dear Miss Gatty,

I have not thoroughly read "Jan of the Windmill"; but I have looked thro' it. I put off studying it until some quiet evening at Kemsing should find me in a fit and yearning state of mind for such a work.

It is at Kemsing—there garnered for the coming winter's consumption. Is not that wise? I was glad to have it—like a farmer likes to have a sheaf of wheat pitched into his barn.

I shall be very happy to see you and Mrs Ewing, and Mrs Gatty, too, if she cares to come—at my workshop—I make no pretentions to having a fine studio. *This* is not mine. And I shall be pleased to offer you a cup of tea on any afternoon of next week which you like to fix—between ½ past 3 and 6. But I shall have little work to shew you. My notebooks—what I have here—are scarcely exhibitable.

Will you kindly let me know on which day you will honour my *atelier*?

If there is rain about or suspected, or if it is foggy, please bring umbrellas. The rain comes thro' the roof, and the fog condenses and does the same.

Believe me, with kind regards,

Yours very truly,

R. Caldecott

[121]
Kemsing
17 January 1880

My dear Miss Gatty,

I am very pleased at receiving your congratulatory note. News will travel and I expected that you would hear of my schemes for happiness.

Thank you all for sending good wishes for *our* future life. I have not time this morning to give you any of the particulars for which you yearn—except the name—which is at present—Marian Harriet Brind—she 'resides' about 7 miles from here (nothing to a good horse).

I hope this will do to go on with until I have the pleasure of seeing you on Thursday next—on which day I shall be happy to do as I am asked—i.e. dine in Finboro' Road, No. 131.

I write this in haste so as to acknowledge the invitation—your note having reached me slowly by way of Langham Chambers. I am in rustic retirement here and my habits are simple and child-like (and my expression bland—at least I think so—I feel so)—*vide* top of this note.

You give me credit for power of expressing my thoughts—or rather of saying something—in pen and ink with rapidity and wish me (if I do not use already—which I don't) to use a potent pen. "Invaluable at this juncture!" I am not sure—nonsense comes rapidly enough, and I think that the pauses required for dipping in the inkstand enable the inditing mind to polish and give more weight to the noble and affectionate sentiments which it is compelled by the overflowing heart to stick on paper, cram into an envelope, and confide to the man who winds the postman's horn.

He will be winding it soon—twice a day here—Pardon this hurried letter (I am just buckling on my spurs for *the* journey) and with all my hopes that you have all got on so far in the year with joy and in the company of health, and that the rest of it may be happy to each.
Believe me to be
Yours very truly,
Randolph Caldecott

[122]
Wybournes, Kemsing
21 February 1880

145

My dear Miss Gatty,

I thank you very much for your addition to Our library—1stly because I am pleased that you wish to make me a present "on the very important occasion"—secondly, because I am glad to possess a copy of this particular book, which I have never read, but heard of, and now tasted of with a longing for a full meal—and thirdly, because it *is* an addition to *Our* library.

In the retirement of this secluded village—in the shade of a pilgrim's yew tree—in the sweet concealment of a bower of roses—with all the sounds of joyful nature in summer-time around us—we ought to find Mrs Gatty's book[7] particularly suitable. I think we shall. I like natural history, too; and from what I have already seen of the notes I feel sure that I shall study them with interest.

I am very glad to hear that Mrs Ewing is well enough to have fixed upon a day for her arrival in town from Yorkshire, and I look forward to the pleasure of seeing you both on the 2nd. Miss Brind will most likely not be in town then: so that the chance of her being at Mrs Blackburn's is doubtful. I shall be sorry if she be absent, for I should like you to meet.

With kind regards to each of you at No. 131. Mrs Gatty has lost her cold—that which kept her from the R.A. Old Masters Ex.—I hope.

Yours very truly,

Randolph Caldecott

P.S. I will return the Myth Book soon—I am obliged to you for sending it to me. R.C.

2P.S. Thank you for returning sick-boy-donkey-doctor sketch.[8] R.C.

[123]

Wybournes, Kemsing, Nr Sevenoaks

13 November 1880

My dear Miss Gatty,

Will you kindly tell me where you are—I wish to send you a little book? Also please to tell me the name of your little nephew—I think it is Jack—at 131 Finboro' Road—I want to send him a book, too.

How is Mrs Ewing? Is she in England? She will be glad to hear that I have been doing something military lately.

Windy, wet and unkind weather to-day—or I should have gone a-hunting.

I hope you are well and your brother and Mrs Gatty and other friends.

Yours faithfully,

Randolph Caldecott

[124]
Wybournes, Kemsing,
Nr Sevenoaks
16 November 1880

My dear Miss Gatty,
    Joy and sorrow struggle for the mastery within me—Joyful am I because you and Mrs Ewing like the *Huntsmen* and because you have bought plenty of copies (N.B. Royalty!)—sorry are we to hear that Mrs Ewing has been so poorly—I hoped she was at Malta by this time—and we are sorry that we are not in London to let you 'bore' us with your toy—your searching micro-scope—I did not know you practised on that instrument, and sorry am I that I cannot have the pleasure of receiving the personal adoration of "my ardent admirer" whom you expect to see you—further sorry are we that we cannot see Jack in his gay coat and at the same time call and ask Mrs Gatty how she is. Mrs Caldecott has been wishing for news of her. We suppose that she is well, as you say nothing to the contrary, and we wish to express our pleasure at the possession by Jack of a baby-brother—we shall have more pleasure when we see that he is as handsome as Jack.
    I hear of several people besides Miss Sulivan off to Egypt for the coming winter—*we* meditated upon it—since doing so, however, work has closed on me with iron grip. I have been and *promised*—so must perform.
    Yes, I *am* glad that you have the reading of M.S. novels to do, as you like it. I hope you do not remember them after you have read them. There was once a man who once said that however much he received for illustrating a book he ought to get twice as much for reading it. I hope your remuneration is in accord with this feeling.
    "The dialect" of the *Huntsmen* is not quite pure: Lancashire and Cheshire and usual English mixed.
    Tell me what you think of "Sing a song". I have not enough to send 1 to Mrs Ewing, to whom and yourself Mrs Caldecott sends her kind regards with mine, and our hopes for Mrs Ewing's rapid and complete recovery.
Yours very truly,
Randolph Caldecott

Wybournes, Kemsing, Nr Sevenoaks
17 July 1881

My dear Miss Gatty,

I did not know the true history of "Aunt Judy"—and I did not *think* very much about the true meaning of Mrs Ewing's suggestion—as I ought to have done—I did not notice that she—the old lady (not Mrs Ewing)—was intended as a reader.

The sad result of haste and pressure!

It would be quite as agreeable to me to make an old lady reader—or a younger lady as "Aunt Judy",[9] putting the latter in prim costume to inspire respect amongst the juveniles.

But how can an elder sister be Aunt Judy to her younger youthful sisters whom she entertains? The heat prevents me from understanding this—I cannot *think*—I can yawn and dream and say "it *is* hot!"
Yours faithfully,
R. Caldecott
P.S. I have a mighty quantity of work to do by the end of the month—whatever the weather may be. R.C.

Wybournes, Kemsing, Nr Sevenoaks
7 August 1881

My dear Miss Gatty,

I hope to make the cover for A.J.'s Mag. this week: and I will try to make the illustration you want—in 2 or 3 weeks time, if that will do.

We broke a shaft of our carriage on Thursday—if we had not we should probably have seen you at 7oaks or fetched you here (if you'd have come). We go to F. Locker's, Weylands, Cromer, tomorrow for 8 or 9 days.
Yours faithfully,
R. Caldecott

Wybournes, Kemsing, Nr Sevenoaks
23 August 1881

My dear Miss Gatty,

I am sending to-day the cover design for A.J.'s Magazine to David Bogue —as you tell me to do—with one of the tinted papers which I think the best— I do not like this one *quite*, however. Others may enjoy it, though.

This cover design could not have been sent before without doing me damage in the eyes of engraving Evans, for he has been for some weeks past in daily expectation of instalments of my Picture Books,[10] which he is anxious to finish—all that I have to do now, except touching proofs, is to make a design for a volume of 8 books altogether.[11] I understand that if Mr Bogue likes this design he will put it at once into Evans's hands.

The drawing for the story[12] I will make in line in a few days—this week it will be in your hands, I hope. It is to be tinted, I think?

We go to Exmoor early in September.

I hope you are enjoying the neighbouring county.

Yours busily and faithfully,

R. Caldecott

[128]
"Royal Oak", Winsford, Dulverton, Somerset[13]
9 September 1881

My dear Miss Gatty,

I am very glad that you like the drawing of the old Gaffers. I have been expecting E. Evans to send me a proof of the cover and the Gaffers for tinting to this hostel—not ready yet, I suppose.

Business. I am going to charge £12 12/– for the use of drawing of Gaffers and tinting proof, &c. If, however, the munificent donor thinks it well I will include the *"original drawing beautifully coloured" as a picture for £17 17/–. Do not consider it otherwise than as a matter of business—and order the O.D.B.C.* or not as the donor desires.

Very pretty place this. Stag hunting on moor—Exmoor—long way off—on Wednesday.

Fly-fishing yesterday. To-day we *drive* to a meet of staghounds.

Here until middle of next week. 10 miles from station.

Hope you had a pleasant time at York meeting. [14]

Our kind regards—very kind regards. Adieu!

Yours faithfully and autumnally,

R. Caldecott

[129]

Wybournes, Kemsing, Nr Sevenoaks

28 October 1881

Dear Miss Gatty,

Thank you for seventeen guineas—payment for coloured drawing to illustrate "Daddy Darwin's Dovecot" in Aunt Judy's Magazine. May the said magazine and its Editor live long and prosper!

Yours faithfully,

Randolph Caldecott

[130]

Casa Paoli, 12 Lung' Arno della Zecca Vecchia, Florence

2 December 1881

My dear Miss Gatty,

You will receive at Warwick Road in 2 or 3 days the O.D.B.C. of 2 Gaffers. I hope you will like it. It started for London yesterday morning early, in fine weather, after a showery night which succeeded weeks of almost cloudless splendour.

I am glad Mrs Ewing likes the said illustration to her story—I must write to her in acknowledgement of her letter which I read with pleasure a day or 2 ago.

With our kind regards,

Believe me

Yours very truly,

Randolph Caldecott

[131]

6 Via de' Servi, Florence

27 December 1881, evening

My dear Miss Gatty,

I am overwhelmed with confusion. It has occurred to me that I have not replied to your note of the 6th inst. Forgive me. In it you ask me if I will let you have the original drawing of the last scene in Mr Carlyon's Xmas; [15] and if so, whether you can have it before the Xmas day just past and gone. Indeed, owing to my forgetfulness you cannot have it before last Sunday; but if you will pardon me I must beg you not to want it at all. I *do* wish to keep the set together and if I took one drawing out it would never be replaced, I fear, except under tremendous pressure. I do not like messing with work past and done with—except just to pocket any pecuniary proceeds which may fall in and which only require a few lines of stamped acknowledgement. It is little things like the replacing of this drawing in the set that run away with my time so sadly. Why, I should almost rather promise to make another drawing for Aunt J.'s Magazine, I would indeed almost rather.

Don't think me ungracious—especially do I not wish to be so to you who look with so kindly and flattering an eye on my humble efforts to amuse the age we live in. I am very glad to read your commendations of various things and I hope to try your friendship and critical faculty more severely next Christmas.

29th morning

There are many interruptions—even in Florence—to calm and steady employment—and of all interruptions one which I dislike most is that which interferes with the finishing of a letter when it is begun and begun in the right spirit—I have tried to be as nice as possible in the early part of this letter and I was going to be as gaily light and pleasant at the closing thereof as this festive and bell-ringing season would admit. So I will be yet—or rather, would be if I could; but this is morning, and as life wears on, I find myself not as light-hearted in the morn as I was of old time, so that you lose very much by reason of my determination to finish this note now, which I do in order that it may reach you as soon as possible with *our* kindest wishes for the New Year and our earnest hopes that all your undertakings therein may be successful.

Present our good wishes for the season to our friends around you, and pray live in the trust that my next letter will be written in the more joyous and sympathetic mood that peaceful evening usually brings to
Yours faithfully,
Randolph Caldecott
P.S. Grim morning is more suited to the invention of the humorous and burlesque scenes and incidents which *some* of my employers desire in my work.
R.C.
2nd P.S. We are sorry to hear of Miss Sulivan's accident—and hope she is well now—I fear we shall not see her if she goes to Rome: for we have abandoned our idea of visiting that city this winter. Should we go to Cannes we shall like to meet Lady Brougham and her daughter—and it will not be our fault if we do not, I think, after what you say. R.C.

Broomfield, Frensham, Farnham, Surrey
29 October 1882

My dear Miss Gatty,

Just found it as I was about to write and ask you for the names of your new publishers! The last *Aunt Judy's Magazine*. I want to send my subscription for next year.

"Laetus sorte meâ" has been enjoyed by us: but in my small opinion I considered the story ended before or without the birth of the baby.

I hope you have not suffered much inconvenience from the liquidation of Mr Bogue—I was much surprised to get the notice.

Such an annoying time we have had—moving from Kemsing. Not straight yet by a long way. Waste of time and money and thought to a serious extent.

We hoped to have seen you and Mrs Ewing from Sevenoaks before we left K.

With our kind regards to all of you—not heard for a long time—all well? Believe me
Yours faithfully,
Randolph Caldecott

Broomfield, Frensham, Farnham, Surrey
18 February 1883

My dear Miss Gatty,

You are very welcome to use the "Household Cavalry" sketch—E. Evans will supply you with an electro or whatever is necessary—I am asking him to do so.

The little Book to which it belongs will—I hope—be out—I fear—in all its crudity at Easter: therefore you will be after it or about the same time. I was not aware that I suggested Mrs Ewing's using it *before* the book. It will be necessary, I suppose, for you just to acknowledge in print from whence it comes—so that it shall not seem to the great public or the publishers that *I* am using it twice? You know best. The book will be called "A Sketch-Book of R. Caldecott's".[16] Don't be rough on it when it appears—or I will not lend you any more—I do not know, though, that I would refuse anything for Mrs Ewing to write to.

I enclose 2 more proofs—these subjects with the "cavalry" forming a group of 3.

We shall be delighted if Mr Hippisley favours us with a call. We have had visits from much of the retired military.

Please tell Mrs Ewing that E. Evans has not yet answered the questions which I asked him after receiving her last letter. He was coming over here from his country seat yesterday; but I had to put him off. And have I not been into shops and shops after soldiers' costumes? And am I not empty-handed yet? But will I not go to the Print Room, Mus. Brit. when I am about to *begin*?

Our kind regards.
Yours very truly,
R. Caldecott

[134]
24 Holland Street, Kensington, W
27 April 1885

My dear Miss Gatty,

We are very sorry to find from your note that Mrs Ewing is so far from well yet. Believe me that we are anxious on her account and hope for better news soon.

Do not trouble her with anything further at present about "Lob" drawings if you think she should not be bothered. If she prefers to be bothered and to make a further remark or 2 on the subject perhaps you will let her know the contents of this letter.

(In any case, I send to E. Evans to-day the 7 drawings which are approved for him to go on with.)

I should like to have a little further criticism of the 4 drawings kept apart from the 7, so that, if possible, I could modify or alter them.

The drawing-room scene is a little "tight" and not simple enough in treatment—this I can perhaps do over again. N.B. The rather fat lady on left was not intended for one of the little old ladies.

In scene with lawyer and 2 ladies—are ladies not satisfactory, or lawyer—or all? He is dressed as country lawyers were wont to be attired at that time.

In baby-finding scene—I do not think the hand of lady is wrong. It has a mitten on it, and I thought I was happy in shewing the shape of the wrist. It looks just a little funny—I could bring the arm and elbow *out* a little more. You do not praise the babe's leg. It is copied from the leg of one of Luca della Robbia's most beautiful Infant Saviours—and he is very great at infants —the best of all the Italians—I think.

If the sailor is not considered a pleasing subject to depict—I'll leave him

out. I could make my drawing of him more winning as to expression of face—
and I think the figure would give variety to the book and please some people.
I think a little of the rugged gives force and contrast and counteracts the
namby-pamby. No more now, but I hope for good news soon.

Yours,

R. Caldecott

P.S. Please excuse scraps. Another question you ask—I made a new drawing
of tea-party and sent it to Evans. I did not put more sentiment into it, so I
thought it would not interest you—I felt sure that it was a better drawing
than the 1st attempt, and had something in it I wanted to shew. R.C.

[135]
24 Holland Street, Kensington, W
11 June 1885

My dear Miss Gatty,

Here are 9 drawings to *Lob*—1 of them is, however, but a second version
of another, and you will please to mark that which you like the better.

The child and wreath I suggest as a finial to the book, and it can be
reduced a little in size.

I fear that Mr Evans will feel somewhat "done" when he sees all the
drawings (he has had the others in his hands for some time) because he has
promised to engrave them on wood, and they are more important and have
more work in them than former books. I do not propose to do any more—
except perhaps a cover-design.

I have put a little more work into these than I intended because I have
felt that I was working towards helping to keep Mrs Ewing's memory green
—although many more important things will tend to do that.

I have at Broomfield a book which Mrs Ewing kindly lent me—it is
called "Johnny" or Jonny "Gibb". When next I am at Frensham I will
return it.

Herewith you have also the letterpress of *Lob* which I have been using.
It has corrections here and there all thro'—so I suppose you will wish Evans to
set up his type from it, and I will send it to him, if you so wish, with the drawings. On page 28 I have taken the liberty of pointing out "woods" instead of
"fields": but you will alter it or not as you think fit, of course.

You ask me for some details of money paid me. I have put down on a
separate paper what I have received and what is owing me on account of
Jackanapes and *D.D.D.*

I hope you are getting resigned to your loss (Mrs R.C. sends her love)
and with kind remembrances to Major Ewing.

Believe me to be

Yours very truly,

Randolph Caldecott

24 Holland Street, Kensington, W
13 June 1885

My dear Miss Gatty,

Thanks for returning and commenting on the drawings so quickly. I again send you the 'Highlander and boy' which I have altered according to your suggestion. I do not think *I* can make it better than it now is. The costume is from a Waterloo picture. I at first made the kilt rather short because I have often observed that soldiers of unusual height wear usual-sized garments. I have added considerably to the weight of the body, and I have altered the nose. Is not this a Lowland nose now?—the old nose I have seen in Highlanders, who are akin to the Welsh, I believe.

I read in the story of an officer with a sword "clattering after him" and from the description of his dress I suppose him not to be a field-officer. If not, would he not wear a claymore. Perhaps I am quite in a muddle over this.[17] Very likely.

As to more military scenes, I do not think I mentioned any number, because I had not then considered that part of the book and the cockatoo portion. Now I am of opinion that to put more than the 2 I have made (the boy running in snow and this enclosed) would unduly illustrate that part of the book and not fairly distribute the cuts over the whole. Then that part is but short and the most dramatic scenes—the outpost duty on cold night scenes—are almost undrawable. The chief figures in this military portion are Mac. and John, and it seems to me unnecessary to repeat them—more especially as they are often drinking. The death-bed scene I consider to be too well told by the author to be trifled with by the illustrator—apart from the seriousness of the subject.

The title and cover design (which will be one) will have the Highlander somewhereabout: but I think he should not be prominent, for I hear opinions that his is not the most interesting part of the book.

As to Mr Evans, I am really of opinion that by the time he has the title design we shall have seriously trespassed upon him—that is, if he is going to do his best with the cutting and deliver the book at price arranged.

As to accounts. The S.P.C.K. will not yet pay for the last 10,000 *Jackanapes* delivered, I fear; but they ought to have paid before this for the last 10,000 of *D.D.D.*, according to Mrs Ewing's arrangement as I understand it.

In reply to your questions, you will see by my remarkably clear statement that I have put down all the money I have received and have stated how many copies have been delivered to S.P.C.K. The difference between what I have received and 1d royalty all through being what is due to me (i.e. when funds are distributable).

The mistake between £90 and £100 up to 23 June means nothing. I mentioned it because there might be found some mem. of Mrs Ewing's bearing thereupon. I fancy she was thinking of the original bargain—which was that I was to receive £100: but if the circulation passed 20,000 I was to receive 1d a copy royalty all thro. Although she had been paying me royalty-wise yet I fancy at that time she considered that I ought to have already received quite £100. I hope this explanation is really lucid. To make it clearer I will try if you wish.

Meantime—Yours very truly,

R. Caldecott

[137]
24 Holland Street, Kensington, W
17 June 1885

My dear Miss Gatty,

I am glad you agree to my alterations in the Highlander. May I trouble you now to tell me if these words are right for the title—hyphens and all? Altho' I have fondled the printed tale for a long time past I am a little doubtful about the hyphens and a possible apostrophe—on second thoughts I put it on a separate bit of paper.

"Comparisons are odorous" and you must not think that my repetition of an opinion or two about some parts of the book compared with others means that I think any part not very good. On further consideration I do not think that I can alter my opinions about the illustration of the military parts and the book as a whole as I expressed them in my last letter. I arrived at my opinions after due meditation and leaning of the head upon the hand.

I regret that the difficulties of which I spoke seem to me so important. Do you know that I have not drawn *Lob* lying by the fire? If I cannot get him in the title I must put another little drawing in somewhere. E.E. seems pleased with the drawings.

I am sorry to read that it is probable that *Aunt Judy's Mag.* will soon cease to run. You must have had much trouble with it and "given" a great deal to it. That is why I once asked you if you were paid for your own articles (I hear that Bogue is again in difficulties). I fear that a drawing or 2 or 3 of mine would not stay the decease of *A.J.M.*[18]

Believe me
Yours very truly,
R. Caldecott

LOB LIE-BY-THE-FIRE
or
THE LUCK OF LINGBOROUGH
or is it
O' LINGBOROUGH

[138]
24 Holland Street, Kensington, W
21 June 1885

My dear Miss Gatty,

Certainly I have told E. Evans to consider the engraving of the drawing you mention as for *A. J. Mag.* and if you will tell me where he is to send the block when ready I will advise him. I hope you will accept the drawing[19] as a contribution from me—both its use in the mag.—and the original sketch. (E.E. will send his bill for engraving with the block, doubtless.)

I should have made the title and the 'lob' by this time, but the present severely cold weather has upset me.

I had the pleasure of meeting Miss Sulivan at Mrs W. B. Richmond's yesterday—she has recently returned from Spain.

Yours very truly,

R. Caldecott

P.S. If I had a good proper likeness as a help I should like some day to try a medallion of Mrs Ewing. R.C.

[139]
Broomfield, Frensham, Farnham, Surrey
15 July 1885

My dear Miss Gatty,

What bothers we illustrators are! I am sorry you have had any difficulty over identifying the illustration enclosed. But it is only one out of the set. Perhaps—I say, perhaps—if I had been entrusted with the adjusting of the cuts to the story—as in the cases of the other books—all might have seemed to fit and to be appropriate.

This wood-engraving, which seems to me good as a reproduction, represents "the bailiff", who is described as a hard-featured man (in other words) with a "speckled straw hat". This hat is mentioned more than once in the book, and I thought that I had treated it in my drawing realistically and lovingly. The bailiff is spoken of as contemplating the difficulty of keeping the juvenile LOB at work and the said LOB is spoken of as preferring to "run races with the sheep-dog". This is the spot where I fondly thought my illustration would naturally come in. The drawing was, I think, one of the 7 first put aside by you and Mrs Ewing as the pick of the first squad sent down.

I have not yet received proofs. When I do I will go carefully over them—I note your remarks—*white* lines are, however, unmanageable—*black* can be altered readily.

The cover, the finial and the soldier are being engraved.

I return proof: but I do not quite understand whether you wish me to send it to you or to Mr E.E.

Yours very truly,
R. Caldecott
P.S. Just had a letter from E.E. Asks if Highlander is for *frontispiece*—if so he will not reduce it. R.C.

[140]
Broomfield, Frensham, Farnham, Surrey
25 July 1885

My dear Miss Gatty,

I only wish to remark that you must have been thinking all manner of evil of me for not acknowledging the arrival of the photographs. They reached my hands a few minutes ago for the first time. Mrs Caldecott has been to town where she found your packet calmly reposing. The house-keeper selected it as amongst those postage things "not to be sent on". I am sorry. The photographs are very interesting—and I'll write about them soon.

I have seen proofs of most of "Lob's" cuts—they are fairly good, I think. Better than they might have been by a long way.

When all are engraved I'll see to their positions.
Yours very truly,
R. Caldecott
P.S. Some letters of ours have recently been lying for an undue time under gingerbread dragoons and Noah's arks at Frensham P. Office.

[141]
Broomfield, Frensham, Farnham, Surrey
1 August 1885

My dear Miss Gatty,

I wish you a happy new August.

I am very much obliged to you for sending the photographs of Mrs Ewing for me to look at. I return all but the one which you kindly say I may keep. They are all very interesting.

I should like—as I told you—to attempt a medallion portrait of Mrs Ewing, and for my purpose the 2 up-looking profiles by Hollyer would be the greatest help. I can either borrow these from you when the time comes for me to begin—which will be when there is a lamp-lit time before dinner—late autumn or early winter—or I will ask you, according to your good suggestion, to get copies for me some time when convenient.

I have to-day received from Mr Evans proof of letterpress with most of the cuts of *Lob*—all that are engraved—and places marked where the others are to come. I will get him to change the frontispiece and put 'woman and child' first—also to alter positions of 1 or 2 others. The party is in quite wrong place—should be towards end of book—and I do not think it best to

158

put every cut right in middle of page. Some may be nearer top than bottom and vice versâ. What do you think? I shall perhaps drive over to Evans's on Monday.

If you are writing soon please tell me how you would direct a letter to Miss Browne—the Bishop's daughter—to prevent confusion with her aunt. Yours very truly,
Randolph Caldecott
P.S. Your old copy of *Lob* I will return.

[142]
24 Holland Street, Kensington, W
13 October 1885

My dear Miss Gatty,
I am much obliged to you for sending cheque Forty-one pounds, 13/4 royalty on 10,000 *Jackanapes* delivered in July last.
R. Caldecott
P.S. I need not say that I have been much interested in your Memoir of Mrs Ewing.[20] There are certain things therein mentioned which I regret that I did not know before. I feel sure that the memoir will be appreciated in many quarters.

Mr Evans sent me a proof on grey paper of the cover for me to mark a bit of white light thereon.

If I had not been particularly busy when I was asked about using this design for the cover I should have very willingly made a new one—I did begin one.

We have left Broomfield—as you have heard—a small sale of odd things, such as a mowing-machine which won't work, &c, will take place on Friday.

In a week or 2—either on 24th or 31st—we shall probably go to America.

Mrs Caldecott encloses kindest regards. Shall you be in town during this month?
Yours very truly,
R.C.

[143]
24 Holland Street, Kensington, W
26 October 1885

My dear Miss Gatty,
Do you think you could lend me one or 2 of those other photographs of Mrs Ewing which I said might be useful to me in making a medallion—the exact profile—looking up—for instance.

I should like to take them to America with me. We leave here on Friday—and L'pool on Saturday.
Yours very truly,
R. Caldecott

24 Holland Street, Kensington, W
29 October 1885

My dear Miss Gatty,

My friends who have been cheering me this evening have left and only the clock ticks. We leave here tomorrow; but before I go I must thank you for your kind wishes for a pleasant journey. We intend not to stay in New York long on arrival—altho' we have many introductions and I know a few people there already—we will do that great city in the spring. Also Boston. I should like to meet your friends the Thorons and the Asa Grays.

(As you name it—if you have anything for me—my money—before our return in six months or so please send it to F. B. Seaman, Esq., Union Bank of London, Ltd., Holborn Circus, E.C. He will acknowledge receipt thereof.)

I am very much obliged to you for sending and offering to lend me the photographs of Mrs Ewing. I keep 3 for the present and return 2 herewith. During the dark minutes before dinner or supper in the orange groves of Florida and California I hope to be able to try a medallion for reproduction in metal on my return. Some considerable attention is now being paid by able men to the reproduction in bronze of modelled works.

With our kind regards, believe me

Yours very truly,

Randolph Caldecott

P.S. Mr Walter Frith introduced Mr Dunville to me a week or 3 ago and he took away a number of drawings. R.C.

1. Charles Green (1840–1898); an illustrator whose work often appeared in the *Illustrated London News* and the *Graphic*. He worked closely with Josiah Whymper, the wood-engraver, father of Edward Whymper, the mountaineer.

2. *The Professor at the Breakfast Table* by Oliver Wendell Holmes, first published in 1860.

3. His first ideas for the *Jackanapes* illustrations.

4. Mrs Ewing was to join Major Ewing, but she became very ill in France and returned to England to convalesce.

5. Evans had returned the original drawing for the *Jackanapes* illustration to Caldecott.

6. *The Mad Dog* and *The Babes in the Wood*.

7. *British Sea Weeds*, published in 1863.

8. It appears on p. 44 of *A Sketch-book of R. Caldecott's*.

9. Caldecott had been asked to produce a cover design for the November 1881 issue of *Aunt Judy's Magazine*.

10. *The Queen of Hearts* and *The Farmer's Boy*.

11. It was published as *R. Caldecott's Collection of Pictures and Songs*.

12. For *Daddy Darwin's Dovecot*.

13. The following sketch was developed into the illustration on p. 35 of *A Sketch-book of R. Caldecott's*.

14. Of the British Association.

15. The story appeared in the *Graphic* Christmas number for 1881.

16. Of it Edmund Evans wrote (16 October 1897), 'This was a separate speculation of ours, but it did not sell like the toy series [the picture books]; I could never tell why.'

17. In a pencilled note on Caldecott's letter Major Ewing obviously agrees that Caldecott is in a muddle. The note reads, 'A field officer of a highland regiment wears trousers. A claymore is a sword of a peculiar description.'

18. Publication ceased in August 1885.

19. It was of a child laying a wreath at a gravestone, which carries the lettering 'J.H.E., May 1885'.

20. *Juliana Horatia Ewing and Her Books*, S.P.C.K. 1885. It is quarter bound in cloth with paper sides, for which Caldecott made a three-colour design. His drawing mentioned in letter 138 appears on p. 136 of the memoir.

MR GILCHRIST

[145]
Broomfield, Frensham, Farnham, Surrey
9 December 1884

Dear Mr Gilchrist,

I am sorry I was not at Holland Street when you called—I have been there but little lately. With pleasure I will lend you some drawings for your Exhibition at Hampstead if you will kindly let me know when you want them.

It is rather a pity—as you think—that Combe has given up his hounds. I have to go a little wider now—as a rule. To the meets of the Hampshire Hounds sometimes—they have a better country for galloping: and I have a galloper now.

In Mr Simmons' company I saw a fox killed last Friday (Mr S looks blooming). The Chiddingfold hounds met at Frensham Mill on that day.

We shall be happy to see you when convenient to call in Holland Street. We shall not be staying there much until March, however.
Yours very truly,
Randolph Caldecott

[146]
Broomfield, Frensham, Farnham, Surrey
13 February 1885

My dear Gilchrist,

I have left a collection of odd drawings to be called for at Holland St. by Bourlet on the day you name. 9 frames altogether. If too many—perhaps you will be able to call and select, *after Wed. next*, because 2 sets are not yet mounted. Or you can only hang what you want when you get them. I think 4 of the frames are about 30 inches (or a little under) in length—the others smaller—one quite small. I do not want to overdo you—but you ask for 12 or 15 *"drawings"*—I have taken this to mean *frames*.

I am sorry that I was not in town when you called the other day—I must be luckier during the Season. It will not be convenient to me to attend the conversazione I regret to say.

If we are here I hope we may see you some day during your contemplated sojourn at Haslemere.—Give us that pleasure.

Yes, I have been preparing to go abroad some time next month: but I have not been very well of late and shall not go unless stronger.
Yours very truly,
R. Caldecott

FREDERICK GREEN

1834–1905

Caldecott first met Frederick Green and his wife Sophie (*see* letters 174–178) on one of his winter visits to the south of France. Though Green was a dozen years older than Caldecott they became close friends, and it is only in these letters that Caldecott refers to his wife by her Christian name.

[147]
46 Great Russell Street, London WC
21 August 1877

My dear Green,

Thank you for your note received last evening.

You have not found a house near where you are now, then?

I am afraid that I shall be unable to see you for some while, for I must go out of town—northwards—about next Monday "in the discharge of the active duties of my profession".

You don't say aught about the Cannes frontispiece. The engraver, like all other 'swells', is out of town again: but I will leave the sketch at his place and it will be done as soon as possible. I shall only make a slight drawing, or it will take much time to engrave.

I am glad to receive your united condolences. At the rate I am improving I think a few days more will find me again an upright person.

With kind regards to each of you,
Believe me
Yours faithfully,
R. Caldecott

[148]
Crown Hotel, Harrogate
22 September 1877

My dear Green,

You must pardon me for not answering your letter of the 1st before now. I have been in daily expectations of receiving a proof of the engraving from my sketch of Cannes. This morning it has arrived. I at once enclose it to you. As I told you, I wished to make it look like an etching, and not like the usual kind of view. But it is not quite as I wished it—my fault, I am afraid. I am now writing to the engraver to ask him to improve his mountains a little.

I shall be glad to hear from you if you have any suggestions to make with regard to it—as to the copyright of it, that is of no consequence to me, and such as it is, I freely give it to you, and some day I will give you the original sketch.

The engraver, J. D. Cooper, of 188, Strand, W.C., wants to know where to send the block to.

So after my hearing from you, and when he has touched the hills, the block can be sent to where you wish.

I intended to give you the block engraved—but as you have arranged with the publishers to pay for the engraving—all the better—considering the terms of your agreement—not very profitable to you, I am afraid.

Perhaps I had better settle the matter with the engraver. He is a friend of mine.

About the other part of your letter. I will talk very soon if you will excuse me for the present. I leave here in a few minutes. Until Tuesday I shall be at J. Nunnerley, Buerton Hall, Audlem, Nantwich, Cheshire.
Yours faithfully,
R. Caldecott

[149]
with G. Tudman,[1] Esq., Ash Grove, Whitchurch, Salop
27 September 1877

My dear Green,
On receiving your letter of the 24th I at once wrote to Cooper and enclosed him the proof marked with a small alteration at the corner of the building—as suggested by you. I did not intend the wing to appear so large. I have not the photograph[2] with me, but I think it was a little indistinct in that particular part.

I hope you will be successful in building a comfortable house, or in finding one already built which will suit you. I hear that it is very difficult to find one at Clifton—Kent and Sussex must have some advantages over Somerset.

I thank you and Mrs Green very much for your hope that I will pay you another visit at Cannes during the coming winter and I shall be happy in accepting your invitation if I can make it convenient to go south again. I am waiting for signs of active rheumatism to give me a shove southwards: but probably I shall go in any case. At the present, however, I am very busy— or ought to be—and have much work to overcome during the next 2 months. With kind regards, also to Mrs Green and the boys,
Believe me

Yours faithfully,
R. Caldecott
P.S. I am gratified by your remarks about the books—B. Hall[3] and Old Xmas[4]—and I will reply at length on another occasion. R.C.

[150]
with W. B. Etches,[5] Esq., Broughall House, Whitchurch, Salop
2 October 1877

My dear Green,
   I received the enclosed leaf from the Guide on Sunday, and I believe that I am in time to catch you at Paris or I would have written earlier, in spite of my numerous rushings to and fro.
   As you say you have not seen the pictures in the houses at Grasse I am the more confident in suggesting the following emendations of the letterpress.
   I think that perhaps instead of the paragraph beginning "In the house, &c" this would do—
   "The walls of a room in the house of M. de F. are covered with small decorative paintings—many of them in a monochrome of blue—probably the work of Flemish artists. Some of them are pretty and the room is well worth a visit."
   I would say "*large* oil paintings by Fragonard"—and lower down "fitted to the spaces or divisions of the wall". And after "more serious" I would say "They are good examples of Fragonard's kind of work, and are much &c".
   If, however, you feel that any of my suggestions will not accommodate themselves to your own ideas, pray throw my alterations over. Improve the grammar—where necessary—if you use my remarks. According to my recollection I have made these changes in your description.
   46, Great Russell St., W.C. will always find me.
With kind regards,
Believe me
Yours faithfully,
R. Caldecott

[151]
Splendide Hôtel, Menton
23 January 1879

My dear Green,
   The tears shed on leaving Cannes were hardly dry on my cheek before

165

its manly furrows were again filled with a melancholy and a briny torrent. This hotel is called the "Splendid"—it is only so in name now. I entered it filled with the joyous reminiscences of that gay time which I once spent here. As I marched on the evening of my arrival along its galleries towards the dining-room up rose in my mind's eye the bundly form of old Mrs Winslow —not of soothing-syrup fame—next to whom I sat aforetime for six weeks, and up rose the stately figures of several spinsters and their companions whose lugubrious countenances and hushed whispers gave such a funeral aspect and tone to the best end of the table; but who were such a valuable foil to one charming, fair-haired, long-necked, graceful girl. Her sister married a joiner; but what of that? I should have been glad to see *her* again and I really half-expected to see her neck, curving swan-like as she pressed her chin back in the accustomed way when I entered the room for dinner. At the top of this letter you will see the company that dined that night. I searched in vain in the gloom and darkness of the other end of the table for even the ghost of her of the long neck. Then I regretted lost opportunities, and wept. I minded not my companions—a dock engineer from Hull, and a lady powdered as to her face and covered with a mantilla as to her head. Her husband should have been present—a R.N. captain with an asthma which gives out groans and shouts of a heart-rending description. This would have completed my woeful state. I should have regretted leaving the wild excitement and the cheerful hospitality of Cannes if I had not my living to get. We are picking up. 10 dined last night. The Huller is gone. Powder-face was there, 2 big young Britons, 3 ladies unmarried who have quite emerged from girlhood (1 of them scrapes the violin, the others are musical), a Canadian (elderly) and his wife, a florid young Dane, and myself. The food is good, I think. It is better than before. A Hungarian family and some Russians occupy the best rooms—we never see them. I have a small chamber, a bed, and a small salon adjoining which is comfortable for working in. No gorgeosity around. 15 fcs a day with board. I shall probably stay nearly 3 weeks— perhaps more—yet.

Thank you for the *World*. I begin to think that Whistler is not the man to do any good to artists by his championship against the critics. T. Taylor should have said no more than that W. had garbled his—Taylor's—article.[6] Whistler's replies seem to me too silly for more than the reading of his private friends.

Let me say that I miss the Villa Rosalie and thank you and Mrs Green for your kind attention during my stay at Cannes. I am glad to hear of general convalescence and I hope to hear of no more sickness. With kind regards to all the Roses and Greens.
Believe me
Yours faithfully,
R. Caldecott

[152]
Wybournes, Kemsing, Nr Sevenoaks
7 October 1879

My dear Green,

I am filled with joy to read that you have ridded your house of the title of S. Park. Thornfield[7] is better. It will remind me of "Jane Eyre".

I have been longing to 'pop' over and see you all: but I have lately been unavoidably messing about at various places instead of being at home: and my trap is too heavy for the mare—who herself sticks at nought—to drag over to your place and back in a day—as I should like. And I am anxious to get into full swing with some work which is on my mind and for which I am making studies here while the weather is fine before I shall feel contented enough all round to pay more visits. However, I hope to dodge a day very soon and have a look at you and your house. I hope you like it—Mrs Green also. I will tell you when I see you of my hopes and fears with regard to this place. It is in a sequestered spot indeed. I shall expect you to come and see it—I have enough things around me to make existence more than tolerable —but I am a simple-minded man. Nothing more (important) I shall do before Xmas, I think, in the way of furnishing. 1 sitting room for 1 man.

I hope you are all well—and with kind regards to Mrs Green, your brother, and the boys,
Believe me
Yours faithfully,
Randolph Caldecott

[153]
Wybournes, Kemsing, Nr Sevenoaks
6 January 1880

My dear Green,

It has often occurred to me lately to write and ask how you are all standing this climate of ours—rather better since Xmas than before, the weather

167

has been, I think—but my occupation of making drawings to amuse, or perhaps instruct (by a roundabout way), the great public is naturally an absorbing one, and my occupation—or rather pleasure—of paying my 'devoirs' to the future Mrs R.C. have together taken up—apparently—all my time. A man's time is taken up with duty and pleasure usually. You see what has been, and is, my duty, and you hear ditto ditto my pleasure. So pray forgive me—all of ye—that I have not wished you each a few seasonable compliments before this. I greet you, and wish you happy New Years!

How does Mrs Green like your new house in winter? And has Fred got quite better—he must have ere this? And how is your brother?

I was in London for more than a month and then in the north for a week before Xmas and 8 or 9 days of the festive season I passed in this county:[8] but not here. I have not got the house quite cosy enough for winter yet—a few draughts are sneaking about—but I am adding small comforts and necessaries and ornaments gradually—and in a couple of months' time the place will be more ship-shape. By-the-bye, most of the rooms are *very* ship-shape at present—referring to the aspect of a ship's deck on calm and peaceful days. I have one sitting room—the dining parlour—nearly all right—all except the chimney smoking and a draught under the door, and the cupboard-door away in London.

I hope to see you here to have a look at me when we can arrange it. And your brother. When I am straight I shall expect a visit from the whole family circle: but before then if you want an out and will come, I shall be very happy to see you. I am working here now.

Hoping you are all well, and with kind regards to each,
Believe me to be
Yours faithfully,
Randolph Caldecott
P.S. Armstrong has taken a caravan of 4 spinsters to the Riviera. R.C.

[154]
6 Via de' Servi, Florence
7 January 1882

My dear Green,
I was glad to hear from you the other day and I should have answered your letter earlier but I wanted to consult Armstrong on a little point before writing to you.

Blue is a very difficult colour for decorators—i.e. the layers-on of the colour—to deal with, so that it would not be wise to let them trifle with that colour—unless it were mixed in their pots ready for use. Under the circumstances it would perhaps be the best to have the colour of the frame of the picture the same as the rest of the woodwork. Indeed it should be so in any case, and therefore I would so make it.

You might have 1 or 2 blue things on the mantelpiece or a *bit* of blue in the furniture to balance the picture if you find the blue in it somewhat solitary when the room is done.

I sent the pattern of colour, which you enclosed, to Armstrong and he suggests that it "might with advantage be made just a little warmer by the addition of just a little ochre".

All this is with the notion of your having the 2 rooms the same in colour —as you seem to wish. If you cared for it, the ceiling of the morning-room might be made blue without the risk of such bad effects as the painters would probably produce by putting blue on the walls or woodwork.

T. Armstrong, who is now boss at Department of Science and Art, South Kensington Museum, will be glad to give you any advice if you think it worth while to call on him. Should you think of doing so, it would be best to write and ask him if he is likely to be in town when you go up, for he is contemplating visits of inspection to the schools of Art at Edinburgh and "Dublin bedad" very soon.

Anything further which you may favour me with on the subject I will reply to at once.

I am very glad to hear that you like the picture so much and that it looks well on your walls. I wish my patrons to be satisfied.

I am very busy with various things here—where we shall probably stay until middle of April—taking, however, a trip or 2 to some of the smaller Tuscan cities before going home.

We hope you are well and send kind regards to each. (Mrs Blackburn has scarlatina).

Yours faithfully,

R. Caldecott

P.S. The weather has been very cold—severely frosty—here for the last fortnight. They are skating somewhere about. The sky sunny and clear and the Lung' Arno 2½ coats warmer than the shaded streets. We know plenty of people and have as much going out as we wish for. Some of the people are pleasant and interesting. On Sunday evening 3 authoresses came in to see us. They behaved themselves very nicely. R.C.

P.P.S. I hope Mrs Green does not suffer much by reason of the English winter. R.C.

[155]
Bush Inn, Farnham, Surrey
11 October 1882

My dear Green,

Pray excuse me—I have been in such a muddle as to my whereabouts that I have hardly had a fitting opportunity to send you the artist's address— which I received on Monday. It is E. J. Lambert,[9] 52 Rawlings Street,

Chelsea, S.W. I write to him by this post to tell him that he will probably hear from you, and to prepare his mind for that event.

Left Wybournes (perhaps I have told you) beginning of last week. In Broomfields in such a way as to necessitate my sleeping, breakfasting and dining here—3½ miles off—and Mrs R.C. to be at Chelsfield. We have varied a little by passing 2 or 3 nights at 24 Holland St. which is barely in order for occupation. Broomfields house is so dirty that we cannot put our furniture and things in order yet. And the Bogles only left on Friday last— 2 servants there still—cows departed to-day and some dogs—tomorrow other beasts. Our horses at an inn 1½ miles away. Captain Bogle been ill— not able to come down to settle up with me and his creditors. Defend me from Captains! Mrs B. been down to-day in rain. Why do I tell you all this? Pretty place—Frensham. My wife comes tomorrow. Kind regards to Mrs Green, boys and yourself,

Yours,

R. Caldecott

P.S. If it were not for my immense administrative ability matters would be in a much worse mess. R.C.

P.P.S. Perhaps it might be most convenient to you to ask Lambert to meet you somewhere in the neighbourhood of Lincoln's Inn (or wherever portrait is) and then to take him to inspect and give his opinion about copying the same. R.C.

[156]
Broomfield, Frensham, Farnham, Surrey
3 February 1883

My dear Green,

I must seem to you lazy in replying to your note of 19th. In truth, I have not been able to consult Armstrong as to a fit and proper person to be entrusted with your portraits. When we were in town last week he had to rush off to Paris. I am very glad to hear that Lambert has given you satisfaction: but I am not able to say that you might sit to him yourself or that Mrs Green might. If we are able to pay you a visit during the coming summer, as you very kindly wish us to do, and you have not by then had your own "pattern" taken I would have a 'shy', or 'shie', at it myself. But I fear that I ought not to approach Mrs Green brush in hand—my brush is not a very reverent one.

However, don't let these remarks prevent you seizing an opportunity of having both pictures done. This will be a very busy year to me and at same time I have some engagements which may prevent us from being able to accept your hospitality for more than a day or 2. The studio will be begun shortly, I hope. Estimates being considered.

Thank you, we are well—except Mrs R.C. having found a small cold yesterday. I take a day with the hounds occasionally.

I am sorry I ordered a map of this district—which is a very complicated one—otherwise I should have been obliged to you in that line.

More soon—meantime we hope you are all quite robust and happy—and we send kind greetings to each.

Yours faithfully—post-boy waiting,

R. Caldecott

[157]
Broomfield, Frensham, Farnham, Surrey
12 July 1883

My dear Green,

When Mrs Green's kind and hospitable note arrived the other day I was on the point of writing to ask how you do, for we heard from Mrs Thurburn that you were not just as well as I could wish; and I should have told you something of our plans for the summer. We only came down here last week and next we go away again. It is usual for us to pay a visit of a fortnight to my father-in-law's at Chelsfield during each recurrent summer. The day for us to go this year is Saturday the 21st: but we can only stay 10 days there. If agreeable to Mrs Green and you, may we be down upon you on Wednesday next to stay until Saturday afternoon?

I could then—if you wish me to so do—have at least 3 good sittings from you—after which it would be well to let the paint dry a bit—therefore, if suitable to your convenience, I could be down amongst you for another day or 2 before leaving Chelsfield, and perhaps complete the picture. We have to go to Cromer for 2 or 3 days after leaving Chelsfield and then we must return here in order that I may get on with some delayed work.

Our Cromer invitation[10] is an old one and we are *expected* there for a week or two: but we cannot manage that.

I should like to stay longer with you—as you are so kind—but, if we are not careful, we shall let the chance of seeing some of the beautiful parts of this county during the summer slip away. In August we have some friends coming here and I believe I must go to Yorkshire in August or September. I cannot get along very fast with my work, somehow—and I have promised a good deal.

We hope you and Mrs Green and the boys are well and summery.
Believe me
Yours faithfully,
R. Caldecott
P.S. If Wednesday will be suited to you, how about the 5.2 train at T[unbridge] Wells? We shall have to leave here before 1 o'clock to catch it. If we use that train I might begin to rub in your portrait before dinner!!
R.C.

The Court Lodge, Chelsfield, St Mary Cray
25 July 1883

My dear Green,

Thank you for your note—it has just arrived as I was meditating writing to you about the trains.

I should like to combine pleasure—as gained by watching the games of polo—with professional occupation: therefore I will leave here on Friday at 2.34 (I think) and reach Tunbridge Junction at 3.10 or thereabouts.

You will perhaps be able to afford me an hour or 2 at the portrait that afternoon—and another sitting on Saturday morning.

If this will not be convenient in any way to you, please send word. Meantime, with kind regards to each,
Believe me
Yours faithfully,
R. Caldecott

The Court Lodge, Chelsfield, St Mary Cray
30 July 1883

My dear Green,

I have just time to write to say that I cannot very conveniently pay you another visit during this week. The picture will be all the better for waiting and hardening, and I will some time further on, when it will suit you, run down again and complete it, if you will let me.

I am much obliged to you and Mrs Green for the trouble you have taken about me and my wants lately. I found your letter of kind suggestions await-ing my return. Letters sometimes reach the P. Office here in evening: but are not delivered until next day.

That view of the polo playing was a great treat and I experienced lively sensations of envy and admiration, and a desire to give it artistic effect.

Our kind regards to Mrs Green and the boys, and until I am down again, adieu to each!
Yours faithfully,
R. Caldecott

[160]
Broomfield, Frensham, Farnham, Surrey
9 September 1883

My dear Green,

It is very kind of you and Mrs Green to wish us to revisit Thornfield again so soon and to offer us the inducements of a ball and of a quiet work-room for me: but we may not have the pleasure of being again at your house just yet. We are going visiting this week and have some more visitors coming here during this month. I am also very busy now—people for whom I promised to make drawings are so unreasonable as to ask me to fulfil my promises in reasonable time. Amongst others Agnews[11] ask me if I can let them have 2 water colour drawings 24 in × 18 before end of month in time for an exhibition of theirs. The drawings are not begun: so they will not get them yet.

The portrait I shall run down and look at again when opportunity shall serve. It will be all the better for drying and more successful by not being hurried.

I hope the boys are progressing with their cycle management and are well— also Mrs Green and yourself— I thought summer had gone— so it has—to-day is only like an autumn day after all!

(I may add that the work which I am engaged on now requires me to stay here— it is more convenient.)

Kind regards to each.
Yours faithfully,
R. Caldecott
P.S. When can you and Mrs Green get over here? If this month be fine try to give us the pleasure.

The Archery Ball.

173

Broomfield, Frensham, Farnham, Surrey
27 September 1883

My dear Green,

How about your driving over here?

I believe that Mrs Caldecott goes away to keep her sister company at Shanklin for next week: and, if it would be convenient to you and Mrs Green, I might pay you a visit at the latter end of the week with the object of finishing that work of art which reposes in your table drawer, and you would perhaps like to drive over here in my company afterwards. I just mention these projects for your consideration and if you have anything to say for or against, or in modification please say it and I will make my arrangements accordingly.

Hope tricycle and bicycle are well and Mrs Green and yourself.

No more now, except to observe that the equinoctial gales are now on.

Yours,
R. Caldecott

Broomfield, Frensham, Farnham, Surrey
1 October 1883

My dear Green,

Thank you for your note. If it will be convenient to you and Mrs Green, I will be with you on Thursday evening—leaving Charing X at 4 p.m., according to my June Guide. I'll verify it tomorrow in town, whither I go in the afternoon (Tuesday). 24, Holland St., Kensington, drop me a line to, if you please.

A happy new October to you all!

Yours,
R. Caldecott

Broomfield, Frensham, Farnham, Surrey
21 October 1883

My dear Green,

I was and am still very much obliged to you for the cap, which I have been about to acknowledge receipt of every day since it came. I also have an assortment of hats about. One feels that the hat one puts on before breakfast is not suitable for evening, the hat one strolls about the garden in is not what one would venture into the fields with. The ordinary walk along the highway requires a different hat from that in which one would proceed to the town in, church hat differs from riding hat, &c, &c. Eh?

As you are so kind I will confess at once that the length of my lower leg from the tendon below the knee to the ground when my boot is on is $18\frac{1}{2}$ inches.

below the knee to the ground with when my boot is on is $18\frac{1}{2}$ inches   This is nearly

This is nearly as good a leg as you drew; but it is not like mine—mine is more symmetrical—thus

it is not like mine — mine is more symmetrical — thus

Marian thanks you

Marian thanks you for the present of the ring-rest which you kindly made for her and encloses kind regards for each of you.

I had a very pleasant time on my last visit to Thornfield (as heretofore) and have to thank you and Mrs Green for your kindness in very many ways.

Those were very enjoyable drives which we had.

[The rest of this letter is missing]

[164]
Broomfield, Frensham, Farnham, Surrey
30 October 1883

My dear Green,

I have considered the subject of the gate. For myself—I should have it painted either creamy white (a warm white—not a pinky white, tho') or oak colour (not necessarily grained). I think white always looks neat and tidy (if cleaned or renewed at proper times, of course; just as a white shirt always looks neat and tidy when it does not happen to have been worn an improperly long time). White can be best seen at night—which I think an advantage. When driving home at dark it is pleasant to be able to be sure that the gate is open or shut as you dash madly at the house. The iron parts being black would connect, as it were, the iron fencing with it—I should think.

I should not have any of these 'aesthetic'[12] tints or shades—they seldom look well with bushes and trees. Oak colour, or pale buff would go all right. A crude green is not suitable to that construction of gate (and, as I have hinted, fancy greens don't go with foliage).

I offer these opinions—as you ask me—but do not be bound by them, if you have any notions.

We hope you are all well and send kind regards to each.

Yours faithfully,

R. Caldecott

[165]
Broomfield, Frensham, Farnham, Surrey
6 November 1883

My dear Green,

Thanks! At first Smiths[13] said they would not take *Jackanapes* in *paper* covers. Then they said they would not put "anything" more of the kind—coloured boards or otherwise—on their stalls until Xmas. They were "glutted".

Other booksellers asked for "coloured boards".

Here they are asking—nay, imploring for tinted boards!

The 2,000 first printed and bound in *paper* all sold off in fortnight or so—and the publishers—Society P.C.K.—ordered 500 more copies from E. Evans. Meanwhile, tinted boards were being prepared for rest of 10,000 edition, printed; but unbound.

Cost of new cover (same designs) borne by author, engraver and printer, and *me*. Oh ho! It should be out now!

Framemaker was to have told me when frame ready. I wrote to him yesterday and told [him] to send it to you, as it *must* be ready. I hope he is not ill and workless—I want 2 small frames ready in fortnight exactly.

Mass of correspondence to-day: so pardon rapid note.

Best regards to each. Hope all are well.

Yours,

R. Caldecott

[166]

Broomfield, Frensham, Farnham, Surrey

20 November 1883

My dear Green,

Pray do not trouble much about the shirt. We shall be at Chelsfield at Xmas and it might find us then and there.

I am glad to hear what you say about the portrait—it will be much improved when varnished further on in its life.

As you insist on it—I must tell you that fifty guineas including frame, or nothing, is the price that I should have. It is many years since I painted a portrait for five and twenty.

I shall be in town on Thursday and Friday and Saturday morning— taking up work lately done.

Hounds ran a fox to ground in one of our woods opposite house yesterday afternoon in our absence.

Stormy to-day—I hope Mrs Green is not yet depressed by severity of our climate—and that all of you are well.

Kind regards to each. My wife went to town this morning.

Yours,

R. Caldecott

[167]

Broomfield, Frensham, Farnham, Surrey

5 December 1883

My dear Green,

Surely I seem long in answering your note of 26th alto. As to *Julia*[14]— I had intended giving you an idea of what I should charge for a picture of her before I let you consider yourself committed to the purchase: but I do not want any such committal—I will paint her when opportunity shall serve and give you the offer of her. For a picture 10 to 12 inches high I should ask you 30 guineas. There is only one figure in it—so I could do it for that. But you should not have the picture unless you swore solemnly that you liked it when done. And if this sum seems too much *now* you will say so, I expect.

I think you had a fancy for a shade of yellow as a dress. If I make a yellow dress I must give her dark hair—which is not in the wood-cut.

Much obliged when leg-rest reaches me. We hope all are well and happy. Cold weather coming now. What do *you* think about rosy sunsets, golden sunrises, &c?

Our kind regards to each.

Yours,

R. Caldecott

[168]
24 Holland Street, Kensington, W
19 June 1884

My dear Green,

You are very kind; but—I am sorry to say—it is quite impossible for us to accept your invitation—pleasant though the prospect you open out may be. I am very busy with some little book drawings[15] and if I delay them authors and engravers and publishers will be wild as hares (we have also 2 or 3 engagements in town next week). I hope that you and Mrs Green do not think me ungracious or unappreciative when we point out difficulties in the way of accepting your friendly invitations. You perhaps do not remember that I cannot leave anybody in charge of my business and that I can never recover the loss of time if I miss a morning's work—I cannot do as many can —i.e. make up for it by longer days afterwards. Positively I cannot afford to accept many invitations and we are therefore obliged to decline nearly all. I am engaged in business more closely than most professional men because they can arrange for a holiday free from business cares—I can only take as much holiday as is needful for health and this I do by bits of each day and by an occasional whole day.

I have lost time lately by being somewhat "unfit". A visit to my father-in-law's at Whitsuntide did not agree with me. On our return here we started off to Littlehampton and Ryde—the former a failure in itself—the latter not pleasant because of very cold winds and some rain and storms. Soon came back. *Now* I *cannot* go away from home—fit or unfit!

We are going to make hay this year, about 11 acres—and shall be at Broomfield during the time it is down—beginning about end of month, 29th or 30th. I must be off and on again here afterwards.

Of course I shall be happy to pay you a little visit soon as possible and some time when convenient to you and Mrs Green in order to varnish and touch up the portrait. Pray do not think I do not like visiting in the pleasant way you do it for us. Our kind regards and thanks to each and all of you. Let me know when you can do the drive to Broomfield. I think August will be best.

Yours,

R. Caldecott

P.S. Pardon rapid letter!

Weylands, Cromer[16]
6 August 1884

My dear Green,

We are paying the visit of which I spake to you when I last saw you—
we were to have come here last year; but scarlet-fever broke out and our
friends left the place earlier than usual. On Saturday we go for a short visit
to my brother's near Cambridge, Horningsea Vicarage—to bless him and
his wife before they go to Barbados early in September. He is to be the
principal of the Codrington College in that island. We shall leave Cambridge
Tuesday or Wednesday next—Tuesday, probably—12th.

I was about to propose to you—before your welcome note of 3rd reached
me—that next week would be a very fine and convenient time for me to run
down to your house and drive with you to Frensham. Mrs C. goes through
to Broomfield: but I shall probably stay a day in town—but if I did not and
went down to you on Tuesday evening I fear there would not be time if you
must be at home on the 15th.

Write and tell me if you think the thing can be managed after you read
this note.

Jolly warm here. Glad you had two pleasant drives—that returning home
at night is all very beneficial—proper food, sympathetic faces—but the
railway [journey] each morning to the carriage is not the correct thing
about a driving tour. That getting-up in strange villages—unless the
accommodation is very bad—is a pleasant sensation on a fine fresh morning.
And the start to drive at an early hour is best thing in fine summer weather.
Sorry to hear that you have been sometimes seedy—quite right and hearty
now, I hope. Our kind regards to each of you. Mrs Green must be revelling
in this warm temperature.
Believe me
Yours,
R. Caldecott

[170]
Broomfield, Frensham, Farnham, Surrey
18 August 1884

My dear Green,

That's it—please start as you say—24th, 25th or 26th—the 24th would
suit me the best—if I am to return with you—(which is part of the programme—the pleasant part to me—that and the entertaining of you here—)
for I must not be longer away from home than I can help—owing to the
departure of my brother and wife for Barbados College. We shall see them
off at Southampton 2nd Sept. and—at present—I am uncertain about the
days of seeing him before then.

Please let me know further particulars as soon as you can when you decide about them, and believe me
Yours in haste—with kind regards all round—
R. Caldecott

[171]
Broomfield, Frensham, Farnham, Surrey
22 August 1884

My dear Green,
As you ask me, I would advise you to come by way of Hog's Back and Farnham Town. That will be a very easy way to find. We are about 4 miles from Farnham. When you get about or nearly 2½ miles on the road from Farnham you will find at the bottom of a hill (a longish pleasant descent) a road to the right with a Finger Post "To Frensham Vale"—Go along there *to the right* and after a bit bind *to the left* up a steep hill—then enquire at cottages (but straightest way forwards is the one).
As you will not care about mid-day travelling perhaps, we will expect you about 6 o'clock—the journey will take you about 2½ hours at outside—as the weather is warm. Less probably. Much less in cool weather. Then after a cup of tea—if agreeable—we may take a little drive from here—if you get here at 6—and return to dinner refreshed and hopeful—or do not arrive until later, if you prefer the cooler hours. I should propose to start back on Monday morning early and go by way of Godalming to Guildford or somewhere—wait middle of day—and make another journey in evening. But you will let me know what is agreeable to you. Perhaps we might reach Horsham for the night. As you like.
We are disappointed of a visitor and I fear Marian will be alone during my absence.
All right about the boy.
Our kind regards to Mrs Thurburn, who, we hope, is well.
Yours faithfully,
R. Caldecott

[172]
Broomfield, Frensham, Farnham, Surrey
23 September 1885

My dear Green,
The JOY which thrilled me on receipt of your letter was tempered by hearing of Freddy's accident and Mrs Green's headaches. Time, and a *short* time, will cure both, I truly hope. This summer has been a strange one—and an 'upsetting' one to many. I don't wonder at Mrs Green's headaches, and I am inclined to grumble when the E. wind brings on my bosom-aches.

I am sorry you are in such a bad market for house-letting. I suppose you will go away leaving it unlet—if nobody will take it. Our landlady wants to let her house at back here—top of hill—£350 a year (dropped from £600). Cheap, if it were furnished more comfortably—only one applicant, I believe. Thought she might let it and keep this place as a *pied-à-terre*. As it is, we are not as well off as if a tenant were succeeding us; for, except 2 things, the landlady will 'take to' nought. Nice friendly woman, tho'. Family cracked generally. So a sale—a sale ahoy! is now the shout. We are taking away chief articles of furniture (there are not many in the cottage, in sitting rooms, of course) and the best beds and bedding—other things—unimportant, but will count up—to be sold. Also 15 tons of hay, dog cart, plants, tools, bees, fire assurance policy, packets of old letters, paint-rags, &c, &c. And from the neighbours will probably come to be sold a mare and foal, a Jersey cow, &c. We have fowls to sell—too. A grand day for Frensham!

Do you want any worn-out things? A few old hens, a cane-seated chair or two—caved in? Empty bottles? A lawn-mower that won't work? A toothless rake? Good deep wheelbarrow, suited to habits of progression of a benighted reveller?

We shall be in Holland Street most probably between now and Xmas for much of the time: but our movements in the future are not very closely fixed —not fixed at all, indeed.

I am glad you were amused by *Dog-cart* story. I have been wondering.

My hunting-mare went down to Shropshire yesterday to a friend's stable, for the present. Cob and carriage we shall perhaps drive to Chelsfield next week—stay at Reigate one night.

With our very best regards to Mrs Green and the boys and yourself, I now say adieu!

Yours very truly,

Randolph Caldecott

P.S. Please send a couple of tortoise-shell pigs to put in sale—they'll fetch it up. Parcel post—prepaid.

[173]
24 Holland Street, Kensington, W
26 October 1885

My dear Green,

Quite well? Hope Freddy has got better from accident. How about Rome —and abroad generally?

On Saturday next we leave Liverpool for United States—"Aurania", Cunard line—(leave here Friday 10.30 or 11 a.m.) intending go to New York and down by Philadelphia, Baltimore, Washington, Richmond, Savannah, to Florida—on to New Orleans and California in Spring—by Colorado, &c, to New York and Boston. Home about May or so.

Think it will "do"?

Hope Mrs Green will not be averse to the idea, because we have taken passage.

Yours,

R. Caldecott

1. Mr Tudman was manager of the Whitchurch and Ellesmere Bank when Caldecott was a clerk there.

2. Photographs at this time had to be copied in line by an illustrator before a wood engraving could be made.

3. *Bracebridge Hall.*

4. *Old Christmas.*

5. Letters to William Etches are on pp. 56–72.

6. Tom Taylor, editor of *Punch* and art critic of *The Times*, had appeared in the Whistler *v.* Ruskin libel case. 'All Mr Whistler's works are in the nature of sketching' and the *Nocturne in Black and Gold* was only 'one step nearer to pictures than graduated tints on a wall-paper' were two of his comments at the trial. The acrimonious correspondence in the *World* hinged on Whistler's report of Taylor's criticism of Velasquez. Taylor followed his first complaint with a mock apology, but Whistler's barbs undoubtedly won the exchange.

7. The Greens had recently gone to live at Tunbridge Wells.

8. With his future parents-in-law at Chelsfield.

9. Edwin Lambert, *fl.* (1877–92); primarily a landscape painter.

10. To stay with Frederick and Jane Locker.

11. The fine art dealers who held—and still hold—an annual exhibition of water colour paintings.

12. The Aesthetic Movement, precursor of Art Nouveau, and so well satirized by du Maurier with his family, the Cimabue Browns, was in full swing.

13. W. H. Smith, who had so many railway bookstalls, and whose order, then as now, was critical to the retail success of a book.

14. The 'fair Julia' of *Old Christmas.*

15. He had already made some drawings for *Daddy Darwin's Dovecot* and had more to complete.

16. Caldecott and his wife were staying with Frederick and Jane Locker.

SOPHIE GREEN

1838—1930

The wife of Frederick Green (*see* letters 147–173).

[174]
Hôtel de Gênes, Gênes
10 April 1877

My dear Mrs Green,

As the train went out of Cannes on Friday last I thought I saw a few towels waved from the Villa Rosalie. I may have made a mistake, because I was sitting on the opposite side of the carriage. Anyway, I saw some towels, and I concluded that "good luck" and "good speed" were meant for somebody. If from Villa Rosalie, perhaps for me. So I felt quite comfortable—although sorry to leave—and passed on my way. The waiting at Ventimiglia I was prepared for, but I was not prepared to wait an hour at a young station this side [of] Savona and then to be shoved over a broken bridge on the edge of the rocks one carriage at a time—sea roaring, men calling, torches blazing. An hour and a half late at Genoa. Well, I grew calm over that: but was soon again disturbed by finding that one of the straps of my bag had been bagged on the journey—a fine, broad, strong, healthy strap—removed from under the brass retainer. They told me that it was always so in this country so I cooled again, but I did not feel quite sure about the "good luck" and "good speed".

However, the delight of being in Genoa was something. At first it looked busy and dirty, and the people ugly—but it improves in these respects. Looking back on a long and wandering life I can say that this is the noisiest place to sleep in I ever knew. The hawkers yell in the streets, midnight revellers bawl and scream, late arrivals and stay-outers bang heavy doors and shout along the echoing passages, cats squawk on the roofs, and the people in the next chamber have little 'at-homes' from 12 to 1—midnight— Four people were drinking and conversing loudly last night until 1—and I heard every word, every bubbling of the drink out of the bottle through the thin partition wall which received and carried around the sounds like a drum. I must fly as soon as possible. I have changed my room once.

I have not yet called up on the people at the Villa Spinola who were to help me if necessary—I shall do so tomorrow, and shall then perhaps know when to move eastward. I think I must stay at Rapallo 2 or 3 days at least.

I will write to your brother-in-law so that he may let me know when he is coming this way.

Let me thank you all very much for your kindness and attention during my pleasant sojourn at your house. With kind regards to each.
Believe me
Yours sincerely,
R. Caldecott
P.S. I have just received the enclosed note from the water-colour painter of whom I spake. A fearful chopping below has commenced—preparing mince-meat for seven thousand persons, I think. I rush away. R.C.

[175]
Hôtel d'Europe, Rapallo, Italy
Sunday, 15 April 1877

Hôtel d'Europe.
Rapallo, Italy.

My dear Mrs Green,
I have 2 letters to thank you for. The 2nd reached me this evening.

I am so glad to find I have a sympathizer with me in my misfortunes. The rows were bad enough before, they increased after I wrote to you in such complaining strains. As if the native hubbub was not enough, somebody imported a few paroquets who shrieked and shriked right into my window. I could have stabbed a nightingale. I was glad when 2 nightingales died that were imprisoned in a cage. I was reduced to such a sad, wretched, low condition that I smiled grimly as I saw the public funeral of a musician on Saturday morning. I began to state my woes in poetry, commencing— "Midst pezzotti and palaces though I may roam" &c. (The 'pezzotto' is a muslin scarf or shawl worn by many of the Genoese women—thus

The *ladies* let them fall easily as they like; the *commoner people* bring their arms outside them; but the ladies—mostly—only wear them in summer. These are not good representations, perhaps I shall shew you better.)

Let me return to my griefs. How I did rush at the train to Rapallo! How afraid to be late!

Directly I received Mr Walter Green's telegram I fixed the time of my departure from Genoa; and I had a private garden to visit, and an invitation for Sunday.

I heard that the *Graphic* people were not publishing my valuable contributions[1] in due continuation: but I asked them to send the numbers which would contain my work to your house. The number you have received is between whiles, I suppose. I do not want it, thank you. The letter will no doubt be sent on from the Hôtel de Gênes—they have already sent on one note. I left there yesterday at 4 p.m.

There was an American family there one night: but I've told you enough of my hardships.

This place struck me as quiet. I got so low down at Genoa that I was obliged to go to church—English—this afternoon. I thought for only prayers: but I got the 7th part of a sermon. 6 ladies—less 1 parson's wife = 5 ladies, 1 man and myself—total 7 people. 3 hymns! I was rather sorry for the parson—that was why I patronised him.

I am looking forward to meeting your brother-in-law tomorrow—and I hope to see the rest of you at Villa Rosalie as I return homewards—in accordance with your kind expressions on that subject. I thank you much for your enquiries about my health—better soon—and with kind regards to all. I am yours very sincerely,
R. Caldecott
P.S. I hope you will like Mr Croft's[2] works.

[176]
Hôtel d'Europe, Rapallo
21 April 1877

Dear Mrs Green,

In response to your expression of a wish that I should tell you of my movements, I beg to say that at present I meditate leaving this beautiful bay on Monday or Tuesday next.

The country and the sea are very charming, and the weather has been very moist—during the days of Monday, Tuesday, Wednesday and Thursday —with a slight sprinkling of water and a few thunder-growls on Friday.

The weather on Monday evening when Mr Walter Green arrived was sympathetically reproduced on Tuesday and affected him into leaving at midday for Florence. He thought it good weather for travelling. We had intended to go to Porto Fino—a fishing village at the point—a spot which I particularly wished to survey.

Not until to-day could I manage it. To-day I, accompanied by a young man who is staying here, went thither in a small boat. We had a very pleasant ride, a slight breeze, and plenty of sun.

I wish to be in London in about a week's time. So I think of leaving here on Monday evening and sleeping at Genoa—Hôtel de Londres this time—and by the only attempt at a swift train on Tuesday—7 something a.m.—going on to Cannes 3 something. There I shall call, and if you can put me up at the Villa Rosalie, as hospitably suggested, I shall be very happy to wait until next day, and then continue my journey to Paris, where I hope to have a day or two.

I give you no time to reply: but I shall stay at Cannes in any case. With kind regards to family circle,
Believe me
Yours sincerely,
R. Caldecott

[177]
46 Great Russell Street, London WC
4 May 1877

46, Gt. Russell St,
London. W.C.

4 May 1877

My dear Mrs Green,

I reached Paris very comfortably after my agreeable rest at the Villa Rosalie, and there I found your note dated 20 April, sent from Rapallo, where it had arrived after my departure. In the note you said that your husband was unwell at the time of writing. So you see that until I reached Cannes I did not know of his ill-health. I hope he is all right now or anyway is rapidly moving in that direction. One cannot expect, much as one may hope for, miraculously rapid recoveries. Perhaps the bracing air of Old England will finish the cure. I cannot say *balmy* air to encourage you now you contemplate coming over. It was very cold when I arrived, and is rather worse to-day: and the sun seems gone and a shadow to have fallen

187

over the earth. It suits me though, I think, but I cannot help thinking also that the bright skies and sunshine of your part of France suited me when I was there. I hope you will find gayer weather when you arrive—otherwise you will be confirmed in your opinions of this atrocious climate.

I stayed in Paris until Monday. Since then I have been preparing for the summer campaign, and shall soon be in the midst of the busy rush after wealth and glory.

With kind regards to all, and many thanks for your kindness and attention to me,

Believe me
Sincerely yours,
R. Caldecott

[178]
6 Via de' Servi, Florence
17 December 1881

Dear Mrs Green,

I am glad to hear from you, although you do not say you are enjoying the English winter—which must always be a burden to you. The little books[3] I could not send to the boys before I left because they were not ready—I hope you all really like them. I am now—amongst other things—engaged on—or rather about to begin—some more for next year. These—this year's—were in the engraver's and printer's hands rather too late and suffered in consequence. Better done [with] more care next time, I hope.

Yes, we know a few people here—there were several of our acquaintance in Florence when we arrived, and since then we seem to add others each day to the list. Some of them are quite bearable—1 or 2 approach the "interesting", and about 3 are "nice". I am sorry that the Marchesa Ricci is not here. A few artists I am knowing in addition to 2 or 3 that I knew formerly.

Mrs Caldecott thinks that there are too many ladies and not enough gentlemen amongst the little crowds whom we meet. I admit that the view before my eyes is somewhat too often obstructed by the same grey-fronted, ribbon-surmounted countenances; but I have no time to seek for the bright, intelligent, sparkling rays that are emitted by hopeful young eyes. Oh dear No!

We are pretty comfortable. We left a sort of pension—where were 2 girls known in the 7oaks district. A large, clean, "respectable" house it was —some fossilised dames were located there. Here we have rooms: a bed chamber, a dining room, a study, a salon and a dressing room, with windows facing south west, and have food and service provided for us in a very convenient way. An Italian's house—Brazilian vice-consul—an English wife. (How the hawkers and street vendors of goods do shout!)

We are very pleased to hear of the continuation of Mr Barlow's instructive career. This age is becoming too trifling and frivolous—so something serious is to be huzzed. My brother—from Cambridge—comes for Xmas here. He is solid. Our very best wishes to you all for a jovial season— Pudding and Turkey to the boys: but let them be careful—as they value their future happiness.

With kind regards from both of us, believe me

Yours faithfully,

Randolph Caldecott

P.S. My compliments and good wishes for the social season to Mrs Thurburn. R.C.

1. The *Letters from Monaco*, which appeared irregularly in the *Graphic* during March, April and May 1877.

2. John Croft *fl.* (1868–73), water-colourist; exhibited at the Royal Academy and Suffolk Street Gallery.

3. *The Queen of Hearts* and *The Farmer's Boy*.

KATE GREENAWAY

1846–1901

Miss Greenaway came under the influence of Edmund Evans about the same time as Caldecott, and her first book which Evans engraved and printed was *Under the Window*, which appeared in 1879. It was an immediate success and each year until the end of the century saw the publication of one or two children's books with her illustrations, and often her text. Evans suggested that she and Caldecott should co-operate on a book (she had already done so successfully with Walter Crane, another Evans protégé) but the project was not completed.

[179]
46 Great Russell Street, Bloomsbury
30 September 1878

Dear Miss Greenaway,

The 2 children of whom I spoke were recommended to me by a Mr Robertson, of 6 Britten Street, Chelsea, himself a model. One is a 'saxon boy' of 6 years old—called A. Frost; the other is a 'vivacious girl of an auburn colour' entitled Minnie Frost.

I do not know anything of Mr Robertson either as a professional model or a private gentleman. He called on me twice for a few minutes at each time.

The brown ink of which I discoursed will not, when thickly used with a pen, keep itself entirely together under the overwhelming influence of a brush with water colour. I have found this out to-day. But the liquid Indian ink used for lines will stand any number of damp assaults. This I know from much experience.

Believe me,

Yours very truly,

R. Caldecott

P.S. I hope the above information may be of use to you.

JOHN HARRISON

[180]
Wirswall, Whitchurch, Salop
23 June 1864

My dear John,

The intention of this note is to tell you that you must come to the "Ladies' Club" next Wednesday and that you are to sleep here, as Mr and Mrs Brown[1] will be very happy to see you.

To make your visit as pleasant as possible Mrs Brown intended to write to the Misses Bolshaw and invite them also, but she believes that Miss Sarah Nunnerley has already done so. In addition to this, Mrs Brown *has* invited Miss Davies, so you see that your best wishes have been consulted.

You will doubtless in this perceive some of my usual solicitude for your comfort, and my customary neglect of anything which may tend to promote delight in myself. Of course your turnips have been up a long time.

Mrs Brown sends her love to Mrs Harrison, who I sincerely hope is very well, and says that she will come over and see her when Mrs B. Senior arrives, and she is expected shortly.

Trusting that you have that calmness of mind which belongs to a clear conscience (it's doubtful) I remain for ever and ever amen,
Yours very faithfully,
Randolph Caldecott
P.S. Excuse my haste

[181]
Wirswall, Whitchurch, Salop
16 February 1865

My dear John,

You requested me to write to you about things in general as often as time

My dear John, You requested me to write to you about things in general as

permitted me. I take advantage of a few spare moments snatched from the many hours required by this world's vanities and humbugs to make glad my soul within by thus sending you a few lines—few, because little or nothing of interest has lately happened for me to record; and few, because though my thoughts and wishes are many yet my pen fails to commit them to paper.

In the first place let me say a few words upon the Whitchurch Ball. I enjoyed myself very amazingly, and so, I believe, did all who were present. Though there were not so many as might have attended, yet we passed a very pleasant, delightful, cheerful, jolly evening—still, had your presence lent its enlivening glow to the festivities our cup of pleasure would have been even fuller.

Secondly, I must speak of what everybody does when there is nothing else to say. The weather. Our salubrious climate by it variableness gives to all they who—not unfortunately—lack very powerful conversational ability an ever new and interesting subject upon which to discourse and contemplate. How nice to interchange ideas thus: "Cold!"—"Yes."—"Almost as cold as yesterday."—"Yes, and if it is as cold tomorrow as it was yesterday it will be almost as cold as to-day."—"It will indeed."—"Our glass is rising."—"So is ours."—"But it will come down again when it can't get any higher." "You're right, it will."—"Good morning, cold isn't it?"—"Very, good morning." How improving to both parties is a conversation like the above!

Talking about improvement reminds me to ask you if you have succeeded yet in bringing within the pale of civilization the inhabitants of the land in which you now sojourn?

I'm getting awfully tired of winter with its cold winds, and I shall hail the advent of spring with a joy unspeakable. Naturally belonging to the class of human beings denominated "lazy", I can't bear having to move about fast to keep warm. I like "to lay all work aside and stretch me in the sun and dream, &c," as one of the later poets saith.

I hope that Mrs Harrison is well, also Mr John Hassall, to both of whom make my most cordial regards and my most reverent respects.
I remain, my dear John,
Yours for ever,
R. Caldecott

[182]
Whitchurch, Salop
13 June 1865

My dear Jack,
Hope you are salubrious, and that this weather agrees with you. Your brother to Blair Athol: can't do it, can he? Tain't all in blood, you see.
You never drop a fellow a line just to say you are in the land of the living; but you always were "very forgetful", in fact the most forgetful of the forgetfulest.
I want to tell you to be sure to go to Beeston on Monday next, as it is

very possible that I may put in an appearance, which of course ought to be an inducement for all the country to go.

You might have told one that you were going to be married so soon; I never heard a word about it until the other day. Well, I wish you health, wealth and prosperity; long life to enjoy your wife; squads of young 'uns to cheer your hearth; and everything that will tend to your comfort.

Give my love to Mrs Harrison and Mr Hassall, and say that as soon as the bothering building is finished I am coming over.

Times are very bad in this quarter of the world, although since you left we are not so random.

McGregor has made your old quarters look very different.

Shows what a man can do!

Goodbye,

Yours forever,

R. Caldecott

[183]
Manchester and Salford Bank, Manchester
2 June 1868

{ arrival of W. Slimpkins } { for the week-end. }

Dear John,

I have talked about coming to see you—you asked me, if you remember —and so I intend to be down upon you next Saturday week, 13 June; and our mutual friends Mr Brown and Tom Nunnerley intend paying you a visit at the same time. So kill the fatted calf about Friday week, and you may as well tap that 18 gallon cask in the far corner—if it will not be enough we can make out with the remnant of that '47 port. The weather will be warm so let everything be very cool and comfortable, for I like to travel at my ease. The gooseberries will be sour so you need not be afraid that I shall make much havoc with the fruit.

I think you may drop me a line to say that you are aware of our purpose and that it will suit you too, and Mrs Harrison also. If it does not, tell me at once, so that I may get over the disappointment.

Upon hearing from you I will again commune with our Wirswall friends.

I hope you are all well and with love to Mrs Harrison and Mr Hassall.
I am, dear John,
Ever yours,
Randolph Caldecott

[184]
46 Great Russell Street, London WC
27 August 1873

My dear John,

Looking calmly round in search of some becoming toast to drink my last evening draught to—a regular custom of mine—my thoughts flew to you. I immediately drained the flowing bowl to your health and then the spirit said "Write unto him!" And so I write.

My dear old boy, how are you? Forgive me for not answering your last

195

note earlier; but I have been rambling about of late[2] and could tell thee things that would 'part thy matted locks and make each individual hair to stand on end'.

[Part of this letter is missing]

They [the Germans] enjoy eating and drinking out of doors to a good band of music and clouds of tobacco smoke. The evenings are not damp and the beer is very enjoyable.

It seems a long time since I saw you, John. I suppose you are hammering and digging away at the Church House Farm. I hope it goes on well. My pursuits have changed, perhaps you know.

I am now engaged in instructing the minds and elevating the tastes of the generous and discriminating public—not only the British Public, but the public of the United States of America.[3] I met some delightful Americans at Vienna, and have promised to call upon several. One young fellow from Kentucky I shall go and see for a week-end. I will look in at you on the way.

You know how devoted I was to business when I was a quill-driver; well, now I am still more devoted, and hope by a strict attention to business and by still supplying the best article at the lowest price to merit a continuance of the favours which the nobility, clergy, &c.

It is too much—family, this is too much!—to expect you to write: but I hope you will do so, if it is only three words to say that you can't forget me if you would, you won't forget me if you could, &c, &c.

I trust that Mrs Harrison and yourself, and Mr and Mrs Faulkner and family are all well, and with kind regards to each, remain
Yours faithfully,
Randolph Caldecott

1. Caldecott lived with Mr and Mrs Brown at Wirswall while he worked at Whitchurch.
2. He had been to the International Exhibition at Vienna with Henry Blackburn.
3. Caldecott was now 'London Artistic Correspondent' for the New York *Daily Graphic*.

THE SECRETARY OF THE HOGARTH CLUB

For some twenty years the Hogarth Club was one of the most important London clubs for artists, with facilities for exhibiting the work of its members, among whom were Rossetti, Burne-Jones, Frederick Leighton and Ford Madox Brown.

[185]
46 Great Russell Street, WC
6 November 1874

Dear Sir,
    At the close of this year please withdraw my name from the list of members of the Hogarth Club, and thereby oblige
Yours very truly,
R. Caldecott

To T. Gray Esq.,
Secretary to Hogarth Club,
84 Charlotte St., Fitzroy Square, W.

MRS JONES

A widow with a large family who lived at Audlem, Staffordshire. There are also letters from Caldecott to her daughter, Emily, on pp. 201–5.

[186]
46 Great Russell Street, Bloomsbury, London WC
25 November 1872

My dear Mrs Jones,

I thank you very much for sending me the letters from the "South Australians" to read, and I now return them to you. I am glad to read that Mrs Middleton (I suppose now it is so) was not very ill on the voyage. I presume it would be improbable that she should be ill after having got so far on the way. There is something pleasant in reading of the concerts, but not so of the

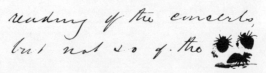

(N.B. I never saw one of these lively beings: you will, however, perhaps see what I mean and dare not name.) I would have applauded most lustily.

On the idea that Mr and Mrs Middleton are residing happily at Emu Plains, I wrote a letter to Mrs M. and posted it in the beginning of last week.

198

Although I am not in Australia, yet I have not been to Bowdon for a long while: but I know I can rush there in a few hours—barring railway accidents.

Since I saw you I have been wandering in many lands,[1] and have had many adventures—on mountains, down mines, in secluded vales, and in crowded towns. Once (here I must whisper and impose secrecy), once I was with an English literary man (with whom and his wife I travelled to many places), well, once I was with him as the evening closed in slowly on the ancient town of Blankenburg, and we walked cautiously along the streets of that usually quiet little place. A fair was being held, many persons were assembled, numberless cake stalls obtruded their wares on our foreign tastes, thousands of toys stared at us, loads of apparel invited us. Sometimes we bought, but on we went and at length we were opposite to a strange mechanical contrivance. We disbursed coin of the realm, we ascended from the ground, we sat aloft in security, strains of soul-stirring music thrilled through our very bones, with no power of our own we began to move, we went faster, faster, and faster. We clove the air, we whirled round and round. We were galloping on wooden hobby-horses!

So no more at present—with the exception of my kind regards to yourself and family—from
Yours faithfully,
Randolph Caldecott

[187]
46 Great Russell Street, London WC
14 October 1873

My dear Mrs Jones,

You kindly asked me to call again when last you spoke—so I just look in for a few minutes. It's getting late in the evening, as usual; but I have been so much occupied, or, as the Frenchman said, I have been a Cupid. The weather is colder. I think so: but your wonderful pen and ink delineations of circus people betray too great a knowledge of those sinful and benighted wanderers. The gentleman in a light suit at the top of this letter now fills the part which I have thrown up after an unprecedented run of popular favour. Clowns are very sad men, and I am sad sometimes. The wickedness and frivolity which surround me are fruitful themes for the philosophic pen and the cogitative ink.

I hope that your family circle has each of its links well oiled—I mean—I hope that you are all very well. Also the Middletons of Emu Plains. I am about to write to that land by the next mail.

Give my kind regards to each.

Good night! Here and there.

I am, my dear Mrs Jones,

Yours faithfully,

Randolph Caldecott

1. Caldecott had been to Saxony-Anhalt with Henry Blackburn and his wife, gathering material for *The Harz Mountains, a Tour of the Toy Country*, which Blackburn wrote and Caldecott illustrated.

MISS EMILY JONES

The eighteen-year-old daughter of Mrs Jones (*see* letters 186–7).

[188]
46 Great Russell Street, Bloomsbury, London WC
9 August 1872

My dear Miss Emily,

I suppose that no apology is necessary because of my writing to thank you for your delightful letter and for enclosing Mr Barton's note—for which I write to thank him.

I am sorry to hear that Mrs Jones is unwell. Let us hope she will soon be restored to us in all the bloom of her usual health and spirits!

Most people are selfish—everybody more or less. Now I belong to the "less" party, and therefore I was not annoyed because you had put such a vague address on *your* envelope—*mine* now, carefully put away with other treasures amongst the lavender, bad sixpences, camphor, and spare teeth—I say, I was not annoyed; for the letter was opened by an apparently respectable man who rejoices in the same surname as myself, and who has been located in this street for a good part of the present century. Of course he is entitled to all letters insufficiently directed. There are very few of the name in London: but he is the chief of the name in Bloomsbury—at present. After he had derived as much pleasure and profit from its perusal as possible—in his wonder and joy he had encompassed an extra cup of tea at breakfast—he naturally thought (good easy man) that I might benefit by reading it—the letter. So he sent it to me during the morning and I afterwards called to thank him. He urbanely answered "Don't name it!" He is no relative, though doubtless of the same noble family originally. Here is his portrait.

I should like to have seen the interesting sketch which Mr Danegagian has perpetrated.

You say that part of the family is away and you feel lonely. A little loneliness is beneficial. It enables the mind to look into its store closet and see how the preserves are. Perhaps there are none. Then some must be made. If there be a good supply they are possibly getting mouldy. They must be used.

As I get more into the sere and yellow leaf I feel the old propensity for jam returning. Second childishness at hand, you think.

Well, "I wish I were a child again, with a child's truth and trust. Unsoiled by life's degrading stain, and time's relentless rust."

Better to have under one's nose the orange dust of the stamens of the large garden lily which childhood smelt in sunny hours than to have on one's moustache the unwiped streak of orange marmalade which remaineth over and above after the last bite of the well-spread bread. N.B. I am at supper.

I commence to travel in other lands next week. If I never return and Bowdon knoweth me again no more, may I beg of you, as the first of April comes round in each year's successive twirl, to find out if the moon be visible. If it be, then drop a sympathetic tear to my memory on the nearest reliable person's shoulder.

Don't think I am insane. I am trying to be merry. Ha! Ha! I will now leave the subject of myself.

To whom can I fly, though? I can fly to Bowdon in spirit: but that suffices not.

Well, I hope all are well except Mrs Jones—I don't mean that I hope she is ill but that all the others, about whose health you whispered not a word, are doing nicely.

So now I will say "Goodbye" —merely temporarily—and request all to receive my affectionate regards.

I am, my dear Miss Emily,
Your shattered friend,
Randolph Caldecott

Sketch in Germany - taken
at the end of August 1872.

46 Great Russell Street, Bloomsbury, London WC
13 January 1873

Home again.

Dear Miss Emily,

Your letter produced an astounding conglomeration of joy, regret, and delight. I look forward towards the day when I shall be allowed to read and gaze at the journal which you so kindly and thoughtfully intend to send to me. If you delay sending it very long the weight thereof will be greatly increased by the minute, but multitudinous, atoms of foreign matter which adhere to objects much handed about and fondly thumbed.

I am very glad to hear that the voyagers arrived safely, and to hear that your sister wrote cheerfully. I congratulate Mr Middleton on having received so excellent a helpmeet, and the colony on gaining such a valuable addition to its Christian circles.

I understand and sympathize with your emotion in chapel when the wedding was announced.

Your letter I received a few days after its date, for I was staying in Shropshire when it reached me.

I have been stalking about amongst some old friends, who have been, and are, very kind and hospitable—so much so that I could hardly tear myself away—I did so at last on Thursday, without leaving a piece of the flesh behind. Indeed, so hard from repeated pummels has my heart become, that a needle and thread are of no use to it—nothing less than a tenpenny nail will fix anything there. This, however, by the way.

I can fully understand Miss Louie's disappointment at not seeing—ahem!—me. Perhaps she is recovering a little as the days grow longer. By the time when the sylvan anemone shakes the coming spring's morning dewdrop from his eyelid, and the wild hyacinth is thinking of wagging his bells at the breakfasting rabbit, probably the spirit of Miss Louie will be somewhat composed. Let us unite in hoping so.

Please to tell your sister Louisa that for several days I have been wondering what it was that made me feel as though I had been disappointed, or had forgotten something, or had left undone some of those things which I ought to have done. Suddenly, at breakfast yesterday morning, the muscles of my arm became rigid, the toast arrested on its road to destruction was poised in mid air, the sugar in the cocoa-cup gave over melting, and the bacon fat ceased from freezing, for a remembrance of what had not happened passed through my brain. I had not heard the singing of a plaintive ballad to which I had been looking forward for many years—I mean months!

With kind regards to your Mama, Miss Louisa, Miss Isabella, Miss Florence, and Messieurs Arthur and Charles, and a happy new year and many of 'em to all.

I remain,

Dear Miss Emily,

Yours faithfully,

Randolph Caldecott

MR LANG

A much older clerk at the Manchester and Salford Bank's head office, who was one of Caldecott's closest friends when he was a bank clerk.

[190]
Hinton's Royal Spa Hotel!!!, Shanklin, Isle of Wight
5 October 1875

My dear Lang,

How are you? I've not forgotten you, old man; and I've been reminded of you more particularly by the gentle Clough, in a letter of his'n which I *read* on Saturday last only. The Lord knows when it was *written*, for I don't —except so far as the knowledge that he was not sober at the time goes. I always noticed something in his manner which rather puzzled me: at last I suspected: now my worst suspicions are confirmed. Howsomedever, I prefer a free-drinker and a union-of-souls-sort-of-chap to a miser or a cold-blooded cove. Give me the hellion rather than the cold-arsed angel.

Clough—poor fellow—said that you and he contemplated tramping in Derbyshire or somewhere. Perhaps you have done so—perhaps you are at it now. I hope you have been, or are, happy.

I, poor devil, left London—being filled with the migratory spirit—at the beginning of September, and since then have journeyed in many lands. I have sojourned at Zermatt. I have walked over a snow-covered glacier, 11,000 feet, into Italy, down a fine narrow valley for many miles to the plain of Piedmont—down the Val Tournanche—been to Turin, to Milan, to Como, to the Villa d'Este (and saw a young Gaddum[1]—to whom I was introduced— win two or 3 races at a regatta, one a canoe race in which the competitors had to upset during the race), to Bellaggio, to Lecco (in a rowing boat on a fine Sabbath morning), to Verona—a fine town which I shall revisit, to Venice (9 days)—which I shall revisit, to Chioggia—down the lagoon in the Adriatic, where I missed the steamer and had a fine voyage back in an open boat with rough weather and darkness. I myself got a crew of 4 men who rowed and put up the sails when practicable—the wind being strong against us—and landed in pouring rain and driving wind on the quay before the Ducal Palace at Venice at 10 o'clock p.m.

I returned to London on Saturday last and came here on Monday. I have a drawing of a mermaid to do and a bas-relief of some gulls to model and a frieze of gulls, &c, &c to paint—so here I study. I shall be in London for a week or so again from next Sunday. It's hard work this moving about.

N.B. This is a *most* comfortable hotel, the landlord and staff are personally attentive, the food very good indeed. I and my sister are staying here.

Regards to all and Clough and Dutch,
Yours faithfully,
R. Caldecott
P.S. This is all about myself, tell me about yourself.

1. One of a well-known Cheshire family, a more recent member of which was Sir John Gaddum (1900–1965), the most outstanding British pharmacologist of his time.

JOHN LENNOX

[191]
Aberdeen Street, Thorncliffe Grove, Manchester
27 September 1868

My dear John,

    I feel that I ought to write to you: but I don't know what to say, except that I am very thankful to you and other kind friends who so nobly and, shall I say, disinterestedly provided me with the means and opportunities of enjoying myself, which I did indeed. You have laid up for yourself treasure where neither moth nor rust doth corrupt—namely in my grateful bosom and diary, where I have put down what things did happen unto me during my sojourn of fourteen days or thereabouts in Shropshire and Cheshire.

    At the heading (N.B. a goat) of this letter you will see two heads. Pray don't misconstrue their meaning. I was not disgusted with the way in which my holidays had passed; but with the thought that they were over, and that I, who am not naturally formed for work, should be again toiling for my daily bread. A thought occurs to me here—what the deuce are we all working and sweating for? Why give ourselves so much unnecessary trouble about "little things"? What more do we require besides health, food and clothing?

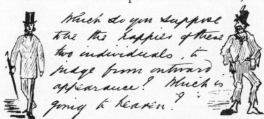

    Which do you suppose to be the happier of these two individuals, to judge from outward appearance? Which is going to heaven?

    To change from the gay to the sublime—I went last Tuesday night to see the Haymarket Company give the "Contested Election".[1] Bucky (an endearing name for Buckstone)[2] was very fine and so was Compton.[3] This latter, by a peculiar dry manner, is quite a favourite with the Manchester

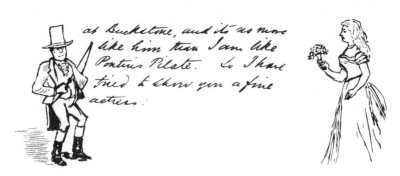

public. I wish I could portray either of them. Here's an attempt at Buckstone, and it's no more like him than I am like Pontius Pilate. So I have tried to show you a fine actress; but, as this is also a failure, I shall not tell you her name. You had better come over to see this company—they will be here all this week.

I suppose you will receive a "Will o' the Wisp"[4] this week. As I know at present, there will only be one sketch by me—the rest of the space being this month devoted to a new artist, who I dare say will eclipse me. And then, Randolph, farewell! a long farewell to all thy greatness.

My modest contribution is a quiet satire upon those ladies who want to vote in the elections for Parliament.

When you next write, address at the bank—I shall leave here shortly— the incoming tenant is going to take my things at a valuation.

Kind regards to Miss Emma and Miss Annie Hill, whom I hope are well. I am, dear John,
Yours very faithfully,
Randolph Caldecott

[192]
Manchester and Salford Bank, Manchester
23 August 1870

My dear John,
Since I wrote to you last I have refused several offers of companionship to one or other spots, and have been feeding my imagination with the delights of a ramble by sea or land in your sweet society. I thought of going by boat

to Penzance in Cornwall, then by boat to London, so to Hull, and on to Aberdeen, and oft repeated to myself "What larks!" This expedition, however, I gave up: and then finally very nearly almost quite settled to go by boat from Liverpool to Glasgow on Saturday evening—3 September—and then spend a week amongst the fine scenery of Caledonia stern and wild—the Trossachs, Loch Tay, the Western Isles, or the Caledonian Canal.

A friend of mine returned on Sunday from Scotland, having gone as above, and I was about to write to you to-day, after hearing his account, and propose a week's trip to Scotland: but your letter to say that you can only spare a week-end has set me on my beam end.

I want to go to Scotland or the Lakes of England to see what I hear so much about, &c, &c, and should like to get out of this hole on the Saturday straight away to some sequestered spot trod only by the British Tourist and paved only with beer-bottles.

I am much obliged to you for your proposal for me to return with you to Buerton: but I must see some more of the world, and if you cannot accompany me for a week even I must tramp on in the calm quiescence of my own solitary thoughts and in the sober enjoyment of my own observations.

Re-think over the matter and write directly. I don't know where we could go for a week-end.

I hope you are all well, and with regards to Miss Nunnerley, remain Yours faithfully, Randolph Caldecott

[193]
46 Great Russell Street, Bloomsbury, London WC
10 April 1872

My dear John,
    I couldn't look you in the face if I were to meet you, and my pen fairly blushes when it thinks how long it is since that truly delightful week-end which I passed at your house —when shall I pass another? —finishing up with an

exhibition of arms—not fire-arms—although they fired one with admiration.

Well, I apologize for not writing sooner—so we'll say no more about it.

How are you? I say, old chap, you will see that I have left the city of Manchester—I had hard work to get away—fellows made little parties to wish one farewell and success.[5]

And as for the ladies—why, that's nothing to do with you.

So I am now a gentleman for a while—such a nice change! I have no news to tell you at present: but hope to hear some from you soon.

This place is opposite to the British Museum, quiet and central.

I accidentally met Dick in Oxford St. this morning—he was going to look how the shops were dressed and thereby earn an honest livelihood by copying them—and I—poor devil—was going to the Park.

Farewell! Regards to Mrs John.

Yours faithfully,

Randolph Caldecott

[194]
46 Great Russell Street, Bloomsbury, London WC
6 April 1873

Dear John,

This is R.C. when he feels as though he was going to "take to drink". (N.B. He very often feels so)

How are you? You ought to feel flattered that in the calm of a Sabbath evening my thoughts fly to you. And yet I don't know, either; for at first they flew to drink. Ah, it's a grand thing to be able to fall back upon when the world is cold and unappreciative, when a fellow looks yearningly for sympathy into the eyes of his countrymen and meets only indifference and contempt. Then is "a bigbellied bottle the cure for all care" as the gay and festive Burns sings.

I hope, John, that when people shall say unto thee "Oh, he drinks all his time", that you will remember the words of the poet

> "Oh! blame not the bard, if he fly to the bowers,
> Where Pleasure lies, carelessly smiling at Fame.
> He was born for much more, and in happier hours
> His soul might have burn'd with a holier flame."[6]

This sentimental strain shows a fine (and probably unsuspected by you) vein of feeling. Struggling in the battle of life has lacerated my tender heart-strings, and now a single bottle brings a tear in one eye and a wink in the other. At such times do I think of my absent friends, and I have now thunk of you.

How the devil are you? Can't you speak? By heaven-smelling Venus, if you don't write soon I will forsake you and bury myself amongst a set of Bacchanalian Bohemians to whose elevating society I may be elected, as I was induced last night to have my name entered in the books as a candidate. I rather liked their appearance.[7]

I am a member of one rather respectable lot of folks: but they are tolerably quiet in their wickedness. This other gang—good men and true though they be—make a horrible row when assembled.

I have been to the Oxford and Cambridge Boat Race once, but I learnt much as to how to go next year, if I am still kicking. I was nearly squashed to death. Never was in such a crowd before. Lots of people got in the water when the tide rose and when the wash of the steamers passed. The race was a very easy thing for the light blue.[8]

I did not do much work visible to the naked eye when I was in the country lately: but I made some notes, and have completed three little hunting pictures in oil since I returned (besides other things), and more of a similar kind are wanted. Yet I think a man ought to live in the country to paint sporting subjects, so when I can afford it (!) I shall take a nice little box in some retired neighbourhood and pay it frequent visits. How jolly it will be!

That you are all well is my hope, and with kind regards to Mrs John and Mary, I remain, dear John,
Yours faithfully,
Randolph Caldecott

[195]
46 Great Russell Street,
London WC
21 September 1873

Dear John,

I remember receiving a letter from you a little while ago. I forget most of what you said, but I know that it was very good. I believe that I larfed a few. Choose how, there was some kind offer of hospitality renewed. I only wish that I could pay you a visit now, and pursue the W.P. through the T.T. or track the S.P. to his F.L. My soul now rambles—night though it be— over the breezy fields of Buerton. However, I cannot at present give you notice of my anticipated descent, for I am very busy—not accumulating wealth, Oh John, but wearing my life away in the pursuit of fame and fortune. Gaze on this, shed a tear, and take another egg.

I've four powerful blisters on my right hand now—Pheugh! Why talk of this. Work all day and dine with choice spirits at a secluded French restaurant, where conversation on all known and unknown subjects may be joined in, any language spoken, choice anecdotes retailed, and the landlord's daughter carefully winked at. No more of that, Lennox.

I like German officers, and have found them polite and accomplished men. The South Germans—Austrians—being the most graceful in figure and manner.

unbiassed Englander.

I wonder whether it is true that the Prussians are spying out the land.

Audlem.

Fancy Buerton Hall being the headquarters of General Friedrich Carl Ludwig Schlapfenberg-Blitzen! Imagine the dismay of an Audlem beauty at the attentions of Count Schwarzendam und Blazdtiereizen.[9]

The unfortunate cigar shop of Buerton will be cleaned out and smoked before the proprietor can sing "Rule Brittania"! (That's my way of spelling it, anyhow.)

I will warn you when I come to pass a few quiet days or months—as the case may be—with you. I am looking out for a studio now and so am not settled down.

I now say Adieu! Gute nacht, ich bin schläfrig.[10] I hope all are well. Kind regards to Mrs John.
Yours faithfully,
Randolph Caldecott

VIENNA.

215

46 Great Russell Street, London WC
21 January 1874

Dear John,

How are you? I received your letter with joy—much joy! I like scandal.

I was sorry that I could not get down to Bradley Green last week. I was much too busy. Heard you had a nice party. 'Hans Breitmann gave a bardy, vere is dat bardy now?'[11] John Harrison did not turn up. He wants kicking. I should have been disappointed if I had gone down. As I have observed before, he and I are about the only two unattached fellows of the old detachment.

But I have about given up hopping, it does not suit my health, and I am relapsing into a steady going shuffler. A nice quiet month at Buerton will be very pleasant when I have no work to do. Now I have to work hard at multitudinous matters—possessing a workshop, a stove, four chairs and a gas-meter all to myself. I paint, model, draw on wood, sculp, &c, &c. Lately I have been working too much at night, and I have just knocked off for a while for the benefit of my eyes. Last night I went out to a friend's and found the centre of attraction a lady called Mother Isabel. Tonight I have been at the house of my friend who was in Metz during the siege.

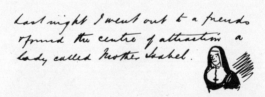

You talk of foxes. A while ago I was twice down into Leicestershire, over the Quorn kennels and stables, the master getting out hounds for me, and the huntsman holding them whilst I sketched. I was at two meets—staying with some people who—man and wife—both hunted regularly. I shall make a drawing,[12] and this reminds me—however, see postscript.

Soon will appear a new weekly illustrated paper[13]—large—price three-pence. I have already had much talk about it and made some remarkable suggestions to the editor. I shall have something to do on it. It will cheer Audlem up very much—its object being to entertain without being flippant, to instruct without being boresome, and by a carefully com&c, &c.

You hint at Xmas-Eve midnight revellers. You must hear the story of the revellers, and your blood will curdle, break, and form into a very substantial cheese. Believe not the inhospitable and unbusinesslike. Sit not in their seat. Four of us will swear that it was known that a cousin of the landlord's was rapping at the door. I was incog. I care not. But anybody ought legally and friendlily to have been let in—for is it not written "Knock and ye shall find!"

I give ye my love. Kind regards to Mrs John and all the family.
Yours faithfully,
R. Caldecott
P.S. I was reminded above—I am making a large hunting drawing and I must draw part from the living model. I want a pair of breeches to draw from. I can get some here, but they won't do. Have you got a pair that you could lend me for a fortnight? Not to ride in, [but] to draw from. An old pair will do. If so, send 'em at once. If not, send me a line to that sorrowful effect at once. R.C.

[197]
Hôtel de l'Epée (Sword Hotel),
Quimper, Finistère
30 August 1874
10 p.m.

My dear John,
It being the habit to pop off to bed in good time here, I am in my bedroom ready for repose; but it occurs to me to write unto somebody—I select you.

After a sea voyage between the isles of Guernsey and Jersey I arrived at the port of St Malo in Brittany.[14] After a dip in the briny ocean in a neat costume I left my brother Alfred on the quay and I sailed away in a small

boat to Dinard, took coach to Dinan—stayed two or three days and came on through St Brieuc, Guingamp, Morlaix, St Pol de Léon, Rosscoff, Lesneveu, Folgoët (a village with a very fine cathedral, and a horse-fair going on—more than 2,000 horses chiefly about 14½ hands and many grey and its varieties—about a quarter of a mile square of a mingled crowd of men and horses and a few women), Landerneau, Brest, and on to here to-day. The public coaches and the hired vehicles are very curious and dusty looking.

A friend and his wife joined me on the way at St Brieuc and we live like fighting cocks. Only two good meals a day, at the table d'hôte, a rousing breakfast, generally of stew, prawns, other fishes, steak and cresses, mutton, fowl, French beans, salad, fried potatoes, cheese and fruit, with at some places cider thrown in, and at others wine. General price for that about 2½ francs.

Dinner a little larger—soup, a fine melon, fish, duck, &c, &c at about 3 francs. Waited on by women, sometimes very stout, in large caps of clean and awful structure, differing at every place we stay at.

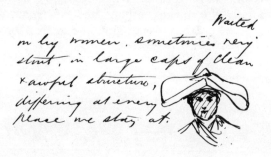

(The fine old cathedral with two tall spires here is now ringing its curfew not far from my window—a deep sonorous bell.)

At St Brieuc my chamber looked on to the Champ de Mars and I was awakened by the drums, for a general was reviewing the troops—2 regiments. The general and his aide-de-camp in plain clothes sat next to me at dinner that evening.

I have made walking excursions into remote villages and have been amused and interested. I actually made such a grand joke to some people winnowing on the top of a hill (letting the corn and chaff fall and the breeze carry away the chaff) that they were pleased and all the villagers came to see me and grin pleasantly. The belle of the village was introduced to me as she carried and ate her dinner out of a porringer like this:

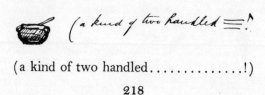

(a kind of two handled..............!)

218

It has been wet to-day—if fine tomorrow I go about the neighbourhood and then on to Quimperlé and from there a day or two's march into the interior.

The country people speak a language like Welsh and many do not understand French.

I hope you are all well, and with kind regards, remain
Yours faithfully,
R. Caldecott

1. By Tom Taylor; editor of *Punch*, 1874–80.
2. John Buckstone (1802–1879); actor-manager of the Haymarket Theatre, London.
3. Henry Compton (1805–1877); a celebrated member of the Haymarket company, 1853–70.
4. A Manchester rival to *Punch*.
5. In the drawing which follows Dutch is second from the left; the bald-headed man wearing glasses is Lang; Caldecott is standing, leaning on the table.
6. A song by Thomas Moore (1779–1852).
7. In the drawing below, second from the left is Thomas Armstrong, next to him is Whistler, then Thomas Lamont; George du Maurier leans with his elbows on the table.
8. Cambridge won by three lengths; it was the first year in which sliding seats were used.
9. Both names are pidgin German concocted by Caldecott.
10. 'Good night, I am sleepy.'
11. The opening words of a song by Charles Leland.
12. The illustrations made of the Quorn appeared in the *Graphic*.
13. The *Pictorial World*, first published 7 March 1874.
14. It was the first visit Caldecott and Blackburn made together to Brittany, which resulted in *Breton Folk*, published in 1880.

FREDERICK LOCKER-LAMPSON

1821–1895

For almost forty years Frederick Locker extended or rearranged a collection of his poems, *London Lyrics*, and for a privately printed selection of these Caldecott made some illustrations. Locker's output was slight: at its greatest extent *London Lyrics* runs to less than a hundred pages, but he had a considerable reputation and was one of the possible contenders for the Poet Laureateship on the death of Tennyson. On the death of his wife's father, Sir Curtis Lampson, in 1885, he added his wife's maiden name to his, and became known from then on as Frederick Locker-Lampson.

[198]
46 Great Russell Street, WC
5 February 1878

Dear Mr Locker,
    Thank you for the copy of your "London Lyrics". If you will call some day when you are coming this way—as you suggest—I shall be very glad to talk about the proposed illustrations.
Yours very truly,
R. Caldecott

[199]
46 Great Russell Street, WC
13 February 1878

Dear Mr Locker,
    I am sorry to say that I am engaged to go to a theatre to-night: but on Friday, the other day you name, I shall be happy to dine with you, and look over your collection of engravings, &c.
Yours very truly,
Randolph Caldecott

[200]
46 Great Russell Street,
London WC
22 August 1878

My dear Locker,
    I am glad to hear that you are thinking of me in so kind a way as to hope

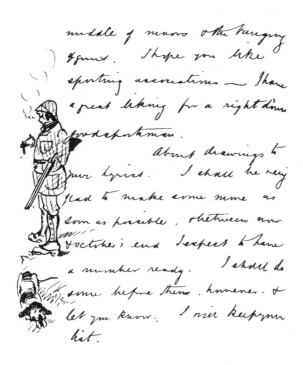

middle of moors & the banging
of guns. I hope you like
sporting associations — I have
a great liking for a right down
good sportsman.
        About drawings to
your Lyrics. I shall be very
glad to make some more as
soon as possible, & between now
& October's end I expect to have
a number ready. I shall do
some before then, however, &
let you know. I will keep your
list.

that I have enjoyed myself in Brittany and been better in health for the visit
to that land. I have had a pleasant time of it, thank you, and I strongly
suspect that I am somewhat better in health. We visited too many places to
allow me to take the 'outing' calmly as I should have liked. It was desirable
for the book, however, that as many different aspects as possible of the inhabitants should be procured.

I think Scotland would have been nicer for a *holiday*. I am glad to hear
that the mountain air suits you, Mrs Locker, and the children. Of course you
have often experienced Scotch weather—I only once: but I had all sorts in
rapid succession. No doubt but you are in the middle of moors and the banging
of guns. I hope you like sporting associations—I have a great liking for a
right down good sportsman.

About drawings to your Lyrics. I shall be very glad to make some more
as soon as possible, and between now and October's end I expect to have a
number ready. I shall do some before then, however, and let you know. I
will keep your list.

About end of October I shall go to the Riviera, I think—giving up these
rooms at Michaelmas.

Although I am busy I am pleased that you ask me to make more drawings.
Yours faithfully,
Randolph Caldecott

Hôtel Gray et d'Albion, Cannes
30 December 1878

Dear Locker,

I send you a few sketches—not because I think them particularly worthy of transmission but because I want to shew you that your *Lyrics* command my attention. Were I to wait before writing to you until happier moments might produce more valuable results you might remain some time in ignorance of my efforts—my well-meaning efforts—in this direction. You asked me to send you any attempts—complete, rough, or hasty—which I might make. Here are some. They are not fanciful. They are realistic. If in any you perceive ought worthy of reproduction kindly let me know and I will work it out. If you think my mind runneth in a wrong groove, help me out of it, and indicate the proper one. Then shall I slip along more easily and truly, perhaps.

The snow-scene may be seasonable to you. I say "may be" because we hear that you have all sorts of weather—snow, frost, sleet, rain, fog, &c, &c. Here we have had more rain than the invalids arranged for. It does not interfere much with my comfort (I find no rheumatism about) for I have much to occupy my time in the way of work—yet these places are not very conducive to work. When the sun shines it is pleasanter to wander along the shore or through the pine-woods than to be scribbling and scratching one's pate in a small room with a poor asthmatic groaning and moaning in a chamber to the right, and with a family talking, grumbling and squabbling in a chamber to the left. Oh, these thin and single doors! Who knows them not?

For some of the most important of the *Lyrics* I think illustrations can only be made in the atmosphere of London—I speak of realistic designs.

Some enthusiastic folks in this hotel are getting up a few *tableaux vivants* of children for the 1st—to-day I am informed that they depend upon me for posing the groups. A flattering but undesired trust!

With kind regards and good wishes for the coming year, believe me,

Yours faithfully,

Randolph Caldecott

P.S. I shall jog on to Mentone very soon, and sojourn there. R.C.

3 January 1879

P.S.

Just as I was making up the envelope enclosing the other sheet and the sketches, your letter of Xmas Eve arrived, and I was very glad to get it— 1stly because an exile (I feel somewhat of one) likes to think that he is not forgotten in his native land and is missed from his accustomed haunts, and 2ndly because of the interest in my drawings which you kindly express. That was the evening of the 30th and I have not until now been able to add this postscript. The wild and exciting way in which the old year went out and the new year came in has not allowed me a moment to sit down and calmly correspond. This morning I—not being at all tired—am resting after the fatigues of a ball held here last evening. A gayer crowd, people who more earnestly yearned to plunge into some giddy whirl of pleasure I admit having seen. Yet we had a ball. It is a large hotel, and is full. Our mighty men of valour— in the dancing and gymnastic line—were called out and numbered. One Belgian soldier (recruiting his health after receiving injury to his lungs by a fall in a steeplechase), an English dragoon (so asthmatical as to require a medicinal cigarette between dances), an intelligent Israelite of middle-age (wanting a borough), and myself (forbidden to take unnecessary exertion). A glorious roll-call—total 4 persons! As a reserve we went out into the highways and fetched people in—men of agility and endurance. To our dancing ladies—total 4 also—we added a number drawn from the remotest corners of Cannes. We surrounded the room with spectators on 1 stick and with spectators on 2 sticks, and with chatty persons of mature age. An agreeable party was the result. The dancing ended at 12.30—a very wild hour for Cannes.

The tableaux went off well according to the complimentary remarks of the audience—I was stage-manager and am not sure about it. The curtain was divided in the middle and drew up on each side cornerways—at the 1st

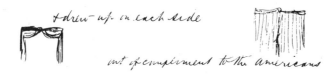

attempt a fine effect was produced by a large pin attaching the 2 sides of the curtain in the middle in order to keep it from gaping being left in.

Out of compliment to the Americans I had arranged for the mother of the New Year to come down early and teach our pianiste "Yankee Doodle". But during the afternoon the New Year fell into a pond and required all his mother's care. New Year (American)—aged 5—turned up at time and did his part all right.

I have some friends who live in Cannes.[1] They make my sojourn pleasanter. In the hotel the people are not very interesting. Agreeable, though. Dr Lyon Playfair[2] is here now. Sothern[3] the actor was here. An Irish Archdeacon Bowen, a Hampshire Bonham-Carter, a retired Australian judge, some Americans, and a few noticeable cases of bronchitis and asthma are our most valued possessions. I am very well, thank you. R.C.

2nd P.S. *Patchwork*[4] I am looking forward for.

[202]
Splendide Hôtel, Menton
26 February 1879

Carnaval de Mentone.

My dear Locker,
    We have been having a gay time here—Sat. and Monday last. There was a general row, a long procession of cars, carriages, cavaliers, clowns and others—very much foolery in the way of 'confetti' throwing—some struggles after music—and they called it the Carnival. I made myself as ridiculous as many other bearded, and even as many grey whiskered and bald-headed, boys. Had all my friends who think I am delicate seen me capering about they would have rejoiced at the apparent recovery of youthful energy and mirth. One of our party got such a dose from a sack while scaling a balcony that his brother and I had to hold him up by his legs and shake the stuff out of him in the middle of the street. In the above elaborate drawing I am represented as retired from the thick of the fray for a moment to wipe the dust out of my eyes. It got in once. On reflection the whole thing seemed very foolish: but I am certain that it did my liver good.

    And now we have cold winds, and much snow on the mountains—they are mostly covered $\frac{1}{2}$ way down: but I think we are better than the folk of Genoa and much better than you of London in the way of weather. So I do not repine. In fact, cold rather cheers me.

    I thank you for the cheque, but I think it was not necessary. If I remember, out of the things I sent you there were only 3 subjects fit for reproduction, and for those your cheque of January sufficed. So, as I hope to do some more, I will consider this as payment in advance, but that is not right.

    You speak of Miss Greenaway—there will appear (soon, I suppose) a very pretty book[5] by her of children's life and habits and pastimes.

As for me—I have been neglecting my proper work and have been wasting my time of late, I am sadly afraid, over a picture. But by getting up earlier and working well before lunch during the next 2 months I hope to pull up.

I was about to write to thank you for sending me "Patchwork" which is doubly welcome as I am an exile. I have derived much pleasure from some of the patches, and have more to come, for I have not read straight through—I pick it up and read where it opens at. It is the sort of book to have about one when on the move. There are patches in it which will haunt me for ever.

I hope your little ones are well now, and with kind regards to yourself and Mrs Locker, I remain,
Yours faithfully,
Randolph Caldecott
P.S. I shall leave here in less than a fortnight—unless Armstrong is coming out.

[203]
Albergo d'Inghilterra, Rome
17 March 1879

My dear Locker,
About the business part of your note of the 1st let me say that I shall certainly make—or try to make—a drawing to the "Pilgrims of Pall Mall"[6] as soon as I conveniently can do so, and after that I still have money in hand. We can talk of this when I see you in London, which I hope will be towards the end of April or beginning of May. I propose to stay here until the middle of next month—all being well.

I was sorry to hear that you had not pushed the general sickness out of the house. I hope by now that you are rid of it and also free from the rheumatism in your hand. I do not see any need for rheumatism at all, and especially in the hand.

I came here for a change of air—finding my digestion going on badly at Mentone. I do not rush about all day seeing places and works of art, for I am obliged to carry on some little drawings with which I am sadly behind.

I was disappointed with my first views of Rome—my imagined view was different—but I am becoming reconciled to the city by means of its glorious details, large details some of them are too.

Can I do aught for you here?
Believe me to be
Yours very truly,
Randolph Caldecott

5 Langham Chambers, W7
20 June 1879

'It's such very disagreeable weather after all'
— some people think. R.C.

My dear Locker,

I suppose that you thought that you might be able to see a wee bit of sun if you went to Cromer which is—I am told—the only place in England where one can possibly see the sun rise out of and set into the sea.

You will have a better chance there—therefore—of getting a ray out of him—or rather, of basking in any ray that he may put forth.

I expect to be in London between the dates you name, and I shall look forward to going down to Chesham St. to see you and Mrs Locker during that time. You left so soon: but many people have gone. The du Mauriers were off last Tuesday—the sickness of Mrs D.M., I am sorry to say, has delayed their going.

As for me—I have been on 2 or 3 visits into the country; and I am just about to complete the arrangements for taking a house at Kemsing—3½ miles from 7Oaks and 1½ from Kemsing stations.

I think it will be good for my health and good for some work which I want to do. This place—which is purer as to its atmosphere now—I shall keep on also—hoping to afford both, because I must be in town often.

And further hoping that Mrs Locker and the children derive good from the sea air—with kind regards.
Believe me,
Yours faithfully,
Randolph Caldecott

[205]
Trouville
25 August 1879

Dear Locker,

Your note and valued present arrived at L[angham] Chambers as I was preparing to wing my way here. So I put off—being pressed for time—writing to say that I think you are very kind to send me the etching—and in such an unexpected and pleasantly surprising way. I do like the etching and shall regard it with an admiring eye when it hangs on one of my walls at Wybournes, (village of) Kemsing, nr Sevenoaks, whither I drive from town on Saturday next in my old-fashioned dog-cart. It will be a little over 20 miles—a pleasant drive—if fine—with a lunching place on the way. By the way of the 'new cut', 'the Borough Road', the 'Old Kent ditto' or something cheery of that kind.

I suppose that you are having a bracing and dustless time of it on some moor or in some forest. I would rather hear the call of a partridge, or the whirr of a grouse's wing than the whistle of the prisoned parrot or the shriek of the caged cockatoo, which is now my fate. These birds—to me uninteresting—are confined in cage or by leg in the garden-like courtyard upon which my windows give. A man is with me—he is a nice man—he riseth betimes in the morning and goeth out into the market place, returning with great slices of melon or bunches of juicy grapes upon which we feed while the earth is getting warm and ready for our 'loaf', loll, or lounge on the sands.

Leave here Wednesday. Wishing you all—Mrs Locker and your infants—health.

From yours faithfully,
Randolph Caldecott

[206]
Wybournes, Kemsing, Nr Sevenoaks
9 November 1879

My dear Locker,
Your note has reached my hand this morning. I am very glad to read

therein your remarks about the Picture Books[8]: for I was anxious to know your opinion about them. During the time between the making of the drawings and their publication I have felt somewhat sad about them. More on this subject when I see you, which will be on Thursday at dinner—when I shall be happy to present myself at Chesham St.—if you find on receiving this that that day still suits you.

I hope to hear from Mrs Locker on that day that you are all braced up for the winter by your autumn sojourn in Scotland.

The postman comes early on Sunday morning to take away our letters, so I must end here.

Yours faithfully,

Randolph Caldecott

P.S. Perhaps you have not seen Blackburn's Brittany[9] book. I shall carry a copy to you for you when I go to your house. R.C.

2nd P.S. I have had a grim joy yesterday in seeing a strong plough tearing up the couch-grass and weeds on my piece of fallow.

I go to 5 Langham Chambers on Monday, and I shall be there chiefly for some time to come—for the sake of my work. R.C.

[207]
5 Langham Chambers, W
12 December 1879

My dear Locker,

Thank you; but I shall not be able to see you on Monday evening. I should like to do so. I shall, however, be out of town, for I go that day to Prescot in the county palatine of Lancashire, intending to sojourn there and in the neighbouring counties of Cheshire and Shropshire for the space of one week. At the end of that time you will, doubtless, be fixed somewhere for the Christmas season. I shall probably go down into Kent then.

I am glad you *approve* the *Graphic*. The 'hunting business'[10] or 'Brighton',[11] I wonder.

Yes, I have heard from America. The engraver looks upon the commission[12] as "complimentary"—has been ill or would have replied sooner. He—J. P. Davis—will send the engravings in 2 months—from 19 Novr.

I wish you, Mrs Locker, and your infants a merry time.

Yours faithfully,

R. Caldecott

[208]
96 Park Street, Grosvenor Square
19 May 1880

My dear Locker,

Yes, we have returned![13] We are trying to settle here for 2 months: but, before doing so, we must go down into Kent—Chelsfield and Kemsing—for 2 or 3 days, and we must go on Friday or Saturday—we cannot tell which day—it hardly depends upon ourselves (it is still a little strange, this talking in the plural) therefore we cannot have the pleasure of dining with you, as you kindly wish, on Friday or Saturday. Your note of welcome is pleasant to receive, and we are sorry that we cannot accept its invitation.

Armstrong is still on the Riviera or at Florence or Milan and will not get back until 3 or 4 more weeks have fled.

I wonder why Davis—the American engraver—has not written with the drawings and proofs and blocks. I will arouse him.

Yours faithfully,

R. Caldecott

As he is — I fear.

As he ought to be — I am sure

Yours faithfully
R. Caldecott

with F. W. Brind,[14] Esq., The Court Lodge, Chelsfield, Nr Chislehurst
25 July 1880

My dear Locker,

I too am glad you have the drawings and blocks from New York, and I am further pleased that you like the engravings—when used much will depend upon careful printing.

Enclosed I send you the engraver's—why not name him?—Davis's—letter. He is a nice man, I think. Will you, or shall I, find out what a Britisher would charge for the work? If *I* do, I think I must ask you to let me have one of the sets of proofs which you possess to shew to somebody. I have 1 set already, you know; if you will let me, I should like to keep these clean and surrounded by their capacious margin.

When the Bird drawings[15] are ready for Mrs Locker's inspection where shall I send them to? They will be ready in a few days.

We are not yet settled at Kemsing—things have been delayed, and we have no horse yet. On Saturday, however, we go there—it is 7 miles or so from here.

I hope you all find Cromer healthy and inspiriting (we are very high here and catch any breezes that are awake).

"Darby and Joan"—as you call us—send kind regards to Mrs Locker. Yours faithfully,
R. Caldecott

[210]
Wybournes, Kemsing, Nr Sevenoaks
5 August 1880

My dear Locker,

I am very glad that you and Mrs Locker like the Bird drawings. Edmund Routledge wrote to me yesterday asking if I particularly wished Cooper to engrave them, or would I let Evans engrave them and print them in black and sepia.

I wrote in reply to say that if Mrs Locker likes the idea of black and sepia, Evans had better do them—with the expressed desire on our part that he takes much care in the engraving.

Evans does my *Picture Books* and K. Greenaway's you may remember. I will write to him expressing the above desire if it is decided to let him have them. I think he will try to get them good.

If you will kindly leave—as you propose—or send to H. Blackburn, 103 Victoria St., the proofs of Davis's engravings he will study them, I know: I write to-day to him asking for his kind attention in the matter; and I will say that you wish to have the proofs again.

Thank Mrs Locker for her letter to me—and pardon a hasty note—'tis the morning and the time of labour.

Yours faithfully,

R. Caldecott

[211]

Wybournes, Kemsing, Nr Sevenoaks

1 October 1880

My dear Locker,

Thank you for $15/-. It was not much over that sum—I forget how much exactly, so we can't settle it any further.

I am reminded that the hop-pickers have gone away with their unrural noises, we have gathered in our oats and the *Ground Game Act*[16] has come into operation at Kemsing—at Wybournes. That is all our news.

We hope you are *all* going on well, and will continue to do so, in spite of the call of $15/- at such a time.

Yours faithfully at post time,

R. Caldecott

[212]

Wybournes, Kemsing, Nr Sevenoaks

24 November 1880

My dear Locker,

It's a great pleasure to me to find that the last new books of Pictures[17] seem to give as much—or nearly as much—delight as the former books. The "giant" of which you once spoke has not yet "strangled" me, I believe.

I think that if I were to try I *could* appeal more to the least educated. One

231

of the reasons why you do not see my books on outlying station stalls is, I think, that not enough are printed at first to supply the demand. A mere 60,000[18] of each to begin with!

The *Graphic* Xmas Number 2 pages by me[19] would have been better in more tints: but when I made the drawings I was told that I was too late for several colours. I have tinted the originals in as many colours as I like and have them by me in a frame.

Thank you for your information about Routledge's remarks. As for myself, my price is just the same on the last books as on the first.[20] There has been no change, and I arranged the price with E. Evans after finding out how much could be afforded me out of the sum that Routledge's would pay for the books. I tried hard last winter to get R's to pay more. They say the sellers[21] won't pay more to them. I fear that the only way for me to get more is by raising the price of the books—putting them in stiffer cover apart from first and last pictures. Or should I threaten or stick out or something? Do you think ½ of the present sale would be found for a $2/- book?

Evans wishes me to do 2 more on same terms to complete another volume of 4.[22]

I have not yet found 2 new subjects. *I want them.*

Did I tell you that my brother[23] was elected a fellow of St John's Coll., Cam. the other week?

Yours very truly,

R. Caldecott

[213]
Wybournes, Kemsing, Nr Sevenoaks
Christmas, 1880

My dear Locker,

We wish to let you and Mrs Locker know that we wish you and your children (and all your friends around you, of course; because if all are not merry in a company the festivity is not successful and is not satisfactory to the benevolent mind) A Merry Christmas. So, in default of being able to buy the usual card in the village I have made the above sketch "hoping it will do".

The village, by-the-bye, has been in much commotion during the last few days. On our return to Wybournes on Sat. evening we heard rumours of a dark and dismal tragedy. Bodies found by the earth-disturbing plough. Police sent for, &c, &c. Further talk of male and female, side by side, near the Pilgrim's Road, buried about two years, robbery, gypsies, hop-pickers, tramps from Maidstone jail, &c, &c.

This afternoon I spent alone in the vestry of our ancient little church, which possesses a bit of old glass and a venerable, delicately-carved screen. Out of a sack lying under the table I took about $\frac{3}{4}$ of a bushel of mud and bones and tried to arrange them on the table into complete skeletons. But there were only 2 whole bones in the lot—namely, one femur and a bone of the foot. Portions of *one* skull only—but I must not trouble you with the details— I will tell you that I concluded—after bringing immense knowledge to bear upon the subject—that the bones represented 2 men in the prime of life—one of them very tall and a little younger than the other—who were slain whilst pursuing the army of Canute as it fled towards the sea after a battle with Edmund Ironside's soldiers which took place about $2\frac{1}{2}$ miles from the field where these 2 warriors were carefully and decently buried, circa A.D. 1016. I further decided that they were men of the better sort and probably "in society".

This dreadful affair having been properly explained, the villagers are settling down to prepare for Xmas.

We appreciated very much the kindness of yourself and Mrs Locker in letting us live so comfortably in Chesham St. last week, and we thank you for your personal attention to us. With our good wishes to each,
Yours faithfully,
Randolph Caldecott
P.S. "John Gilpin" has been translated into German and an edition of my Picture Book published in that language. Would a copy interest you?

[214]
Wybournes, Kemsing,
Nr Sevenoaks
3 February 1881

My dear Locker,
    We thank you very much for your present of a copy —and one of the first

printed—of "Lyra Elegantiarum".[24] It is a very useful book to have lying
about handy—becomes a pleasant chatty friend—does not resent being un-
noticed—changes not his colour if abruptly put down when one has had
enough of him for the time being. All his little stories and remarks are to the
point—not enlarged by mere wind.

Will you some time, and that as soon as all things make it convenient to
you and to Mrs Locker—will you do us another favour—will you and Mrs
Locker send us your photographs? We want them and should be glad to have
them when you are "in copies".

You have kindly talked of sending the "Needy Knife Grinder"—I
believe I have read him.

As to the Queen of Hearts, I am hesitating about making a shilling
Picture Book like my last of it or making a more decorative and complete
thing of it (in the future)—introducing the various kings, queens, knaves
and their little games and costumes.

This between ourselves. If you have anything to say on the subject,
please say on. I shall listen with more than eagerness. If you have not, never
mind.

Snow not yet gone out of narrow north and south running lanes—but so
dirty to behold. Unsightly!

I hope you are all well—with water from unfrozen pipes and no snow
coming thro' your ceilings.

Our kind regards.
Yours faithfully,
Randolph Caldecott

[215]
Royal Oak, Winsford, Nr Dulverton, Somerset
8 September 1881

My dear Locker,
I am much obliged to you for the copy of Wordsworth. I have renewed

234

my acquaintance with him and derived pleasure and profit thereby. Also—thank you for a *Critic*.

Mr Austin Dobson has written to me about a drawing—he has abandoned the notion of which he spoke to you. Wants a drawing in *Bracebridge Hall* manner—suggests a scene from "Tony Foxhunter" or Goldsmith's essay on Beau Tibbs (an old favourite of mine). I shall try to do one before end of this month.

On Monday we came here in pouring rain—open waggonette from Dulverton station—10 miles—heavy rain all night. Weather then improved—yesterday very fine—I was driven 12 or more miles to a meet of the staghounds—and then rode a pony with them. Got on to the moor—Exmoor—very fine views and clear air.

I enclose a bit of print which I found amongst some papers the other day—it may amuse you—kindly return it some day.

The dogs are a specimen of a photo-process from an old pen translation of mine of a photograph from a Landseer—It is of no value—do not trouble to return it.

We hope you have pleasant weather at Rowfant and send kind regards.
Yours faithfully,
R. Caldecott

[216]
6 Via de' Servi, Florence
8 March 1882

My dear Locker,

I have just been sealing a letter with the Etruscan Scarabaeus which you once gave me and I am thereby reminded to thank you for 2 or 3 "Critics", in which we have found something interesting. In one was a Boston notice of a book by the President of Manchester Literary Club[25] which I was asked to illustrate a few months ago, "Country Pleasures". The Americans seem to understand it. It really is a fresh, pleasant, open air book.

By this time we hope Mrs Locker is very well again and that you and the little ones are not complaining at all.

The weather is very bright and warm and sunny here—too warm almost.

Do you know Lady Winchelsea—she has 2 very fine girls with her, a daughter and a Miss Shelley—we are going to take tea with her, Miss Poynter[26] also, do you know her—Miss P's—books? She is an agreeable acquaintance and we have seen her pretty often. Mr Perry[27]—of antique casts fame—has been here and I liked him and learnt something from him.

The enclosed may amuse you—or it may not—here it goes to you, anyhow. My time is up.
Yours faithfully,
R. Caldecott

Wybournes, Kemsing, Nr Sevenoaks
9 July 1882

My dear Locker,
   I am sending to the Fine Art Society the original drawings of the

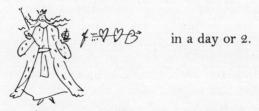 in a day or 2.

I promised to send them: but if they do not sell the whole lot together, and I decide to break up the group, I will *send* them to you so that you may be the first to inspect them when they are in the market on those terms—*as you asked me to do, I think*. Perchance you may wish for a little drawing. Perchance not. I think it most likely, however, that I shall wait a while before breaking up the party.
   I will do this with any other sets which I may think well to offer in bits— that is, just send them for your gentle inspection and severe criticism.
   I am sorry now to have to say that I fear we cannot have the pleasure of paying the visit to Weylands which we had quite decided on. This looking for another country-mansion takes up more time than I can honestly afford. I have already lost 4 whole days by the necessary going to and fro and found nought yet. And we have taken a small house in Kensington[28] for a studio— the preparation of this and the leaving of Wybournes will also cause much loss of time between now and Michaelmas—therefore I with much regret have come to the wise conclusion that we must forfeit the pleasure of the visit to the sea which you and Mrs Locker so kindly proposed to us.
   I am very busy just at present—finishing off some of the drawings for my books of this year.[29]
   Mrs R.C. writes to Mrs Locker.
   (This week I have to go to Chester for 2 or 3 days—more time lost!)
Believe me,
Yours faithfully,
Randolph Caldecott

Wybournes, Kemsing, Nr Sevenoaks
25 July 1882

My dear Locker,
   I was not in town as you supposed when you last wrote: but I will no

longer conceal from you our address at Kensington—it is 24, Holland St.—a small house in a small street at the back of the large church. There is nobody in the house now and no furniture.

I am thinking of building a small studio in the garden.

"The very desirable Bijou Gentleman's Cottage residence" has not yet turned up.

I enclose for your acceptance—if you will—one of my attempts. It is an application of the fable of the *Cock and the Jewel*.[30]

Don't see any chance of going to Cromer, thank you and Mrs Locker— to whom our kind regards and we are glad to hear that the children are well. Yours faithfully,

R. Caldecott

[219]
Wybournes, Kemsing, Nr Sevenoaks
5 August 1882

My dear Locker,

Very much obliged to you for writing about Sir Curtis Lampson's cottage; but I did not write to him because we think that neighbourhood not dry and high enough for us. This subject has been most carefully and constantly considered by us of late.

I am glad to see the *Miranda* doing well.

Mr Blunt's Arabs[31] were not in such demand as he hoped, I am afraid. I should like to have been at the sale.

We feel that we ought to be at Cromer now—we are not there unfortunately, and in a few days we go on a cottage inspecting expedition to Haslemere and thereabouts.

Hoping you all keep well, believe me,

Yours very truly,

R. Caldecott

P.S. *The Farmer's Boy* original drawings[32] went to Manchester last week and the people—a firm of Stationers—took them at once—all the set. R.C.

Broomfield, Frensham, Farnham, Surrey
17 December 1882

My dear Locker,

Behold an entirely new and quite original design for Christmas!

I want to thank you for the journals which you have kindly sent us of late. All welcome—except the *Field*, which I take in every week and read most solemnly. As far as my knowledge goes it is the best paper for acrimonious correspondence. The Kennel Club people have been very busy writing letters during the last month or 2.

Mrs R.C. saw the *Truth* to which you kindly refer me. I never buy that paper.

Our kind regards, and good wishes for a festive and healthy Christmas to all at Rowfant.

Yours very truly,

Randolph Caldecott

P.S. We go to Court Lodge, Chelsfield, St Mary Cray, for Xmas.

Broomfield, Frensham, Farnham, Surrey
21 January 1883

My dear Locker,

We shall be happy to dine with you on Wednesday—7.45 I note the hour. It will not be foggy in town, we hope.

Yours faithfully,

R. Caldecott

Broomfield, Frensham, Farnham, Surrey
18 February 1883

My dear Locker,

I am much obliged to you for sending the *Century*—do you want it back again?—silence will mean that you do not. If you do, we shall get one to keep.

Oh yes, I read and admired "Atalanta in Camden Town" in *Patchwork*.

As to the Title-Page of my selection of Fables—they are not treated very seriously—so that it is not necessary to have a severe title.

I fear that "select Fables" would suggest a very respectable gathering of highly instructive Fables with morals elegantly and wisely pointed—in which, for instance, "the man and his 2 wives" could not come—harmless though it be. And I do not want people to be deceived into the notion that they are going to buy all the Fables of Aesop. So I think we shall have to say 'Some of Aesop's Fables with modern Instances' &c, &c.

This is more in the spirit of my designs, sketches and scribblings—and yet is not too irreverent—I admit its tendency towards flippancy.

"Twenty Fables" &c would be too auction-like and cause irritable folk to ask "Why twenty?" "What twenty?" and to fancy that they are the 20 I like best.

Keeping out the words "1st Selection" is judicious: because, if these don't take, of course I will not trouble the world with others.

I am grateful to you for your remarks on the subject.

Mrs R.C. sends kind regards to all of you.

Yours very truly,
R. Caldecott

24 Holland Street, Kensington, W
11 April 1883

My dear Locker,

I am very glad to have your opinion of the *Sketch book*[33]—especially when you take the trouble to particularize, which shews that you compliment me by a careful scrutiny of the sketches—at the same time I am aware that they are not solid enough to stand up before a prolonged and serious contemplation.

That you have not been well and were not when you wrote has concerned me much, and as you thought you might be coming to town about now I shall call and enquire about you at Chesham St.

We are here for some time.

All around you are well, we hope

Yours faithfully,
R. Caldecott

Grand Hotel, Paris
Whitmonday [14 May] 1883

My dear Locker,

When I return to London on Wednesday or Thursday I shall find the book[34] about which you have been kind enough to write, and shall first enjoy it for itself and then proceed to contemplate it from the point of view which is desired by you and the Tennyson family.

If I feel bold to undertake any illustrations you may be sure it will be a pleasure to me to be associated—however slightly—with a work by Miss Thackeray and Mr Hallam Tennyson. I will write to him in a few days, therefore.

The above address may seem worldly and gay; but I found a room here on arriving in Paris late in the evening and have proved it to be so quiet and comfortable and 'handy' that I have retained it.

I wish you all a pleasant Whitsuntide.

Yours very truly,
R. Caldecott

Broomfield, Frensham, Farnham, Surrey
7 December 1883

My dear Locker,

I am glad to hear that you are well again—I hope this cold weather agrees with you—I am sure it makes you look kindly on some things.

The *Graphic* Xmas No. I also think about the best they have issued—taken all round. My contribution[35] comes fairly well—as seen by lamplight: I have not yet looked at it in the bright light of day.

I shall be very pleased for you to have the drawing which you compliment me by wishing to possess. As you suppose, I might make another if anybody happens to want the set. It is not, however, to me an easy task to copy one of my own drawings—the slighter the drawing the more difficult, of course.

I *believe* these drawings are still at the *Graphic* office. I will ask them to send the packet to Holland St., where we shall be next week for 2 or 3 days, and I will send or leave the chosen drawing at your house.

The morning is beautiful as I write—cold, sunny, bright—but I should go up to town *now* and be there as long as the hard weather lasts if we had not a visitor staying with us at present. She is clever as an amateur water-colour painter and it would not seem respectful or sympathetic if I were to leave this week.

We hope all are well and send kind regards.
Yours very truly,
R. Caldecott
P.S. I have no doubt that the Cromer house[36] will be the means of you living a long life. R.C.

[226]
24 Holland Street, Kensington, W
27 April 1885

My dear Locker,

We saw Sir Richard Hamley[37] at the Grosvenor Gallery on Saturday and he seemed to say that you are not as well as your friends could wish. We are sorry to hear this. The weather has been of fine quality of late and suited to most people—so perhaps you are better for it. We enjoyed it down at Broomfield up to Friday last.

It is a little lonely down there and I must be in town sometimes to do a little sketching from models—therefore we shall be here for the next two months or more—chiefly.

It is also agreeable to see certain people about once a year—in many cases agreeable because one only sees them once a year. It is not easy to see the friends of one's choice as often as one would like and I feel this to be a drawback to existence.

I hear that you have a stronger interest in Rowfant than you had hitherto; but I suppose you will be migrating to Cromer soon.

Will you be kind enough to ask Mrs Locker where I shall send the sketch for the Hospital Bazaar Book?[38] We hope she is well and reconciled to her recent loss, and that the children are blooming.

Mrs Caldecott sends kind regards all round.

Yours very truly,
Randolph Caldecott
P.S. Much obliged for some *Critics* sent by you
I have a small picture at the Grosvenor Gal. R.C.

I have a small picture at the Grosvenor Gal. R.C.

[227]
24 Holland Street, Kensington, W
11 May 1885

My dear Locker,

I am very glad to hear from you altho' I grieve to find that the report that you have not been well of late is too true. Rowfant must be very fresh and bright now: but I fear you will feel the cold wind there as much as we do here. I am susceptible to the slightest change of weather.

Please tell Mrs Locker that Mrs Tyssen-Amherst[39] called when I was out and left a message on a card, and in consequence I sent the sketch for the Hospital to her—I could not call upon her at the time, as she suggested, but I shall do so another day. I have since received a letter of thanks from Lady Frederick Fitzroy, and I have offered to colour the original drawing for sale at the Bazaar when it has been reproduced.

I am just about to send off an oil-sketch for a Boys' Home, and soon I must make a drawing—or send some already-made sketches—for a Cottage Hospital in Shropshire.

Before the end of this month I have to send in a small water col. drawing for an album to be given to Princess Beatrice on wedding as present from Institute of Painters in Water Colours. So you see I am quite busy.

I can well understand a long time of sorrow for Sir Curtis's[40] death. He was certainly a man to be much missed when taken from his friends. Always genial and kind, I judged. We hope Mrs Locker is well, and beg our kind regards to her. Lady Fred[k] Fitzroy says she cannot trouble her at present with a letter about the Hospital Book.

I hope to see you soon and quite well again.

Yours very truly,

Randolph Caldecott

12 May. Just had news of burning of the dwelling-house and part of extra buildings of Codrington College, Barbados, where my brother is Principal. R.C.

[228]
Broomfield, Frensham, Farnham, Surrey
18 July 1885

My dear Locker,

We think it very kind of you to ask us to Cromer again this year—especially as we cannot help supposing that you are hardly firmly settled in your new abode, and, whether you are or not, as it is quite likely that there is a large demand for quarters in that desirable marine mansion. But I am afraid we cannot have the pleasure of accepting your invitation, and this is why.

We are about to give up this "charming bijou cottage residence suited to a gentleman fond of country pursuits" as it was described to us—and we are very anxious to make certain arrangements with our successors—we have many things—live and dead—which we should like them to take to. At present, however, we do not know who they will be—our landlady herself or tenants like (if it be possible) ourselves. One has to appear very knowing, to say little, but ask much, when bargaining over horseflesh, garden tools, sets of harness in good condition, corner-cupboards, and prime, well-harvested upland hay. By the way, we have been very successful with the grass this summer, and I gloat, in prospect, over the money I shall receive for the stack —or rick. One set-off is the approaching wedding of our landlady's daughter (they live close by)—we are not on intimate terms; but as I shall have to deal personally with the old lady in the matter of leaving the house &c in good condition I believe it will be excellent policy to make a handsome wedding present.

The vagueness as to date of our departure and the uncertainty as to our successors make it seem desirable that we should be on the spot ready to try to take advantage of anybody or anything that might turn up. Our predecessors swindled me, and they were somewhat chousled by former tenants (I have heard)—and in some things I am conservative and dislike innovation.

But the waiting will be turned to good account, I hope, in other ways. When one is about to leave a place one often discovers that the most has not been made of it. This is the case here. There are many objects, views, bits of building or landscape, besides beasts and birds, which have been so handy to my sketch-book that I have neglected them. Some of these I must seize upon before it is too late—so that I intend to be very busy as long as we are here. One or two old ladies have begged that I will not forget to introduce certain 'bits' of this neighbourhood into future Picture Books; and to oblige them and to retain my present fair state of health are other reasons why I have given up two or three proposed or possible visits for this summer.

We hope that you are well now and that you are all thoroughly enjoying the sea-air and we enclose kind regards to each.

Yours very truly,

Randolph Caldecott

P.S. I am beginning to feel old—it is through discovering once or twice lately that I have not been the youngest man in the company. R.C.

My dear Locker,

Your hint is a good one: but fear not! We are duly impressed with the necessity of not going out too much. We are not in a "vortex of dining out" I assure you, and will not get pulled in—if chance should come. What we can do without strain will be a pleasure to us—no more.

When your verses reach me they will be welcome.

Yours—feeling quite summery,

R.C.

[230]
24 Holland Street, Kensington, W
18 October 1885

My dear Locker,

It was the suggestion of you and Mrs Locker—you will remember—that we should go to America. We shall sail by Cunard ship "Aurania" on 31st inst.

I propose to take an easy tour—be guided by circumstances, of which the climate may be the chief. It may be pleasant to go quietly down the Eastern States to Florida and eventually on through New Orleans to South California, then up to North California and through Colorado and home by Boston?

I will give you news from some of the places.

At present I am hoping that my experience on the vessel may not cause me to call a man—when I am very angry in the future—"the son of a sea-cook"—a time-honoured, but somewhat disused, epithet.

Yours very truly,

Randolph Caldecott

[231]
Hotel Bellevue, Philadelphia
18 November 1885

My dear Locker,

We were very much obliged for your good wishes sent in a letter, and we have to announce that we have not suffered shipwreck, altho' we had not an agreeable passage altogether. We met head-winds and got the skirts of some stormy weather which delayed other steamers. Ours was a day late. Mrs. C. was not very well. I was not sea-sick at all; but was a little light-headed and lost some rest. I felt the confinement of the cabin for a day or two, and hated the plunging of the remorseless, resistless vessel. There was no getting off. We hope there will be an overland route discovered by the time of our return.

We saw several people in New York who were known to me before. We were at Cyrus W. Field's house on Sunday—he has offered to be of use to us if he can be. New York and Boston we propose to 'do' in the spring.

F. B. Seaman, Union Bank, Holborn Circus, looks after my affairs and sends on letters.

I hope the *Picture Books* arrived at Rowfant.

Yours,

R. Caldecott

1. Mr and Mrs Frederick Green; *see* letters 147–178.
2. Sir Lyon Playfair (1818–1892). When this letter was written he was Member of Parliament for the Universities of Edinburgh and St Andrews.
3. Edward Sothern (1826–1881); an actor particularly well known for his performances as Lord Dundreary in Tom Taylor's *Our American Cousin*.
4. *Patchwork* was a collection of verse edited by Frederick Locker and published in 1879.
5. *Under the Window*.
6. One of Locker's *London Lyrics*.
7. The sketch was developed into a cartoon for *Punch*, 2 August 1879.
8. *The Mad Dog* and *The Babes in the Wood*.
9. *Breton Folk*.
10. A series of four coloured illustrations which appeared in the Christmas number.
11. Eight illustrations in the 13 December issue.
12. To engrave illustrations by Kate Greenaway and Caldecott for an edition of *London Lyrics*.
13. From their honeymoon.
14. His father-in-law.
15. For *What the Blackbird Said* by Jane Locker.
16. Among other clauses it prohibited the use of fire-arms at night and restricted the use of spring traps.
17. *Sing a Song for Sixpence* and *The Three Jovial Huntsmen*.
18. The first pair of picture books, *John Gilpin* and *The House that Jack Built*, had an initial printing of 30,000; the first printing of the second pair was 50,000.
19. Five illustrations of *The Wychdale Hunt Steeplechase*; they were printed in three colours. Caldecott also designed the cover of the Christmas number, which was printed in brown.
20. It was three farthings.
21. The booksellers.
22. This was published as *R. Caldecott's Picture Book No. 2*.
23. Alfred Caldecott.
24. A collection of verses by Locker and published first in 1867.
25. George Milner, who was president of the club for thirty-six years from 1879, and who published some novels and much poetry.
26. Eleanor Poynter, authoress of, among others, *My Little Lady*, *An Exquisite Fool* and *The Failure of Elizabeth*.

27. Walter Perry (1814–1911) at whose instigation the Victoria and Albert Museum had recently acquired a collection of casts taken from historic sculptures.

28. At 24 Holland Street, Kensington.

29. *The Milkmaid, Hey Diddle Diddle* and *Baby Bunting*.

30. It was one of Caldecott's selection from Aesop.

31. Wilfred Blunt kept a well-known stud of Arab horses at Crabbet in Sussex.

32. Four of the water-colours were sold at Christie's in June 1886 for £54 12s.

33. *A Sketch-book of R. Caldecott's*.

34. *Jack and the Beanstalk. See* letter 243.

35. Caldecott contributed the story and eleven coloured illustrations of *Mr Oakball's Winter in Paris*.

36. After spending several summers at Cromer in rented houses the Lockers bought 'Weylands'.

37. General Sir Edward Hamley (1824–1893); military theorist.

38. *In a Good Cause* published for the benefit of the North Eastern Hospital for Children. Caldecott drew the frontispiece.

39. Wife of W. A. Tyssen-Amherst, M.P., who organized the production of *In a Good Cause*.

40. Sir Curtis Lampson, who was Mrs Locker's father.

JANE LOCKER
1846–1915

The wife of Frederick Locker, and author of *What the Blackbird Said*, which Caldecott illustrated.

[232]
Splendide Hôtel, Menton
11 January 1879

Dear Mrs Locker,
    The above view will give you a more correct idea of the splendour of this hotel than a page of writing, I think, could possibly do. It represents our *table d'hôte* last night. I fled yesterday from Cannes, which—although called a very quiet place by most visitors—I found to be too lively for one who has much work to do and a desire to do it. In your note, which I read with great pleasure, you kindly hope that I am not working too hard. I was not guilty of that crime at Cannes—I felt inclined to sin in that direction—so I left my friends and my acquaintances and came here. This hotel is indeed a calm spot—but the food is good and I have a pleasant little room or two where I can do a little work comfortably. I know the inhabitant of one villa here—an American —and I think there are 2 people whom I know in an hotel—so when I feel very lonely I shall hunt them up. There is much snow on the rocky hills near the town and the weather is rather cold—but the aspect of everything (nearly) around is very fine and worth coming to see—I have been here before and know the district pretty well.
    You very kindly enquire about the effect of the sea breezes and bright skies upon me. All at Cannes—especially the landlord—said I had improved much in outward appearance during my sojourn there; and I have nothing inward to complain of.
With kind regards. Believe me to be
Yours very truly,
Randolph Caldecott

[233]
with Horace Mann, Esq., Hayes Grove, Nr Beckenham
27 June 1879

Dear Mrs Locker,

I am very sorry that I cannot be at your house tomorrow afternoon—
especially as I am invited to stay to dinner and as you leave town so soon.

I have arranged to go to Chelsfield in this county of Kent to-day and to
remain there until Monday, when I return to town.

The drought—as long promised—has not yet begun here, and it is very,
very windy for midsummer.

Believe me,

Yours very truly,

R. Caldecott

A Midsummer Walk
on Hayes Common
R.C.

[234]
Wybournes, Kemsing, Nr Sevenoaks
5 March 1880

Dear Mrs Locker,

Thank you very much for the present which you and Mr Locker have sent me.

It is a very pleasant surprise indeed. How have I deserved it?

I like it for itself too—and so does my wife that is to be—It will look well in this old fashioned country home, which I hope to have in really habitable condition by the early summer. I could wish—although I like old-fashioned things—that the roof and pump had not been quite so old-fashioned. A monster who has just been talking with me assures me that the roof is all going to the bad: and I have been forced to get a new pump at a fearful cost. But then I have snowdrops in the garden; and the old man (or lad's love), the honesty, the lilies, and the yellow roses will all come out and cheer me in the summer days: and the working of the fallow land will bring out a healthy agricultural zeal and excitement.

Now to other matters—since I had your note asking me if I can make the blackbird drawing[1] soon I have been trying to see my way to making it before the 18th—but up to this moment I have not been able to write and promise it. And I cannot yet promise it, and I am sorry to say—although I hope to be able to do it.

The page drawings for only 1 of my *Picture Books* will be ready before my wedding-day—I had intended having both done: for the engraver and colour printer want them to go on with. I wish to make the drawings for the 2nd as soon as possible, and I expect to be able to make your frontispiece at the same time—I include it with them—I hope that will be soon enough for you.

The *Graphic* people are waiting for 2 pages for their Xmas No. from me.[2] I *fear* that I must ask them to persuade themselves that the public can do without me for once.

I am grateful to you for your good wishes for my future—my new life—and remain
Yours very truly,
Randolph Caldecott

[235]
Wybournes, Kemsing, Nr Sevenoaks
23 July 1881

Dear Mrs Locker,

If the accompanying drawing does not carry out your ideas please let me know. If it seems to you worthy, I suggest that it be engraved by J. D. Cooper, 188 Strand, and that the drawing be returned to you, and that I have a proof to look at—but I will send it to Routledges with these directions rather than let you be troubled, if you will kindly return it to me. At the same time I may mention that it would save time and danger by post to forward it direct to the Broadway[3] instead of repassing it thro' my hands. All this in case of your approval.

Mrs Caldecott and I will accept your invitation to Cromer with pleasure for several good reasons. I am very busy at present and we have an engage-ment or 2 to keep soon: but in about a fortnight I think we shall be able to pay you a visit if the time will be convenient to you—this will be discovered by correspondence a few days beforehand.

We hope Cromer will fully restore your health after your recent illness.

This letter I send to Eaton Square—knowing that Mr Locker will be there on Monday—and perhaps you—coming up to town as a sad mourner. Yours faithfully,
R. Caldecott

[236]
14 Sheffield Gardens, Campden Hill, W[4]
3 June 1882

Dear Mrs Locker,

Pardon me for not answering your note before—We have been very uncertain as to our movements but now we know that we shall be at Kemsing again on Monday for a while.

If you will kindly send there the sketch of the story, *or the story itself when written*, if that will be time enough—I shall do my best to make 2 or 3 or 4 small illustrations to it—in rather an open style of work: but as good as I can make them, although they may *appear* slight.

Please give me as long a time as you can to do them in. They will not take long to make, however, when I *can* get at them: so do not think you are "imposing" the work upon me. I shall be happy to do it.

We hope Godfrey has got over the worst of the measles and that the other children keep well.

A visit to Cromer again will be a great pleasure and we shall try to manage it, thank you.

Heavy weather here, which does not suit me.
Yours very truly,
Randolph Caldecott

1. For *What the Blackbird Said*, by Mrs Locker.
2. The 1880 *Graphic* Christmas number did, in fact, contain two pages of drawings for *The Wychdale Hunt Steeplechase* by Caldecott, but because of delays it was printed in only three colours. Caldecott also designed the cover for this special number.
3. Where Routledge's offices were in the city.
4. Caldecott was staying with Thomas Armstrong.

THE EDITOR OF THE *MANCHESTER GUARDIAN*

The *Manchester Guardian*'s review of *The Three Jovial Huntsmen* sparked off correspondence on the origins of the rhyme. It was ended by a letter from Edwin Waugh who explained that 'I wrote three or four verses in addition to the old version, and tinkered a little at the rest. There is certainly a kind of rustic rustle and a quiet touch of simple humour in it; but at the best, it is nothing to make a fuss about—whoever wrote it.'

[237]
Wybournes, Kemsing, Nr Sevenoaks
24 November 1880

Sir,

Your notice of my work—as is shown in my picture books and elsewhere —has hitherto given me unalloyed pleasure and gratification, and in your journal of the 20th inst. you continue to give me praise by saying some very encouraging and flattering things about the quality of the designs in "The Three Jovial Huntsmen", just published; but you add thereto some comments which may cause my friends who are amongst your constant readers to shake their heads over my seeming falling off in virtue and generosity.

You use these words: "The text is, we believe, though no acknowledgement of the fact is made, the production of Mr Edwin Waugh." Now, my friend, Mr Waugh, has written, by the help of his fertile imagination, a version of this not at all unknown ballad upon the lines handed down by tradition, and it is printed in his cheerful little book called "Old Cronies". In a letter to me he said, "With respect to the song, 'The Three Jolly Hunters', I have written two or three additional verses, and altered some of the others a little. Of course, you are quite at liberty to use it in any way you like." I have, therefore, taken out six of his verses, disrespectfully changing a word here and there; also mark the difference of title; and have added two brand new verses of my own. Your readers can judge from this statement of what my text truly is—whether I could have explained it in a suitably brief preface to my simple picture book, or whether I was called upon to explain it at all. I may here remark that I supposed all Lancashire people knew "Old Cronies" by heart.

And towards the close of your observations is the passage: "Mr Caldecott has been greatly helped by the excellence of the engraving, which is, we believe, the work of a well-known Manchester artist (whose name might, perhaps, have been given). Mr Caldecott can afford to be generous to his *collaborateurs."* Mr Edmund Evans, the engraver and printer of the book, who sends me the piece of your journal in which the notice appeared, is glad to have your opinion of the engraving, because it is his work, with the exception of three of the small uncoloured designs—that on page 28 being one, I think —which were engraved by the artist to whom you give credit for the reproduction of the whole. The said artist[1] is a clever engraver, and I persuaded Mr Evans to take advantage of his proffered help.

When I say that the profits of the other people connected with these books are larger than mine, I hope that those who still think I want all the glory will be comforted by knowing that I do not get all the money.

As I have only troubled you with facts and not with opinions or beliefs, I feel sure you will publish this letter, and thereby oblige, yours &c.,
Randolph Caldecott

1. John Heywood, who had engraved some of Caldecott's illustrations to other verses by Edwin Waugh.

MISS MARIA MUNDELLA

Polly Mundella was the daughter of A. J. Mundella, Liberal Member of Parliament for Sheffield. She was a friend of Mrs Ewing and Miss Gatty (their father was vicar at Ecclesfield, near Sheffield) and it was at her house that they met Caldecott for the first time in July 1879.

[238]
5 Langham Chambers, W
23 July 1879

My dear Miss Mundella,
    I shall be happy to take tea with you on Friday—even if there will be authoresses present.
Believe me,
Yours very truly,
Randolph Caldecott

MATTHEW NOBLE

One of Caldecott's fellow clerks at the Manchester and Salford Bank.

[239]
Rusholme Grove,
Rusholme, Manchester
13 June 1869

My dear Noble,
 From what Beechey says you seem to wish somebody to write to you.
I should have written long, long ago: but it was suggested that I had
better not—I could not quite see why, though. However, I apologise for my
neglect, and hasten to assure you that it is with great pleasure that I sit down
to the duty this fine Sunday evening, when all good folks are at worship, and
where I should like to be; but I don't feel good enough.
 I am very glad to hear that you are so much better than we expected.
Don't you enjoy the pleasant summer days? I hope so, and that they suit your
health. I would it were always summer for invalids; and for myself too, if I
had nothing to do. How glorious to be in a country house in the fine, hot,
drowsy summer, and no business or care to distract one! Eh?
 I am rambling with my pen: but, I have no news much. There was a large
gathering of people at the Pomona Gardens yesterday to show sympathy with
the Conservative lords in their contemplated objection to the Irish Church
Bill. Dutch, Potter, Memhittrick, Jesse and I went, cheered and shouted, got
tired and dusty, hungry and thirsty, and then went home.

 Politics are a mistake
in summer. They are all
very well in winter,
during a long damp evening.
People can sport away
at their convivial meetings
and get jolly warm with it:

but it wouldn't do like this. Too much exertion!

You see I have not much.

You see I have not much to write about. Anyhow this letter will intimate that I wish you to be getting on well, and that I am happy that by Providence you have got so far towards recovery.
Believe me to remain, my dear fellow,
Yours very faithfully,
Randolph Caldecott

[240]
Manchester and Salford Bank, Manchester
7 January 1870

My dear Noble,
I dare not think how long it is since I received your note in answer to mine of some time last spring: but if I have not been writing I have been thinking of you, and you heaped up coals of fire upon my head by sending me your love the other day. I am a very affectionate youth and therefore enclose my love to you—it is not visible, 'tis so sweet and undefinable a thing that even a look sometimes smashes it and leaves not a wreck behind.
Although it is "balance-time" yet I am gushing, you see. Having a fine poetic sensibility without the proper means of bringing it out makes me at times morose in manner of conversation: but, by Jove, Sir, it adds a peculiar charm to my erratic pen. I don't do much in verses—I have written very many first lines for fine poems, yet never got any further with some glorious ideas for great epics.
By-the-bye, I may just give you a few lines written to a young lady after receiving her photograph—the sole merit of their production is mine and all rights of translation are reserved—
"When wind and rain are falling fast
Upon the houseless creatures,
I'll pull your 'carte' from out my chest
And gaze upon your features."
We are all going on in the grumbling, jog-trot, lazy, loafing, monotonous manner peculiar to this hole.

The sweet bonds of friendship between clerks are now and then temporarily broken assunder by the bad-temper engendered of a round of dreary, shut-up, daily drudgery. The noble soul will, however, soar above such petty work and meandering among the ever-recurring sentiments of a thoughtful mind will find sufficient intellectual food upon which to fatten and grow fat. Hem!

All other news soon. I sincerely hope that you are well in health and spirit.

Farewell!

I am, dear Noble,

Yours ever,

Randolph Caldecott

ALFRED WILLIAM PARSONS

1847–1920

A fellow-contributor of Caldecott's to *Harper's Magazine* and a collaborator with Edwin Abbey, Parsons exhibited paintings regularly at the Royal Academy and the leading London galleries.

[241]
Broomfield, Frensham, Farnham, Surrey
13 March 1885

My dear Parsons,
    Sorry I shall be prevented by circumstances over which I have no control from being at your Pictures tomorrow: but I wish you a happy Private View!
Yours,
RC

FREDERIC JAMES SHIELDS

1833–1911

As a painter, Shields was much influenced by the pre-Raphaelites. He had lived in Manchester from 1867 to 1875, where it is likely that he and Caldecott met. Many years before Caldecott's intended visit to Porlock, Shields had executed a celebrated series of water colours whilst staying there.

[242]
Wybournes, Kemsing, Nr Sevenoaks
18 November 1880

My dear Shields,

I am long in thanking you for your kindness in sending me—and so promptly—so much information likely to be useful to me as a visitor to Porlock. I was very glad to have your note and I should have felt hardly a stranger on alighting in the village street with your directions in my pocket.

As I was about to set out from here the weather became very bad and I myself was taken unwell, so I have had to postpone my visit to that beautiful coast. Next September I shall try to get down there and your note and map I shall keep by me and then make use of.

This is hardly the sort of weather for the country; but plenty of work to engage the attention makes any sort of a day slip by only too quickly.
Believe me to be
Yours very truly,
Randolph Caldecott

HALLAM TENNYSON
1852–1928

The only son of Alfred, Lord Tennyson. *Jack and the Beanstalk* was Hallam Tennyson's first book and it was published after Caldecott's death with illustrations made from his initial sketches. Tennyson's other books were largely about his father, family and friends. He had a good collection of pre-Raphaelite paintings, and was later to serve as Australia's Governor-General 1902–04.

[243]
24 Holland Street, Kensington, W
23 May 1883

Dear Mr Tennyson,

I have been considering the subject of illustrating your verses on *Bluebeard* and *Jack and the Beanstalk* from my point of view.

It is pleasant to me to be told that their success as a separate publication would be increased by the addition of designs by me—this would perhaps be so if I happened to be happy in my performance, but I never feel sure of such a result (nor do other people I suppose).

Would you like me to try two illustrations to each subject, or would you prefer that I should fully illustrate the stories? In the latter case the cuts (unless quite small) would take up more of the book than the verses.

Perhaps you have a clearer notion of what the book should look like—if so, I should be glad to hear what it is, and also when you think it should come out. Then I could tell you what I might be able to do. I should be happy to be associated with you in the book: but I have already made many plans for the work of the immediate future.

Yours very truly,
R. Caldecott

[244]
Broomfield, Frensham, Farnham, Surrey
8 August 1883

Dear Mr Tennyson,

The weather was too rough for us today, we are sorry to say.

If tomorrow, Thursday, be fine we shall take the chance of finding you at home at luncheon time.

Yours very truly,
R. Caldecott

EDWIN WAUGH

1817–1890

Called the 'Lancashire Burns', Edwin Waugh first made a reputation in 1856 with a song in Lancashire dialect *Come Whoam to the Childer and Me*. He subsequently published songs, poems and tales in both—as he would have it—'Lancashire and literary English'. He corresponded constantly with Caldecott, sending him a weekly copy of the *Manchester City News*. Waugh was the writer of *The Three Jolly Hunters*, which Caldecott modified slightly and published as *The Three Jovial Huntsmen*.

[245]
Splendide Hôtel, Menton, France
16 March 1877

Dear Waugh,

Thank you for your letter and enclosure—the good wishes are welcome, and I am pleased to hear that people have been kindly enquiring after me.

I feel quite proud that I know Percy—we shall see a reflected legal glory in his face when he comes down from the mount.

I think the proof of engraving of the vignette is good. Of course it is blacker and more even and uncompromising than the original drawing, because that unavoidably has little differences in the colour of the inky strokes. Printers' ink is equal, and perhaps better. Over the page I have marked where I think a little may be cut out. I keep the proof sent: and if convenient some time, I should like 3 or 4 more proofs from the block.

I shall be here until the 23rd I think. Then away!

I hope you are well and all friends. With kind regards,
Believe me,
Yours faithfully,
R. Caldecott

The stocking of the woman—please cut out 3 lines across the stocking as above—I wish a shoe to be shewn. R.C.

261

[246]
Broomfield, Frensham, Farnham, Surrey
7 January 1883

My dear Waugh,

Actually I was leaving a letter out of your name—and the "you" of all! Dear me! The truth is—and I always prefer the truth when practicable and troubleless—my business (!) correspondence leaves me no time for the feast —which I always feel it to be—of writing to a friend—a sympathizer and one who keeps stirring up my interest in good old things and ways and people and places of character as you do by your kind postal gifts. And now for *the* "Whistlebinkie"—thank you very much beforehand.

This—Broomfield, Farnham—is our new abode—nearly had a fight with our predecessor—hope he'll be a predeceaser!—a Captain Bogle—slashed blotchy face and over 6 feet of him!

Hope you are having a very pleasant time at New Brighton. I wish you— guess!—a happy new year!

Yours (Armstrong's address is 14 Sheffield Gardens, Campden Hill, W) faithfully,

R. Caldecott

MR WILLIAMS

Obviously a schoolfriend of Caldecott's (*see* para. 2 of the letter below).

[247]
46 Great Russell Street, London WC
19 February 1878, night

My dear Williams,

I am very conscious of being a dreadful ruffian for not acknowledging earlier your letter of the 27th of Sept. last. I returned here in October after rambling about, and found your letter with a heap of others—which had not been sent after me. I read it and put it down on the table in a conspicuous place that it might get early correspondential attention. And there it has remained through the winter, calmly staring at me, assisted by bottles of ink —black and brown—colour boxes, pamphlets, sketch-books, notepaper, prints, envelopes, scraps of poetry and a comedy (not mine), india-rubber, rolls of paper, a piece of old rag, and a set-square. Now I have re-taken it— your note—up. I see with regret that you asked me a question about some 'Dutch Mordant'.[1] I really don't know anything about etching materials. Several years ago I got 2 or 3 plates and just scratched upon them—un-prepared—with a dry point.[2] That is all my experience. You also asked about a printer. A. Delâtre is the best I have heard of in London. He printed me some proofs of my attempts. Legros,[3] Whistler,[4] and other etchers use Delâtre to print. He is an artist. I will try to find out if he is in London, and if so, I will send you his address. I am glad to hear that you do some work in that way, and I should like to see some of the results when opportunity serves.

I have to thank you for your photograph. I think I detect in it a likeness of my schoolfellow—barring the beard. The chief reason why I have not replied to thank you before is that I have not had a photograph of myself by me for years—I had 1 taken about 5 years ago. The results were not alto-gether pleasant. The picture is beautiful enough; but my manner of disposing of the copies produced much jealousy and heart-burning amongst my acquaintances, and I vowed to punish the world for its littleness by not sitting any more for my 'pattern'.

However, I contemplated yielding to the earnest solicitations of many friends, and having my photograph taken at Cannes—where [there] is a good photographer and where I intended to be about this present time— thinking that the sunny climate of the south of France would be more likely to be productive of a valuable memorial than the foggy weather of this great city during the winter months. But I have not gone southwards, and therefore I shall feel compelled before long to have an interview with a London photographer, after which I shall be glad to send you a 'carte' in exchange for yours, which I am very pleased to possess.

You were right in supposing the *Graphic* supplemental notes from Monaco to be by me.

I am very much occupied in a variety of works, some of which I hope will be successful. I hope you do not now suffer from that weakness about the eyes of which you spoke.
With regards to your mother and all,
Believe me,
My dear Williams,
Yours faithfully,
Randolph Caldecott
P.S. Here is a portrait to be going on with. R.C.

A gentleman called to-day to know if I would paint 2 sphinxes to try effect at base of Cleopatra's needle. "Too busy." R.C.

1. A solution of hydrochloric acid and potassium chlorate used to etch intaglio printing plates.
2. A heavy steel needle with which a copper plate is incised to produce an intaglio plate. The angularity of line is softened by the burr which is created naturally by the incision.
3. Alphonse Legros (1837–1911); painter and etcher, Professor of Fine Art at the Slade, 1875–92.
4. James A. McNeill Whistler (1834–1903).

WALTER WILSON

[248]
Wybournes, Kemsing, Nr Sevenoaks
18 July 1882

Dear Sir,

At Mr W. L. Thomas's[1] request I send you a photograph of myself for your use in preparing the proposed group of the Members of the Institute.[2]

I should have great pleasure in giving you a sitting and by those means making your acquaintance; but I have lost much time of late and therefore cannot do so.

When you have no further need of this photograph I should like—if convenient to you—to have it again, as it is not mine.

I am, dear sir,
Yours very truly,
Randolph Caldecott

P.S. Pale complexion
    hair light
    beard fair
    height 5ft 11in.

[249]
24 Holland Street, Kensington, W
13 March 1884

Dear Wilson,

I shall be happy to hear it if you have anything to tell me about Mrs Wilson's intentions as regards the costume which she wishes to assume in our procession.

I am sorry to say that I have been disappointed about one lady upon whom I have been calculating. I am 2 ladies short now, therefore; and I want another man or 2.

Yours very truly,

R. Caldecott

P.S. I go to Broomfield, Farnham, Surrey, tomorrow until middle of next week. R.C.

1. The publisher of the *Graphic*.

2. The Institute of Painters in Water Colours. It received its Royal Warrant the following year, 1883.

LEONARD CHARLES WYON

1826–1891

Leonard Wyon was chief engraver at the Royal Mint from 1851 to his death. He was one of an outstanding family of engravers: for virtually the whole of the 19th century one of the Wyons was chief engraver at the Mint or chief engraver of the Seals. Caldecott designed the reverse of a medal for the Afghanistan campaign (1878–80) which Wyon engraved. The letters and the sketches which accompany them relate to this commission. The reverse of the medal shows an elephant with howdah, mounted troops with lances, and foot soldiers, with a mounted officer in the foreground. It carries the legend 'Afghanistan 1878–79–80'. The obverse was designed by Sir Joachim Boehm and bears a crowned head of Queen Victoria.

[250]
Wybournes, Kemsing, Nr Sevenoaks
4 February 1881
9. a.m.

Dear Mr Wyon,

I forgot to write last night to tell you that I yesterday sent by rail to you the bas-relief of the Medal design. I thought that perhaps you might want it in order to begin the engraving.

I shall be in town again on Tuesday next and then I shall go up to see you—unless you send me word to say that it will be unnecessary on that day and you would rather see me a little later.

I wish to carry further or explain any details or parts of the relief as you may desire, and I shall be ready to do so—as soon as possible after hearing from you.

If no word reaches me before Tuesday (our 1st postal delivery is before 8 a.m.) I shall carry out my present intention of seeing you then—I shall probably be in town in any case.

I have raised and lowered the model in the parts pointed out by you.
Yours very truly,
Randolph Caldecott

[251]
Wybournes, Kemsing, Nr Sevenoaks
13 March 1881

Dear Mr Wyon,

After a little delay—I am sorry to say—I send you some of the details from which I have made the Afghan design. Kindly tell me if they are not

267

clear or full enough for you and mention any particulars which you may specially want.

Details of the mounted officer I will send you soon.

I am not wrong in supposing that you are not waiting for them. I hope. Don't trouble to write if all goes well.

Believe me,

Yours very truly,

R. Caldecott

[252]

Wybournes, Kemsing, Nr Sevenoaks

24 March 1881

Dear Mr Wyon,

I enclose you some details of the officer—I thought I should have been able to send you better *from town*—but I have not been there since I had your

last note. If you want further particulars of this man and horse I will get some when next I go to town.

Yours faithfully,

R. Caldecott

ANONYMOUS

Published in the *Manchester City News*, 20 February 1886, under the heading 'Advice to a Literary Beginner', it was prefaced by the following: 'If you think the following copy of a letter from the lamented Mr Caldecott would be interesting to any of your readers, please print it in your pleasant paper. It may possibly amuse those who, like all us literary people, have met with the disappointments so inevitable to us at the beginning of our ascent up the ladder. The letter will tell for itself that I once asked for Mr. Caldecott's friendly influence in such a matter myself, when I first began my ascent. The kind and earnest tone throughout is only a repetition of the sentiments we all have known him to possess.' M.

[253]
London
1878

Dear Miss M.,

Your packet reached me safely, and as I call to mind very readily my feelings in times gone by, after I had posted a piece of literary or artistic composition to some friend acquainted with the dread editor of some magazine, or even to the dread editor himself, I think it only your due that I should write to you without delay about the sketches of country life which you have kindly allowed me to read, and my opinion of which you flatter me by desiring to know. You ask me for my candid opinion; in these cases I always try to be candid. Editors of magazines, I know, are smothered by the quantity of literary matter poured in upon them, and as a rule they only read those papers which bear a name already favourably known to them. If a friend of an editor hints that he has in his pocket a manuscript which he would like him to read, the editor seizes his hat and rushes away to keep some vague appointment which he has suddenly remembered. To persuade an editor to read the work of a new author is a feat which can only be done by a person having great influence over him, or by a man in whose judgment the editor trusts, vowing that the said work is very excellent. Now I have not the necessary influence over any present editor to persuade him to read your MSS. to oblige me. And as to the editors with whom I am acquainted, I cannot say that I would care to trouble them with them, because after carefully reading them myself I have come to the conclusion that they are not quite up to the standard required.

I think it right to tell you this in a plain and earnest way, so as to save you any suspense which might end in disappointment. To go more particularly into the matter, which I hope you will allow me to do, I think that your papers are, as they stand, hardly interesting enough for the mass of readers, though to me they draw out pictures which please, and also revive old associations. Their fault, however, if I may speak of faults, is not so much in subject as in style. You have chosen simple subjects, in which is no harm, of course; but simple subjects in all branches of art require a masterly hand to delineate them. The slightest awkwardness of execution is noticed, and mars the simplicity of the whole. When a thrilling story is told, or a very interesting and novel operation described, faults of style are overlooked during the excitement of hearing or reading. Is it not so? Now it is very curious how similar and strange events happen in different places, and how an account of what happened in one place gets told far away and the name of another spot substituted. I send you by book-post a story similar to yours about the church, written years ago by my friend Edwin Waugh, who lives not far from you. His previous narration of the tale utterly takes away from you, unfortunately, any chance of telling it in print. These things do occur sometimes in periodicals—I mean repetitions—and nobody is to blame.

Oh! these magazines, of how many efforts have they been the graves, I wonder? I have buried cherished morsels of literature and many drawings in their gloomy depths. But I am glad of it now.

I have by me a very good comedy in MS. written by a gentleman in your neighbourhood, and I have much difficulty in getting it read by people who might help it forward in the world. They often keep such things a year or two, and then return them unread, if inquired about. But I am hoping to get it looked at in influential quarters; looked at, if nothing more. The author has already printed and published one comedy. Then on my table here lie two pieces of poetry written by the tutor of a young gentleman whom I met on the Riviera last spring. He trusted these to me at Genoa, and I have not yet been able to get them off my hands. Believe me, there are many authors and authoresses trying to push their works forward to be seen or read by the world, and but few are heard, and fewer remembered. Another friend of mine two or three years ago sent me a MS. which he had read amidst the applause of a gathered circle of chums. They were delighted! They praised and cheered! I read the MS. and was obliged to write a melancholy letter, giving an unfavourable opinion on many important points—an opinion agreed in by two or three others whom I had consulted. My friend was not pleased, and showed it; but a little while after he wrote to thank me for opening his eyes. Do not think that I fancy myself a lofty critic. And do not consider me a final court of appeal; but believe that I have tried to give honestly, what you frankly asked me for, my opinion of your MSS. which I herewith return, and thank you for giving me the pleasure of reading them.

I may further be allowed to remark, that the style of writing required by all periodicals, papers and magazines, quite apart from the subject, is only acquired by study and experience. People do not fall into it naturally; and there is nothing so subtle as style in every kind of work. You speak of illustrations. It is usual for publishers to make the arrangements with the artists.

Authors and their illustrators are seldom in unison; and often speak despite-
fully of one another. This is sad.
Now believe me, yours very truly,
Randolph Caldecott

ANONYMOUS

These letters were published in *Randolph Caldecott, a Personal Memoir of his Early Art Career* by Henry Blackburn. They were probably written to Augustus Whittenbury (a clerk at the Manchester and Salford Bank), William Clough and, the letter dated 16 November 1873, to Edwin Waugh.

[254]
46 Great Russell Street, London WC
27 April 1873

My dear

I was delighted to receive your letter—quite a long one for you. I hope that you had a fine time of it at the ball. Dancing is not absolutely necessary to a man's welfare temporally or spiritually; so if you be a 'wobbler', wobble away and fear not, but see that thou wobblest with all thy might, then shall thy zeal compensate for lack of skill. I've nearly given up gymnastics. I only danced twenty-one times at the last ball. . . . . . .

I now find that during quadrilles my mind wanders away from the subject before it, and I am continually reminded that I ought to be idiotically squaring away at someone instead of cogitating with my noble back leaning against the wall. Sed tempora new potater, &c. I hope you are all well, and with kind regards, remain
Yours faithfully,
R.C.

[255]
Hogarth Club, 84 Charlotte Street, Fitzroy Square, London W
5 August 1873

Dear

The poet sings 'Oh! have you seen her lately?' to which I answer 'Yes'. But, whether or no, I returned today from a fortnight's sojourn in Buckinghamshire and the first thing I was going to do was to write to you and say that I have no acquaintance with the happy medium who resides in my very old rooms in Great Russell Street. I have left those rooms, and am a wanderer and an Ishmaelite. I dare not take those rooms when she leaves. I called at the house just now and found another note from you. I had a good look at Europe during my Vienna expedition.[1] I was away a month and saw many towns, and conversed with many peoples and tongues. I could say much, but will defer till we meet over the flowing bowl. Since I came back I have been staying with a friend[2] at Holborn Circus, and also with some friends[3] at Farnham Royal, near Slough, a lovely country place. There I have been working off some sketches of Vienna and England for the use of the neighbouring country of America.[4] But I could not help being interrupted. Fancy a being like this bobbing about! Howsomedever, I am again in town at Bank Chambers, Holborn Circus, EC, where I may be consulted daily. Please observe signature on the box, without which none others are genuine, post free for thirteen stamps. So you see that I have had a seven weeks' delightful mixture of toil and pleasure, and now ought to have a bout of toil only. There is a book waiting to be illustrated.

R.C.

[256]
46 Great Russell Street, London WC
16 November 1873

Dear

I have nothing to say to you—nothing at all. Therefore I write. I don't like writing when I have aught to say, because I never feel quite eloquent enough to put the business in the proper light for all parties. Having a love and yearning for Bowdon and Dunham, and the 'publics'[5] which there adjacent lie, I think of you on these calm Sunday evenings about the hour when my errant legs used to repose beneath the deal of the sequestered inn at Bollington. How are you? I was pleased to see that the *Athenaeum* gave a long space to your book, although I presume you did not care for the way they reviewed it. That is nothing. I have been very busy—not coining money, oh, no!— but occupied, or I should have descended into the country during last month.

'Graced with some merit and more effrontery; his country's pride, he went down to the country.' My summer rambles shall be talked of, and the wonderful works in the regions of art shall be described when next I see you. Till then, farewell! This short letter is like a call.

Yours,
R.C.

46 Great Russell Street, London WC
9 August 1874

My dear

It is so long since I have heard from you that I have concluded that you must be flourishing in every way. No news being good news, and no news lasting for so long a time, you must have a quiver full of good things. How is . . . . . ? The woods of Dunham? The gaol of Knutsford?—the vale of Knutsford, I mean.

A fortnight ago, when all the ability were leaving town, I returned from a six weeks' pleasant sojourn in Bucks., at Farnham Royal. I was hard at work all the time, for I have been very much occupied of late, you will be glad to hear, I know. In process of time, and if successful, I will tell you upon what. I wish I had had a severe training for my present profession. Eating my dinners, so to speak.

I have now got a workshop, and I sometimes wish that I was a workman. Art is long, life isn't. Perhaps you are now careering around Schleswig or

some other-where for a summer holiday. I shall probably go to France for a business and pleasure excursion.[6] Let me hear from you about things in general or in particular—a line, a word will be welcome. I hope you are all well; and with kind regards, remain
Yours faithfully,
R.C.

46 Great Russell Street

My dear
 The ancient Romans said, or ought to have said, that ingratitude was the greatest of human crimes. But, my dear fellow, I am not an ingrate. I have not forgotten you—unless, as the poet sings, 'if to think of thee by day and dream of thee by night, be forgetting thee, thou art indeed forgot'. I did receive your last collected joke, and a very good joke it was—for a Manchester joke. I'm sorry that I have not power to use it, but it will keep, although it will tread on some people's feelings when used. The fact is that this same joke nearly brought me to an untimely end. I went out hunting on the day I received it, and at one fence and ditch I had quite enough to do to avoid a rabbit-hole on the taking-off side and some barked boughs of fallen timber on the landing side—not to mention some low-hanging oak trees. Well, just when I was in the air I thought of your joke and smiled all down one side; my hunter by King Tom, out of Blazeaway's dam, by Boanerges—took the opportunity of stumbling, and before an adult with all his teeth could get as far as the third syllable in 'Jack Robinson', my nose was engaged in cutting a furrow across a fine grass field, some eight acres and a half in extent, laid down after fine crops of seeds and roots, and well boned last winter. However, in less than half a minute (having retained possession of the reins) I was again chasing the flying hounds.
 About the middle of February I went down into the country to make some studies and sketches, and remained more than a month. Had several smart attacks on my heart, a little wounded once, causing that machine to go up and down like a lamb's tail when its owner is partaking of the nourishment provided by a bounteous Nature. Further particulars in our next—no more paper now. I hope you and . . . . . are well, and with kind regards, remain
Yours faithfully,
R.C.

1. To the International Exhibition there.
2. F. B. Seaman.
3. Henry Blackburn and his wife.
4. The illustrations were published in the New York *Daily Graphic*.
5. Public houses.
6. To make sketches for the illustrations to *Breton Folk*.

CHRONOLOGICAL LIST OF THE LETTERS

If it has been possible to place the undated letters chronologically according to their content, this has been done.

1864

23 June	John Harrison

1865

16 February	John Harrison
13 June	John Harrison

1868

2 June	John Harrison
27 September	John Lennox

1869

13 June	Matthew Noble

1870

7 January	Matthew Noble
23 August	John Lennox

1871

29 June	Thomas Armstrong

1872

16 January	Henry Blackburn
10 April	John Lennox
9 August	Miss Emily Jones
25 November	Mrs Jones

1873

13 January	Miss Emily Jones
5 February	William Etches
29 March	William Etches
6 April	John Lennox
27 April	recipient unknown
5 August	recipient unknown
27 August	John Harrison
21 September	John Lennox
14 October	Mrs Jones
22 October	William Etches
3 November	William Etches
16 November	recipient unknown

1874

1 January	William Etches
21 January	John Lennox
4 April	William Etches
22 June	William Etches
9 August	recipient unknown
30 August	John Lennox
6 November	Secretary of the Hogarth Club

1875

9 May	William Etches
19 August	William Etches
5 October	Mr Lang

1876

6 October	William Clough
17 December	William Clough

1877

16 February	William Clough
16 March	Edwin Waugh
10 April	Mrs Sophie Green
13 April	William Clough
15 April	Mrs Sophie Green
20 April	William Clough
21 April	Mrs Sophie Green
4 May	Mrs Sophie Green
15 August	James Cooper
21 August	Frederick Green
22 September	Frederick Green
27 September	Frederick Green
2 October	Frederick Green
9 November	William Clough

1878

5 February	Frederick Locker
13 February	Frederick Locker

1878 (continued)
19 February	Mr Williams
3 May	William Clough
22 June	William Clough
21 August	Henry Blackburn
22 August	Frederick Locker
29 August	William Clough
30 September	Miss Kate Greenaway
1 October	William Clough
13 December	William Clough
30 December	Frederick Locker
undated	recipient unknown

1879
11 January	Mrs Jane Locker
23 January	Frederick Green
26 February	Frederick Locker
17 March	Frederick Locker
28 March	William Clough
3 April	William Etches
24 May	William Clough
20 June	Frederick Locker
27 June	Mrs Jane Locker
23 July	Miss Maria Mundella
31 July	Miss Horatia Gatty
4 August	*from* Mrs Juliana Ewing
21 August	*from* Mrs Juliana Ewing
25 August	Miss Horatia Gatty
25 August	Frederick Locker
27 August	William Clough
29 August	Miss Horatia Gatty
5 October	Miss Horatia Gatty
7 October	Frederick Green
10 October	Miss Horatia Gatty
7 November	Miss Horatia Gatty
8 November	William Clough
9 November	Frederick Locker
19 November	Miss Horatia Gatty
12 December	Frederick Locker

1880
6 January	Frederick Green
17 January	Miss Horatia Gatty

1880 (continued)
21 February	Miss Horatia Gatty
5 March	Mrs Jane Locker
11 March	William Clough
19 May	Frederick Locker
22 June	Robert Drane
23 July	*from* Mrs Juliana Ewing
25 July	Frederick Locker
5 August	Frederick Locker
5 September	William Clough
1 October	Frederick Locker
13 November	Miss Horatia Gatty
16 November	Miss Horatia Gatty
17 November	*from* Mrs Juliana Ewing
18 November	Frederic Shields
24 November	Frederick Locker
24 November	*Manchester Guardian*
25 November	Mrs Juliana Ewing
Christmas	Frederick Locker

1881
3 February	Frederick Locker
4 February	Leonard Wyon
13 March	Leonard Wyon
24 March	Leonard Wyon
13 May	William Clough
17 July	Miss Horatia Gatty
23 July	Mrs Jane Locker
7 August	Miss Horatia Gatty
11 August	William Clough
23 August	David Bogue
23 August	Miss Horatia Gatty
25 August	William Clough
25 August	William Clough
4 September	William Clough
8 September	Frederick Locker
9 September	Miss Horatia Gatty
28 October	Miss Horatia Gatty
23 November	*from* Mrs Juliana Ewing
2 December	Miss Horatia Gatty
4 December	Mrs Juliana Ewing
11 December	William Clough

1881 (continued)

17 December	Mrs Sophie Green
27 December	Miss Horatia Gatty

1882

7 January	Frederick Green
8 March	Frederick Locker
24 March	Mrs Annie Fields
24 May	Mrs Juliana Ewing
3 June	Mrs Jane Locker
6 June	Mrs Juliana Ewing
9 July	Frederick Locker
18 July	Walter Wilson
25 July	Frederick Locker
2 August	Mrs Annie Fields
5 August	Frederick Locker
22 August	William Clough
11 October	Frederick Green
29 October	Miss Horatia Gatty
29 November	Mrs Juliana Ewing
5 December	Mrs Juliana Ewing
9 December	*from* Mrs Juliana Ewing
15 December	Mrs Juliana Ewing
17 December	Frederick Locker
19 December	Mrs Juliana Ewing

1883

1 January	Mrs Juliana Ewing
7 January	Edwin Waugh
21 January	Frederick Locker
29 January	Mrs Juliana Ewing
3 February	Frederick Green
18 February	Miss Horatia Gatty
18 February	Frederick Locker
25 February	William Amyot
4 March	Mrs Juliana Ewing
4 March	Mrs Juliana Ewing
7 March	Mrs Juliana Ewing
10 March	Mrs Juliana Ewing
13 March	Mrs Juliana Ewing
19 March	E. J. Baillie
21 March	Mrs Juliana Ewing
24 March	Mrs Juliana Ewing
26 March	E. J. Baillie

1883 (continued)

11 April	Frederick Locker
14 May	Frederick Locker
23 May	Hallam Tennyson
8 July	William Clough
12 July	Frederick Green
25 July	Frederick Green
30 July	Frederick Green
8 August	Hallam Tennyson
21 August	Mrs Juliana Ewing
9 September	Frederick Green
27 September	Frederick Green
1 October	Frederick Green
12 October	Mrs Juliana Ewing
15 October	Mrs Juliana Ewing
18 October	Mrs Juliana Ewing
21 October	Frederick Green
30 October	Frederick Green
6 November	Frederick Green
20 November	Frederick Green
29 November	Fine Art Society
5 December	Frederick Green
7 December	Frederick Locker
9 December	Mrs Juliana Ewing
16 December	Mrs Juliana Ewing
31 December	Mrs Juliana Ewing

1884

22 January	Mrs Juliana Ewing
7 March	Mrs Juliana Ewing
13 March	Walter Wilson
7 April	Mrs Juliana Ewing
28 May	*from* Mrs Juliana Ewing
19 June	Frederick Green
19 June	Frederick Locker
21 June	*from* Mrs Juliana Ewing
23 June	Mrs Juliana Ewing
6 July	Mrs Juliana Ewing
10 July	Mrs Juliana Ewing
6 August	Frederick Green
15 August	Mrs Juliana Ewing
18 August	Frederick Green
22 August	Mrs Juliana Ewing

1884 (continued)

22 August	Frederick Green
21 October	Mrs Juliana Ewing
undated	*from* Mrs Juliana Ewing
29 October	Mrs Juliana Ewing
3 November	Mrs Juliana Ewing (*from* Mrs Caldecott)
5 November	Edmund Evans
6 November	*from* Mrs Juliana Ewing (to Mrs Caldecott)
8 November	Mrs Juliana Ewing (*from* Mrs Caldecott)
16 November	William Clough
24 November	*from* Mrs Juliana Ewing
28 November	Mrs Juliana Ewing
29 November	*from* Mrs Juliana Ewing
7 December	Mrs Juliana Ewing
9 December	Mr Gilchrist
undated	*from* Mrs Juliana Ewing

1885

2 January	*from* Mrs Juliana Ewing
4 January	William Clough
4 January	Mrs Juliana Ewing
25 January	Mrs Juliana Ewing

1885 (continued)

13 February	Mr Gilchrist
1 March	William Clough
13 March	Alfred Parsons
25 March	Mrs Juliana Ewing
20 April	Major Alexander Ewing
24 April	Mrs Juliana Ewing
27 April	Miss Horatia Gatty
27 April	Frederick Locker
11 May	Frederick Locker
11 June	Miss Horatia Gatty
13 June	Miss Horatia Gatty
17 June	Miss Horatia Gatty
21 June	Miss Horatia Gatty
30 June	Edwin Abbey
15 July	Miss Horatia Gatty
18 July	Frederick Locker
25 July	Miss Horatia Gatty
1 August	Miss Horatia Gatty
18 August	William Clough
23 September	Frederick Green
27 September	Edmund Evans
13 October	Miss Horatia Gatty
undated	Frederick Locker
18 October	Frederick Locker
26 October	Miss Horatia Gatty
26 October	Frederick Green
28 October	Mrs Dawson
29 October	Miss Horatia Gatty
18 November	Frederick Locker
undated	William Clough

INDEX